KINGDOM COME

J.N. CHANEY
TERRY MAGGERT

VARIANT
PUBLICATIONS

LAS VEGAS, NV • GARDEN CITY, KS

CONNECT WITH J.N. CHANEY

Don't miss out on these exclusive perks:

- Instant access to free short stories from series like *The Messenger*, *Starcaster*, and more.
- Receive email updates for new releases and other news.
- Get notified when we run special deals on books and audiobooks.

So, what are you waiting for? Enter your email address at the link below to stay in the loop.

https://www.jnchaney.com/backyard-starship-subscribe

CONNECT WITH TERRY MAGGERT

Check out his website
http://terrymaggert.com/

Connect on Facebook
https://www.facebook.com/terrymaggertbooks/

Follow him on Amazon
https://www.amazon.com/Terry-Maggert/e/B00EKN8RHG/

JOIN THE CONVERSATION

Join the conversation and get updates on new and upcoming releases in the awesomely active **Facebook group**, "JN Chaney's Renegade Readers."

This is a hotspot where readers come together and share their lives and interests, discuss the series, and speak directly to J.N. Chaney and his co-authors.

facebook.com/groups/jnchaneyreaders

CONTENTS

1

I SAT BACK from the terminal, raising my hands in triumph as I surveyed the data scrolling before me.

"*Yes*. Perimeter is *down*. Deactivated." I turned to Perry. "How long?"

"One hour, thirty seven minutes."

"And fourteen seconds, in case you care," Netty added.

I kept my arms raised and flexed my fingers, turning it into a stretch. "Time flies when you're having fun."

Perry bobbed his head. "Right? I've been beside myself with excitement for the past ninety minutes, wondering what part of the screen you'd tap next. Upper right, I'd think, but no, you'd go for the *lower* right, and I'd be all like, wow, I did *not* see that coming."

"Gripping stuff," Netty added.

"You didn't have to sit here and watch me, you know," I said.

"Van, you *told* me to sit here and watch you so I could give you an after-hack assessment."

"Oh. Uh, then exceptional work carrying out my orders, faithful—"

"If you say *feathered friend*, there will be repercussions, Peacemaker Tudor," Perry warned.

I pointed at him and clicked my tongue. "Copy that, tough guy."

Torina unlimbered her long legs, dark hair pulled back in a style I called *space necessity*. With her gray eyes twinkling, she exited the *Fafnir*'s cockpit and made her way back into the crew hab, then the galley where I'd been doing my little hacking exercise. She picked up a cup to pour herself some coffee. "So, success? Did we break into the bad guys' system and steal all their secrets?"

"Nope. Van turned off a security light. And it only took him nearly two hours. He made faces the entire time. It was quite the drama."

"Uh, excuse me, security *perimeter*, thank you very much." I stood, stretching my back this time, then took the cup out of Torina's hand when she'd finished pouring it. "And I'd love some coffee, thanks."

She glared and grabbed another cup. "I still don't get the point of this, Van. You've got Perry and Netty, who can both do this hacking stuff. It would have taken them, what, a few minutes—"

"One minute, twenty-six seconds, but who's counting," Perry clarified.

"—to turn off that security light?"

"Security *perimeter*, and that's not the point. I may not always have them available. And besides, I'm a hacker, so I should know how to *hack things*." I took a sip of coffee, then grimaced and offered it back to Torina. "Ugh. Too much sugar."

The look on her face made me pull my hand back before I lost it. "But that's okay, I'll drink it anyway. It's just that—I guess it's just that back on Earth, I was pretty damned good at what I did. But everything I learned about busting into computer systems, or keeping other people from busting into them, all went out the airlock the moment I stepped aboard the *Fafnir*. None of the system architecture was the same, every program is basically its own operating system, and it's—" I shrugged. "I just want to get some of that old magic back."

"Van, you don't have to impress us. You never did."

I started to offer her a grateful smile but stopped. "Wait—I never *had* to impress you with my abilities, or I never *did* impress you with them?"

She smiled and sipped coffee, just as Netty cut in.

"Van, we're getting a distress call from the freighter *Plodding Fool*. She's a class 5, privately registered here in the Eridani system. She's calling for assistance, saying she's being attacked."

I put the coffee down and headed for the cockpit. "Where is she?"

"She's in the vicinity of Tarsura, a moon of the outermost gas giant. Think Venus, if it orbited Jupiter. Her captain says they're trying to use Tarsura for cover."

I looked at the tactical overlay as I settled into the pilot's seat. Torina took her place beside me and started pre-firing diagnostics on the weapons. We hadn't been in a fight in nearly a year, since the protracted and bloody Battle of 109, so aside from occasional test shots, our guns had stayed silent that whole time.

Zenophir's walrus-like whiskers twitched as she observed Netty beginning pre-flight checks. Zeno's thick body was clad in coveralls

3

that spotted the tears and stains of a working engineer, but her eyes were keen as she issued two crackling commands for Netty's course selection—and with that, we were underway. "Kinda figured you'd want to go and help these folks out," she said, and I gave her a thumbs-up. We'd been together long enough that at some point, we'd crossed that ineffable boundary between *crew* and *team*. I trusted Zeno and the others to make the right decisions, and I hadn't been disappointed yet.

"How long to intercept, Netty?" I asked.

"Best case, three hours, ten minutes, and change," she said as the *Fafnir*'s drive rumbled to life.

"Okay, start broadcasting that we'll be there *shortly* across the comm channels. And leave it at that, *shortly*. Maybe we can spook whoever's attacking them."

I turned to Perry. "I didn't know there were active pirates here. I thought the Eridani Federation put a lot of effort into keeping their space safe."

Perry shrugged. "Nobody's perfect, Van. Besides, if everyone thinks that, they kinda let their guard down, right?"

"I suppose—"

"What the hell's all this about, anyway?" a new voice cut in.

I turned to the grumpy voice. Icky, who'd obviously just woken up, clambered into the cockpit and settled into her place behind Torina.

"Pirates attacking a freighter. We're going to intercept," Zeno said.

Icky brightened. "A fight?"

I shrugged. "Maybe."

Icky cracked all four sets of knuckles. "Hope so. All this flying around transferring prisoners and lugging old rocks and sticks back to wherever they came from is *bor*-ing."

"Those old rocks and sticks are the cultural heritage of a dozen different worlds, Icky. They belong where they came from, not being knickknacks in that Traversia Corporation boardroom where we found them."

"Whatever. It'd just be a lot more interesting if it involved busting some heads."

"*It'd just be a lot more interesting if it involved busting some heads.* Ladies and gentlemen, I give you Icky's philosophy of life," Perry said.

"Keep it up, bird, and I'll show you some of my *philosophy* in action."

———

I squinted at the overlay. "She's *in* the atmosphere?"

"They did say they were going to use the moon for cover," Torina said.

"Well yeah, but diving down *there*? Doesn't look friendly at all."

"It depends how you define friendly. If you find six hundred kilometer per hour winds and frequent, high intensity lightning discharges friendly, then Tarsura would be downright charming," Netty offered.

"I'm a fan of the semi-organic flying boogers, myself. Quite the array of, ah, fluids hurtling around in the upper atmo," Torina said.

"Flying boogers? That are, presumably, frozen?" I asked in disgust.

"Sort of. I'd hate to be the one to clean our windshield if we took a dive in there. Lots of long-chain organics that we might find offensive to our sense of smell," Torina added.

"I'm offended by boogers in general as I have none," Perry announced.

"Elitist of you. What's that?" I asked as we eased down to the greasy upper winds.

We arrived to find the aftermath of a battle. The *Plodding Fool* had managed to land some solid hits on her attacker, a class 4 up-gunned workboat—or, actually, a *former* class 4 up-gunned workboat, now a drifting wreck about a million klicks above the roiling storm clouds. It had launched an escape pod that was broadcasting its own locator beacon, but we decided that whoever it was could sit tight while we tried to rescue their supposed victim.

"Netty, are we getting any comms at all from the *Plodding Fool?*"

"No voice or video for over an hour now, just her transponder broadcasting an automated distress call. And even it's sporadic. There's a lot of electrostatic potential in those clouds, which is probably screwing up comms."

"So there might not be anyone actually alive down there," Torina said.

"There's a chance." I pondered the situation for a moment, then shrugged.

"I'd rather not come all this way just to let someone die a couple of hundred klicks below us. Netty, based on what I'm seeing on my panel, the conditions down there are within the *Fafnir*'s performance envelope, right?'

"Just. Drop even another twenty klicks or so deeper into the atmosphere, that becomes a no. And the aforementioned semi-organics are heavy. They'll cause serious drag as well."

"Yeah, well, we still have to try," I said, tapping at the flight controls and committing the *Fafnir* to the safest and quickest atmospheric insertion Netty could calculate that would take us down to the *Plodding Fool*.

The cloud tops loomed closer as we fell from orbit. The *Fafnir* shuddered briefly as she passed through the first tenuous wisps of gas, then settled into a steady bass rumble once we hit the atmosphere proper. The ship plowed through the thickening vapors, incandescent streamers of plasma spilling off her nose and flickering across the canopy and along the hull, with the odd ripe *splat* as the *Fafnir* was decorated with some local flavor.

Dropping further, we passed between two towering banks of cloud lit by restless flashes of lightning, the coruscating whites and blues fading to more menacing tones lower down. The first winds shook us, pushing the *Fafnir* one way, then the other.

"Not much worse than Earth atmo," I said.

"Wait for it, Van. The good part's just ahead," Netty said.

"The good par—?"

I was cut off mid-word by a sudden rightward slam as wind gusted against the *Fafnir*'s broadside flank. The inertial dampers handled it easily, but it was still disconcerting to see the view ahead suddenly snap sideways. And then up, and then steeply down. Up again, and to the left, and then hard back to the right.

I tapped at the thruster controls, struggling to keep the *Fafnir* flying down the long, arcing pipe Netty had calculated as our best descent.

"Van, might I recommend that Perry or I take over? The winds are only going to—"

The *Fafnir* abruptly barrel rolled, while slewing hard to one side.

Despite my best efforts, she slipped out of the pipe and plunged toward Tarsura's unseen north pole.

"—get worse."

"No argument here, Netty. You have control," I said, lifting my fingers from the command screen.

"I have control." She immediately began thrusting in quick bursts, edging us back into the pipe. My reaction time was measured in fractions of a second, but hers were in milliseconds. Moreover, I had to see and process the wind and flight data on the master display, where she just thought it all. When it came to delicate piloting, there really was no contest.

Even so, Netty struggled to keep us flying more or less in the direction we wanted to go. And now some new enemies entered the field. Lightning lashed the clouds around us, gigavolts of electrostatic power discharging in colossal blasts of energy. Peals of thunder slammed against the hull. At the same time, the atmospheric pressure began to quickly build, squeezing the *Fafnir* like a giant vise. Netty had compared Tarsura to Venus, but compared to this, the latter was downright sedate.

I glanced at the overlay, where even the *Fafnir*'s scanners were having trouble burning through the titanic flares of electrical discharge. "Netty, dead-reckon it. How far?"

"Based on inertial nav, about thirty klicks."

I nodded and we flew on. Crackling arcs of lightning now pulsed around the *Fafnir* like flickering strobe lights, slashing around and across our course, while hurricane winds tossed us like a toy boat on a choppy lake. Icky muttered something, and I glanced at her.

"Problem?"

"Not yet, but this combo of pressure and winds are starting to get a little scary. If either goes up much more——"

"There," Torina said, pointing ahead.

The *Plodding Fool* had emerged from a swirling wall of cloud, a dark shape silhouetted against the inconstant flashes of lightning. Thunder walloped us again and again, pounding on the *Fafnir* like a drum.

"Van, we are *never* going to be able to dock with that ship!" Zeno called over the racket.

I had to fight just to keep my eyes on the other hull, which slid and jinked like mad across the sky as we pitched and yawed and rolled.

"No shit. Netty, any comms yet? Maybe we can tell them they don't need to hide anymore, and to start pouring on the thrust for an escape——"

Again, I cut off my own words. A big chunk of something detached from the *Plodding Fool*, whipped away, and vanished into the clouds.

"Van, she's breaking up. And we're not going to be far behind her if we don't lift out of here," Netty said.

As if to underline it, the *Fafnir* suddenly groaned, a low, plaintive cry of metal being stressed to its limits.

More pieces came off the *Plodding Fool*. Each exposed a greater volume of her to the supersonic gusts, which ripped off additional plating——

Until, just a few seconds later, there wasn't enough of her left to even contemplate a rescue.

I knew when we were beat. "Netty, get us the hell out of here!"

The *Fafnir* immediately pitched up—then down again. Netty

fought for control, but the furious winds had had a taste of space-ship, and they wanted more.

"Van, I need to light the drive," Netty said.

I winced as lightning arced across the *Fafnir*'s bow, looking close enough to singe my hair. At the same time, thunder clapped so loudly it made my ears ring. Lighting the fusion drive inside an atmosphere was perilous at best, since it was basically a continuous, directional thermonuclear explosion. There was a reason it was profoundly illegal on every inhabited world, one of the few things everyone in known space agreed on and generally respected.

But if Netty said we needed to do it, I believed her. "Kick it!"

Netty did, and another blast of thunder, one of our own making and the biggest yet, walloped the *Fafnir*. I saw a half-dozen systems flick to yellow on the status board. But the *Fafnir* shot upward, and the winds and lightning quickly died. Less than thirty seconds later, we punched out of the clouds. Glowing jets of vapor trailed us into orbit, the strange phenomena called sprites erupting from the storm tops. And just a minute after that, Netty cut the drive as we settled into the placid calm of stable orbit.

"Well, that was fun," Zeno said.

"For certain, very specific definitions of *fun*, sure," Torina replied.

I stared down at the clouds, wondering how long it would take the debris that had once been the *Plodding Fool* to reach the unseen surface.

I sank back in my seat. "Shit."

Torina shrugged. "We can't save everyone, Van."

"Doesn't mean we can't try, though, and we did," Zeno added.

"Yeah." I turned back to the overlay, where the escape pod from the ship that had attacked the *Plodding Fool* still beat out a monotonous distress call. "So let's do the next best thing and nab the bad guys that caused all this shit in the first place. If any of them are alive, I've got some creative punishment in mind."

"Go on, boss, I'm listening," Icky enthused.

I waved at a repulsive smear on the cockpit. "Wash and wax the ship. By hand."

Icky tilted her head in respect. "And I thought *I* was mean."

WE BROKE ORBIT, aiming ourselves at the distant beacon, and recovered one of the up-gunned workboat's crew, a skeletal alien with beef-jerky skin. His head—face, whatever— was clad in a gas mask rebreather. He was the same race as Koba, the shuttle pilot who'd tried to kill Torina and me during one of our very first jobs together on Dregs. Whatever they called themselves wasn't exactly clear, so everyone generally referred to the emaciated race as Skels. They had the dubious distinction of being widely regarded as being more criminal than the Yonnox, which was quite a feat.

"The Skels have some cultural imperative to flout laws when and wherever they can," Perry had once told me.

"Why?"

"Don't know. No one does. And the Skels won't say, or maybe they can't say. But if there's a rule, they're somehow obligated to break it, almost as a matter of principle."

"That… doesn't sound like a winning formula. Just anarchy. How the hell do people like that even form a civilization in the first place? I mean, being civilized *implies* rules."

"Simple—they're basically parasitic. They evolved on the same planet as the Gajur and seem to have just leeched off their civilization without ever forming much of one of their own."

"Huh. And just when you thought they couldn't get any more charming."

This particular Skel was badly injured, and there were some severe burns we hadn't even noticed on his leathery skin. We slathered him with first-aid gel, bandaged him up, and stuck him in the brig where Netty could keep watch over him. Then we turned our attention to the *Fafnir*.

"We took some damage to the backup comm array and had two stealth coating sheets de-bond. Three of the reactive armor modules are loose, too," Netty reported.

Our stealth coating was a prize we'd seized from some miscreants a couple of years before. Since then, we'd lost about twenty percent of the original installation. It still made the *Fafnir* stealthy, but not as much as she once was. And we had no spares, so we needed to save what we could.

"Can Evan take care of it, or do we need to go outside?"

"I'll put him to work and let you know."

Evan was a new addition to the *Fafnir*. Essentially a variation on Waldo, our general maintenance bot, Evan—actually EVAMS, for extra-vehiclar activities and maintenance system, but Evan just flowed off the tongue better—was designed to live outside the *Fafnir* and do routine exterior in-flight maintenance and urgent repairs. He lived in his own little garage on the *Fafnir*'s ventral stern, just ahead of the rad shielding that protected the ship from the stellar fury of the fusion exhaust.

"Sounds good. Meantime, I guess we need to hand off our

wounded Skel friend back there to the appropriate authorities—which would be the Eridani Federation, right?" I asked Perry.

"It would, but it's a long trip back to the inner system. It'd be faster to carry on to Spindrift and hand him over to the Eridani mission there," Perry replied.

I nodded. Spindrift had been our intended destination anyway. And since we were much closer to our twist point than we were to the Eridani planets back in-system, Perry's suggestion made sense.

"Sounds like a plan. Netty, if you please."

She calculated a new course, lit the drive, and started us away from the pale, featureless crescent of Tarsura. From a million klicks away, there was no hint of the violent winds and lightning that perpetually lashed its turbulent atmosphere, just the soft, diffuse glow of starlight reflecting off the perpetual clouds.

I made a point of spending a moment watching it recede behind us anyway. It only seemed fitting. It was, after all, more than just a planet.

It was a grave.

2

I KEPT my tone as neutral as I could. "Again, he committed his crimes—which I might remind you include piracy and murder—in your jurisdiction. And per the Eridani protocol agreements with the Peacemaker Guild, that means we're supposed to hand him over to you."

I gestured at the gurney. "So, here you go. He's all yours."

The head of the Eridani mission on Spindrift, an older human woman who'd apparently lost the ability to smile, fixed me with a flat glare. "And just what the hell are we supposed to do with him? I've got four staff here, plus myself, and that's it."

"Look, sparklepants, I don't make the rules, I just enforce them."

Still glaring, she finally thumbed my data slate, accepting the prisoner transfer. Then without another word to Torina, Perry, and me, she ordered one of her underlings to wheel the Skel into the Eridani mission's suite of offices. The door closed with a heavy thud.

"You're welcome," I said to it with annoying cheer, then glanced at Torina. "Serves us right for having the audacity to enforce their damned laws."

"That *was* a lot harder than it needed to be," Torina agreed. "The good news is that Icky and Zeno managed to snag a table at *The Blast Crater*. They're busy fending off people trying to grab the empty chairs, though, so the sooner we can get there—"

"We need to hurry to a bar and have some drinks? Oh no, tell me it ain't so," I said, and we hurried away from the Eridani mission, back toward Spindrift's main level and concourse, and its most popular watering hole.

As usual, we attracted a slew of reactions when we entered, our b-suits and Peacemaker logos on clear display. Most were curious but wary, some were outright hostile, and a few—the ones I always enjoyed the most—were briefly alarmed before looking away and studiously avoided any further eye contact. As fun as that was to see, it also meant petty, bullshit crimes not worth our time. The truly interesting bad guys were usually bland, innocuous, or both.

We joined Zeno and Icky and ordered a round of drinks. While we waited, I took a moment to scan the crowd around us. It was rare for anyone to openly challenge a Peacemaker, but it did occasionally happen, especially when there were intoxicants involved. But no one seemed particularly interested in us, so I turned my attention back to the crew. Perry, who could split his attention about a hundred different ways without effort, would keep an eye out for any burgeoning trouble.

Our drinks arrived, then we paid the AI waiter and made to dig deep into some social time. But I held up my drink first, waiting until everyone was quiet and watching me.

"A moment for the crew of the *Plodding Fool*. I know all the facts aren't in, and I know we don't really know who shot first or what really happened, but still."

Zeno nodded. "Yeah, hell of a way to die."

We took a moment, the bar buzzing around us. The bartender had some 3V trans-system news thing playing, blaring out commodity prices. I'd have assumed porn or some sort of sports would be the broadcast of choice, but since most of the people drinking here were merchants and traders, I guess it made sense.

We drank, then put our drinks down.

"Have to admit, I'm not used to excitement these days. That flight down into those winds—" Torina shook her head.

Zeno nodded again, vigorously. "Glad it's not just me. When you haven't had anyone shooting at you in a while, you kinda lose your edge. I mean, that lightning had me jumping like *I* was the one being hit every time it flashed. Sumbitch but that took me back." She gave a shudder, then tipped the rim of her glass to me. "We've got a good thing here, Van. I was scared but... not to the point that I thought we weren't going to make it."

Torina gave a slow, warm smile. "We *do* have the right crew. The right ship."

"And we're in the right place, too," Perry added, then gave me a one-eyed amber wink.

"As in, this bar?" I asked, confused.

Perry gave a subtle—for him—nod toward a humanoid woman three tables over. "Damned fine scenery compared to the wind-driven snot rain of Planet Doom, or whatever it was called."

I stared around the table, then back at Perry. I lifted both hands and patted the air. "Hold. Up. I need you to pump the brakes and tell me just what you mean by *scenery*. You mean that… woman? Over there?"

Perry gave a small shrug. "Yeah. And?"

I felt a bewildered stare flatten my face. "Uh, Torina? Zeno? Anyone? Is this a new thing? The whole, um, attraction to women?"

Zeno shook her head. "No. He's always been a bit randy."

"What?"

Perry gave an exasperated sigh that would have done a teenager proud. "While I cannot and never will engage in mating, exactly seventeen-point-five percent of my personality matrices are geared toward an accumulation of what my Peacemaker partners have found, ah, to their liking over the years."

"Excuse me?" I asked, setting my drink down.

"I love it when Van looks dumb like this," Icky enthused. "For the record, my ideal mate can fight, has at least four arms, and, um, can really fight."

"Thank you for the illuminating chat about your ideal booty call," I said.

"Don't mention it," Icky said, waving her glass.

I looked over at the woman who'd drawn Perry's attention, seeing that Torina was sizing her up as well. "Thoughts, dear?"

Torina lifted her brows. "He's got good taste for a bird. She's stunning."

"I—huh." The woman *was* beautiful—tall, long black hair cut to one side with a silver thread in it and high cheekbones over caramel eyes. "Why her, Perry? I mean, why her type?"

"My matrices accumulate. Like memories."

"Like any person, your tastes evolve?" I asked.

"They do. For instance, you'll be pleased to know my first

human partner would have—and I'm paraphrasing his own words here—fought a lake full of alligators for a shot at a redhead," Perry reported.

Torina made a *hmph*. "Most men go through a redhead phase. It's in their genes."

Zeno snorted. "For ours, it's the bristles. They see long bristles and fat paddles and—"

"I—we get it, Zeno. Thank you. Good to know that being *thicc* has universal appeal," I said.

"If there was ever a need for confirmation of your personhood, this is it, bird. I'm sorry you can't—"

"Carry out the sticky, weird parts of your genetic swap shop you call mating? No thanks, I'm good. I am partial to Ford Mustangs and arguing about whiskey, but those are tertiary aspects of my ongoing development. Just like people can like painting without being an artist, well…"

I lifted my glass to him. "You know art when you see it," I said, staring at Torina, who chose that moment to blush.

"I do, and Van?" Perry held up a wing, head cocked as he looked over my shoulder again, his entire frame utterly still.

"Go on?"

We fell silent and waited. Perry turned toward the bar. "Van, we need to get back to the ship."

I looked at my drink that was barely touched. "Why?"

"That's why," he replied, his wing now pointing back at the bar.

I turned to follow it—

And found myself looking at my own face on the 3V feed.

TORINA IMMEDIATELY YANKED out her data slate and accessed the 3V feed. She found the story under the "news" category, right near the top.

PEACEMAKER IMPLICATED IN SERIOUS CRIMES

"Van, maybe we should head back to the *Fafnir* before we—" she started, but I shook my head.

"Just play it."

She did.

A voice-over started with stock footage of Peacemaker stuff—ships with the logo, people in Guild b-suits, a long, still image of Anvil Dark.

"'—wanted for his alleged involvement in serious crimes,' Torol said in a statement." The image changed to that of a young, slick human male who was impeccably dressed and standing behind a podium. He oozed charm right through the feed, but it was that sticky, almost greasy sort of charm I associated with used car salesmen and the most accomplished of politicians. Torina paused it.

"I know him. That's Jun Torol, Satrap of the Seven Stars League. He was just elected—oh, three or four months ago. My father did some fundraising for him."

I made a spinning gesture with my finger. "Torina, let's go—"

She resumed the vid. Torol stood front and center, but I saw a restless, almost furtive woman, another human, lurking in the background. I assumed she was an aide or an assistant or something, someone just incidentally caught on the imager. But about five seconds of watching her told me she wasn't a mere underling. Her body language was too direct, too forceful, causing her to lean slightly toward the podium as though she wanted to be the one speaking.

Although I could have been wrong. The woman was a bundle of nervous energy, never still for more than a second or two, so maybe I was reading too much into it—

No. I wasn't. I knew it as soon as her eyes looked straight into the imager. They were bright and hard and cold, the eyes of a raptor hunting its prey. It struck me that these two were a set—he was the squooshy velvet glove, and she was the brutal iron fist inside it.

I asked Torina to hit pause again and pointed at the woman. "Who's *that?*"

"No idea. I don't think I've ever seen her before."

"Uh, Van? I think some people have started to notice that you're the guy who was just on the news," Perry said.

I glanced around. Sure enough, we had a few people watching us and whispering. I saw someone point, indicating us to someone else. That person said something to someone else, and so on, a slow motion chain reaction of recognition and interest.

"Okay. *Now* it's time to leave, before this whole bar knows we're here," I said before standing and heading for the door.

We made a quick exit, trailing glances like sticky cobwebs. I kept going until we'd rounded a corner. No one in the concourse outside the bar had offered more than the usual passing glance afforded a Peacemaker, but that could change really fast.

"Play the rest of it, Torina?"

"—formal charges of piracy and murder are being delivered to the Peacemaker Guild even as we speak," Torol, the Satrap, was saying in a smooth, warm tone. "We are further requesting that the Guild strip Tudor and his crew of their qualified immunity so that we can pursue our own charges against him."

He paused, giving the imager a moment to take in his square jaw, dark eyes, and artfully tousled hair. "It is our hope that Tudor will do the right thing and turn himself and his crew in to the authorities. We are giving him one standard day to do so, whereupon we will ask the Guild that he be found."

Another pause. "I realize that charges of this nature are rare. The Peacemakers are a vital force providing an indispensable service to known space—objective, dispassionate administration and enforcement of the law. We are asking them to set aside the fact that this is one of their own and carry out the revered and ancient task that has been given to them. We're confident that they will do the right thing. Thank you."

The image cut away back to the 3V logo, with a voice-over that wound the segment down and segued into the next.

We stood in silence for a moment.

"When the hell did we piss in *his* dinner?" Icky snapped, her voice taut with outrage.

"Crudely put but a good question. Torina, can you think of any reason why the new Satrap of the Seven Stars League would go multi-system with something like this?" Perry asked.

"The Seven Stars League does have a history of corruption," Zeno noted.

Torina sneered. "The Seven Stars League *is* the history of corruption. In fact, if you look up corruption in the dictionary, it just says '*See the entry for the Seven Stars League.*'"

"Sure, but it doesn't explain why this guy in *particular* is gunning for us," Icky said.

"Someone's gotten to him," Zeno stated flatly.

Torina blew out a breath. "Probably. We knew the Fade would eventually regroup, especially with No-No still out there somewhere. And they do have a history of trying to work their evil magic through other, generally legitimate parties, like they did with Traversia."

"All of which is very well and fine, but it leaves us with a question," I said.

Zeno nodded. "What now?"

"Yeah. Although, I think I might know the answer to that, at least in the short term. Let's go, we're going to pay a visit to our surly friends in the Eridani mission." I gestured for everyone to follow but added a warning to keep very, very alert.

"Van, I'm gonna fly high cover," Perry said, then he flung himself into the air. He'd sail from structural beam to conduit above us, watching for trouble.

"You think that whole attack on the *Plodding Fool* was a setup?" Torina asked.

"I don't know. Maybe. I mean, we don't know for sure that anyone was aboard her now, do we?"

"Yeah, but luring us into the atmosphere of that moon, hoping we'd end up being killed? I mean, there's indirect, then there's making a plan around things you can't possibly control," Zeno said.

I had to agree. "I know. But keeping with the indirect theme, the idea might not have been for us to die—especially if the Fade's new plan is to not kill us in the first place."

Icky grumbled. "If they don't want to kill us, then what?"

I let out a slow breath. "That, dear Icky, is a very good—and unsettling—question."

Sure enough, the Skel prisoner we'd handed over to the Eridani mission was gone.

"Yeah, he just suddenly jumped up, burst out, and ran. We thought he was unconscious. Apparently he wasn't, though, and he got through the door before any of us could do anything besides just kinda stare," the mission head said.

I didn't bother to pursue the matter. Even if the Skel was still on Spindrift, finding him would be a massive undertaking, one that the little Eridani delegation didn't have the resources or, it was pretty clear, the interest to pursue. And the Cloaks, the Spindrift security force, would be no help. Notwithstanding Torina's assertions about the epic corruption of the Seven Stars League, the Cloaks would definitely give them a run for their money.

We hurried back to the *Fafnir*, not least because we were starting to attract an awful lot of curious looks. At least it seemed that way, but suddenly being an infamous celebrity across known space has a way of making every glance seem like a suspicious stare.

As of now, there'd been no reward offered—yet. I suspected that was probably coming in a day or so, after we didn't turn ourselves in.

"I don't get it. What good does it do them to fake a pirate attack, plant that Skel, have us pick him up and bring him here to Spindrift —" Icky started, but I abruptly cut in.

"We were right in the Eridani system and were bound to turn

him over to the Federation. So the logical thing to have done was for us to take him back, in-system, and hand him over there. Instead, we brought him here, to Spindrift."

"You think that the Eridani Federation's in on this, too? As trans-system governments go, their reputation is pretty good."

I shrugged as we started walking again. "No idea. Maybe someone in the Eridani bureaucracy was on their payroll. It only takes one with enough authority, right? Or maybe there was an ambush or something waiting for us, and we went the wrong way."

All we could do for now was speculate. We finally made it back to the *Fafnir* to find Netty had already done the preflight checklist and had her powered up and ready to fly.

"I heard the news and figured you'd want to get gone sooner rather than later," she said as we settled into the cockpit.

"Excellent instincts, Netty," I replied, clearing her to start maneuvering away from the docking port. I wondered if Spindrift traffic control would try to keep us here on some pretext, but the AI just offered a terse acknowledgement and unlocked the port.

The *Fafnir* turned and pointed her prow starward. Netty accelerated us away from Spindrift but asked the next obvious question.

"On our present heading, we'll reach the star Theta Boötis in about eighty-six thousand years. Or did you have some other, not-quite-so-time-consuming destination in mind, Van?"

"I do."

"And that would be?"

"Nowhere. I mean that literally. Nowhere at all."

3

IT REALLY ISN'T hard to hide in space. Space is the very definition of big, and most of it consists of absolutely nothing, aside from wisps of gas and the odd mote of dust. So it was easy to twist the *Fafnir* to a point roughly halfway between Spindrift and Anvil Dark where we could just drift in the virtually infinite anonymity of space. We could do this forever and never be found.

Which was effectively the same as being dead, so it wasn't a long-term solution. But it did give us a chance to get in touch with someone we trusted, so I reached out via comm, and got an instant response. That was good.

The tone of the response was. . .mixed.

"What the hell is it with you and drama, Van?" Lunzy asked.

I smiled and shrugged. "I'm a complicated person."

"You're also a wanted one. But that's only part of the reason the Guild is in a panic. Two veteran Peacemakers have gone missing."

I sighed. "Let me guess—more Masters."

"Not this time. It's a bonded pair of S'rall, which is half of the S'rall contingent in the Guild."

I nodded. The S'rall were a relatively reclusive, grumpy race that originated on a desert planet. We had an in with them, having rescued one of their nobles, a princess, from digital servitude several years ago. She'd been one of the very first of the stolen identities we recovered, in fact. It turned out some of her own people were behind it, which led to a series of executions whose brutality still didn't bear thinking about too closely.

"Where were they last known to be?"

"They were doing a transit job, a simple delivery on behalf of the Quiet Room. They never showed up at their terminus."

"Huh. What were they delivering?"

"Not what but who, and the answer is that I don't know. The job was posted at a hundred thousand bonds, which is awfully high for carrying a passenger. It set my threat alarm off, if you know what I mean."

I whistled. "Yeah, no kidding. Any chance you can find out who they were carrying?"

"I'll try. If I do, I'll let you know." Lunzy leaned a little closer to the imager. "For now, though, Van, just stay out there. Don't come near Anvil Dark. This place is as tense as it's ever been. I'm heading out myself in a few minutes and won't be coming back until things cool down some."

"Understood. You remember my place? If you need to, go there."

"Eh, might take you up on that. It's always nice to have options."

"The security word is corn, if anyone asks."

"Corn."

I smiled. "Yes indeed. Corn."

Lunzy nodded. "Be careful, Van."

"Always."

She signed off, and I turned my attention to Netty.

"Netty, contact Dayna at the Quiet Room, please and thank you."

We waited. It took about ten minutes, but she finally announced a comm link. Before she activated it, though, she gave a warning.

"It's not Dayna."

I frowned. Dayna was our regular Quiet Room contact. "Who is it?"

"Some Gajur named Polixis."

I glanced at Torina, who just narrowed her eyes.

"Put them on," I said.

The display lit with the image of a Gajur. "Peacemaker Tudor, allow me to introduce myself. I am Polixis, your new account representative with the Quiet Room."

"What happened to Dayna?"

"She has moved upward and onward in recognition of her excellent work. Now before we proceed, I do have some questions regarding your account security. Where are you currently?"

Torina raised a warning finger, but I was way ahead of her.

"On a mission, and that's all I can tell you. Operational security, as you'll appreciate."

"Of course. Well then, can you come to Procyon so we can go over some details of your account and address some issues?"

"What sort of issues?"

"These are matters that really should be discussed in person."

"I understand. We'll be able to be there in"—I made a show of looking offscreen—"let's make it nineteen hours."

"Ah. Could you be more specific about your time? My own schedule is very busy, and I'd hate to have to keep you waiting."

Again, I looked offscreen. "Torina, can we make this trip in any less than nineteen hours?"

"We—" She hesitated, then shook her head. "No. Nineteen hours is our best time, and we can't really be more specific because of—well, you know."

I nodded. "Sorry, nineteen hours, maybe a little more. And if we have to wait, then we'll wait."

"Very well. I will see you then."

When he signed off, I turned to the others. "Bets that he's looking at a star chart right now, trying to figure out what's a nineteen hour flight away from Outward in Procyon?"

"Van, is this more of your famous Iowa spy nonsense?" Icky asked.

"Of course it is. Remember that city we sometimes fly over, Des Moines? It's a hotbed of espionage. The whole state is lousy with spies and counter spies."

Icky frowned. "Really?"

"You mean you didn't know?"

"Don't be so dismissive. Des Moines has three distinct spy rings working there right now, and a fourth starting to gain traction," Torina said.

Perry turned to her. "Wait, what? Really?"

Torina sighed "No, silly bird, of course not. But if you're fooled that easily, then best let Van and me handle the espionage."

"Suits me. The trouble with that whole *lying for a living* thing is that it can be hard to know when the workday is done. Trust me, I know," Zeno put in.

"So, Van, what exactly do you want to do besides sit here basking in the charm of a random point in interstellar space?" Netty asked.

"Why, we're going to Procyon, just like we said," I replied.

Icky shook her head. "Now I'm really confused. We *are* going to Procyon? But I thought that was just a ruse."

"We're going there to watch the shipping lanes and see who comes calling on the bank, am I right?" Perry said.

"The bird gets it. That's it exactly."

Perry turned to Torina. "Who's the clever and devious one now?"

"Uh... Van? It was his idea, after all."

Perry uttered a single, "Hmph." I'm sure he would have grumpily crossed his wings if he could.

I smiled. Alone in the vast nothing with just my crew, it suddenly felt... safe. But the smile didn't last because we couldn't *stay* out here.

"Okay, Netty, we need to get to Procyon before anyone else does. Kick it, please, and don't spare the fusion horses."

———

THE CLASSIC STAKEOUT trope from TV cop shows really is a thing. In the show, it's compressed down to minutes or even seconds, of course, but every impression is given that it's tedious to the point of mind-numbing.

And that's true, it is. The *Fafnir* hung in another nondescript part of space, mostly powered down, this time in the Procyon system well outside the orbit of Outward, the outermost of the system's four habitable planets. The Quiet Room's branch office—no one was really sure where their head office was, or if they even had one—was located on a large moon orbiting Outward, and it was the approaches to and from there we were scrutinizing.

Of course this wasn't TV, so it wasn't as though Torina and I sat in the *Fafnir's* cockpit with binoculars and paper cups of bad coffee, watching out for the bad guys to make their move. Okay, maybe the bad coffee. Something had gone wrong with the maker, and neither Icky nor Zeno seemed to know how to fix it.

I ranted about it a bit, too. "You're telling me you can tune a fusion reactor that involves plasma burning at thousands and thousands of degrees—basically, a controlled thermonuclear explosion inside a bottle—to a fraction of a percent, but you can't get this damned thing to stop making shitty coffee?"

Icky and Zeno shrugged. "Sorry, Van. It's a basic spacecraft system, not a power plant, or drive, or weapon system, so… yeah, kinda outside our area of expertise," Zeno said.

"Besides, neither of us drink that crap. Tastes like hot sweat," Icky said, making a face.

"How would you know what hot sweat tastes like? And for that matter, whose sweat tastes like coffee—and you know what, never mind. I don't want to know the answer to *either* of those questions."

So we resigned ourselves to drinking shitty coffee and played cards, and slept, and generally futzed about while Netty and Perry maintained their unblinking attention on the space lanes to and from Outward. And that was the part missing from stakeouts on TV —AIs. They made the life of a cop a lot easier.

Zeno interrupted me as I was settling in for a nap. "Van, got a second?"

"I don't know, got a busy couple of hours of sleeping to get out of the way."

"Indulge me. Remember that gross satellite you guys brought me to examine the first time we met?"

"I do. What about it?"

"Well, it was super stealthy, and part of the reason was that it was somehow recycling its own internal heat into power generation, and doing it really efficiently. I've been tinkering with a system like that for the *Fafnir* back in engineering, and I've got one up and running."

I'd been half-reclining on my bed, but that made me sit up. "You mean we don't have a heat signature anymore?" I was more than impressed, I was excited. Heat was the one emission from a spaceship that fundamentally couldn't be stopped, at least not without switching everything off and letting it cool to an ambient temperature. Out here, that wasn't much above Absolute Zero, which was just a *bit* on the chilly side for my taste.

Zeno held up a hand. "Before you get too enthused, it's only running at four percent efficiency. We can do better, but we're never going to reach one hundred percent. It just isn't physically possible."

"Anything helps, Zeno, so yeah, keep at it, please."

"I was hoping you'd say that, which is why I'm hoping you'll say yes to my next question—can we spend some money on it? I've done everything I can with parts I've been able to scrounge."

"How much money?"

"End of the day, say, fifty thousand bonds or so."

I whistled. That was a lot of cash, plus being on self-imposed exile from Anvil Dark and no longer able to rely on the Quiet Room, I wasn't anxious to start spending what we had on-hand. "My answer is yes, but I'd kinda like to see a… a budget, I guess."

"Ooh, how bureaucratic of you. Master Gerhardt would be proud."

I stuck out my tongue at her, but Netty cut off any further conversation.

"Van, there's a class 9 light freighter inbound for Outward. A class 7 whose performance suggests she's carrying some extra mass, maybe armor, is on a fast intercept course."

I stood. "On my way."

We settled into the cockpit but kept the *Fafnir* powered down, aside from life support and passive scanners. I saw the two ships on the tactical overlay, a pair of icons rapidly converging.

"That 7 wants to meet up with that 9 something fierce," Perry said.

I grunted in agreement. "Netty, could they be intending to rendezvous?"

"If by rendezvous you mean a pleasant little meetup to exchange passengers or cargo or information, probably not. Based on their relative performance, their rendezvous isn't a friendly one. That 7 is traveling way too fast, and it's *still* accelerating."

"So a fight, a class 7 against a 9. Talk about the mouse that roared."

"Aren't mice those cute little creatures with the big ears and the tails?" Torina asked.

I nodded. "They are, although I'm a farmboy and don't find them that cute. They're pests."

"Besides, I don't see any big ears on that class 7," Perry put in.

"What the hell are you talking about, bird?" Icky asked.

"I—it—" Perry sighed, a mannerism he'd now perfected. "It's just a riff on Van's metaphor. Mice are tiny and mostly inoffensive creatures, so one of them roaring and attacking something much bigger—" He stopped. "Why the hell am I explaining this?"

"The class 7 has opened fire. Four missiles in pairs, meaning two launchers," Netty cut in.

I whistled. A class 7 was a small hull to be carrying two missile launchers and their reloads. That suggested that this one wasn't just up-armored but up-gunned as well.

"Van, we're watching a violation of interstellar commerce laws, unjustified use of weapons in a designated space lane. Procyon's a signatory to the applicable protocols, so—"

I cut Perry off. "We need to do something about it."

"Even if it means blowing our cover?" Icky asked.

Perry nodded. "Yup."

"But those two ships might have nothing to do with us."

I turned. "Sorry, Icky, but Perry's right. We're law enforcement, remember? And there's a law to enforce right in front of us. Netty, full power-up, please. Light up the active scanners and start us inbound on this scrap, best possible delta-V."

The *Fafnir* rumbled to life. As soon as the active scanners began to ping away, we got a much clearer picture of the battle.

The mouse that roared, indeed. The class 7 was badly outmatched by the 9 but was pressing home its attack anyway.

I switched the comm to a general broadcast. "All ships currently illuminated by our active scanners, this is Peacemaker—" I was going to say Tudor but gave my credential number instead. "I am instructing you to heave to and prepare to be boarded."

"Does that ever work?" Zeno asked.

"Only if they're good guys, or at least know they've got nothing to hide. The bad guys usually don't. Makes them easier to tell apart," Perry said.

We accelerated toward the impending clash. Long before we could intervene, though, the battle was joined. The class 9 deftly shot down three of the incoming missiles with point-defenses, while the fourth detonated too far away to have done much damage. It responded with a barrage of missiles and laser fire back at the class 7 that swamped any lingering resistance. Less than five minutes after it had opened fire, the class 9 had pounded its adversary into drifting scrap.

I repeated my demand for the 9 to cut its drive, but its only response was to accelerate away, hard, obviously en route to the nearest possible twist point. I didn't need Netty to tell me that. Unless it had an abrupt change of heart, there was simply no way for us to catch it.

I turned my attention back to the crippled class 7. "Now I wonder just what the hell that was all about."

"And if it was somehow meant to involve us," Torina added.

I shrugged. "Hard to see how, but I wouldn't put anything past the Fade. Anyway, the answer's out there," I said, gesturing to the overlay. "So let's go and see what's left. I'm in the mood for a little profit."

THE CLASS 9 had been thorough in its violence. Its class 7 adversary was a write-off, worth nothing more than scrap. We couldn't even try to strip some data out of her because a mass-driver slug had slammed through the ship's data core, reducing it to pebble-sized fragments. The only things of value we could retrieve from it were some odd parts and its fuel, helium-3 and anti-deuterium, which somehow both remained in containment. The rest of it had been pounded into so much junk.

Two of her crew had survived, though, a human and a Nesit. Both were badly injured by flash burns and fragmentation effects, but Perry was still able to compare both to our databases. Neither was a hit, meaning they either weren't bad guys or had managed to fly below the radar if they were.

"More importantly, they're hurt way beyond our capacity to treat them," Torina said, applying first-aid spray to the human, who we'd laid out on the *Fafnir*'s galley deck. "We can keep them sedated and stable for now, but—" She looked up at me and shook her head gravely.

I nodded back. I was no expert, but I still knew enough to tell that neither of them would live more than a few hours without proper medical care.

And that presented us with a problem. The nearest decent medical care was on Outward, but that would take us into close proximity to the Quiet Room and whoever might be watching for us to arrive there in—

"I'll be damned. It's nineteen hours, our fictitious arrival time," I observed. "Got a question for you, Netty. Is there anywhere else in this system that might have decent medical care that we can reach in, say, under three hours?"

"The next planet outward from, um, Outward, has a terraforming research station in orbit. It's a self-contained facility and likely has a full infirmary. Might even have grafting capabilities."

As she spoke, she put the data up on the display over the galley table. I leaned on the table and took it in.

"Kleskof's World. One-point-two-five Earth masses, breathable atmosphere—huh, how come *it's* not Outward—oh." I read the mean surface temperature. It was minus twenty Celsius, ranging from highs just above freezing, to a record low of minus ninety-seven.

"A little on the chilly side, isn't it," I said.

"Indeed. It orbits just outside Procyon's Goldilocks Zone."

"Which is why they're trying to terraform it by pumping greenhouse gases into the atmosphere to try warming it up," Perry added, hopping on the table.

"Huh. Wait a minute." I straightened. "So we're talking a bunch of terraforming scientists and techs, right?"

"Plus support staff, yes," Netty replied.

"Okay, let's do it. Netty, get us underway, if you please."

"What about that class 7? The debris cloud is a nav hazard."

"Just send a message to Procyon traffic control. Let them earn all those fees they charge. We've got an errand of mercy to run."

"OKAY, what the hell is that doing here?" I asked.

We were on our final approach to the terraforming station

named Kleskof Prime. It seemed like any number of other orbital platforms, about half the size of a city block, maybe, with docking facilities for a half-dozen ships. There were three present—one freighter, a second ship bristling with scanners that was obviously a survey ship, and a third. It was the third, a class 9, that snagged my attention.

Sleek, dark, and venomous-looking, like the business end of a poisonous snake, it mounted two laser batteries, two rotary missile launchers, four point-defense batteries, and some sort of chunky weapon even Zeno couldn't immediately identify.

"A particle cannon, maybe, but no design I've ever seen before," she said.

An obvious warship, its presence here at what should be a research facility set all sorts of alarm bells ringing. But she was also docked and powered down, so she posed no immediate threat.

"She's registered to a Tau Ceti-based company called Group 41," Netty reported.

"Group 41? Yeah, that doesn't have sketchy written all over it," Zeno muttered.

I nodded as we slid into our berth and gently bumped against our assigned docking port. "Yeah, I suspect they aren't in the scented-candle and throw-pillow business."

"Not unless the scented-candle and throw-pillow business is a lot more cutthroat than we realized," Torina added.

"You've never seen multi-level-marketing essential oil sales on social media back home. Makes interstellar war look *polite*," I said, staring at the warship.

"Oh, like when those women say '*Hey, girl, ready for a life-changing business opportunity?*" Torina asked. When I raised my brows, she grinned. "We've got them on my planet too. They usually hit you up about ten years after you're out of school."

Perry snorted. "Humanoids are *vicious*."

I turned to him. "Can't argue with that. We're scrappers by nature. What about this Group 41? Anything?"

"No and yes. No, because Group 41 is wholly owned by a single shareholder, so it doesn't have to disclose… pretty much anything, really, to conform to interstellar commercial law."

"How about the *yes* part?"

"Yes, we have a little bit about them in our intelligence database. Group 41 is a security consulting firm."

"So, mercenaries."

"No and Yes."

"Perry—"

"Yes, they're guns for hire, sure. But no, unlike Groshenko and Pevensy and those types, they aren't primarily in the war-fighting business, at least not on a large scale. They're more the sorts of guys you'd hire for a personal protection detail or to guard some sensitive facility and do it off-the-books."

"They're kind of the spec ops of mercenaries," Zeno said. We all turned to her.

"You know these guys?"

"I know of them, or at least the type. I've never dealt with this Group 41 before, but back before I met your grandfather, I did some freelance work of my own, mainly weapons procurement for an outfit like this one. *Legal* weapons procurement, I might add."

"So there aren't very many of them, but they're really, really good, is what you're saying."

"Exactly that."

I turned back and looked out the canopy at the sleek, sinister vessel two berths away.

"So that brings me right back to my first question: what the hell is that doing here?"

4

I STEPPED through the airlock ready for trouble, with The Drop loosened in its holster and my hand resting on the pommel of the Moonsword. Torina and Icky followed, ready to back me up, while Zeno kept the *Fafnir* flight ready.

Our greeting committee consisted of an officious-looking scientific type and a pair of techs with medical crash gear. One of the latter was Yonnox, reminding me of the strikingly altruistic emergency medical tech we'd met on Dregs, who selflessly administered to the underclass that filled the warren of ghettos around the spaceport. I'd come to believe that the Yonnox were generally a scummy race, but it turned out they were, instead, a race of extremes—either entirely scummy or incredibly selfless. Either saints or sinners, with not much in-between.

We offloaded our two wounded and handed them over to the station's medical techs, while the officious scientific type produced a data slate.

"I need you to sign this, affirming that you have no particular expectation of health outcomes for the injured parties you've transferred to us and relieving us of all liabilities if those outcomes are negative."

I took the data slate. Its screen was full of tiny text, like a user agreement on a piece of Earthly software.

"Do you, uh, have a lot of sick and injured people dropped off here?" I asked, reading from the top. By the end of the first paragraph, it had all blurred into eye-glazing yadda-yadda—just like an Earthly user agreement.

"No, we don't. Why?"

"Well, because you guys have a five thousand word disclaimer all ready to go, so either you're the fastest typists in known space, or you already had this on file," I said, continuing to skim. I didn't see anything about agreeing to indentured slavery or paying out vast sums of money, so I finally just thumbed it and handed it back without reading it in detail.

Just like an Earthly user agreement.

The scientist, a humanoid female with a name tape that read Burton, returned a thin smile. "We have the appropriate forms available for any and all reasonably envisioned contingency."

I bet she was fun at parties.

As far as I was concerned, we'd done what we'd come here to do. I wanted to see if we could get some information out of our two wounded friends, but both were likely going to be unconscious for some time, possibly days. I hated to lose the opportunity to question them, but the idea of hanging around here waiting wasn't very appealing. I was about to just return to the *Fafnir* and depart, but something stopped me in my tracks.

A group of Fren-okun had just come around a corner, walking along the docking concourse and chattering excitedly amongst themselves. I caught a few words, including *heroes* and *the best warriors ever!* In both cases, the Fren were obviously referring to themselves.

That piqued my interest. The Fren were, frankly, a goofy race—except for a certain percentage of their elderly women who turned out to be whip smart, almost diabolical geniuses—but I'd never imagined them as especially warlike, or even especially good at *being* warlike. Hell, I couldn't imagine them being allowed to operate a toaster oven, let alone military grade hardware.

I turned back to Burton, who was in the process of leaving. "Excuse me, but while we're here, do you have, like, a cafeteria or restaurant or something aboard? I could use a break from what we've got on our ship, and—"

"One level down, follow the markers to section 4-A. It will be on your right through the last set of blast doors," she said, then finished turning and walked away without a backward glance.

I turned to Torina and Icky. "Hungry?"

They exchanged a glance, then both shook their heads.

"Not particularly, no," Torina said.

"Excellent. I'm buying," I replied and started for section 4-A.

———

"This tastes like damp laundry and sadness," Torina said, picking at her meal. The station's *Food Services Division*, which was what the placard on the bulkhead beside the entrance proclaimed, was an entirely automated affair. You could either take packaged food out

45

of mechanical dispensers or give your order to an AI for fresh food. We went with the latter.

Which I began to regret as soon as we sat down in the cafeteria-style galley. It turned out a greasy spoon was a greasy spoon, regardless of whether it was alongside a bumpy Iowa country road or a space lane in the Procyon star system. Mind you, the view from the second one was better. One wall of the cafeteria overlooked the icy splendor of the frozen planet below, a mottled wasteland of gleaming white and dour bluish rock.

"Okay, Van, so you wanted us to dawdle and spend some time here because of those Fren. And here we are, dawdling—"

Torina grimaced and pushed away her tray.

"—and gagging a little."

"Dunno, I think it's pretty good," Icky said, shoveling something that looked like chopped-up drywall into her face.

Torina raised an eyebrow at her. "Why am I not surprised," she said, then turned back to me. "Anyway, now what?"

I shrugged. "Not sure. Just acting on a hunch. There's obviously more going on around here than meets the eye. I mean, that sleek little warship out there, some Fren patting themselves on the back and proclaiming that they're heroes—"

"Some Eykinao wearing uniforms."

I nodded. "That would be odd, yeah."

Torina nodded. "No. I mean, right over there, there are two Eykinao wearing uniforms."

I glanced where she'd indicated, only to see two of the strange, somewhat broom-like aliens called Eykinao had entered the cafeteria and were examining the food selection. They were speaking to one another, but I couldn't make out the words, so I turned to Icky.

"Icky, can you—uh, stop filling your face for a second? Thank you. Anyway, you've got sharper hearing than any of us. Can you make out what those two are saying?"

"Uh… something about earning bonds, saving their families, stuff like that. You gonna eat that?" She pointed at Torina's tray.

Torina nudged it toward her. "Enjoy."

I stood, then ambled up to the food dispensary and stood a short distance from the Eykinao. After a few seconds of strategic listening, I overheard one of them saying, "—sure it's enough, though. Maybe we should ask for more."

"I'm not asking anything, I just want to get my money and get out—"

The second Eykinao cut himself off when he noticed I was standing nearby. I turned, smiling, and took in their strange uniforms that were a drab, blocky camo pattern. They were sporting a badge that looked like a stylized flower. "Hey, fellas. So what brings you to this lovely vacation spot?"

"This—you are here for a vacation?"

"I'm, uh—well no, I'm not. I'm here on business."

"You are a Peacemaker."

"I am."

They both seemed to stiffen, though whether that meant the same thing it did in an Eykinao as it did in a human, I had no idea. We'd only encountered the strange race a couple of times, mainly in the context of a scam being run by the Fade involving unnecessary fertility treatments. I certainly didn't have enough experience with them to start reading their body language.

"There has been a crime committed here?" one of them asked.

I shook my head. "No, nothing like that. There was a battle

47

between two ships not far from here. We rescued two survivors from one of them, and this was the closest place that had decent medical facilities. How about you guys? Those are uniforms, right? Do you work here?"

"We are only here temporarily."

Again, I wasn't sure if their reticence was racial, or if they were actually trying to be evasive about something. My instincts told me it was the latter, though, so I decided to try something.

"Ah, okay. Well, since you're here, I might as well ask—there's a ship in dock, armed to the teeth, belongs to something called Group 41, apparently. We have intelligence that they might be of interest in another investigation we've got underway. Would you know anything about it? Because if so, you'd be helping my crew out."

Even though the Eykinao have an entire ring of eyes, I could still tell that one gave the other a meaningful look. A few gestures are universal, like a glance meant to impart something sketchy.

"You must speak to the Major. He will answer your questions," the other one finally said.

"Ah, the Major. Okay. Where might I find him?"

"He is probably on the surface. That is where the induction is occurring."

"The induction?"

"Yes. We are now working for The Bulwark. We are to be inducted on the surface and then deployed to our first contract—"

The other Eykinao made a noise, cutting his fellow off, probably because he thought he was sharing too much information. I decided I'd pressed enough.

"Thanks, fellas, you've been really helpful," I said, then returned to the table.

"So they said—"

"Icky was filling me in as you were talking to them. Oh, and in case you were interested, she talks with her mouth full," Torina said, wincing in horror.

"Wha? I can talk an eat at a ame ime," Icky protested through a wad of damp drywall that, based on her expression, was *haute cuisine*.

"Eww. Anyway, it seems pretty clear that those Eykinao are involved in some sort of military or paramilitary group called The Bulwark, which is headed up by a Major, and somehow related to that Group 41 ship out there," I said.

Icky swallowed. "Don't we have enough bad guys to deal with? The Fade, the Salt Thieves, the Sorcerers, the Cabal—" She stopped. "And what's with all the sinister names? If I was going to start up some criminal outfit, I'd call it the Wu'tzur Charity Pet Rescue, or something like that. I mean, sheesh, you're trying to be all sneaky and low-profile, and you call yourselves the *Sorcerers?*"

I shrugged. "I don't help them pick their names, Icky, I just thwart their schemes and lock 'em up."

"Did you notice what word those Eykinao *didn't* use when they were describing what they were doing here?" Torina asked.

I nodded. There was one word soldiers used pretty much universally to describe what they were doing when they weren't operationally deployed, and the Eykinao never used it.

"Training."

Torina nodded. "They kept saying *induction*."

"What's the difference?" Icky asked.

"Induction is the stuff you do to join the military in the first place—the paperwork, background checks, that sort of thing. It makes you a soldier in name, but training is what makes you a soldier in fact," I replied.

"Without proper training, you're just cannon fodder," Torina added.

Icky shrugged. "Maybe they just misspoke."

"Possibly," Torina admitted.

"But you don't think so," Icky said.

"I don't *not* think so, either. There's something going on here that's not just terraforming research. Torina, how about you use your silver tongue and go see what you can find out from the people that actually run this station. Icky, you're with me."

Icky wiped her mouth with the back of one hairy hand. "Doing what?"

I waved grandly. "We're going to see if we can join the army and see the world."

Torina took Perry, who'd been snooping around the station's public data network, to visit with the station management and see what she could learn from them. In the meantime, Icky and I went to the airlock where the Group 41 ship was docked, intending to ask a few questions, nice and friendly.

We were greeted by a human male sporting blocky camo with the flower insignia and a name tape that said *Darwan*. He stood at the airlock as though on guard, giving an all-purpose, utterly insincere smile that flicked off like a thrown switch the moment he saw I was a Peacemaker. That was a useful bit of information in itself because someone more on the ball wouldn't have batted an eye.

Rookie move, kid.

"Hello," I said, introducing myself and Icky. I hadn't bothered to change into civilian clothes because we'd arrived in a Peacemaker ship, so I didn't try to conceal anything else about our identities, either. That was another experiment. I wanted to see if this person recognized my name from the 3V broadcasts and, if so, what their reaction would be. And if it wasn't a good one—well, I had The Drop and the Moonsword, and Icky lugged along her hammer, which, after all, was just a tool.

But my name got no reaction, just a cool, unchanging stare back.

"Can I help you, Peacemaker?"

"To satisfy my curiosity, yes. What brings you folks here?"

"I'm not prepared to answer any questions without proper—"

I raised a hand. "Relax. This isn't an investigation, and I don't for a moment think you're doing anything illegal. I'm just genuinely curious since, really, your ship is pretty slick and hard to miss."

The man's eyes narrowed slightly. "She is a fine ship. State of the art, in fact."

"I can believe it. So you guys must be some sort of… mercenary company, I guess? I have a good friend in that line of work, a former Guild Master named Groshenko."

"You know Groshenko?"

"I know Petyr very well."

The man's face softened a touch. "I worked with Groshenko for a while before I joined The Bulwark. He's a good man."

"He is that. But about The Bulwark?"

"Private security contractors."

"Ah. The spec ops of mercenaries," I said, borrowing Zeno's phrase.

Darwan's face softened a little more. "I… suppose you could put it that way, sure."

I pointed at his insignia. "The flower, it must be significant, huh?"

He looked down at his sleeve. "It is. It's adapted from the Oda Clan symbol of ancient Japan."

An explicit Earth reference. *Huh.* I just stared blankly. "Apologies, I'm not really up on my Japanese history." Which was true. I had no idea who or what the Oda Clan was or why it was notable.

"The clan of Oda Nobunaga, the first of the Three Great Unifiers of ancient Japan. He was one of the fiercest, most skillful warlords of the time—of any time, for that matter. The boss decided it fit the idea he had for The Bulwark, that we aren't afraid of anyone, and it sends the exact message we want."

"Which is?"

"Don't get in our way."

I felt Icky bristle at my side, but I maintained a pleasant smile.

"Point taken. So, what brings a group like you here?"

Darwan opened his mouth, but he suddenly stopped and cocked his head, clearly listening to something, probably a hidden ear bug. Then his face went hard and blank again.

"Sorry. I've got things to do," he said and turned away in dismissal.

"But I was hoping you could tell me—"

He turned and strode into the airlock, which started to cycle closed. Icky immediately jammed her sledgehammer toward it, as though to block it from closing, but I pulled it back.

"What? I thought you wanted to get some information out of these guys?"

"We did," I said, before turning and walking back into the station.

———

"So that's apparently the deal. This Group 41 is paying the terraforming research group that operates this station for its use as a transfer point down to the surface," Perry finished. She and Perry had recounted what they'd learned, and so had I, moving us into the comparing notes stage.

"They're paying *well*, too. I could tell from the look on the station manager's face. He was definitely worried we were going to do something to interrupt the flow of cash," Torina added.

Zeno nodded. "Not surprised. These sorts of operations are never funded as well as they should be. The extra cash is probably letting them have amenities out here that they otherwise wouldn't."

"Some of it might be going into a few strategically selected pockets, too," I suggested. "You don't need to bribe a lot of people. Just the *right* people."

"True enough, but what do you want to do, Van? I mean, these guys come across as sleazy, sure, but most mercenaries do," Torina said.

"Not to mention the fact that they're not doing anything obviously illegal," Netty added.

I pursed my lips in thought for a moment. They were right—as intriguing as all this was, it didn't really reach the bar of being a case. Even recruiting cannon fodder, as reprehensible as that might be, wasn't illegal. The Fren and the Eykinao we'd seen clearly weren't under any direct duress, and they weren't slaves. They might be desperate for money or adventure or whatever, but if they chose to be cannon fodder, that was their call.

But still—

There was something about this not sitting right with me. The logical person to ask was Groshenko, and I decided to put in a call to him. But he often took time to answer, and, in the meantime, we might be able to learn something useful. Besides, I was in no hurry to go anywhere I might be immediately recognized. The nice thing about this terraforming station was that it was out of the way, a sort of frontier outpost that wasn't necessarily up on the latest news.

I turned to the others. "Break out the cold-weather gear. We're going to take a little trip down to the surface."

"We'll need clearance from the terraformers, and they're going to ask us why," Perry said.

I turned to Torina. "Care to employ your silver tongue again, my dear?"

She scowled. "How did I end up becoming the diplomat of the group?"

"Look around you. Perry and Netty are AIs, Zeno's still part recluse—"

"And a big part, at that," she admitted.

"—and Icky's—" I grimaced. "Icky has some of that whatever the hell it was from the cafeteria stuck in her teeth."

"So? I'd love to be the diplomat," she shot back, pulling a tool from her belt and picking her teeth with it. "I'm a natural."

"We're speaking about language skills, not aroma," Perry said with his own natural tact.

"Thank you," Icky beamed.

Torina narrowed her eyes at me. "What about you?"

"I'm the brains of the group."

She smiled, then patted my shoulder. "Sure. We'll go with that."

"THEY'RE RIGHT over the ridge ahead—" Perry started and abruptly cut off.

I glanced up into the hard, gray sky. Wind gusted around us, driving clouds of ice crystals that rattled off my b-suit. "Perry, you okay?"

"Yeah. It's just choppy up here—yikes!"

I found him, a dark spot against the scudding clouds that abruptly slid sideways.

"Yeah, the captain's definitely switched on the seat-belt light— holy shit!"

"Perry, come on back down here before you get blown to the next continent," I said, trudging through the snow toward the crest of the ridgeline. Torina and Icky followed me, a few meters behind and to either side.

Torina had convinced the terraformers that we'd been wanting to test out some new equipment in a cold-weather environment, and that this was an ideal opportunity. They'd balked until she sweetened the deal with a couple of thousand bonds, which, I had no doubt, was going straight into the station manager's pocket. Whatever. It got us down to the surface, and that was good enough. It did mean Icky was lugging a backpack full of odds and ends that we could test here on the frigid surface, though.

We reached the crest, and the wind slammed into us full-force. I only felt it as a rising and falling pressure against me, though, since the b-suit and helmet kept me at a comfortable temperature. It was a spacesuit, after all.

Icky dropped her backpack, and we made a big show of doing things with the contents, but I put my attention on the far side of the ridge. I could see a few dozen figures in the distance, arranged in something presumably meant to resemble a formation. I remembered my own army days so vividly that the skills I acquired might as well have been physical laws—watch your assigned arc of responsibility, maintain at least five meters spacing and don't bunch up, look through foliage and not around or over it, don't skyline yourself against a crestline, pass along commands and hand signals to the next guy in line and confirm he sees and acknowledges it. They were all simple rules intended to keep you in the fight and effective in battle. These were the building blocks of being a soldier, and they were, even years later, autonomic.

Those distant figures were doing *none* of these things.

"They might as well be marching around on a parade square," I said, zooming the view through my helmet's heads-up. Sure enough, they were arrayed in a line, marching across the frozen tundra like they were searching for a lost kid. Ambling along, the soldiers—a term I used with hesitation—held their weapons in a riot of different positions, none of them quite at the alert. A handful of figures followed along, and these ones were moving like experienced soldiers. It looked as though the leaders were cajoling the line of soldiers ahead of them, urging them on while sheltering behind them, using them as a sort of fleshy screen.

We stayed on the ridge for a while, supposedly doing our cold weather testing while we watched the bizarre performance in the valley below. Perry wheeled overhead, scouting. Maybe these were such brand new recruits that this was their first taste of the field, the very leading edge of a more rigorous training regimen. But after being marched back and forth several times, they were all loaded aboard a trio of shuttles on the next ridgeline to our north.

As they clambered aboard the boxy ships, I studied a group of figures standing to one side, conferring. From their collective body language, I could tell which of them was the focus, the center of everyone's attention. Whoever he was, he was in charge. Finally, they boarded the shuttles, the airlocks cycled closed, and they began spooling up their drives.

"That wasn't military training, that was a LARP," I said, watching as the first shuttle lifted in a cloud of dust and snow.

"A LARP?" Torina asked.

"Live-action role playing. It's make believe, but in real life. Kind of like... improv."

"You mean, like acting."

"Yeah. Exactly."

Icky moved to join us watching the shuttles lift into the clouds. "So what you're saying is that these Bulwark guys, whoever they are, are basically trash at what they do."

I shrugged. "Maybe. But they can afford to operate that ship docked up there, plus uniforms and equipment, plus pay for their soldiers and whatever they're paying the terraforming people to use their facilities. So either it's some rich dilettante playing soldier, or they're making genuine money. And then there's the Oda Clan thing."

"That flower symbol of theirs?" Torina asked.

"Yeah. I looked them up. Four hundred-odd years ago on Earth, in the country called Japan, their leader was named Nobunaga. Through cunning and sheer force, he took on a bunch of ruthless and ambitious warlords all vying for control of Japan, and came out on top. Along the way, he earned the name *The Demon King*."

"So? Anyone can find something or other in the history books and name themselves after it," Icky said.

"You're right. But—I don't know." I watched the last shuttle vanish into the clouds high above. "My gut tells me these guys aren't just posers or wannabes. I think that shitty, so-called *training* we just watched was deliberate and calculated. They only wanted to give these new recruits of theirs enough *training* to get them marching across somewhere, to do something, and if they get killed in the process—"

I turned away from the tundra below that was still pocked with footprints.

"Well, Oda Nobunaga got named The Demon King for a reason, didn't he?"

5

WE CHECKED in on the two injured crew from the class 7 that we'd rescued when we returned to the terraforming platform. One of them wasn't likely to survive, while the other wouldn't be conscious for a long time. Even then, when he did recover, the medical assessment was that he might regain consciousness but not much actual awareness.

It meant that the clash between the class 7 and the class 9 it had attacked was, for the moment, another mystery we had to throw on the heap of mysteries we'd already encountered. We also found that The Bulwark's warship, and the freighter docked alongside it, had departed immediately after the shuttles returned from the surface. That was all a mystery too, but one without any obvious connection to us or any of our cases. And we had more than enough to keep us busy without chasing down yet more trouble, so we just filed Group 41 and the Bulwark away for future reference.

Which would have left us at a loose end had it not been for a call Netty received from herself.

"My instance aboard the *Iowa* reports that someone has boarded the ship, apparently searching for something," she said, catching me in the middle of showering away the plasticine stink of wearing a b-suit.

I shut off the water and watched it sluice down the drain and into the reclamator. "Someone? Can she—er, you—or both of you, I guess—"

"It's sufficient just to refer to me, Van, singular. I'll know what you mean."

"Right. Can you be more specific about this *someone*?" I asked, stepping out of the shower and toweling myself off, trying not to flail my fists or smash my elbows against the bulkheads of the *Fafnir*'s cramped lavatory as I did.

"Six individuals boarded through the starboard amidships airlock. I didn't detect them until they breached the doors."

I stopped. "Didn't detect them? Like, at all? No inbound ship or anything? What'd they do, walk?"

"Sorry, Van, I don't know. I was only using passive scanners, per your direction, so if they were using a sufficiently stealthed ship and taking advantage of the rocky debris around the *Iowa* for cover, they could have approached without being detected—which they obviously did, since here they are."

I started yanking my clothes on, anger building with each passing second. The *Iowa* was mine. It was an extension of my farm, and the *Fafnir*, and violating the sanctity of my spaces was a short path to my unreasonable side. "Okay, tell the others we're getting underway, heading for Sol."

I finished getting dressed while Netty got everyone rounded up and briefed them on the situation. When I emerged from the lavatory, my hair damp and face flushed with anger, I found the rest of the crew at their action stations. The *Fafnir's* drive was already thrumming, accelerating us toward the closest twist point. This far out in the Procyon system, that wouldn't take long.

"Netty, do you know what these assholes are actually *doing* on the *Iowa?*" I asked, sliding into the pilot's seat.

"They appear to be searching for something—and quite exhaustively, I might add."

"Tossing the joint, boss," Perry added.

"Thank you for the noir flavor, bird. Any damage showing up that we know of?" I asked.

"What sort of access do they have? Do they have control of the ship itself?" Zeno added.

"No. They've made no attempt to hack or access the *Iowa's* core systems, at least not yet."

"So they don't currently have access to her drive, nav, weapons, any of that."

"That's correct."

"That's something, at least," Torina said.

I exhaled, thinking. With the help of Icky's father, we armed the *Iowa* to the teeth using salvaged weapons from an ancient battle site near a lonely neutron star called Arx. She went from a pair of point-defense turrets to batteries of lasers, mass-drivers and particle cannons, and a single weapon whose secrets we were still unraveling. Zeno determined it was some sort of plasma-discharge cannon, a weapon that could pump out focused thermonuclear detonations, which would be absolutely devastating at short range. We hadn't actually fired it yet, though, and would probably dismount it from the *Iowa* before we did.

We then returned the *Iowa* to her parking orbit near the dwarf planet called Orcus in Sol's Kuiper Belt. A second instance of Netty watched over her, keeping her ready to fly anytime we needed some especially heavy firepower. It meant we didn't have to rely on others—Schegith or her cousin, Groshenko, or other Peacemakers—whenever we expected a scrap too intense for the *Fafnir* alone to handle. But it also meant that the *Iowa* was effectively mothballed in the meantime, powered down and relying on passive scanners only. That seemed to be an Achilles heel we were going to have to address.

But first, we had to take back our own ship.

WE APPROACHED THE *IOWA* CAUTIOUSLY, using the cover of an icy rock the size of a small town to get to within a few thousand klicks. Netty still had full control of the ship, aside from a few lesser internal systems, such as security doors. Whoever was aboard was obviously determined to find something, although what, we had no idea.

"Okay, so if we keep the bulk of the *Iowa* between us and the ship that's docked with her, they shouldn't be able to detect us approaching, right, Netty?" I asked, studying the imagery of our battlecruiser on the central display.

"That would be the case, except that they've deployed a small scanner drone to keep watch on the space around the ship."

"Drones. They're too cheap and effective for my taste, especially when the enemy has them." I looked at the tactical overlay. "It's going to take us about ten minutes to reach her from here? That's enough time for them to prep an unpleasant reception."

"Or get away. They might not want a fight," Torina said.

"Yeah, but I kinda do. And on top of that, I'd like to close out some of these questions. I don't need mystery. I want *answers*."

"Van, Netty and I have been conferring, and we think we can hack that drone and keep it blissfully unaware of our approach," Perry said.

I glanced at him. "I can't help thinking there's a *but* somewhere in there."

"*But*, if we blow it, we'll let them know we're here almost immediately."

"That wouldn't make things any worse than they are now, correct?"

Torina gave me a sidelong look. "You're going to let Netty and Perry do the hacking, right?"

I smiled. "As much as it wounds my pride to say it, they are *way* better at it than I am. I'll reserve my hacking for occasions where they can't."

I turned to Perry. "Whenever you're ready—"

"Oh, we're done."

"You're... done?"

"Yeah."

I glared. "First, well done. Second, I'm annoyed at you for making it look so easy."

"Yeah, well, you annoy me for being able to experience the sun and the wind as more than just pressure and temperature differentials."

I let my face soften. "Really?"

"Pfft. No. They're just pressure and temperature differentials."

"You're being a bit of a tool, bird."

"Hurtful but fair, boss."

I turned to the others. "Okay, folks, this is gonna take all of us. Netty, start us in. We're going to suit up and get ready to kick the respective asses of whoever dared to board our ship."

WE HAD a tense moment while slowly sliding past the enemy scanner drone that was less than a hundred meters away. Perry and Netty kept it blind to us, though. We had the advantage of home turf when it came to hacking, and we had it for the next step— clearing the *Iowa* of these intruders.

I hefted The Drop into a firing position aimed at the airlock door. "Remember, everyone. I want at least one of these scumbags alive."

I got terse acknowledgements. We'd suited up fully, strapped on every bit of armor we had, and loaded ourselves with weapons, power cells, and ammunition. Torina and Zeno had goo guns slung, ready to use to incapacitate some of our foes. Icky wielded her sledge-hammer in one pair of hands and a boarding shotgun in the other.

"Okay, Netty, anytime you're ready," I said.

"I'm opening the airlock doors—now."

The *Iowa*'s inner and outer doors slid open, and, The Drop raised and ready, I stepped through—

And into a hail of gunfire.

SOMETHING SLAMMED into my right side like a thrown fist. Something else snapped off my left vambrace, the one made by Linulla, and ricocheted away. Rounds sparked and clanged against the bulkheads around me. I didn't even think, I just aimed The Drop at the source of the gunfire and squeezed off a round with a thunderous boom. Then, in my tactical brilliance, I kept firing until The Drop's action locked to the rear.

The incoming fire stopped. I saw why. A sentry gun, set in the cross-corridor just inside the airlock, had been rigged to fire from right to left, into the flank of anyone boarding. It was called enfilade fire, and placing the weapon where we couldn't see it until it opened up was called defilade. It told me that whoever was aboard knew something about tactics.

"Van, are you okay?" Torina called out.

"I—yeah." I slipped out The Drop's magazine, snapped a new one into place, and let the action slide closed, chambering a new round. "Yeah. Took a couple of hits, and I'll probably be bruised, but I'm still in the fight."

Zeno moved to examine the sentry gun I'd wrecked with my return fire. "Standard, off-the-shelf type, not military-grade." She glanced back at me. "You're lucky they cheaped out, Van."

I touched my right side, just below my ribs, and was rewarded with a dull flare of pain. "You're not wrong."

"Actually, I suspect they didn't bring along heavier gear because it's bulkier and more cumbersome to carry. I suspect this was more of an early warning setup," Perry put in.

"Which means we no longer have the advantage of surprise," Torina replied.

I nodded. "Maybe not, but we do have an ace up our sleeve. Netty, can you tell where they are?"

"Two on the bridge, two in engineering, two amidships. Those last two were probably searching the cargo hold, but they've started forward. If you move up a deck to intersection four-alpha-two, you'll cut them off before they can reach the bridge."

"And now that ace is on the table. Come on, folks, let's go say hi to our visitors."

WE SPLIT into two pairs at intersection four-alpha-two, Torina and I to the right, Icky and Zeno to the left. Perry lurked further forward, peeking around the corner down the longitudinal corridor that ran from just ahead of engineering to just behind the bridge. It was the uppermost of four corridors that ran most the length of the ship, the others being along her belly, and one down each beam.

Two bogies just appeared, four junctions down. They're coming toward you, side-by-side, with long arms. One's a laser rifle, not sure about the other. Some sort of slug thrower, Perry said in our headsets.

"Roger that. Let's let them come right up this junction—"

Van, they've got a small drone running ahead of them. They're using it to check each cross corridor. They're three junctions down now.

I glanced around. "Okay, change of plan. Icky, Zeno, duck into that compartment just behind you to your left. Torina, let's you and I move back to this next intersection and take cover there. We'll let them go by, then we'll attack from behind."

With quick and quiet efficiency, everyone moved into their places and waited for Perry to give us the word they'd passed us by.

Two junctions away now.

A pause.

They're at the next junction. Yours is next.

Another pause.

The drone's entering the junction now.

I heard a faint whirring but didn't dare stick my head around the corner. I just waited, gripping The Drop tightly. I'd drawn the Moonsword as well and held it in my off hand.

And they're past you, starting forward.

"Van, the two in engineering have started forward now," Netty confirmed.

"Okay, everyone, places please. Let's introduce ourselves, shall we?"

"I love it when you use manners. So Britishy," Torina said with a low laugh.

"Wait until I show you my curtsy. Okay, showtime. On me."

I slipped around the corner and started back toward junction four-alpha-two.

Torina had unlimbered the goo gun, as had Zeno. Icky was going to hang back, our reserve.

I stepped around the corner, into the main corridor, just as one of them turned to look right at me. I had a brief impression of dull, charcoal gray armor and a blank visor, then he snap-fired a shot from his laser rifle at nearly point-blank range.

The intense pulse of coherent light snapped against the overhead above me. He fired again, and this time the shot struck the bulkhead to my right. An instant later, Torina and Zeno fired their goo guns, splattering both of our opponents with gouts of sticky foam that almost immediately turned to thick sludge and hardened. One ended up stuck to the bulkhead. The other lost the use of his arms and his weapon, so he turned and ran, desperately calling for help on his comm.

I raised The Drop and planted the sight in his back. I hated to shoot someone like this, but we couldn't let him reach his comrades—

The corridor ahead of him vanished into a scintillating burst of dazzling light. He stumbled and smacked against the bulkhead.

"Watch my rear!" I shouted to the others and charged after him. At point-blank range, I raised The Drop again but this time triggered the underslung beam projector, which I'd already dialed to its strongest stun setting, for humans, anyway. I caught him squarely, but his armor protected him, so I kept going at full speed and launched myself in the air.

Like a middle linebacker, I *blasted* the invader, rattling his entire frame against the bulkhead with a dull *bonnnnnnngggg*.

Perry deactivated his dazzle mode and skittered to a stop before us, me on top of the target, who was, no surprise, as still as a tomb.

"Nice tackle. Saved that one for a few years, eh?" Perry asked.

"Always wanted a clean hit over the middle. Congratulations, friend. You made my personal highlight reel," I said, putting a knee on the guy as he wiggled a bit under my weight.

"I wouldn't do that," Perry said, extending a foot, talons spread. "I'm feeling pokey."

Something grabbed me and firmly pushed me aside. It was Icky. She grabbed our opponent and lifted him, then slammed him against the bulkhead, his feet scrabbling at the air. Grinning, she pushed her face right into his visor.

"Excuse me, but I think you took a wrong turn and ended up aboard my ship. How careless of you."

His field of view filled with Icky's bared teeth, the figure went still.

I glanced back at the other bad guy, still stuck to the bulkhead. Torina and Zeno had him under control.

I took a breath. "Okay, two down, four more to go."

"What do you wanna do with these two?" Icky asked.

"Torina and Zeno are going to glue them firmly in place, and you're going to stay here and keep an eye on them. That'll give them time to think about what they've done."

Icky shot the guy a murderous glare, then nodded without taking her eyes off him. "You're about to enjoy some of my close, personal attention, shithead."

I turned to Torina, Zeno, and Perry. "I'd say this situation is secure. Icky, leave some pieces big enough to question, okay? Now then, let's go. I want my bridge back."

WE RAN into another sentry gun, set up just outside the bridge. As the rounds sizzled past, I ducked behind the junction. "Netty, a little warning about these damned things would be nice!"

"Sorry, Van, but I can only tell you where the bad guys are, not what they're doing."

Something clattered along the deck. A grenade.

"Grenade!" I bellowed, diving backward.

When it detonated, the junction and both intersecting corridors rang with shrapnel. I felt something smack the heel of my boot, hard. As the flash cleared, I aimed The Drop.

Perry, further to the rear along the longitudinal corridor, called out. *Here they come! They're making a break for it!*

Two armored figures appeared at the junction, pouring out fire as they went. The next few seconds were a confusing swirl of gunfire and movement. I heard Zeno get hit but couldn't spare even an instant to check on her. Torina lunged at one of the bad guys and grappled with him, but his armor prevented her from delivering any debilitating blows. The other bad guy raised a gun to shoot at her point-blank range.

I charged and swung the Moonsword with my off hand. It wasn't the most elegant blow, but it passed through armor, and then flesh, and then muscle and bone. My opponent's right arm and most of his shoulder thumped against the deck. Blood showered the junction in an explosive loop, and then it *kept* spraying as his or her heart thumped away, sending crimson arcs flying in a chaotic mess.

Zeno appeared, goo gun raised, and shouted for Torina to get clear. She let go and dove backward just a little too late. Her foot got caught in the glue blast, and she dropped to the deck on top of the severed arm. Her opponent was firmly enmeshed in the quickly hardening slurry, though, and just gave up, dropping his weapon with a clatter. I saw his visor turn to the severed arm, and the blood, and then back to me. There would be no more resistance—that, I could tell.

"Perry, confirm the bridge is clear, would you?"

"On it, boss."

"Zeno, are you okay?" I asked.

She turned and peered at me through a visor that was a spider web of cracks radiating from a distinct impact point. "Does this answer your question?"

"Could've been worse."

"Yes, having my head shot off would definitely be worse—"

We heard distant gunfire from astern.

"Shit—Icky." I started to run, Zeno right behind me. I heard Torina cursing.

"I'll just stay here then, shall I?" she snapped.

"Join us as soon as you can!"

WE ARRIVED to find the immediate aftermath of a bloodbath. Icky stood in the corridor, her sledgehammer hanging in one hand, her boarding shotgun cradled in two more. Two broken bodies lay in the corridor just beyond her, and there was blood—

A *lot* of blood.

I raced past our first two prisoners, both still stuck firmly in place.

"Icky!"

She turned, then stumbled against the bulkhead. She'd taken two hits that I could see, one in one of her upper, bigger shoulders that looked like a through-and-through, and another that had gouged a chunk out of her right upper leg, the pink muscle exposed in a wicked crescent.

I skidded to a stop beside her—literally, because the deck was slick with blood. "Icky?"

"Ow."

I yanked out a cylinder of first-aid spray from my harness and squirted it on her leg. Zeno did the same for her arm.

"Holy shit, Icky, why didn't you just take cover and call for help?" I snapped.

She gave a tight grin, wincing as she moved. "Van, I have been… dying to beat the living shit out of… of at least some of these assholes who keep… coming after us." She let her head loll back against the bulkhead. "I finally got… my wish."

"Was it everything you hoped it would be?" I asked, emptying the first aid cylinder.

"And more."

Torina appeared, one foot clad only in a sock.

"You're out of uniform," I said.

She scowled. "It got me free of that damned goop. How's Icky?"

"Shot twice, but she got to smack some villains around, so it's all good I guess?"

Icky closed her eyes and nodded. "Damned right it is."

6

I STARED AT THE MAN, a grizzled human with a face scarred by old burns.

"Yotov?"

He nodded. "That's what I said."

"You were hired by a Ligurite named Yotov."

"How many times you gonna ask me this question?" he snapped.

I stepped back. We'd taken three of the six intruders alive. They were mercenaries, clearly, and had the loyalty of mercenaries, which meant not much. Faced with a whole suite of crimes that could send them to the Guild's prison barge for a very long time, they were more than willing to trade information for lesser charges. The one that had absolutely snagged me had been the name of their employer.

Yotov.

Former Peacemaker Guild Master, Yotov had been found guilty

of some egregious crimes and sentenced to lengthy prison time. That had been less than a year and a half ago, though, which meant she still had at least a couple of decades to go.

I gestured for Torina to follow me out of the compartment and had Netty seal it behind us. We'd stuck each of our three prisoners into three different compartments, stripped down to their under-suits. Out in the corridor, I turned to her and Perry.

"Yotov."

"Maybe it's a different Yotov," Torina suggested.

I sighed. "Yeah, maybe. But—Perry, have you and Netty heard anything back from the Guild yet?"

"Nope. Regular, formal channels seem to be closed, so I've put in a query through the AI net. One of them must know if Yotov somehow escaped custody."

"So it's either not her, it *is* her and she's out of prison, or she's somehow able to hire mercenaries from inside her cell," I said.

"There's another possibility, Van. They may just be lying to you for some unknown purpose," Perry added.

"Yeah, that too."

Zeno joined us, wearing a partial grin.

"How's Icky?" I asked.

"Bitching about being stuck in the infirmary while Netty gets her patched and stapled up, so fine. Did you learn anything from these assholes?"

She nodded as we brought her up to date. "Yotov, huh?"

"That's what they say."

"And did they say why they were here? What they were looking for?"

I shrugged. "Yes and no. They were looking for a specific cargo, a small crate marked with a number, 18975-A-T."

"What the hell is that?"

"No idea. And I don't think they know, either. They were just sent here to find it and then bring it back to a rendezvous at everyone's favorite sneaky meeting spot, the outskirts of Wolf 424."

"So what the hell makes Yotov, or whoever hired these assholes, think that this one, specific cargo crate is aboard the *Iowa*, a decommissioned battlecruiser?" Zeno asked.

"Another very good question. The trouble is, like I said, I don't think these guys know."

Torina ran a thoughtful hand along the bulkhead behind us. "Van, what do we know about the history of this ship?"

"Like Zeno just said, she's a decommissioned battlecruiser. So—that, and then she was mothballed when she was decommissioned, and then she ended up in our hands. Why?"

She turned to me. "Are we *sure* she was actually mothballed?"

"I—" I stopped, staring, then shook my head. "No, I suppose we aren't."

"Might be worth looking into."

"Yeah, it just might. Perry, I assume that since we nabbed these assholes here, in the Solar System, jurisdiction falls to the Guild by default, right?" I asked.

"Earth isn't a recognized interstellar authority, so yeah. I mean, unless you want to land outside some police station and hand these guys over to them, which would be a lot of fun to watch." He stopped, then gave me a glance. "But don't do that."

"Much as I'd love to drop our prisoners on the lawn, say, of the

FBI headquarters in Washington DC, I guess we need to get these guys to Anvil Dark."

"You sure about that, Van? Lunzy was explicit about staying away from there," Torina said.

"I know. That's why I said we need to *get* them to Anvil Dark, not that we had to *take* them there."

WE HADN'T SEEN K'losk in a long time, not since shortly after the Battle of 109, which he'd missed because of another case. He showed up to help us with the aftermath, though. For the past year, our paths simply hadn't crossed again, though we kept in touch. He was one of a handful of Peacemakers we felt we could actually trust, a steady, distant presence that gave me a sense that no matter what, we had a small core of people on our side.

We met with him on the fringe of Anvil Dark's star system, Gamma Crucis. He took our prisoners into custody to deliver them to the Guild so we didn't have to. He also took a couple of questions to the station with him, promising to bring us back whatever answers he could.

While we moved the prisoners to K'losk's ship, we were treated to another standoff between Perry and his combat AI, another bird-construct named Hosurc'a with a long, flowing, and admittedly magnificent tail. For reasons entirely unknown to us mere flesh-and-blood mortals, the two had an epic rivalry.

They stopped, facing each other through the airlock.

"Hello, Hosurc'a."

"Hello, Perry."

They stared at one another for a moment, then simultaneously turned and walked away.

"What the hell is their deal?" Icky asked.

I shrugged. "AI drama. It's like ordinary drama but much, much faster."

Icky had more or less recovered from her wounds, her tough Wu'tzur constitution getting her back on her feet within a day. But the through-and-through wound she'd taken in her shoulder was going to take time to heal, leaving her with one arm bound up in a sling. Icky, predictably, hated it.

"I can't *do* anything!"

Zeno clicked her tongue. "Unlike the rest of us, Icky, you have two more arms to use, plus a spare."

"It's not the same—!"

"Icky, what did I say about whining?"

She glanced down at her feet. "Sorry."

K'losk returned in about a day, time we took to just chill in the outer reaches of Gamma Crucis and get some items checked off the *Fafnir*'s maintenance to-do list, which wouldn't actually make any difference because the damned thing never got any shorter. We docked, and he came aboard, bearing gifts.

"I thought you might be tired of whatever you carry around with you for refreshments," he said, producing two bottles of a sour liqueur from Falaxis, a planet that seemed to thrive on exporting nothing but high-end luxury goods, from its famed tapestries to artisanal spirits like this one. I'd developed a taste for the stuff, but it was expensive enough to make it only a rare treat.

"Two bottles? I mean—thank you, K'losk, that's great, but I

can't take these as gifts. They must have cost you a small fortune," I said.

He shook his somewhat lupine head, which always looked like some random add-on to his otherwise insectoid body. "Not at all. *The Black Hole*'s going through a rough patch, so they're selling off all their expensive, low-sales-volume stuff."

I took the bottles but frowned. *The Black Hole*, Anvil Dark's premier watering hole, was normally jammed to bustling. "What's wrong with *The Black Hole*?"

"Almost no business. Everyone's doing their best to stay clear of Anvil Dark."

"Why?"

"Well, that segues right into one of the questions you wanted me to look into. Yotov is, indeed, no longer in custody."

I put the bottles down on the galley table. "She *escaped*?"

But K'losk shook his head again. "No, she was released."

Torina, who'd been nearby reading something on a data slate, glanced up. "Released? She had years to go on her sentence. Even if she was being the model of model prisoners, she shouldn't have been *close* to release.'"

"And yet, there it is. You arrested her on Persuasion, in the Ligurite home system. That gave the planetary authorities there jurisdiction over the case. And the new governor of Persuasion apparently decided that Yotov had suffered enough in her plush, minimum-security suite and commuted her sentence."

"But… we had an explicit guarantee that that wouldn't happen."

"And I'm sure the old Planetary Governor meant it. The new one, not so much."

Torina put the slate down. "It almost never happens, though. As soon as a new Governor decides to reverse something like that, something that isn't actually government policy, they open up questions about how reliable their promises will be going forward."

"And yet, once again, here it is."

Torina's eyes narrowed. "I need to make a call," she said and headed for her cabin.

I turned back to K'losk. "Any other good news?"

"Well, news, but whether it's good or not is up to you I guess," he said, handing me a data slate. "These are three different criminal intelligence reports, collected over four years. They all involve smuggling. But it's not the actual crimes themselves I thought might interest you. Check out the images in each report I've highlighted."

I scrolled through the data until I found the first image he'd marked. It showed a ship, maybe class six or seven, docked at what I thought was probably Crossroads. "What am I looking at?"

"The background," he said and pointed at other ships in the picture. None of the ones at berth meant anything to me. It wasn't until my attention went well into the background that I noticed what K'losk had found.

It was the *Iowa*.

I checked the date stamp on the image. It was a little under twelve years ago.

"Now the next one," K'losk said, reaching over and tapping the slate with a chitinous manipulator. He'd linked the next image, so the display immediately flicked to displaying it. This time, it was Spindrift. I recognized the shape of the docking modules. Once again, the *Iowa* had been caught in the background, this time about ten years ago.

The third image from Crossroads caught the *Iowa* a little over nine years ago.

"These can't be the *Iowa*, though. She was laid up in a mothball orbit somewhere," I said.

"Something was laid up in mothballs, but it wasn't your ship."

I called out to Perry in the cockpit and filled him in when he arrived in the galley. He downloaded the images, then said, "Huh."

"Huh? What does *huh* mean?"

"These three images are definitely the *Iowa*."

"But she was one of a class of ships. How do you know it isn't one of her sisters?" I asked.

"Because she's got that dorsal bulge amidships, the one with the two extra weapons hardpoints. She was the only one of her class to get that upgrade, at least as far as the records show."

"What the hell? She couldn't have been in two places at once. If she was out running around the galaxy, then how was she not missed from where she'd been stashed in mothballs?"

"I can answer that," Icky said, arriving from astern, her tool harness jangling. "When they lay a ship up in long term storage, they switch its transponder to broadcast an ID and a few odds and ends about its basic status. But these yards cover millions and millions of cubic klicks. They don't bother trying to keep a physical eye on every ship."

"You sound like you've got some experience with this, Icky," I noted.

She shrugged, wincing slightly around her injured arm. "My dad and I paid a visit or two to one of these places for parts for the *Nemesis*. While we were there, we might have had a few extra bits and pieces fall into our hold from mothballed ships that weren't actually on our paid manifest."

"You stole them."

Icky stared for a moment. "Liberated, thank you, but my point is that the people who operate these boneyards only know most of the ships parked in them as a transponder ping. So if someone cloned the *Iowa*'s and put something else where she was supposed to be——"

She shrugged, wincing again.

I sighed. "So based on this, when she was supposedly parked in cold storage, the *Iowa* was actually out gallivanting around, doing… something."

"Probably something illegal," Perry said.

"Over the course of about three years, she visited Spindrift once and Crossroads twice. But we can probably safely assume those weren't her only ports of call. Whoever had her replaced her transponder in the boneyard, and for at least three years, no one noticed."

"I presume that someone tasked with the yard's operations was probably involved, or at least on the take," K'losk said.

I nodded. "As for what she was doing, I'm going with smuggling."

"That's a pretty good bet," Perry said.

"And that brings us back to Yotov, and the mercenaries she hired to toss your ship. Yotov must have learned about the *Iowa*'s history and had reason to believe there was something still stashed aboard her, something valuable."

I crossed my arms. "She's a big ship, with about a million possible hiding places."

"Those mercs might have had some info that narrowed the

search down. Or they had hand scanners, so maybe they were looking for something in particular. Or maybe Yotov was just hoping they'd get lucky. After all, the *Iowa's* just sitting, mothballed in a stable orbit near Orcus. We go weeks at a time without visiting her," Perry replied.

"Except they apparently didn't know we'd installed an instance of Netty aboard her and thought it was just the standard, off-the-shelf dimwit AI running her," Icky said.

"And they would've gotten away with it, too, if it hadn't been for those meddling kids," I said.

Icky and K'losk just stared blankly, of course. Perry got it, though, and chuckled.

"Good one, Van. I tell you, I miss those Saturday morning cartoons."

"I wish you'd experienced the heart palpitations from sugary cereal. A true rite of passage, along with cartoons. Anyway, enough about my youth," I said, waving grandly.

K'losk shook his head. "One last thing. I asked Bester to pull the records for anything reported missing between ten and fifteen years ago that was valuable enough that someone like Yotov would go through the effort and expense of sending mercenaries after it. Note the item at the top of the list," he said, handing back the slate. I read what he'd highlighted.

Case 78659-16-BT, currency imprint plates, quantity four, origin Falaxis, value 250,000 bonds per plate, Falaxian ID 18975-A-T.

It took a moment for it to sink in.

I nodded. "What an unpleasant and wholly foreseeable surprise.18975-A-T., none other than the good Master Yotov. So, she somehow knew about these plates—wait. The Falaxians are on the bond system, aren't they?"

"They are now, but they used their own currency in parallel until just a few years ago. Beautiful stuff, too. They printed it on a blend of supple fabric like silk, interwoven with platinum thread and edged with flexible, opalized wood. It's still legal tender on Falaxis, but these days it's mostly a collector's item." Perry looked up at me. "They destroyed all the plates when they switched to the bond system," he went on, then looked at the slate again. "Or almost all of them, apparently."

"Those plates would be worth a fortune now, probably far more than—what was it, 250,000 bonds each?"

I returned the slate. "Yeah. A million bonds, and that was a decade ago."

Icky scratched her chin. "Wait. Are you saying there's a million bonds worth of stuff hidden somewhere on the *Iowa*?"

I shook my head.

"No, Icky, I'm saying there's probably *several* million bonds worth of stuff hidden somewhere on the *Iowa*—and Yotov wants it."

———

WE CONCLUDED that Yotov must have been involved in the original smuggling operation of ten years before, so she knew about the plates. For whatever reason, she either also knew, or at least *believed*, that the plates were still aboard the *Iowa*. And having just squirmed her way out of prison, she was probably desperate for fast cash. It meant that the *Iowa* was still very much a target.

I settled into the *Fafnir*'s cockpit, watching as K'losk's ship maneuvered away. "Okay, Netty, contact yourself aboard the *Iowa* and tell her to go weapons-free. She can give one challenge, then she blasts *anything* that ignores it. Use the new toys we bought."

"Less the experiment plasma-discharge cannon, I assume."

"Yeah. I'd rather not blow the ship up while trying to save it."

"Van, to do that effectively, I'm going to have to have me switch to active scanning mode. Otherwise, I might just get surprised, again."

"A: this is a weird conversation. B: yeah, do it. Yotov already knows the *Iowa*'s there, obviously—and I'd love to know how she found that out—so the priority is keeping her at bay. The amount of firepower the *Iowa* can pump out now should be a pretty strong deterrent, especially since she's going to want to capture the ship, not just destroy it."

Torina reappeared. "I was talking to my father. Guess who just assumed protectorate status over Persuasion?"

"The Seven Stars League? But I thought Persuasion was dead set against that."

"They were. But then along came the new governor, who apparently feels that Persuasion would benefit from the League's care and protection."

"The Ligurites must be thrilled about that—" I stopped. "Wait. The Seven Stars League. That's our oily Satrap who wants to toss me in jail."

Torina nodded. "I thought you'd make that connection. In fact, the new Satrap was elected only two months before the new Governor of Persuasion was installed."

I sank back in my seat. "So we've now connected, what? The incursion on the *Iowa* to Yotov, we know Yotov is connected to

Persuasion, and Persuasion is now connected to the Seven Stars League." I glanced around. "Am I missing something? Could this be all connected to our Crimes Against Order case?"

"Not obviously," Perry said. "I mean, it might be, but it might be a separate case entirely."

"So that's a maybe."

"A *definite* maybe."

I blew out a sigh. "You know, sometimes the idea of just going back to the farm and growing corn is really, really appealing."

"Well, I can't give you corn, but I can give you a distraction, Van. My father has invited us to Helso for a few days," Torina said.

"Uh, correct me if I'm wrong, but isn't Helso another League protectorate? Is that kind of like walking into the lion's den?"

Torina shook her head. "My father's arranged for a diplomatic shuttle to divert from Tau Ceti to pick us up. And once we're inside Helso's atmosphere, the League's jurisdiction, such as it is, ends. And it won't matter much longer anyway."

"Why not?"

"Because Helso has been offered protectorate status by someone else. The Grand Council is voting on it sometime in the next few days, but my father says it's a done deal. Nobody on Helso likes the League."

"A new protector? Who?"

Torina smiled. "We're especially proud of this one."

I sat up. "Who is it?"

Her smile became a grin.

"Helso is the first world to join the new Schegith Protectorate."

As it sank in, I grinned, too.

"Now *that* is the best news I've had in a long time."

7

I LOVED COMING BACK to Helso. I loved it almost as much as going home to Iowa. Between Torina's parents' estate and Master Cataric's Innsu dojo, it was a home of sorts as well.

This time, though, something was different. Instead of being the normally placid and pastoral place I'd come to know and love, the Milon estate was abuzz with people when we arrived. There were aircars—some of them bearing the logo of Torina's too-perfect ex, Boswic—parked all around the place, with people milling about on the terrace. As our shuttle swooped down to land, I turned to Torina suspiciously.

"What exactly is going on down there, Torina?"

She shrugged. "My parents are hosting a regular Helso social event. It rotates around every year, and every year the well-to-do fight viciously to be the host."

I shifted uncomfortably in my seat. We'd left Zeno and Icky aboard the *Fafnir* at Tau Ceti, and only brought Perry along with us.

I'd been looking forward to a few quiet days with Torina, but it seemed that tonight, at least, it wasn't going to be very quiet at all.

We disembarked into a warm, humid Helso evening. The restored lands to the west looked greener and lusher than ever, the far trees fading into an evening haze. I noticed that everyone present seemed to be dressed at least semi-formally, making me immediately feel out of place in my standard-issue Guild worksuit. As a robotic attendant retrieved our luggage and followed us from the landing pad to the house, I gave Torina a wary, sidelong look.

"Torina, what is this social event all about exactly?"

"What makes you think it would be about anything in particular?"

"Are you telling me that it's about nothing in particular?"

"Does it have to be about something in particular? Can't it just be a pleasant gathering?"

"Are you going to keep answering my questions with questions?"

She smiled. "Is it bothering you?"

We reached the door to find Torina's parents in a sort of receiving line. I wasn't exactly a social butterfly. Back on Earth, my concept of a party was a bunch of people standing around drinking, shouting at one another over loud music, and desperately hoping to get laid. I'd only attended one event that could be called a *soirée* rather than a party, and that had mainly been to meet a prospective client who was looking to get some inconvenient data removed from the internet. All I really remembered was champagne, which I detest, canapes, which were addictive, and an ocean of dark suits and glorious dresses. I'd worn a jacket and tie, something else I detested, and made my exit as soon as I could.

This was essentially that, except this time I was trapped. I was staying here at the Milon estate, so unless I pretended to be sick, I was stuck at this thing until it was done—probably at sometime between zero-dark-thirty and dawn.

Of course, I could always arrange for Perry or Netty to come up with an emergency that needed my immediate attention—

"Van, so good to see you!" Torina's mother said, offering her hand in that strangely stilted, formal way and holding it out kind of limp so that I could, what? Touch it? Awkwardly shake it? Kiss it?

I hated these damned things.

I settled on briefly holding her hand. "Good to see you too, Ms. Milon."

Her father offered me a more comfortable hearty handshake and a broad grin. "Van, thanks for coming. It's always good to see you."

Torina hugged each of her parents, then we plunged into the throng of people—probably about half humanoids and the rest a mix of various races—milling about, chattering and posturing and uttering that stupid, tinkling laughter I'd come to associate with these sorts of events.

A robotic waiter passed, and I flagged it down, needing a drink —a strong one. It stopped but raised a manipulator and pointed at a hologram glowing above it.

For the refreshment and enjoyment of those with a taste for powerful acids, less than pH 4!

"Ah. Yeah, I'll pass on the battery acid, thanks."

"I've summoned a waiter more suited to your physiology, sir," this one said and wheeled away.

Another waiter arrived. On a joking whim, I asked for bourbon on the rocks and was surprised to get it. I tasted it, enjoying the smooth burn. "I did not expect this. I resigned myself to something more... alien. *Plova*, maybe," I added, referring to the Helso version of whiskey, if whisky also had a cloying, fruity thing going on.

"I asked my parents to bring in some bourbon just for you, Van," Torina replied.

"Really?"

"Yes, really." She leaned a little closer. "I know you hate this sort of thing, so I wanted to do what I could to help you enjoy it."

"By getting me drunk?"

"And taking advantage of you, yes," she said, her tone solemn.

I blinked. She laughed.

"You really have to lighten up, Van. It's a party. You're supposed to relax and, you know, have fun."

I looked her up and down. She'd put on the more-or-less formal outfit she kept aboard the *Fafnir* in case there was reason to need it, but she had put some extra care into things like makeup. She'd also dabbed herself with a scent that rounded out the picture. Combine that with the grace and charm honed by growing up in a wealthy family—

Well, there were worse ways to be taken advantage of.

We moved on through the crowd and passed a small group of guests in envirosuits, protecting them from our atmosphere, which was toxic to their bodies. Torina's parents kept two large rooms capable of being pressurized with alien atmospheres, which was truly superb hospitality on the part of House Milon. It gave guests who breathed the stuff a place to take off their helmets and do some socializing without them. Several other attendees were telepresent, remaining aboard their ships and attending as mechanical avatars, or, in a couple of cases, holograms projected above mobile platforms like the little robotic vacuum cleaners that terrorized cats back on Earth.

"Torina, darling!"

I recognized the booming voice, and the incandescent grin and perfect hair that went with it. It was Boswic, Torina's ex.

Boswic moved in and hugged Torina in a way that effectively elbowed me aside. I stepped back, sipped bourbon, and tried not to sneer in contempt at Boswic, the Final Male Form, as he saw himself, although more than a few people would agree. He was everything I hated in Carter Yost, dialed up to eleven.

I caught myself. *Everything I used to hate in Carter Yost.* In the past months, Carter had repeatedly proven himself to be smart, resourceful, and brave in ways I'd never imagined he could be. He still grated on me from time to time, but he'd actually become a pretty good Peacemaker. And, more to the point, he was another of the few that I thought I could trust.

Mostly, anyway.

Bowic turned to me. "And this is—Dan, right?"

"Van."

"Van. Right. How does the Peacemaking go? Caught any bad guys recently?" he asked.

"Well, we—"

But Boswic turned back to Torina. "So, are we going to see you standing up to make your Declaration tonight?"

Torina's blandly pleasant smile didn't waver. "Oh, is that tonight?"

Boswic's smile turned sly. "We must have a drink after dinner and get caught up," he said, stepped back, then paused to glance at me.

"You as well, Dan," he said and glided off into the crowd.

I tinkled the ice in my drink. "He's a douche, but at least he's handsome."

"Now, Dan, be nice."

"Hah. Oh—what's this Declaration thing?"

"Oh, a tedious Helso social thing right after dinner, kind of like… speeches."

"Not just a stuffy party, but a stuffy party with speeches. And to think, I only had to travel light-years to get here. Gotta give credit where it's due, though."

"Go on," Torina invited.

"Your folks brought in bourbon, and the food is superb, and you look stunning. So, I'll survive."

"Attaboy, Tudor."

A discreet, melodious chime sounded, and everyone began gravitating toward the adjoining dining room. It was another commodious space, one in which we could have easily parked the *Fafnir*. I wasn't used to seeing these big rooms in use and had always just kind of ambled through them without paying too much attention.

There were place cards, and I found the one with my name on it. I ended up sitting between a chatty dilettante to my right who was all frills and feathers and an entirely uncommunicative grump of a man to my left in a rumpled formal suit. I'd expected to be seated with Torina, but she was at the head table with her parents and a hatchet-faced woman with a severely short haircut who I didn't recognize. The first course was brought by the cadre of robotic waiters and laid before us—a salad whose ingredients had been collected from the reclaimed lands of the Milon estate. I enjoyed it a little more for that, knowing that, if I did nothing else in my Peacemaking career, I'd been partly responsible for some damned good salads on Helso.

My chatty companion prattled on through dinner. I mostly ignored her, until she said something that snagged my attention.

"It's always so much fun to speculate about who's going to Declare for whom," she said, then started to draw a breath to keep going. I cut her off.

"Declare? I heard something about that earlier, about a Declaration. What's that all about?" I asked her.

She giggled. "Oh my, you've come to the Helso Festival of Declaration without knowing what it's about?"

"So it would appear," I admitted. "Van Tudor, my apologies for not being more declarative myself. I'm a—"

"Peacemaker, of course. We all know, Van Tudor. I'm Myklestun Pravic. Call me Mykki. So, to the heart of the matter here—this is considered the pinnacle of Helso social life. The established come together to announce their intended Concordance." She said *established* in a way that instantly made it synonymous with *snobs* or *society*, but she did so with such buoyant charm it was impossible to dislike her.

I put down my fork and shook my head. "I'm sorry, their Concordance?"

"Van? Ah, you really are clueless about all of this?" Mykki delivered this without anything other than compassion, though it still sounded… stuffy.

"Sorry, yes. I'm from off-world."

"Yes, from Earth, aren't you?"

"That's right. Did Torina's parents tell you that?"

"Oh, no. I can always tell people from Earth. They have such a rustic charm."

I smiled again, taking in her clothes, which featured an array of feathers from more birds than I'd seen on Helso. Ever. "We pride ourselves on authenticity. It's one of our charms. Now, back to the… ah, the Concordance?"

"Their union. Their pair-bonding."

"You mean, like, their *engagement?*"

"If the translator is right, then yes, *engagement* would fit too."

"Ah." I felt color rush to my neck and tamped it down with a series of calming breaths.

Then Mykki's engine went into *overdrive.*

She launched into a discussion about who was going to Declare and who they were going to Declare for, but my attention left the discussion behind when I found Torina's oval face in the crowd.

And then, next to her, Boswic.

Oh, shit.

If Torina was required to Declare, based on her culture and the web of politics, then Boswic made a grotesque kind of sense. The fact that I was even wondering about this issue was my own damned fault—

I stood by Torina in battle, and during quiet moments, and everything in between. But I hadn't done anything other than *stand.*

There were still many cultures on Earth in which marriage for love was rare, or at least secondary to things like political or economic gain. And Torina's parents no doubt saw Boswic as an excellent opportunity to reinforce their standing in Helso society by absorbing some of that cachet of his family's wealth and power. The reverse was probably true as well.

I put down my fork, my appetite suddenly flagging. I'd thought of Helso as sort of a second home. But if Torina's future husband was living here, that certainly wouldn't last.

And that assumed that Torina even remained part of the *Fafnir*'s crew. But why would she? Remaining my Second meant a life of constant danger, jammed aboard a ship with a smart-assed AI bird, a dour old criminal, and a mercurial, four-armed monster, all while rubbing grubby, callused elbows with some of the worst that known space could offer. Retiring here to Helso meant she could return to her life of pampered privilege and eventually inherit her parents' business empire. Staying with the *Fafnir* meant the not-inconsiderable likelihood of dying a cold and lonely death in space.

I looked at my dinner.

Nope. My appetite was gone.

WHEN DINNER HAD OFFICIALLY ENDED, another chime sounded, while the robotic waiters wheeled around the tables with liqueurs and various smokables. I recognized the stages of this social gathering, which meant that Earth exported a form of stilted parties for the upper classes, or boorish, stodgy behavior was simply a natural occurrence for humanoids everywhere.

Or at least Earth and Helso, anyway.

The quiet background music that had been playing through dinner stopped, and the severe woman sitting at the head table with Torina and her parents stood, then introduced herself as Zupharat, the Justice of Declarations. As soon as she did, the vibe in the place changed. Where there'd just been people, I now saw pairings, and those who supported or stood to benefit from those pairings. What had been *guests* had become glorified *breeding stock.*

I took a breath and resigned myself to getting through this with as much grace as I could.

"Now then, we shall proceed with the event that has brought you all here, the Declarations. I'm sure everyone is very excited to see who will Declare for whom," Zupharat said.

My frumpy seatmate, sitting on the other side of me from Mykki, *hmphed* and leaned toward me, his pink nose a story of sun and drink. "Like any of it's going to be a surprise. These pairings have been in the works for years, most of them."

I nodded but kept watching Zupharat—and Torina.

Zupharat continued. "We shall, as is customary, proceed in order of—"

Torina stood and walked to the dais where the Declarations presumably happened. It was draped in fragrant blossoms, more bounty of the reclaimed Milon lands. Zupharat stopped and watched her, her mouth opening, then closing again. Clearly, this wasn't supposed to happen.

I glanced at Boswic, who sat twirling a small stemmed glass of some yellowish liqueur and was smiling like the proverbial cat with a canary feather hanging from its mouth. I saw that most of the crowd was switching their attention between him and Torina— except for her parents, who looked—

I wasn't sure how they looked. Maybe a little surprised that Torina had apparently taken the initiative, but they seemed only to be watching her intently.

Torina smiled until the hushed whispers stilled. Then she began to speak.

"Thank you, and my apologies to you, Zupharat. I realize that by stepping up here now, and not in accordance with custom, I am flouting those customs. That isn't an accident. It's to make a point."

She paused, letting that sink in. "We have many... echoes... of our former society, such as this Festival of Declaration. But things evolve. They change. And, as you all know, I've demonstrated that by stepping outside what my family had planned for me, of what you all no doubt expected of me. Now, don't mistake me, I miss my home, but I wouldn't trade it for my life now."

Another surge of whispers. When they died again, Torina went on.

"But that doesn't mean that I'm going to throw out all of the old traditions, and that I won't Declare. I referred to echoes. Some are harsh and unpleasant. Some are echoes of beautiful music, the note of the Synclavion, the most beautiful music I've ever heard. But I have only heard it because my life has followed the course it has. Because of my Declared. My Declared who is honorable, who is brave and loyal, compassionate and generous. He is also not of our world, and if he'll have me, then I will Declare such here and now."

It is a true testament to my own capacity for cluelessness that I still had no idea where Torina was going with this.

"Now, we may have to take our time on this path. It is a dangerous place, where I live and work. But despite the danger, I am learning to care about someone in a way I never thought possible, not at any time while I was growing up here, among all of you, my friends."

My frumpy seatmate suddenly chuckled and leaned over to me. "You'd better tell her yes or no soon, or this is going to get *really* awkward *really* fast."

I blinked at him.

And then I got it, in that way you suddenly see where that puzzle piece was meant to fit, and it seemed so obvious.

I turned to Torina. She was looking straight at me, her smile diminished by an expectant look. She needed me to answer the question she was asking before she went on.

I felt an incandescent smile break across my face, and I gave a single, sharp nod, followed by one word. "Yes."

Torina's smile returned, brilliant and free.

"I Declare for Clive VanAbel Tudor III, of Pony Hollow, Iowa, of planet Earth."

The silence that suddenly draped the room was as quiet as the airless void. It lasted—I'm not sure how long. A few seconds, anyway, before Boswic stood and broke it.

"No! No, I will not have this! She's to be *mine*!" he raged, then turned and came straight at me, his fists balled.

The old me, the me who existed before I found that remote in a desk drawer in the Iowa farmhouse, would have probably tried to defuse the situation, maybe even backed down. That me had only known the shitty, low-stakes conflict of the schoolyard, or the dispassionate, remote-control conflict of hacking in cyberspace.

But I wasn't that guy anymore.

Boswic may have been an impressive specimen of a human being, all muscles and indignation charging toward me like a bull— but I'd faced much, much worse. I'd honed my instincts on implanted memories of combat when I joined the Peacemakers, on hours and hours of grueling training in the Innsu dojo just down the road, on repeated battles on Spindrift and Dregs, and through the cramped airlocks of ships. I stood and waited for Boswic to arrive with an icy calm that he should have feared.

But he didn't. Instead, he accelerated into a trot, shoulders bunched and face twisted with petulant fury.

Then I clocked him with a savage left as soon as he got within reach—but before he could even start to raise his own fists. My fist lashed out, he stopped dead in his tracks, and physics took over as he staggered back and crashed comically into a table. Guests and cutlery and desserts went flying and fell all around him, just like his assumptions. In the stunned silence after he landed, there was only a mewling cry from between his broken teeth, and I heard Torina give a satisfied *hmph* before anyone else could even twitch.

My frumpy seatmate bellowed with laughter. "*Now* it's a party!"

8

Pandemonium replaced the silence of a moment before. Torina's father came hurrying toward us, while other guests—except my frumpy friend, who simply sat back, sipped his after-dinner drink, and grinned—scattered away from the fracas.

I raised my hands in surrender, making it clear I had no intention of pursuing this any further. I turned to Torina's father, opening my mouth to apologize and excuse myself.

But he just pushed past me and stopped in front of Boswic, who'd dragged himself back to his feet, one hand over his ruined mouth. The seething anger in his eyes told me that this wasn't over, and that I was going to have to take him down again. I did the only logical thing. I took my jacket off and prepared to give him an ass-kicking for the ages.

But Torina's father had his own idea. He reached inside Boswic's jacket, yanked out the invitation to the Festival of Declaration, and pointedly ripped it in half.

"How dare you even hint at violence in my home, you wretched poseur. You're a husk. A shell. Manners wrapped over dung!" Every word he spoke was a lash, stinging Boswic to the core.

Boswic dropped his hand to reveal a crimson mess of split lips and shattered teeth, then had the stones to jab a finger at me. "He's the *outsider* here, he's the one that *doesn't belong*—"

"And he's the one who could be breaking you into little pieces now but isn't. He defended himself from you and gave you a pass, which you appear to be too stupid to realize." Despite Boswic towering over him, Torina's father somehow seemed to be the one doing all the looming.

"I've wanted to say this for a long time. I've never liked you, not when you were a snotty teenage brat harassing my daughter, and I *sure* as hell don't like you now. Now, as a member of the Binding Council and the owner of this home, I'm ordering you to get your skinny ass off the grounds before I invite Icky up here from the *Fafnir* and let her work out *her* frustrations on you."

I was impressed as hell—but also suddenly worried. The one-two punch of, well, my literal punch, and now Torina's father giving him the heave-ho, was pushing Boswic into some macho place of true stupidity. I could see it on his face, that his anger was going to turn itself on Torina's dad.

Yeah, not on my watch. I closed in.

Boswic snarled at him and raised a fist. What he said next was about Icky, but he was going to unload on Torina's father. "As if some walking bag of blue carpet shavings is going to—"

I stepped around Torina's dad and hit Boswic twice—once in the gut to double him over, then an uppercut that flung him back-ward. It was a sweet moment, spoiled only by a searing flash of pain from my knuckles. But I gritted my teeth and ignored it, stepping over Boswic and leaning down.

"Trust me, you *want* me to be the one throwing these punches—which I will happily keep doing as long as you're a danger to these people, you prick. Because if I get Icky up here—let's just say she can lift you with one hand while she beats the shit out of you with three others. Do you hear me? Is this getting through?"

Boswic reached deep inside himself and found a shred of reason, because all he did was nod, then begin levering himself up to stand, swaying, before me. The pandemonium continued, but Zupharat and Torina's parents began working to get it back under control. Boswic dragged his sorry ass out of the event, while the robotic waiters zipped smoothly in and began cleaning up the mess. Brawl or not, there was still a Festival of Declaration to complete.

Moreover, the mood of the crowd had changed. The crowd's energy shifted from polite boredom to actual interest, because the evening had taken a turn into unknown waters.

And for the people around me, that meant our night was no longer predictable. It was *spicy*. I watched everyone chattering with excitement as order was restored, some of the guests shooting me searching looks—or looks of open admiration.

My frumpy seatmate summed it up well, touching my arm as Torina and I made to leave.

"Congratulations, you two. Torina, you've picked a winner here," he said.

She took my arm, her face flushed and alive. "I'd like to think so."

He turned to me. "Good punches, by the way, and they've been a long time coming to that coiffed asshole. Thanks."

I smiled around the wince emanating from my abused knuckles. "For?"

"For making it dinner *and* a show," he replied with a wink.

"So you walloped him a second time? Damn it, if I'd known it was going to be a punch-up, I'd have insisted on going with you guys!" Icky grouched.

I hissed a bit as Waldo put a closure through my split knuckle. "And that's why you didn't, Icky. It was a formal dinner, not a Spindrift bar."

"But it could have been both!" she said, then furrowed her brow. "Now, tell me again about that *bag of carpet shavings* crack."

Perry chuckled. "Bag of carpet shavings."

Icky spun on him. "Are you saying that's what I look like, bird?"

"Uh—only before you brush yourself."

Icky kept glaring at Perry, but Zeno touched her arm. "Icky, I kinda think you're missing the bigger picture here. Van and Torina are—uh—sorry, what exactly are you guys now?"

"We've Declared for each other," Torina replied.

"So that means you're, what? Engaged to be married? Actually married? Business partners? What?"

"It's roughly equivalent to the idea of being engaged, I think. At least, it would be on Earth, right?" I asked as Waldo deftly applied a spray bandage to my knuckles.

"That's right. We've publicly stated our intention to be joined."

"Married."

"Sure."

"Well, in that case, congratulations, you two. I'm very happy for you, I really am," Zeno said.

"Me too, boss," Perry added.

"That goes for your favorite disembodied voice, too," Netty put in.

Everyone turned to Icky. She frowned.

"What? Oh, wait. I'm supposed to congratulate you, right?"

Zeno sighed. "You have all the social graces of a point-defense battery, dear Icky. We're going to have to work on that."

She shrugged. "Okay, so… congrats, I guess. Are you two going to be all swoony and kissy-faced now?"

Torina grinned and put her arms around me. "Every—" She kissed my cheek. "—chance—" Another kiss. "—we—" Kiss. "—get."

Icky pulled a disgusted face. "Aw, really?" Then she brightened. "Hey, what's the policy on pants now?"

"Pants?" I asked carefully.

Icky sighed in disgust. "*Yeah*, pants. Like, since you're—whatever, are you going to stop wearing pants? Which means you won't give me any shit about not wearing pants? I gotta say, this would really help the morale of the ship."

"Icky," I said.

"Um, yeah?"

"Wear pants."

She looked up at the ceiling in disgust. "*Fine*. This was a done deal before the fancy dinner, right?"

Torina's grin became a laugh. "I think we've effectively been Declared for one another for a while now."

I nodded smugly. "All according to my subtle plan."

"Pfft. Torina, he was clueless right up until you said his name out loud, wasn't he?" Zeno asked.

"For a few seconds after too, I think."

I stood. "While you gossip about my ability to mask my superior plans, I've got work to do."

"Of course, you're a master of skullduggery and such. What work, by the way?" Perry asked.

"Figuring out what we do next. Being around all these rich people has got me feeling poor. I think some money came spilling out of Boswic's pockets when I slugged him. In other words, I need another job, one that doesn't necessarily depend on the Guild since I'm a wanted man and all that."

"Hey, that's right. Torina, you've hooked yourself up with a guy on the lam," Perry said.

Torina pushed herself against me, then tugged at a lock of my hair. "Always wanted a bad boy. Now, I've got one."

We spent another couple of days on Helso, helping Torina's parents contend with the public outrage at the way the Festival of Declaration had gone.

"In private, though, all we've been getting is congratulations, and more than a few people are apparently happy to have seen Boswic taken down a few notches, that preening bastard," her father said.

Her mother smiled at me. "Van, I am so glad Torina found you and has Declared for you, and I look forward to you being part of the family. But no more dinnertime brawls, okay?"

I stuck my hands in my pockets. "Well, I can't *guarantee* anything, but—"

She slapped my arm, laughing.

Our main reason for staying was that we simply had no other destination. With Schegith taking over Van Maanen's star and Helso as a protectorate, the Milon's location was now just as safe as Schegith's homeworld. Starsmith was another possible refuge, but we had no reason to go there and not enough disposable cash to have Linulla undertake any new projects or upgrades to existing ones. And then there was Earth, which technically wasn't all that safe—we had been attacked there by the Fade, after all—but at least had the protection of interstellar law as a pre-contact society.

And that was about it.

We'd convened at the house, sharing a drink with Torina's father on the terrace overlooking the reclaimed lands. As we sat making small talk about what to do next, Torina suddenly offered a sly suggestion. "Maybe you could interview as a mercenary? Those were damned fine punches you threw."

"Yeah, right," was my immediate reaction, but the others all exchanged glances.

"Wait—you're serious?"

"Sure, why not? If we're going back out into the wilds of the galaxy, we might as well make some money doing it, right?"

"I counsel caution, but it would be a good way of gaining some intelligence," Perry offered.

"Okay. So the only question is, where's the closest recruiter for Group 41?"

Torina stared. "I was thinking more along the lines of Groshenko. That'd be a lot safer, don't you think?"

"Yeah, but like you said, if we're heading back out to the frontier, we might as well get our money's worth."

Torina's father had pulled out a data slate and was tapping away at it. Torina gave him a frown.

"Uh, dad, isn't it pretty rude to sit here conversing with someone on your slate while we——"

He held up a finger. "This is business, and by business, I mean your business," he said and kept tapping away. We waited. He finally smiled and nodded.

"As it turns out, Van, you're in luck. There's a trade festival underway on Tau Ceti Prime, and guess who's one of the registered participants, presumably combing the crowds for fresh meat?"

"Group 41? Really? How did you find that out so easily, Mister Milon?"

"I'm rich, Van. I've got a guy. I always have a guy." He lowered the slate. "And let's dump the Mister Milon thing, okay?"

"Okay... dad."

He grinned. "How about we settle for Tor—you know, my actual name? The patronymic syllable in Torina's name?"

I nodded. "Tor. Works for me."

"I'd recommend calling my mother by her name, Less, as well. She doesn't even like it when *I* call her mom."

"Does this make me look fat?" I asked the room at large.

Torina shook her head. "Fat? No. Kinda scary? Yes. Yes it does."

"Well, I'm going to apply to become a mercenary, so scary is okay, if not optimal."

Torina, Zeno, Perry, and I occupied a room in a hotel complex, adjoining an actual corporate convention center. The center—bland, free of charm, and efficient—was hosting the trade festival with the kind of lackluster process that seemed to pervade every corporate event, no matter what planet it was held on. It never failed to amaze me how much things evolved in parallel, as though there was some sort of DNA imprinted right into the fabric of the universe regarding basic physical laws, the nature of time and space —and the conduct of corporations with their love of name badges, and banners that were always a touch out of date on the coolness scale.

I'd been to more than a few tech industry trade shows back on Earth, a few famous, a few not well-known outside their attendees, and a couple that were entirely off-the-books and invitation only. For instance, I'd once attended a hacker convention in a warehouse in Barcelona, one that officially wasn't happening, despite having a slew of government and corporate types in attendance. It had slowly morphed through the day into an all-night rave, from which I learned two things—one, I don't like techno, and two, people at raves sweat *far* more than they need to while wearing business casual clothes.

It didn't matter, though. All of those shows, and this one happening in an alien star system light-years away, were funda-mentally the same. There were bored delegates standing uncom-fortably in booths, half-heartedly trying to attract the attention of attendees who were overwhelmed by the noise and lights, the colorful posters and maps and things, the shiny pieces of whatever hardware the show was trying to hawk. I'd once attended an event in Indianapolis, and as it had been winding down, they were already setting up for the next trade show, one focused entirely on bathroom fixtures.

The other aspect of the show was the social culture enveloping it like a sloppy embrace. Hospitality suites abounded, where the same companies that had formal booths and presentations on the trade show floor poured booze and finger foods down their would-be customers' throats in another front on the war over business. There was drinking, and parties, and sex—lots of sex. *Shocking* amounts of sex. That fact surprised me most of all, because khaki pants are the least attractive mating garb in the known universe. Add pleats, and you might as well be a monk.

And yet, there were enough one night stands to fill a furniture warehouse.

All of which was to say that I hated attending the damned things. But here we were, me wearing the little projector device around my neck that superimposed a hologram over my features, altering them just enough that I wasn't *quite* myself. It was mainly meant to defeat facial recognition tech, but when I looked in the mirror, I found a stranger staring back at me.

Which was perfect.

I checked myself over. I was in non-descript civvies, which, along with my holo disguise, should be enough to prevent me from being easily identified. I was unarmed, of course, because I wasn't about to start shooting The Drop or swinging the Moonsword amid a throng of innocent conventioneers. Zeno and Torina would stick near me, while Perry provided top cover and eyes on high.

I contacted Icky, who was still aboard the *Fafnir*. "Is that nifty little gizmo of yours and Zeno's ready to go?"

"Fully charged and online, yup. Ready to deploy it whenever you say, boss."

"Hold that thought." I turned to the others. "Okay, folks. Let's go do this. I want to get down to the convention floor before all the shitty coffee and stale pastries are picked over," I said, leading the way out of the room.

We made our way to the convention floor, passing a gaggle of humans and one Yonnox who were obviously all intoxicated—in the middle of the local morning. Either they'd gotten an early start or were winding down to a late finish. We let them stumble by, chattering and laughing, then entered the convention proper.

It was all so *corporate*—potted plants, fake waterfalls, and a sea of people flowing around ranks of booths like ocean currents around rocks. This was a big show, focused broadly on careers, so there were a lot of delegations here and a lot of people wanting to talk to them. I recognized some of the corporate attendees and sponsors, but Perry noticed a notable omission.

No sign of Traversia Bolt-Right, he said from somewhere above us.

"Yeah, funny thing about that. Turns out that when your corporation is infested with criminals, you don't get invited places."

"Isn't every corporation infested with criminals?" Zeno muttered.

Well, sure, but nothing's illegal if you don't get caught.

I ambled through the crowd, pretending to be interested in this booth and that, while generally aiming myself for booth number A189, the one assigned to Group 41 on the handy map of the show. A few booths away, I stopped to watch a stunningly beautiful holographic woman explain why I wanted a career in… manufacturing convention booths and booth hardware. Really?

I shook my head. "This is really meta," I said, turning away and making my way to the Group 41 booth.

A Wu'tzur and a human male who looked like he'd been chiseled out of stone greeted me with curt nods and a muttered, "Sir." They both wore coverall-style military uniforms, again each emblazoned with the insignia I recognized as the Oda Clan of ancient Japan.

I looked around. "Private security contracting, huh? Sounds interesting."

The man glanced at the Wu'tzur, who stepped back. "It can be. Interesting and challenging. Do you have a background in law enforcement or the military?"

"I was in the army for a while, but polishing rocks and painting sidewalks got old pretty fast."

The man gave a smile that flicked on and off. "Yes, sir, the traditional army is well-known for being all *hurry up and wait*. Which army was it?"

"Seven Stars League. I was briefly stationed on Helso, which is about as cushy as postings get. But… again, the boredom was a constant companion. By the second month, I swore time was flowing backward."

He gave a laugh that was just sincere enough not to offend me. "Well, sir, if you're up for a challenge, I can guarantee you won't have time to be bored with our outfit," he said, then launched into his recruiting pitch.

I relaxed a bit. I hadn't seen even a hint of anything to suggest he or the Wu'tzur, who was now speaking with another attendee, had me marked as just another common recruit. My Seven Stars League cover story seemed to be holding up, too.

I hemmed and hawed as much as seemed appropriate, then agreed to attend an indoctrination session at an off-world location. For security reasons, I couldn't know exactly what the location was until I showed up at the ship that would take me there.

"Here's your recruit number," he said, handing me a badge. "Go to berth 106 and present this there. The crew will do the rest." He shook my hand, firmly, two shakes. "Good luck, recruit. I think you'll find this very rewarding."

I nodded with just the right hint of awe. "I'm sure I will."

———

I MET Torina and Zeno at one of the pop-up food courts that dotted the convention hall, well away from the Group 41 booth. They'd heard everything that had transpired over my comm.

"You're not planning on actually boarding that ship, are you?' Torina asked, her face grave.

"Why not? What's the worst that can happen?"

She frowned instantly. "It's a long list. You're not serious, are you?"

I smiled. "Not. . .really. I do my best to be brave, not stupid. *Of course* I'm not boarding that ship. Perry checked with Netty, who says it's a class 3. That's room for, what, maybe a dozen people? So an empty seat's going to leave quite a hole. That'll piss them off."

"And pissed-off people are more likely to make mistakes," Zeno said, nodding.

"Yup. And we're going to follow them and be there when those mistakes happen. Hopefully, it'll let us flush out at least some of the truth behind Group 41."

"Do you think they're connected to our case? To the Fade, or Sorcerers, or—hell, any of the rest of the menagerie of villains we're after?" Torina asked.

I shrugged. "I have absolutely no idea. We certainly have nothing to suggest they are. But I'd really like to know for sure before we decide to just ignore these guys, and find out too late we were wrong. Perry, you ready?"

Way ahead of you, boss. I'm on my way back to the Fafnir *now.*

9

NETTY WATCHED CAREFULLY with her scanners as the class 3 lifted and soared skyward, heading for orbit above Tau Ceti Prime, and then to—wherever it was bound.

"Netty, do we have liftoff clearance?" I asked.

"We do."

"Okay, then. Let's try not to make it obvious. We're all just ships heading out on journeys of our own."

Tau Ceti law required Netty to fly the ship into orbit because the airspace was so crowded. Prime reminded me of a sleeker version of Tokyo but much, much more heavily populated. A slightly more than Earth-sized planet, the population was something like twenty-five billion, and over a billion living in this one urban center alone.

Netty wound us among the traffic, a multitude of AIs communicating at lightspeed to coordinate their movements. The sheer volume of other ships ascending, descending, and proceeding in level flight made the busiest day at LAX or O'Hare look like some grass strip out in the boondocks. The tactical overlay showed icons for nearly 300 ships all in some flight profile, resulting in an aerial furball that no human pilot could hope to traverse without crashing into *something*.

"I've got the ping from that tracker Perry put on our target," Netty said.

I grinned with satisfaction. Our quarry was represented by an icon that pulsed, highlighting it. Perry had exited the *Fafnir* before it left dock, surreptitiously planting an experimental tracking device Zeno and Icky had concocted that would help us keep tabs on it. It would be less important once we broke orbit, but I wanted to make sure it didn't abruptly return to the surface or suddenly jet off to some other part of Prime before heading into orbit.

If the device worked as intended by Icky and Zeno, it would gather data regarding an impending twist and burst-transmit it back to the *Fafnir*. Tracking ships once they twisted was a constant headache because a good set of scanners might, at close range, be able to gather enough data to gain a little insight on the destination. But once a ship twisted, you were limited to guesswork and reports from friendlies, or to put it more bluntly, playing catch-up with few tools at your disposal.

We'd tested it twice, attaching it to the *Fafnir* and twisting, then examining the data it had collected afterward. The first result was pretty good—we were able to discover our own destination to within a few light-minutes. The second one, not so much. The thing had failed during that brief window when space-time was distorting around the twist drive. It needed work that Icky and Zeno hadn't been able to get to yet, so this was a shot. Still, it was better than not trying it, and I believed in the abilities of my engineers. They considered optimization of everything we had to be the holy grail of our purpose—and performance.

We reached orbit just as the class 3 broke his. We followed, easing along in the same space lane, keeping our acceleration to a space-standard delta-V, and trying very hard to look innocuous and forgettable. For nearly three hours, the placid chase wore on. And then, the moment it was able to twist, the class 3 did.

"Now if he's smart, he's not twisting straight to his actual destination. If he doesn't and makes a quick intermediate stop somewhere, we'll lose him. But if you're right and you've irritated him by reneging on their job offer..." Zeno said, ending on a shrug while examining her panel.

We waited.

Zeno finally nodded. "Got it. Netty, I'm sending you a set of twist coordinates, so any time—"

"Actually, Netty, let's offset those coordinates by, say, two light-minutes. Just in case this guy's meeting up with some class 7000 monstrosity, I'd like to have some room between him and it," I said.

"Will do. Twisting in fifteen seconds," Netty replied.

We plunged through that momentary, wrenching distortion of space-time, losing a little more time with respect to the rest of known space, including Earth. Just like Gramps, I was sliding further and further out of sync with Earth every time we twisted—an hour here, three hours there. It added up. I estimated that Earth and everyone on it was now nearly three years older than I was. It wasn't enough to make a difference... yet. But if I kept this up, the people I'd graduated high school with would be retiring at about the same time I'd turn thirty-five or so.

I yanked my immediate attention from time dilation and back

into the *now*. I'd actually expected the tactical overlay to remain blank and this not to work. I saw only one celestial object displayed, a random, uninhabited star with only a numeric designation—but I also saw four ships. Netty painted icons for three class 3s similar to the one we'd followed, and a class 9. Two of the class 3s had snuggled right up to the 9, while the third, our quarry, was en route.

"Okay, let's assume that these class 3s are bringing some more poor saps to be turned into cannon fodder. I won't be a party to murder, which it is no matter what kind of spin you put on it. So, any ideas on how to save these people?"

As we pondered that, something about the arrangement of the other ships plucked at me. I asked Netty to give us a zoomed image. It showed the two class 3 workboats attached to the class 9 by a pair of gantry-like arms that had swung out from a big pod slung under her belly. I frowned in bewilderment at that.

"Netty, what the hell are they doing?"

"The class 9 is refueling those class 3s from an external storage pod. The class 3s only have the range for a single twist, or maybe two very short ones, with the fuel they carry."

I stared at the image for a moment, then took the controls and lit the drive, ramping it up to full power. The *Fafnir* shot toward the cluster of ships.

"You're in a hurry," Torina said, readying the weapons. We all confirmed our helmets were at hand, while Icky unstrapped and moved aft, where she and Waldo could do damage control as needed. Zeno and Netty would watch over the ship and its systems. Perry sat as my tactical advisor and stood ready to back up Torina on the weapons. It all happened without a word, everyone simply and seamlessly knowing and doing their jobs.

"I want to disrupt their little refueling op. We might not be able to stop that class 9 from getting away, but we could still nab the class 3s if they can't twist away from us," I replied, watching the range tick down. With the other ships effectively at a dead stop, we'd be in missile range in less than a minute.

I turned back to the image just in time to see our opponents react, apparently having detected us. One of the refueling workboats cast off, but the other hadn't. The class 9 lit its drive anyway, ripping the gantry free of the class 3, which tumbled away in a chaotic slurry of debris and frozen fuel.

Without warning, the thrusters fired and spun the *Fafnir* around, then slammed us into a sudden deceleration relative to the other ships. I hadn't commanded it, Netty had.

"Netty, what the hell?"

"Trust me on this, Van."

I did, so I just watched the scanners, since the visible image was now obscured by our own exhaust plume. The class 9 was coming straight for us, while two of the class 3s were burning hard, trying to scatter. The damaged class 3, though, had been joined by a new return, an icon representing... something.

"Netty, did we just have a new ship arrive?" I asked.

"No. That will be the refueling pod, jettisoned by the class 9. It's going to be leaking anti-deuterium from that damaged connector, which means that he—and we—don't want to be anywhere near it."

"Good point."

"I make them now and then."

I wasn't sure what to do next, other than watch how the situation developed. Netty calculated, based on the maximum amount of antimatter fuel the pod could likely carry, the effective blast radius if it failed. When she judged it safe, she flipped us again but throttled the drive down to only one third power.

"This will give us some room to maneuver and still keep outside the danger radius of that pod," she said.

I flicked a glance over our screens and made a noise of agreement. With the *Fafnir* once more upended, Netty had restored the visible imagery. I zoomed on the damaged class 3.

It wasn't a pretty sight.

A mere whiff of anti-deuterium had touched her hull, resulting in a blast strong enough to blow out her flank. Bodies tumbled from the wreckage, while the fuel pod spun lazily just a few klicks away.

"Ouch. Tough way to go," Torina said.

Perry cut in. "Van, that class 9 is still charging straight at us. He might just be trying to get away from that pod as quickly as he can—"

"Understandable," Zeno said.

"—but he has lit us up with targeting scanners, so I think he's out for blood."

I nodded. "What were we saying about angry people and mistakes? Torina, you weapons-hot over there?"

"I sure am."

"Then you're also officially weapons-free."

The resulting battle was a lopsided affair, mainly because the class 9 insisted on relentlessly boring straight toward us. We transmitted three warnings and let it fire first, a spread of missiles, to clearly establish it was the aggressor. We exchanged shots and took a few superficial hits with one laser hit that knocked our primary comms array offline. We scored a few hits in return, but nothing solid, so the battle was indecisive to that point. But it turned decisively in our favor when he foolishly got himself in range of our particle cannon.

Frankly, for all the vaunted power of the thing, it had left me less than impressed with its performance. As potent as it was, I felt like I could throw a baseball as far as its maximum effective range. It lived up to its hype this time, though, since the class 9 was making no attempts to maneuver.

"I've got this, Torina," Perry said, taking control of the cannon. His first shot, at less than a hundred klicks range, punched a hole right through the class 9. He slammed shot after shot into it, firing as fast as the weapon cycled. The intense particle beam shredded hull plating with ease, leaving gaping, glowing wounds in the other ship. By the time it swept past abeam of us, it was a shattered wreck, although still underway, since Perry had carefully avoided targeting its engineering section.

"That was fun," he said, switching the particle cannon into standby mode.

"Wonder how long that thing's gonna keep going," Icky said, returning to the cockpit.

"Under power, at full burn? Probably two to three days. Coasting, once the drive cuts out? Well, forever, or until she either slams into something or is ground down to dust by micrometeorite abrasion."

"That's... actually kind of creepy," I said. The thought of this wrecked ship, the remains of its crew on board, traveling more or less forever through space—it had a kind of a *Flying Dutchman* vibe to it.

I shrugged the gloomy image away. "Anyway, let's get ahold of those class 3s that are still flying. We're their only ride home from here, so I expect they'll be willing to make a deal."

"Can I negotiate?" Icky asked, hopeful.

I folded my arms and gave her a stare. "I sense—and this is just a guess, mind you—that you'll offer angry, untenable terms, throw a few insults in, and then hope that you get to crack a few skulls?"

Icky looked abashed. "I mean, yeah. Still get the job done, though. Sorta."

I sighed, getting ready to open the comms. "I know, Icky. You think I never let you have any fun."

She gave a hopeful wave of two arms. "I consider this progress, boss. At least you agree that fightin' is *fun.*"

———

BY JAMMING the passengers and pilots of both class 3s into one of them and then locking it to the *Fafnir* with a hardpoint clamp, we could twist both us and them back to something resembling civilization. We left the other class 3 adrift, and also remained well clear of the damaged fuel pod. I'd considered just destroying it, but since it was effectively in the middle of nowhere, it wasn't a navigation hazard. Moreover, it wasn't worth the cost of a missile. Netty said it would likely blow itself up anyway when its containment generator failed.

"So where are we going, boss?" Netty asked.

I sighed. As far as we knew, we had two Group 41 pilots and a half-dozen new recruits in the attached class 3, but we honestly weren't sure of any of their identities. I decided it was time to face the music and return to Anvil Dark.

"We can argue that they're all implicated in the class 9's attack on us, then hand it all over to the Guild and let them sort it out," I said.

"Van, uh… do you think that's a good idea? I mean, you are a wanted man still, at least as far as we know," Zeno said.

I shrugged. "What are we going to do, run and hide forever?" I shook my head. "No, it's time to find out where the Guild stands on this and if they've got our backs or not."

Perry gave his convincing sigh. "Look out, trouble, here we come, right into your waiting arms."

Icky sniffed. "So what else is new?"

———

We claimed the class 3 we'd seized as a prize, netting us a cool 150,000 bonds. That would definitely help. But the real test would come when we docked at Anvil Dark.

Or so I'd expected, except we received a call from Anvil Dark as soon as we twisted into the Gamma Crucis system, from none other than Master Gerhardt.

"Tudor, I just finished reviewing the report you sent ahead of your arrival."

"Oh. Okay." I glanced at Perry. "Did I send my report ahead of arriving?"

"You did. You thought it would be a good idea, paving the way, as it were."

"Prescient of me." I turned back to the comm. "Alright, Master Gerhardt—and?"

I braced myself for a torrent of bureaucratic bullshit. Instead,

Gerhardt just nodded. "Good work. We've actually been trying to pry open Group 41 for some time now, without much success. You've managed to get us some hard intelligence on them your first time out."

"That's probably because I had no idea you were interested in them. If I had been, it wouldn't have worked out, of course," I replied, smiling.

"Why not? How are those things related?" Gerhart countered, his face gravely puzzled.

"Uh… sorry, I was just being, you know, flippant."

"So was I, Tudor." He smiled. "Contrary to popular opinion, I do have a sense of humor. I just use it sparingly. Anyway, this is such good work—getting us some firm intel on Group 41 *and* saving innocent lives—that you're being promoted again, this time to full Veteran Peacemaker status. Congratulations."

I blinked stupidly, while Torina and the rest of the crew grinned and slapped my shoulders. "Oh. Well, I—uh—"

"Come on, Tudor, where's that glib tongue of yours?"

"On standby while I think of something to say. Oh, how about this? You know those charges that Seven Stars League Satrap guy announced against me? Aren't they kind of a, you know, damper on things?"

"The Satrap of the League did submit a formal extradition request for you since, under interstellar law, you have qualified immunity from prosecution as a Peacemaker by any party other than the Guild. However, the request was in the wrong format, so it had to be resubmitted, and then it lacked certain details, which had to be provided in follow-up documentation—which was provided in the wrong format again, requiring another redo, and I took the time to add a stern warning about the use of improper fonts, like papyrus or anything resembling comic sans, both of which I consider to be near criminal offenses unto themselves. And now it is on the list of items that need to be placed on the Masters' docket. I think... it's number two hundred and thirty-seven on the list."

"And how far down have you reached on the list so far?"

"We're currently considering item number sixty-three. At the present rate we're addressing them, we should get to their extradition request"—Gerhardt made a show of looking offscreen—"sometime between now and the heat death of the universe."

I laughed. Gerhardt returned a cool smile. "It seems that process and procedure doesn't bother you nearly as much when it's working in your favor, I notice, Tudor." He shrugged. "We've decided that you are too valuable an asset to the Guild to hand over to the Seven Stars League on charges of questionable legitimacy. And the League has it coming, frankly. They often refuse to cooperate with us, and now they want us to cooperate?'

"As they sow, so shall they reap," Perry said.

"Thank you, erudite bird," I said, then turned back to Gerhardt. "So the upshot of this is that I'm not going to be clapped in irons the moment I step into Anvil Dark."

"Not by us. Quite the contrary, in fact. You've arrived just in time for the Investiture Ceremony—which, I must admit, I've just moved to tonight so that you are forced to attend it. Do *not* contrive to miss it because a great many people will be scrambling, getting ready to attend, and they will not be impressed if you're a no-show. Dress will be full number ones. The symposium starts at eighteen hundred local time, for dinner at nineteen hundred. I look forward to seeing yourself and your crew there."

I didn't hesitate to agree. "We'll be there."

"Oh, and one other thing, Tudor. Just because the Guild isn't going to support the League's charges against you, it doesn't mean that the League itself won't try to arrest and prosecute you. I'd suggest you stay vigilant."

"Master Gerhardt, we've got so many people gunning for us that the League is just another one to add to the list—and they only want to arrest us. Most of the rest of the list would be quite happy to just outright make us dead."

"Welcome to the senior ranks of the Peacemakers," Gerhardt said, then the comm channel closed.

I sat back. "Well, that's good news, anyway."

"No it's not," Icky grouched.

I turned to look at her, about to ask her why. But Perry cut me off.

"Better get your number ones out of the locker and get 'em all polished up, boss. You're not just going to a dinner, you're going to a ceremony. And I think that explains Icky's lack of enthusiasm." He glanced back at her. "Doesn't it?"

She blew out an exasperated sigh. "Yeah, it does, 'cause I think I know what it means."

"Indeed, you barbarian, and it's not up for negotiation. You are wearing pants."

Icky crossed all four arms and scowled. "I *hate* being civilized."

10

THE CEREMONY OF INVESTITURE checked all the boxes that seemed to be must-dos for any stuffy, formal, military-style event. Everyone wearing excruciatingly uncomfortable clothing? Check. Long periods of time spent standing in one place either at attention or at-ease, waiting for some senior rank—in this case, the Deputy Master in charge of Guild operations—to show up? Check. A long, inter-minable speech from said senior rank to everyone assembled? Yup, check. And enduring all of it just for thirty seconds of walking up to that senior rank, being handed a new rank doodad, saluting, and walking back to the same place you've been standing for the past hour? Check, check, and check.

And that was all *before* dinner.

A burst of music from an instrument native to Falaxis announced to everyone that it was time to file into the dining room. The instrument, which had a name that sounded like someone trying to dislodge a chicken bone from their throat, apparently filled the same role in space as bagpipes did on Earth—a sound everyone hated to love and loved to hate. It didn't manage quite the edge bagpipes did, though, more like a hurdy-gurdy crossed with a zither. It was the kind of instrument that Ren-Faire people would adopt and tote from festival to festival with an air of inscrutable elitism.

Dinner itself was the usual orgy of food and drink, not too different from the Declaration Festival on Helso, just stuffier and with tinier food, all in an array of colors that were, in nature, warning signs. Here at the table, I quickly learned that the food color was utterly unrelated to the flavor and level of spice—a fact I discovered the hard way. I tried a small, innocuous object that looked like a cookie and smelled like celery, and two bites in, I felt as if I'd swallowed a chunk of lava.

"What in the name of all that's *holy*," I wheezed, and if flames had come from my mouth I wouldn't have raised an eyebrow. I've eaten native Thai food. I've eaten a burrito called The Assploder. I've eaten a gas station microwave pizza with ghost peppers and reaper flakes.

And I survived them all.

It wasn't always pretty, but I survived. But those *spicy death cookies*? They were a kind of torture you only hear about in hushed tones from foodies who love pain almost as much as flavor.

Naturally, Icky liked those the *most*, using four arms to toss them down her gut like she was just coming off a hunger strike.

"Here, have mine," I said gallantly.

"Thanks, boss! Culture isn't so bad after all," she enthused, chewing a fistful of *death cookies* with more gusto than I could make myself watch.

"It's... fascinating," Torina said in wonder.

"Like a train wreck. But with a napkin tucked in her shirt," I agreed.

In between sharing small plates, we talked, as the crews were placed together, making the tables abuzz with chatter and laughter. I sat back, taking it all in because it was a rare moment of normalcy in what had become a complex life. Torina looked stunning. Zeno seemed happy. And Icky was wearing pants.

It was a truly festive mood.

And then they began the Parade of Sir Archibald. Sir Archibald was the taxidermied head of a ferocious lizard, a scaldron, which was native to the S'rall homeworld. This particular head had a knife driven straight into its brain amid its triple-eye cluster, and now said brain was gone, replaced by an enameled snuff box. Tradition held that at the conclusion of dinner, Sir Archibald would be taken around the table so that each attendee could snort a pinch of snuff, or whatever passed as snuff among my peers. It was another of those bizarre rituals that somehow catch on in old organizations, taking on a nearly sacred sort of air.

I touched the pommel of the knife when Sir Archibald was brought to our table. "Wonder who did that," I said to Torina out of the corner of my mouth.

"Whoever they were, they had a hell of a story to tell."

"If they'd lived."

"There is that."

I had never in my life tried snuff. I'd barely even smoked, only tried a couple of cigarettes in high school and quickly decided that the experience of breathing in the fumes of burning leaves just wasn't staying on my to-do list. Neither was chewing tobacco, which combined two of my least favorite things—enhanced salivation and the taste of minty boot leather. I'd never considered snuff before, though, always taking it as something reserved for fops in the court of Louis XV or similar.

And yet, here I was, falling back in time with a group of people who took ritual and bonding as a serious thing—which it was, because events like this led to a connection that made you feel like no matter how bad things got out there in the darkness, someone always had your back.

Sir Archibald was brought to me, the young Peacemaker carrying him dutifully waiting for me to snuff my share.

I sighed, then used the little scoop to dig some of the powdery stuff out and deposit it on the back of my hand, the way I saw others doing it. Torina and Zeno, after a moment of wary staring, did the same, and we all proceeded to huff the stuff up our noses.

It was amazing how pulling something up your nose could actually be *more* wrenching than riding a wave of antimatter fueled distortion through space and time during a twist, but here we were.

I snorted. Coughed. Gagged. Sneezed. Snorted some more. Through watering eyes, I saw Torina doing the same. Zeno, though, had a profoundly *meh* expression and shrugged.

"I just learned something new about my own race, that inhaling desiccated plant matter doesn't seem to affect us at all."

"Maybe it's"—I stopped, blinking streaming eyes and clearing my throat—"related to your—oh, *sheeeeeit* is that nasty—anyway, your native rad resistance—"

I cut myself off with a snort. The searing pain up my nose was finally starting to recede.

Torina shook her head. "I've been exposed... to rads. This is—" She grabbed her napkin and, with a *to hell with it* expression, blew her nose into it. "This is worse."

"Excuse me, ma'am, but that's not the way you do it!" I heard the Peacemaker carrying Sir Archibald say. I blinked away tears to find him confronting Icky, who had plunged one of her smaller hands into the snuff box inset in the scaldron's head and lifted out a handful of the dried herbs.

"It's the way *I* do it," she said, then slapped her hand to her face with a puff of snuff while inhaling deeply with the delicate tone of a North Sea fog horn in November.

We all braced ourselves as she pulled her hand away. And I mean all, as in everyone attending the dinner. Her face was covered with brownish snuff, but aside from a single sniff, she seemed as unaffected as Zeno.

I started to relax.

But then Icky's eyes crossed, and she huffed in a ragged breath, her massive rib cage jittering in a staccato beat.

"Incoming!" I bellowed, kicking myself back and away from her in my chair. Torina just stood and hurried out of the beaten zone.

A pause, with the room utterly silent.

Then, like a shot from a mass driver, Icky *sneezed*.

With one whooping, cacophonous sneeze, Icky turned the area in front of her into a winter wonderland—

—if that winter wonderland was a glistening landscape of mucosal debris, snuff, and what I swear was a small fish that had doubtless been stuck between her back teeth for an indeterminate amount of time.

Silence fell on the room as Icky wiped her mouth. And nose. And hair, I think, then looked around at the sea of faces watching her.

She ran her tongue over her front lip, made a face, and said, "It's not as good as the cookies, but it's not bad."

AFTER DINNER, I spent some time schmoozing, circling the room to congratulate other Peacemakers who'd been promoted—initiates to full Peacemakers, others to Myrmidons, and Peacemakers who had achieved some level of veteran status. Becoming a Full Veteran, also known as a First Veteran, put me on par with Lunzy. I was proud of that, sure, but I couldn't help noticing a subtle shift in the way other Peacemakers, some of whom I'd come to know reasonably well, treated me.

For some, their congratulations were tinged with a touch of resentment. I'd jumped over a few on my rise to First Veteran status, so that was understandable. Others adopted more of a sycophantic attitude, marking them as people that were going to be looking to me for favors. Frankly, I found the second group more annoying than the first.

The one that managed to surprise me yet again was Carter. He wasn't on Anvil Dark but sent me a congratulatory note that Gerhardt passed on to me. It read as both genuine and heartfelt and ended with him offering to buy me a drink the next time we were together.

I stood and chatted with Gerhardt while the rest of those

attending the dinner milled around the sumptuous lounge adjoining the Masters' dining room. The amount and volume of chatter had been slowly increasing, probably in direct proportion to the amount of drinking going on, so we had to keep inching up the volume ourselves. But when the conversation took a more serious turn, heading in the direction of talking about Yotov, Gerhardt gestured for me to join him back in the dining room.

We avoided the robotic waiters as they bustled about, cleaning up and resetting the room so it was ready for the next dinner. In a quiet corner, I asked Gerhardt about the former Master.

"How they hell could they just let her go?"

"Reality, Tudor. It's just reality, how things work. She had connections that got the Seven Stars League to commute her sentence, as simple as that."

"But what about the Guild? She was a *Master*. Isn't she accountable as a Peacemaker?"

"She did lose her job."

"Yeah, but you know what I mean. She was corrupt, using the Guild to feather her own nest—"

"Can you prove that?" Gerhardt asked, sipping his drink with a clatter of cold cubes.

"Right this instant? No. But give me some time to dig and I'll find the evidence, yeah."

"Alright, and what else will you uncover?"

I frowned. "What do you mean?"

"You say you'll start digging. Fine. And you may very well find things that implicate Yotov in wrongdoing. Fine. But what else will you find? What other wrongdoing will you uncover? If you find something to also implicate, say, Groshenko, or even your grandfather, I assume you'll pursue those cases with equal vigor, won't you?"

"My grandfather wasn't involved in any corruption or similar bullshit."

Gerhardt awarded me that thin smile of his. "I agree, he almost certainly was not. But I don't *know* it for certain, any more than you *know* it for certain. There is always the possibility, isn't there?"

"I—" I started, but I had to stop myself. I hated that Gerhardt was right. There always was the possibility that Gramps wasn't quite as pure as the driven snow, wasn't there? He'd bent the rules for Zeno, placing her under a sort of unofficial house arrest. Might he have bent others?

I sighed. "This all smells like one big cover-up."

Gerhardt laughed. "Tudor, cover-ups make the galaxy go round. Every institution has its dirty little secrets, even if it's something as trivial as catching a file clerk stealing paperclips. Theft is theft, isn't it? But that clerk is just going to get their ass chewed out and told not to do it again. And, just like that, we have a cover-up."

"Well, sure, but—"

"Tudor, let me put this to you another way. If you dig and dig until you find something you can use to charge Yotov, she will make sure that a multitude of dirty little secrets and instances of wrongdoing will come to light along with it. Like it or not, she and the Guild have an uneasy truce, a kind of détente that's based in reality, not just principle."

I stared at Gerhardt, then shook my head. "And here I thought you were all about doing things exactly by the book."

Gerhardt laughed again, this time in a way that sounded almost genuine. "Tudor, I *do* insist on doing things correctly, because if everyone did that, there'd be no need for conversations like this one. But I haven't become a Master in the Guild by being naïve. I've learned, often the hard way, which battles are worth fighting." He locked his gaze on mine. "I'd suggest you do the same."

"Tell that to Yotov. If she just went her own way and I never even heard her name again, that'd be fine. But she hired mercenaries to toss my ship, the *Iowa*, looking for some damned printing plates."

Gerhardt frowned. "You haven't reported this."

I hadn't. I'd considered the incursion aboard the *Iowa* by Yotov's hired minions to be my problem, not a Guild one. So I explained what had happened to Gerhardt now, finishing with a description of the missing printing plates.

"So Yotov, at least, seems to think they're still somewhere aboard, a leftover cargo from her apparent smuggling days. And she's a big ship, so I suppose Yotov could be right."

Gerhardt pursed his lips in thought for a moment, then nodded. "This has... implications. Potentially significant ones that will require some discreet investigation. Leave that with me, but in the meantime, you need to get back to your ship, the *Iowa*, and find those plates."

"Implications? Okay, and beyond the obvious ones, those would be...?"

Gerhardt returned that thin smile, no genuine laughter this time. "This is your first lesson as a full Veteran Peacemaker. At some point, it stops being about crime and starts being all about politics."

I sniffed. "I always thought they were the same thing."

Gerhardt clapped me on the shoulder. "Welcome to the senior

ranks of the Guild, Tudor," he said, then drained his drink and headed to the bar for another.

———

BACK IN MY cabin aboard the *Fafnir*, I let out one of *those* sighs as I finally unbuttoned my collar and experienced a rush of relief. I shucked my formal jacket and draped it over the back of the chair beside my bed.

My bed was calling to me, a siren song made even sweeter given my full belly topped off with a few rounds of fine whiskey—or what passed for whiskey on Anvil Dark. Before I could strip any further and head toward peaceful slumber, Netty spoke up.

"Van, there's an incoming comm message for you."

I stopped and scowled. "Tell them I'm unavailable. That I'm sleeping. Tell them I'm dead. Then take a message."

"Will do."

A few seconds later, an icon popped onto the screen of the data slate on the desk. That was quick. I started to turn away from it, but having that message sitting there was going to bug me.

I sighed. "The smart thing to do, Tudor, is leave it until you wake up. But you're not going to do that, are you?"

I tapped the icon, bracing myself for some sudden, urgent plea for help or some lead or something that had to be pursued *now*, this instant, before it went cold. Instead, the display lit with the image of a woman, a Peacemaker. I figured her to be in her late forties, maybe her early fifties, with short, dark hair going gray. I didn't recognize her.

"Peacemaker Tudor, I just wanted to take a moment to congratulate you on your promotion. Welcome to being a First Veteran."

She smiled and signed off.

"Uh, Netty, who the hell was that?"

"Peacemaker Jocelyn Wallis, retired."

"Okay. And she's contacting me because…?"

"Because she wanted to congratulate you on being promoted?"

"Yeah, I got that. But who *is* she, and why is she suddenly contacting me?"

"Sorry, Van, I know what you know. I have no idea."

"Huh."

I finished getting undressed, then clambered gratefully into bed. Before I drifted off to sleep, I tried to recall a Peacemaker Wallis, in case I'd crossed paths with her before. I came up a total blank, though. So either there was some connection I was missing, or she just kept tabs on the Guild and got some sort of satisfaction from offering her congratulations to new First Veterans.

I sighed into the darkness. I knew that retirees sometimes had trouble letting go and felt it necessary to try and stay involved in things, even if those things weren't their responsibility anymore. For that matter, she might just be hoping that I could benefit her in some way, now that I was a First Veteran Myrmidon.

I finally shrugged it away. She looked to be about the same age as Lunzy or Gerhardt, so the next time I had a chance, I'd ask them about this strangely gracious woman.

WE RETURNED to the *Iowa* and spent the next three days scouring her thoroughly, trying to poke into every nook, cranny, and crawl-space. The trouble was that, with just five of us able to do it, three days of effort left us with huge swathes of the ship still unsearched. The *Iowa* was a battlecruiser, after all, with *kilometers* of cable and power conduits, void spaces under decks and bulkheads, and huge swathes of empty space between her inner and outer hulls. Even her normal crew complement would have needed days, if not weeks to search her entirely.

We convened in the galley we'd repurposed into our lounge. Zeno arrived with a data slate and a smile.

"Check this out," she said, putting the slate on the table.

It was an image of a metal plate with writing scored into it, probably by a cutting torch. I read it aloud.

"Lead Hand Gorvus sucks his own—I'm not sure what this next word means."

"Does it matter? I think the sentiment's pretty clear," Zeno replied, grinning.

"Where did you find this?"

"It's inscribed into the backside of a hull plate on deck four, aft quarter. Must have been done by some unhappy yard worker while the *Iowa* was being built."

Torina chuckled. "Whoever did this wasn't a fan of Lead Hand Gorus, were they?"

"Nope. And they decided to engrave their thoughts about it for posterity," I replied, smiling and handing the data slate back to Zeno. "So aside from snarky comments about unpopular bosses, did we find anything that even hinted at those damned printing plates?"

Zeno and Torina both shrugged. Perry arrived to announce that he hadn't found anything either. Icky straggled in last. She was carrying a small case, and it was labeled 18975-A-T.

We all stared for a moment, until Zeno broke the silence. "You found it? Where the hell was it?"

"Inside a waste reclamation tank."

"Icky, what the hell possessed you to look inside somewhere like that?" I asked.

She shrugged. "I asked myself, self, where would you hide something that was pretty much guaranteed to be the very last place anyone would look? And, well, here we are."

I reached for the case but stopped. "Uh—you said this was in a waste reclamation tank? Just *how* much of a waste tank? We talkin' fresh here, or… ?"

"Well, it'd been purged, probably when she was decommissioned, and apparently hasn't been used since." She opened the case and extracted a delicate, rectangular plate that was intricately engraved. "It's not all of them, though. There are slots in here for six, but there are only three—"

Without warning, as she turned the plate to show it to us, it snapped into pieces in her grip. One fragment dropped to the deck and shattered.

Icky blinked. "Oops. Make that two."

"Well, there goes a bazillion bonds," Perry muttered, shaking his head.

I snapped a curse. "Icky, I'm deliriously glad you found these, now how about keeping your big meaty mitts off them, huh?"

"Sorry, boss."

Torina peered into the case. "Icky's right. Slots for six. I wonder what happened to the other three?"

"Who'd only steal three of them?" Zeno wondered.

Perry shrugged his wings. "You're assuming they were there to begin with. There might only have been these three." He looked at Icky. "Now two."

"I said I was sorry."

I raised my hands. "It's fine. We still have two plates that we can return to their rightful owners."

Zeno frowned. "I thought we were just going to—let me put this delicately—"

"Sell 'em to the highest bidder?" Torina asked.

I shook my head. "Nope. I had Perry check. Under interstellar law, these plates are the sovereign property of their creators on Falaxis. They're effectively cultural artifacts, so we're obligated to return them."

"Well, shit."

"That's okay. The Kynuvar—that's the race on Falaxis that made these plates and are the rightful owners—still have a generous reward on the books for returning them," Perry said. "So we'll still be paid pretty handsomely. Only two thirds as handsomely as we might have been, but—"

"Can I pay you back over time, boss?" Icky asked.

I held out a hand. "Deal. Ten bonds a week."

Icky shook my hand, and this time she was delicate. "Who will—"

"I'll keep track of the debt, you ruffian," Perry said. "I've seen you count slices of pizza when there are only a few left. We don't need that kind of *creative math*."

"I leave the debt collection in your capable hands. Wings, I mean, Perry."

"Always wanted to be a gangster type," Perry said.

"And now you are. One condition," I added.

"Name it."

"No fedoras. Ever."

Perry dipped his beak, laughing. "Loud and clear, boss. How about shiny suits?"

I rubbed my chin. "As long as they're natural fiber, yeah. We don't do tacky 'round these parts."

11

We returned the two remaining plates to their owners, the Kynuvar, without incident. Falaxis, a planet noted for its artisanal works, especially sculptures and tapestries, was a pleasant surprise in almost every way. Thanks to a quick bit of geochemistry, most of the planet's land surface was richly fertile, making Falaxis an especially productive agri-world with an economy based almost entirely on exports of foodstuffs—everything from the basics, like bulk grains, to fine and shockingly expensive luxury goods. The result was a world of pastoral serenity, with the population spread widely across the surface rather than jammed into teeming urban sprawls.

I took a deep breath of the air, savoring the way it tasted of almost nothing except, well, *air*, underlain by lush vegetation and a hint of fertilizer. If anything, it seemed even cleaner than the air of rural Iowa, which I'd always considered a sort of gold standard for what fresh air meant.

"This place is amazing, like Iowa turned into an entire planet," I said, scanning the flat lands around the spaceport. As far as I could see in every direction were cultivated fields, punctuated by occasional buildings, silos, and storage granaries. Robotic farm machinery trundled around, but there were also lots of people toiling in the fields, digging and weeding by hand, often in small groups, while chatting or even singing. I remarked how that was strange, since even in Iowa most of the farming was mechanized.

Perry had the answer. "It's cultural. This whole continent is under the sovereignty of the Kynuvar, who believe that the growing of food is kind of the ultimate act of creation. To them, cultivating crops is a sort of artform unto itself."

I squinted into the bright daylight and nodded, resolving that I had to get back here during some downtime. The Iowa farm boy in me felt *right* at home.

We met the Kynuvar delegation in the spaceport terminal. What I hadn't noticed while looking into the distance outside was their actual appearance. I found myself facing a group of small, squat, plum-colored aliens with four tiny eyes covered by dark goggles, a small mouth, and wrinkled skin. Each had five slender arms, three of which ended in thin tentacles, which were probably ideal for fine, dexterous work.

Unfortunately, to me, they also looked like anthropomorphic raisins.

Their delegation head received the printing plates with solemn gravity, offering a heartfelt thanks.

"If you happen to recover the remainder, we would certainly appreciate their return as well. Although… I understood that there were three missing, which should leave three. But there are only two here," he said, gesturing with one cluster of tentacles at the case.

I reached into a pouch in my harness and extracted a small bag that rattled as I handled it. "Unfortunately, one of them was broken beyond our ability to repair it. But all of the pieces are here, if that helps."

I felt Icky shift uncomfortably beside me, but I focused on Perry. If anyone was going to cut loose with some smart-assed remark—

But he stayed dutifully silent.

"That is unfortunate. Nonetheless, we are deeply appreciative of the return of our plates." The Kynuvar gestured to one of his fellows, who stepped forward with a case full of bonds. As he did, I was struck with the irony of how handing over some goods in exchange for a bag of cash was, in some contexts, perfectly fine— but not so much in others. It almost made me laugh.

You're thinking they look like raisins, aren't you, Van? How very Earth-centric of you.

No one else could hear Perry, just me, through my ear bug. So much for dutiful silence, since he'd apparently assumed my almost laughing was about that, not bags of cash. And, of course, now that he'd said it—

That's okay, boss. If they start singing I Heard It Through The Grapevine, *you have my permission to howl.*

I snorted. Everyone looked at me. I quickly cleared my throat.

"Sorry, there must be something I'm allergic to here, maybe from those lovely fields," I said with a grand, theatrical wave.

Perry started humming in my ear. I recognized the damned tune instantly, the one he'd just named. Those animated California raisin commercials were mostly before my time, but I knew them well enough to suddenly bark out a laugh. Again, everyone shot me a hard look.

J.N. CHANEY & TERRY MAGGERT

I let myself keep grinning and laughing. "I'm sorry, it just makes me so happy to see this sort of cultural artifact returned to its rightful owners."

"We thank you for that, Peacemaker Tudor," the Kynuvar delegation head replied gravely.

"Now if you'll excuse me, we have to get on our way. There's a problem aboard my ship that needs fixing, quite possibly by throwing it out the airlock."

"We understand, and thank you again."

We turned and left. Once we were out of earshot, Torina turned to me. "What *problem* are you talking about?"

I opened my mouth, but Perry cut me off—of course.

"Don't mind Van, Torina. He's just raisin an issue here."

I spun on Perry. "Listen, bird—"

"Oops. I think there's something he wants to prune away."

"Bird, you better be lucky you're valuable."

"And that you like dad jokes," Perry countered.

I snorted. "Wouldn't say I *like* them. . . "

———

THE LAUGHTER FADED when we received a message from an unexpected source while lifting into orbit from Falaxis. It was from Retta, our friendly Francophone slug riding atop her nacreous ball. She owned a ritzy bar on an orbital called Needle in the Groombridge 1618 system. Her bar bore a hand painted sign that read *La Maison Loin de Chez Soi*—Home Away from Home. Technically, her full name was Countess Henriette Eugenie de Gauthier-Francois, and despite being about as alien as aliens got, she had an obsessive fascination with Earthly French culture—specifically, Paris in the late nineteenth and early twentieth centuries. The bar and Retta were steeped in French culture, resulting in people of all races underestimating her, which was a *highly* desirable trait for anyone in espionage.

Her message was cryptic, though, offering little detail. And it was recorded, so all we could do was acknowledge it. I'd cultivated Retta as a contact for useful information because she seemed to have connections into many things far beyond Groombridge 1618. In fact, her network was superior to anything I'd seen in the stars, and she maintained her web of secrets with the elan of Mata Hari.

If Mata Hari had been a human-sized gastropod, that is.

"Well, I'd been kinda thinking of heading back to Anvil Dark, but I could go for some, uh, *poutine*, I guess."

"Poutine is French-Canadian, Van. I suspect if you tried to order fries slathered in gravy and hunks of cheese curds from Retta, she'd kick you right in the Tolouse Lautrec," Perry said.

I shot him a glare. "Sorry, bird, you've declared yourself an expert in raisins and raisin accessories, so you'll forgive me if I don't take culinary advice from you seriously anymore."

"Well, that, plus the fact he doesn't actually eat," Netty put in.

Torina looked blank. "What the *hell* are you talking about, Van?"

"Perry's an asshole."

Icky spoke up right away. "See, now that's what I've been saying all along!"

RETTA HAD GONE to enormous expense to duplicate the feel of some café on the Champs-Elysees, circa 1900. She had most of it, including the checkered tablecloths and rococo wall paneling fabricated from scratch, but everything in the place that could be considered art was apparently the real deal. Not an expert in French masters, I had to take her word on that. But it didn't surprise me. All sorts of Earthly artifacts had been exported into space, something that could get awkward once Earth achieved true spaceflight and entered the community of known space. The law said that cultural artifacts had to be returned to wherever they originated, and I really didn't want to have to seize all of Retta's paintings.

It seemed I didn't have to, though.

"Mais non, I have paid for all of them. They are acquired *légitimement!*" she replied, when I brushed up against the subject. "I keep *les reçus*, all of the receipts!"

"Oh. Uh, Perry, that makes it okay then, right?"

"The law doesn't say anything about who can legally purchase stuff, no, so she's fine."

In pride of place was her newest acquisition, a super stylized rendering of boats in a harbor by the father of the Impressionist school, Claude Monet. I actually liked it, the way it gave more of the *impression* of what it was trying to portray than the actual thing itself.

"It is almost twin to *Impression, soleil levant*. That was the first great Impressionist painting, yes?" Retta said proudly while deftly wobbling around on her ball.

"There've been rumors of a twin to that painting for ages, but it was assumed lost," Perry said.

I nodded, inspecting it. "Yeah, and I know why—here it is, a dozen light-years from Earth. Great frame, by the way."

"A frame should augment the art, not unlike Torina's new hairstyle. Stunning, love. Truly," Retta gushed.

"New… hair?" I asked.

Torina patted my hand. "You've been busy. And you're a man."

"Almost a brute," Retta scolded, then began rolling away.

"It's from wearing my helmet, not a new style," Torina muttered, low. "You're in the clear."

"Thank you, dear."

"Don't mention it."

We settled into a table. Icky knelt on the floor. The chairs looked spindly, but they were fabricated from high-strength materials she couldn't break. She just couldn't fit onto one of the delicate pieces of café seating. Not while maintaining any dignity, anyway, to the extent that Icky had dignity.

"So, to address our point, Retta, you were rather opaque about why you wanted us to come visit you. What's up?" I asked as a robotic waiter brought us wine.

"I wish to ask, are you familiar with Group 41?"

We all exchanged glances. "Yeah, funny you should mention them."

"Ah, well, then you shall find this *vraiment hilarant*, truly hilarious, no? My little birds have come to my window and sung me a most interesting song. You have heard of the star group called Unity?"

I frowned, thinking. I had but didn't know much about it. It was a group of three planets and several disparate races that had found some way to form lasting economic, social, and cultural bonds. It had effectively eliminated conflict and strife among them, but at the cost of them declaring themselves wholly isolated from the rest of known space. They conducted no trade and had no diplomatic relations outside of their own space, and had made it clear they wanted neither. By interstellar agreement, their space was entirely off-limits to anyone they didn't specifically invite to enter it. There weren't even opportunities for crime or corruption to get their scummy toes through the door, so solid were the relationships amongst these peoples. To the extent I'd thought about Unity at all, it struck me as an idyllic sort of life, albeit at the cost of remaining utterly insular and never interacting with anyone else, ever.

It reminded me of North Sentinel Island, in the Indian Ocean. The indigenous peoples there, the Sentinelese, had voluntarily isolated themselves from the rest of the world, living an existence that was, by modern standards, pretty much Stone Age. But they were stable, prosperous by the standards of their own society, and, by all accounts, perfectly happy. So more power to 'em, I'd say.

"What about Unity, and what have they got to do with Group 41?" I asked Retta.

"Ah, well, the birds sing that Group 41 was there, nibbling at the edges of Unity just a year ago, but now they are gone, all gone. This may mean little, but it may mean much, no?"

"Retta, why couldn't you have just told us this by comm? Why did we have to come here in person?" Torina asked.

"Ah, because Group 41 has a reputation, one almost as severe as the corporation, Traversia, that you dispelled so firmly a year ago. When talking about the cat, the mouse only whispers, yes?"

I smiled. We'd attempted to keep the details of the Battle of 109 as under wraps as possible. Some leakage was inevitable, but Retta knowing about it didn't surprise me. In fact, I suspected she knew pretty much how it all unfolded, and in some detail, such was her own reputation for acquiring and brokering information.

Also, an anthropomorphic slug talking about cats and mice was just, well, weird.

"So, wait. Retta, are you saying that every member of every race that makes up Unity is gone?" Zeno asked.

I stiffened. Had we just been informed of genocide on an interstellar scale?

But Retta laughed. "No, no, la fille drôle, funny girl. The Group 41, they are all gone. The questions, of course, are why were they there? And why are they not there now?"

I eyed Retta suspiciously. "Retta, did you somehow know that we were interested in Group 41? Because this is just awfully convenient."

"Ah, my birds sing many songs, some sweet, some not so much. And yours is one of the sweetest of all."

"I think that's her way of saying *yes*," Zeno said.

Retta laughed a tinkling laugh, probably an artifact of her translator. It was a little jarring coming from a slug of *any* size, let alone one who was eye to eye with me.

"*Mais oui*. But this information doesn't come *gratis*, Van Tudor."

I smiled. "It never does. What would you like from us, Retta?"

"There is a delivery I would ask you to make, to The Quiet Room. It is platinum, sixty standard bars.'

"Standard bars?"

Perry answered. "To the extent that bonds are underwritten by a standard, that's what these are. Some authorities, like Tau Ceti and the Eridani Federation, consider it a standard, like the old gold standard on Earth. Others, like the Seven Stars League, don't. It's complicated."

"And valuable. Sixty bars is a not-so-small fortune," Torina noted.

"Ah yes, they were payment for services I provided to a particular party," Retta said.

"Sixty bars? That must have been one hell of a service," Zeno put in.

Retta laughed. "Some things I provide for free, or even a song. Others are more… costly, yes?" Her voice hardened slightly. "And some, who have not been so nice, pay more for everything."

"So you want us to cart some platinum to The Quiet Room and deposit it? I think we can do that," I said.

Torina raised an eyebrow. "I thought we didn't trust The Quiet Room."

"We don't, which is why we're going to some obscure branch office, not Procyon. Perry, where would the most out-of-the-way Quiet Room office be?"

"They have a branch on Crossroads. It's deliberately kept discreet because some of their clientele wants to remain *aggressively* discreet," he replied.

"Discreet, huh? So, dirty money."

"Not always. Sometimes money is just a little dusty around the edges. And sometimes it's for things that aren't illegal but are still dangerous. Think… an insurgency fighting for freedom from some oppressive regime."

"Sounds perfect."

Retta had one of her waiters fetch a small case made of coppery alloy, reinforced on the corners and edges and locked with an elaborate mechanism. Retta, however, not only used the key to open it to show us the contents, but she also offered me the key to carry.

"Don't you want to send this separately, keep the lock and the key in separate shipments?"

"Ah, but you are one of my clients I consider *agréable*, nice. I trust you, yes?"

Retta then rolled out a sumptuous meal—fresh bread and butter, *coq au vin* and steamed vegetables, a dessert of *crêpes* with fresh strawberries and new cream, and strong coffee and wine—lots of wine. As we sat and dined, it struck me that this was the third elaborately rich meal I'd had in less than two weeks, including the Declaration Festival on Helso and the formal dinner on Anvil Dark. I was going to have to hit the gym a little harder and pursue Innsu sparring with Torina more vigorously.

Or have my b-suit let out a little.

Retta bustled around us in constant motion atop her nacreous ball, making sure our glasses stayed filled. As she rolled about, directing her waiters like a conductor leading a symphony, she hummed a song it took me a moment to place. Perry heard it, too, and began to make music, dulcet tones that sounded like a richly textured accordion. Retta picked up the thread of the tune and began to sing.

Now I recognized it. It was *La Vie en Rose*, the seminal French song by Edith Piaf—of course.

I sat back and listened for a moment. Retta's voice was pure and sweet and blended in perfect harmony with Perry's background tune. It was absolutely enchanting and left us all just sitting and staring, our meals and wine momentarily forgotten. In that moment, a little of the best of Earth was with us, floating in the air until it faded, alive only in our memories from that moment on.

And then it was done, and gone, and we applauded as I raised my wine glass. "That was stunning. Thank you, my friend. And… bird, you play music? I didn't know."

"You never asked. Oh, and I heard you singing—and I use that term, uh, *generously*, boss—when you were working on the *Fafnir* back in Iowa. Especially when your grandfather had you heaving hay around."

"Ah, magnifique! And how was his music?"

"It was enthusiastic!"

"And good?"

"He has good lungs, so you could really hear it!"

"And… good?"

"It was… enthusiastic!" Perry looked at me. "Although, Christmas carols in June, Van? Really?"

I sipped wine and shrugged. "I'm a traditionalist, what can I say?"

Zeno suddenly leaned forward. "Icky, are you alright?"

She'd had her head bowed since the last strains of *La Vie en Rose* had faded. When she looked up, her eyes were shiny, even a little wet.

"Icky, are you *crying?*" I asked.

She shook her head furiously.

"I'm not crying, *you're* crying!"

12

WE TWISTED in to the Crossroads system, which had been my very first interstellar stop after leaving Earth to become a Peacemaker. It was where I'd done my indoctrination, having a variety of memories about law and hand-to-hand combat and no-g operations implanted in me. I'd only been back a few times since, and then only for refueling. Still, the orbital station had a certain feeling to it, a familiarity that few other places managed. I felt more comfortable here than I did at, say, Spindrift or Dregs.

I was feeling those warm and fuzzies, right up to the moment the threat alarm jangled. The tactical overlay lit up, painting two angry red icons boring straight toward us.

"What the hell—?"

That was all I had a chance to say before the *Fafnir* shuddered, loosing two salvoes of two missiles. I glanced at Torina, but she was gaping blankly at her weapons panel.

"I didn't fire those," she said.

"That was me. My bad," Zeno said.

I glanced back at her. "Zeno, what made you put your finger on the trigger like that?"

"I… honestly don't know. Just feeling paranoid, I guess."

But Perry shook his head. "We are not supposed to shoot first."

"Yeah, well, then assholes shouldn't come charging straight at us hammering away with their fire-control scanners, should they? Play stupid games, win stupid prizes," Icky said.

I couldn't argue. Perry was technically right, insofar as we should have issued a warning once they acquired us as a target. But there was latitude to argue that targeting scanners themselves consti-tuted a clear and present threat and could justify an immediate armed response. And considering how many different parties we'd pissed off enough that they wanted to kill us, I was happy to make that argument.

Or, to put it another way, it was better to be judged by twelve than carried by six, as the old adage goes.

The missiles apparently caught our opponents by surprise, too, something I noted.

"Even though our stealth coating is far from perfect anymore, it still makes us a harder target to lock onto. They were probably hoping to get closer, so they got better firing solutions," Netty offered.

The two incoming ships launched missiles of their own, and we began to maneuver in crisp, decisive angles according to my instinct and the crew's advice. For the next few moments, we could only watch as their missiles flashed past, their avionics burning up computational power in an effort to track us. Of the four enemy projectiles, though, only two were able to get a lock. We shot down one, but the second detonated close enough to rattle us with shrapnel. We weren't suited up, so I braced myself for an explosive decompression and a need to grab at the emergency rebreather, but the *Fafnir's* armor took the hits and held.

Our opponents weren't so fortunate. Four missiles tracked one of the ships, and three punched through the target's point defenses. Our trio of birds detonated almost simultaneously, showering the class 7 with so much shrapnel that its drive cut out and its power emissions died. We'd damaged its reactor, drive, or both.

"Well, that evens the odds up," I said, but Torina cursed.

"Van, fire control is offline."

"What?" I looked at the status board. Sure enough, the targeting scanners had gone red, no longer target-scanning.

"Piece of shrapnel must have hit the primary targeting array just right—or just wrong, I guess," Zeno said, stabbing at her panel. Then it was her turn to curse. "And I can't get the controller to switch to the backup array, dammit to hell."

Icky unstrapped. "I'll see if something came loose back there," she said, hurrying aft.

I glanced at Torina. "Okay, dead-eye, you got this?"

She shook her head. "Against a ship that's evading, at this range? With the laser, if I get lucky."

"Zeno, any ideas?"

"Working on it."

I muttered a curse of my own. "Netty, how about you or Perry?"

"We could fire some missiles in passive mode and hope they can get their own lock," Perry suggested.

"Netty? You're the expert when it comes to this stuff."

"We've got eight missiles left, plus two trackers. Odds are we'll get three to lock, and one or two of them will make it through."

"So we need those scanners back online. Zeno?"

"Still working on it, Van."

I bit back a response. Everyone was doing the best they could. We still had point-defenses, which had their own targeting systems, but those were only intended for terminal, short-range tracking. They received data from the main fire controller to set up their defensive shooting. It meant that each of the batteries had an effective window of only a few seconds to take down incoming ordnance.

I turned to Torina, who was snapping out laser shots manually and muttering some really nasty curses. "Netty, call the Peacemaker detachment on Crossroads and see if they can help us."

"Actually, Van, I've done better than that."

"What? What do you mean—?"

The tactical overlay suddenly lit up with a swarm of icons. There had to be nearly twenty of them. And they were closing with phenomenal speed, effectively faster than light, which wasn't possible. And yet, there they were.

"What the hell are *those*?" I asked.

"The Quiet Room maintains its own ordnance, installed in a launcher complex on that asteroid off to our eleven o'clock and high. I asked them for help, and they provided it—in spades, as they say. Those are skip missiles, and they each cost a small fortune."

"*Skip* missiles? Twenty of them? Holy shit!" Zeno said

Skip missiles. I'd heard of them but had never seen them in action and never would have assumed The Quiet Room had them. They were high-end military ordnance of the sort that only governments or the fantastically wealthy could dream about owning. They literally skipped, twisted a short distance, got a lock, then did it again. Since they weren't twisting far and weren't moving very much mass when they did, they were able to work inside a gravity well. We watched in horror as they converged on the other class 7, then detonated in rapid succession. The hapless ship was consumed by blasts of shrapnel, culminating in one final, colossal detonation as the ship's antimatter containment failed.

When the last skip missile went off with a scalding bloom, I stared at the tactical overlay. There was nothing. The barrage had blasted the class 7 to such tiny bits that most of them didn't even register on our scanners.

Icky reappeared. "Fire control should be back online. There was a cable junction—" She stopped. "Wait, is it over?"

"Yup. Turns out The Quiet Room's got a bigger military force than most major powers," I replied.

Torina switched the weapons back to hold. "Which is a little disconcerting, if you think about it. They just fired at least a million bonds of ordnance without batting an eye."

I nodded. "And just because we asked them for help. I mean, I'm all for good customer service, but I kinda think it should be measured in client satisfaction, not kilotons."

WE'D REMOVED the crew of the damaged class 7—a pair of surly Gajur and a sloppily fawning Nesit. The first two had answered all of our questions with what amounted to, "I want a lawyer." The Nesit, conversely, had gushed, so much so that it was hard to know what was actual criminal intelligence and what he'd just made up, thinking it was stuff we wanted to hear. He professed to not know who'd hired them, though, other than a guy on Dregs.

We decided to put a salvage beacon with a Peacemaker Guild seal on the damaged ship, which would alert us if anyone or anything came near it, then carted our three prisoners to Crossroads and handed them over to the Guild station there. The Station Head, the frumpy but good-natured Gus, made an elaborate show of sighing while taking them into custody.

"We're not really set up to handle prisoners here, Van. We're more of an eyes-and-ears thing for the Guild."

"I'd say I owe you one, Gus, but… isn't capturing bad guys our thing?"

"It depends what you mean by *our*. And you do owe me one, Van."

"Fair enough, Gus. Perry, take a note," I said.

"Note taken, boss. Gus is owed one."

When Gus gave us a tired but genuine grin, we left, heading for The Quiet Room.

Perry had been right about the bank's offices on Crossroads—they certainly were discreet. They were tucked away in a remote part of the station, the entrance surrounded by cabling and conduits that made it seem more the door to a utility room than an organization that could blow a million bonds worth of lethal force without blinking. The more I thought about it, the more bizarre it seemed. Why did we rate such a lavish expenditure? How did they even know Netty was telling them the truth about coming to see them?

I got my answers when we were finally ushered into their suite of offices. It was kind of jarring, like stepping from some gloomy industrial works into a high-end day spa. We'd left Icky and Zeno back at the ship to keep her ready to fly. Crossroads wasn't Dregs or Spindrift, being a little more orderly and fractionally more law-abiding, but it was still far from the security of Starsmith, Null World, or Anvil Dark.

I shook hands with the rep who'd been assigned to meet with us, a young, baby-faced human named Jenkin. My first question was the obvious one, about the missiles.

Jenkin smiled. "Ah, well, we disapprove of anyone robbing our clients. Other than us, that is."

"Um—"

He laughed, his cheeks pinking as his eyes twinkled. "Sorry, an old banker joke."

I narrowed my eyes at him and waited, choosing a neutral stance in the face of his attempt to make me feel at ease. I'd been among hackers and customers far too long to truly *trust* a banker until I got to know them, and Jenkin was an uncertainty. For now.

His laugh became a smile as he sat back in his sumptuous desk chair. "We've been alerted that you were on your way by a rather preferred client who insisted we ensure you reached us safely."

I looked at Torina, who simply said, "Retta."

"We have a strict policy regarding the release of any information about our clients, but—yes, it was Retta."

I nodded, impressed. Retta was better connected than I thought, if The Quiet Room considered her a *preferred customer*. I wondered what you had to do to earn the status, aside from the obvious— keeping huge sums of money on deposit with the bank.

"Still, though, all those missiles. That was a little… extravagant, don't you think?"

Jenkin waved a dismissive hand. "We sometimes take interest

payments on loans in goods rather than cash. And sometimes we partner with the makers of said goods in things like… well, let's say field trials."

"You were helping the manufacturer of those missiles test them? By firing *all* of them at a bad guy attacking us?" Perry asked.

Jenkin shrugged, but his eyes were still bright with subtle excitement. "Sometimes these things just have a way of coming together. The synergistic application of banking and manufacturing interest is, quite frankly, one of the spicier events in my life."

Perry turned to me. "Did you hear that, boss? Spicy. Which brings me to a question—in the midst of all this, ah, spiciness, there is the issue of target selection, of course. Unless you think they were just pirates who happened to pick the wrong victim—"

"Right. Who sent them after us, and how did they know we were coming here?" I asked, my tone remaining neutral but firm.

"That, I'm afraid, I can't answer," Jenkin said, and I sensed he was telling the truth. The Quiet Room was invested in us, and thus, our death would ultimately damage their bottom line, not to mention losing the shipment of platinum.

I handed it over, along with the key, and Jenkin called for his assistant, a stout, grayish alien with no obvious eyes, just a profusion of hairs that reminded me of a cat's whiskers. Somewhere in the back of my mind, a memory stirred—this was a Dolux, a mainly subterranean race that used a combination of scent and echolocation enabled by the sensitive hairs to perceive the world around them. They weren't noted for often leaving their buried cities on one of the planets in the Tau Ceti system, though not because they were especially xenophobic. It was more the pragmatic fact that the world above ground was incredibly noisy for them, making it hard for them to even get around.

As the Dolux carried the case away, it struck me that The Quiet Room was just that, as far as he was concerned—an island of relative calm amid the slurry of smells and chaotic air currents that would be the rest of Crossroads. It made me wonder why someone would choose to enter such a difficult environment. It would be like me trying to live my life in a rave, submerged in pounding music and flashing lights. The novelty would wear off fast.

Jenkin excused himself while The Quiet Room dealt with Retta's deposit. Perry, Torina, and I spent our time musing over who had owned those two class 7s and how they'd been able to find and bounce us so quickly. We might have gotten the answer when Jenkin returned with the Dolux, who carried the empty case.

"It would appear that your secured delivery device is… broadcasting," Jenkin said, giving us the specifics. I turned to Perry.

"How come you didn't detect this?"

"Because it's pulsing out microsecond burst transmissions, so if I'm not properly tuned in at the right moment, I'll miss it."

"Can you detect it now?"

"Yup. It's just a carrier, though, pulsing every eight to twenty-one seconds so far in random intervals. It's not carrying any data."

"So it could just be a locator beacon," Torina offered.

"Maybe. We need to get Icky and Zeno to work their magic on it," I said, thanking Jenkin and getting ready to leave The Quiet Room.

"Be cautious, Van, if you please. We're interested in your continued success," Jenkin said gravely.

"Why?" I asked, extending a hand to shake. Jenkin's own hand was small, tidy, but warm and dry. He regarded me evenly, then looked around at my crew.

"Mark Tudor's reputation is excellent, as is that of all your friends. You are, we believe, an asset to the side of what's right," Jenkin said.

"I—thank you," I managed, marking the moment as a chance to confront my own assumptions. When we left, the Dolux gave a half bow, and Jenkin stood, smiling warmly.

"Safe travels," Jenkin said as the door closed and we left as a group, silent as we kneaded the implications of what we'd learned.

Walking back to the docking concourse, Torina shot me a glance. "Why would Retta give us a bugged container for her platinum?"

I shook my head slowly. "Maybe she didn't know it was bugged. Or maybe it was serving some other purpose entirely and had nothing to do with those ships."

But the question stuck with me like cobwebs as we walked on. I trusted Retta—of course I did. But was it because she was truly trustworthy, or because she was charming?

Charm was like any other weapon. If you didn't have a defense against it, you could wind up dead.

"WE'VE SEEN THIS BEFORE," Perry said, standing on the *Fafnir*'s galley table and examining the device Icky had extracted from the case.

I nodded. "It would seem that our old friend, the good High Doctor Markov, is still handing out bugged religious artifacts.

Although there doesn't seem to be anything especially religious about this," I replied, gesturing at the remains of the case.

"I hope Retta wasn't attached to that," Torina said.

I smiled. Icky had disassembled the case in such a way that it could be put back together, but only to a point. When she reached that point, she switched to the *smash and separate* method of examination.

"Van, I've gone over our logs of all the emissions that either impinged on or radiated from the *Fafnir* from the moment we twisted into this system, until those class 7s hit our scanners. Sure enough, I detected fourteen pulses from that box. The first nine were just carriers, but the last five contained small amounts of encrypted data. I haven't been able to crack that yet, and it might take a while."

"Did it receive any data?"

"It did. Those last five pulses triggered encrypted burst responses from one of the class 7s."

"Please tell me it's the one The Quiet Room *didn't* turn into cosmic confetti."

"It was not."

I turned to the others. "Well, that confirms it, then. The case and that attack were linked. The question now is, why? I can't imagine our wannabe Czar Markov is holding out some seething hatred for us so intense that he's coming at us—what, nearly two years since the last time we crossed paths with him?"

"Van, maybe we weren't the target," Perry said.

"But—" I stopped, then nodded. "The money."

"It was a highly secure container. And highly secured containers don't normally get used to cart around dirty socks. They get used to carry things that must be kept *highly* secure. There's a purpose to them."

"That does make sense. So it means that whoever was carrying that thing was going to get bounced. Huh. I'm not used to an attempt on our lives just being a case of wrong place, wrong time. I really must be getting paranoid."

Zeno shrugged. "Hey, when you're a nail, everything looks like a hammer."

WE RETURNED to the class 7, suited up, and boarded her. Her engineering compartment was a no-go zone, some of our missile shrapnel having penetrated the reactor casing and spread irradiated casing fragments all over the place. Netty noted that it had pretty much been a coin flip as to whether the reactor's safeties could shut it down before it lost containment and blew.

"Seems that our three friends called heads and got it," I said. It wasn't a problem for us anyway, because what we wanted was forward, in the cockpit.

Icky and I waited, suited up, while Perry scanned the ship's controls, focusing on the comm. Icky was the best qualified to tinker with our objects of interest, even though it meant there was room for her in the cockpit and nowhere else. Hopefully, if Perry found something, it would save us the laborious process of waiting for her to tear it all apart. That required the ship's key systems to be powered up, though, which she accomplished by running a cable from the *Fafnir* and splicing it into the class 7's main bus.

"Perry, anything?"

"Ask and ye shall receive, boss." He pointed with a wing. "That panel, right beside the comm. It's labeled for environmental controls, but there's a spurious signal coming from something behind it that doesn't seem to have anything to do with environmental stuff."

Perry withdrew, and Icky entered. She did a careful scan to make sure things weren't booby trapped, then opened the panel and peered inside.

"Yup, there's a second comm unit back here. Looks like one of the switches on the environmental panel lets you toggle between using the regular comm unit or this one."

"Clever, but not clever enough," I said, then pursed my lips in thought.

"You know, it would be really interesting to see who's at the other end of the line. Icky, can you activate it?"

She grabbed the loose environmental panel, flipped a switch, and clambered back out of the cockpit. "You're on the air, boss. All you need to do is activate the comm like normal."

I entered the cockpit and did just that. Icky pushed herself partway back in, enough so that her head would be visible over my shoulder.

The screen had gone to a *Seeking Connection—Stand by* message. A moment later, it flicked to an image, one that I immediately recognized.

"Children! How goes the tithing?" High Doctor Markov said brightly, then he realized he wasn't talking to his minions. His face fell.

"Oh dear, you caught me with my hand in the collection plate— you old fraud," I said, grinning. Icky waved.

The image abruptly flicked off.

"What is it with peoples' manners these days? He didn't even say goodbye."

"He's gonna run," Icky said.

"The question is, where is he, and can we get to him before he leaves?"

Perry cut in. "Anticipating that very question, I already have an answer for you. He's at Dregs. And I asked Netty to check the Dregs traffic reports, and she's confirmed he's still docked at an orbital called Bixil's Hostel. It's a sort of orbiting flophouse for those who want to be sleazy but don't want to go all the way down to the surface to do it. So, figure at least four, and probably six to eight hours for him to get to a twist point, while we're already somewhere we can twist—"

"It means we can end this asshole's sleazy career. Mind you, I thought the same thing about Yotov," I said as we extracted ourselves from the cockpit of the damaged ship. While Icky disconnected the temporary power feed, Perry and I headed back to the *Fafnir*.

"I doubt that the good High Doctor has the sort of connections Yotov had. Moreover, he definitely doesn't have her Ligurite gift for persuasion," Perry said.

I whistled softly. "Imagine someone like Yotov going into the church business. With her enhanced gift for gab, that would be truly dangerous."

"I can think of something worse," Perry said.

"Someone like that going into politics?"

"Got it in one, boss."

We cycled the airlock, and I stripped off my helmet as I considered the ugly possibilities. In a way, the Ligurites were one of the most dangerous races in known space. It was a wonder they hadn't carved out a far larger piece of every pie—especially if that pie was made of bonds.

There was another possibility that simmered in my mind, the concept just starting to take shape.

Maybe they *had*. Who knew exactly *who* was behind people like Markov—or the Satrap of the Seven Stars League and his sudden desire to see me jailed? The Satrap was polished and well-funded, and it arrived out of nowhere, factors that pointed to someone behind the curtain.

It was time to unmask Oz. But first, we had to find the curtain.

———

WE PINGED THE NEWEST, least-veteran Peacemaker we could find on the roster and handed over the salvage rights to the damaged class 7 to them. That was partly because we just didn't have the time to deal with it, but I had another reason, one inspired by Gus and his, *you owe me one.*

"What do we want in return?" Perry asked.

"Something better than money. A future favor."

With that out of the way, we twisted to Dregs and plotted a course to intercept any ship traveling the fastest possible route to a twist point from Bixil's Hostel. Sure enough, there was a creaky old class 5 workboat that, had Markov just taken a slow, plodding course away from the orbital, we'd have never given a second look. Nor did it take long for Netty to trace the workboat's registry back to a company with ties to Markov's church.

Zeno, though, was suspicious. "He sends that workboat rocketing off, hell bent on getting away, but isn't aboard it. Instead, he stays at the hostel and waits for us to be too far into the chase to turn back."

"You've got a diabolical mind, Zeno," I said.

"I try."

"Don't suppose you have a solution to that little scenario, do you?"

"Hey, far be it from me to tag a problem without having a solution handy. I have a contact or two on Dregs, including one who hangs around that hostel. I've got a call in to him and—and there he is. Be right back."

Zeno took the message in her cabin, probably because her contact didn't want to be identified. I was okay with that and we just waited, coasting on a compromise course between the fleeing workboat and the hostel itself. Five minutes later, Zeno came back.

"Markov's not very good at this being nefarious stuff. His regular pilot must be down on the surface of Dregs, so he started throwing money at whoever would fly him away. Anyway, my contact confirmed he's aboard that class 5."

"Perfect. Netty, if you please."

We accelerated onto our new course. I was ready for trouble, but it ultimately didn't even turn out to be much of a contest. Markov's class 5 threw itself around in some janky but futile evasive maneuvers, then opened up at us with a single, anemic laser.

"That laser couldn't give us a sunburn let alone punch through our hull. Is there some way we can guarantee ourselves a mobility kill on that damned thing without killing Markov or his pilot?" I asked, rolling and pitching the *Fafnir* faster than the other ship could track us.

"It's a standard class 5, pretty much off the shelf. I've pulled the schematics, and if we can get close enough, I can target a mass-driver round that'll take his reactor offline without blowing it up—probably," Perry said.

"Probably?"

"There are no guarantees in space battles, Van. You should have learned that by now from all of my patient mentoring."

I smiled. "Where would I be without you, bird?"

"Wearing a straw hat, shucking corn, and whittling on the front porch?"

I glanced at him. "I've never worn a straw hat, all the corn gets shucked mechanically, and the farmhouse does have a front porch, but when have I ever given even a hint of wanting to, or even being able to whittle?"

"See? I saved you from all that."

We closed in on the class 5. Torina did her dead-eye thing and shot off the workboat's laser with our own, but she left firing the mass driver to Perry. It wasn't enough to just hit the target. We needed to hit a particular part of it about the size of a garage door. That required a very close range—stupidly close, if the workboat had been decently armed—and better than split-second timing.

The workboat continued to jink. We kept pace, while Perry took control of the mass driver, choosing the moment for his shot as we, too, waited, unmoving and silent.

Now only about twenty klicks away, the two ships gyrated wildly with bursts of thrusters. But with Netty flying, she was able to keep the relative movement to a minimum.

Ten klicks away. Now eight.

The mass driver thumped. Less than two seconds later, a flash lit up the workboat. Its drive immediately cut out, leaving it effectively motionless.

"Good shooting, Perry," I said.

"I know."

"We gonna go crack some heads now?" Icky asked.

I held up a finger. "Netty, is their life support still operating?"

"As near as I can tell, yes, it is. At the very least, they've still got heat in the cockpit."

We sidled up to the class 5 until we could look in through the canopy. I saw two suited figures. One of them, a sensible sort, held up both hands in surrender. The other held up a hand and extended a finger upward in a gesture I knew quite well, having driven in Atlanta rush hour traffic once or twice.

"I wonder. . . who's Markov and who's his angry, underpaid pilot?" Torina said, grinning.

"A gesture like that's definitely not appropriate coming from a holy man, that's for sure," Perry added with a mechanical sniff. "I'm scandalized."

"I am too," Icky agreed. "Does being scandalized give me the right to—"

I shot her a look. "Icky."

"Yes, boss?"

"Rest assured, if there is legal and just headcrackin' to do, I'll get you in position. However, if you could let me do the whole diplomatic-negotiating thing first, that would be great," I said patiently.

She looked at her hammer, then back at me. "I'll take that as a maybe."

"Attagirl. Love the team spirit. Netty, change in plans. I don't even want to board that thing. Tell them we're going to take them in tow, and if that rude pilot—he of the single raised finger—so much as twitches, I'll unleash Icky, missiles, and our cannon. In that exact order."

"Yesssss," Icky muttered as I reached back to high five her without looking.

"He's way ahead of you, Van. He's already made his intention to surrender clear, particularly since he claims he's not guilty of anything," Netty replied.

"You know what? He's right. We'll take them to Anvil Dark, give him a meal and drink and some bonds for his trouble, and he can be on his way. Besides, being stuck with Markov in that cockpit for the next day or so is punishment enough for outstanding sins he *does* have."

Torina gave me a wicked grin. "Netty, can you override their comms and broadcast no matter what?"

"Sure, it's done," Netty answered immediately.

Torina rubbed her hands together with glee. "In the spirit of *helping*, begin broadcasting Markov's sermon on *temperance*. It's marked in our logs as a sleep aid."

In seconds, Markov's sonorous voice began flowing into his own ship, every sentence more pompous and full of shit than the last.

"And in freeing yourself of unpleasant goods like money and jewels and the occasional high-yield real estate investment, you will find that your heart grows lighter with each act of giving—"

"Annnnd, mute on our end but volume up, please," Torina said.

"You… you are wicked, dear." I snorted with laughter as Markov's pilot looked at his employer in disgust, then mouthed the words *are you shitting me?* as the sermon went on.

Icky placed her hammer down with a pointed thump, a look of respect on her face as she regarded Torina. "No need for this. That's worse than anything I could do."

Torina smiled sweetly. "Penance is a lot like Icky's hammer. Sometimes, it hurts."

Gus hadn't held onto the prisoners we'd dropped off with him for long, apparently availing himself of a Guild transport making a convenient run to Anvil Dark. I arranged for Markov to get a holding cell next to theirs, just to see what the reaction would be. And, sure enough, they recognized him as he was marched past.

"High Doctor!" the Nesit called out, but Markov just gave him a venomous look.

"I know. Good help's so hard to find, isn't it?" I said, smiling as he was locked up.

"The universal powers will sustain me and see to my release from this unjust bondage," he shot back. I shrugged.

"Well, tell those universal powers to meet you in arraignment court in about two hours, if they're going to do you any good."

Just for the sheer satisfaction of it, I asked to perp-walk all four of them to arraignment court. That was normally a job for the Guild Bailiffs because I only had to actually be present if certain, especially heinous charges were being read in. But Markov was everything I hated in a criminal—narcissistic, opportunistic, and utterly uncaring of how his actions impacted others. I wanted to *see* him squirm while the charges were laid. A dour robotic Bailiff accompanied me anyway, one of its arms ending in a potent shock baton I'd only seen used once. It could easily have dropped Icky like a sack of wet grain. That baton had *punch*.

Markov's foul nature was underscored by an incident along the way to arraignment. An Auxiliary from another Peacemaker's crew recognized Markov, glowered, then took a swing at him as she walked past. He dodged just in time to have her connect with the Nesit instead.

"That's for selling me a fake water purifier, asshole!" she snapped and moved in to take another poke. I interposed myself.

"Now, now, let's not abuse the prisoners, no matter how much they deserve it."

The Nesit, who'd squealed at the hit, clutched at his face and seethed indignantly. "She assaulted me! That was assault! I demand that she be charged!"

I smiled at the woman. "Oh dear, I'm afraid he's right. Do me a favor and charge yourself, wouldn't you?"

She returned a feral smile. "Yeah, I'll get right on that."

As we carried on, Markov clicked his tongue. "Typical. One justice for the oppressors, and another for the rest of us."

"Yeah, that's what keeps me up at night—the inequities of life. Like, for instance, scumbag grifters pretending to be Russian holy men so they can scam desperate and vulnerable people out of their money. Can you feel it, Icky?"

She flexed her big, capable hands, a grim look on her face. "The oppression? Sure can, boss."

But it was Perry who surprised me as he skittered alongside the

High Doctor. "You don't know oppression yet, you charlatan. But even if you manage to get out of this, you've acquired something you truly *don't* want."

Markov, still feeling himself, looked askance at Perry. "What's that, you upjumped assistant robot?"

Perry's talons clicked as he walked, and after a long moment, he answered. "You have our *undivided attention.*"

REPAIRS to the *Fafnir* went quickly and didn't cost as much as I'd feared. Our fire control scanner array only needed a new part, not a complete replacement. I decided we'd take some time for a bit of R&R, but just as we were sorting ourselves out to head for *The Black Hole*, Max called from Gerhardt's office. He wanted to see me right away.

"Ooh, someone's getting called to the principal's office," Perry said.

I sighed. "You guys go on ahead while I go deal with this."

"It might not be so bad. Gerhardt's been a lot more friendly lately," Torina offered.

"Yeah, but all good things come to an end, don't they?"

I SIGHED my way to Gerhardt's office, reading snippets of legislation and policy along the way and trying to avoid crashing into things as I did, while quizzing Perry about them as we walked.

I knew that our arrest of Markov was just and fair, and Perry absolutely agreed. Still, I wanted to ready myself for any possible objections. Yes, Gerhardt had lately proven to be an unexpected ally rather than an obstructive pain in the butt. But leopards really don't change their spots, they just cover them up for a while.

I entered Gerhardt's office and sat when he gestured for me to do so. He didn't say anything immediately, so I started to speak— but he held up a hand, stopping me. Another fifteen seconds or so passed, then he sat back.

"So you just arrested High Doctor Markov, the would-be Russian king."

"Czar's actually the title he wants to use, but yeah, we did," I said, and started to explain why. Again, though, Gerhardt held up his hand.

I decided to keep the initiative and just kept going.

"Why do I get the feeling I'm about to be screwed here? What is there to discuss? It was a valid arrest in every possible way."

"Are you sure about that?"

I glanced at Perry, exchanged a nod, and turned back to Gerhardt. "Yes, I am."

Gerhardt regarded me gravely for a moment, then sat up and nodded. "I agree. Good work."

"Oh. Really?"

"Do I seem like the ironic sort to you, Tudor?"

"Uh, no. So what did you want to see me about, then?"

Gerhardt rested his hands on the desk, fingers laced together. "Markov, for all of the pain and misery he's inflicted with his hustles and con games, is a bit player in the bigger scheme of things. He's a small fish. How would you like to go after the big one?"

"What do you mean?"

He gestured at whatever he'd been reading on his terminal. "When you filed your report, the archival AI did its usual thing and looked for potential links to other cases, both active and cold. And it got a very interesting hit, or actually, a number of them. It seems that Markov made the same mistake most grifters eventually make and stole money from the wrong people. About six months ago, he started a determined effort to make some money fast, so he could pay back the aggrieved party."

"That would explain why he was in a flophouse at Dregs and not living in luxury in that tacky... palace," Perry said.

Gerhardt nodded. "Indeed. He no longer had the luxury of waiting for idiots and the desperate to bring their money to him. He's been out on the hustle for the past half-year, presumably running every con he can dream up to pull in cash, a large portion of which he sends to whoever he screwed over."

"This is all very interesting, and I'd say poor Markov, but to hell with him. Knowing this now, I don't care if it was a good arrest and would just say throw him back out the door to the wolves if he wasn't going to hurt innocent people because of it. But what's this got to do with big and little fish? I'm assuming the interesting part of this is who he owes money *to*."

"It is. But we have no idea who that is."

I blinked. "So... why am I here then? The arrest was good, Markov owes money to someone so tough shit for him, that someone is presumably more of a bad guy than he is but we don't know who they are—what am I missing?"

"The last piece of the puzzle, that our heroic archives AI teased out of the data. Markov transferred the money to his mysterious debtholders via a series of seemingly random, labyrinthine transactions, all laundered in the usual ways. When you assemble the whole puzzle, it shows that he never sent the money to the same place twice. In fact, the only thing these places have in common is that in each case, one or more people abruptly went missing in the vicinity within a day or two of the transfer."

I sat up straight. Gerhardt smiled. "I thought that might get your attention."

"Can you send us these transfer points?"

Gerhardt tapped at the terminal. "I'm sending the data to Perry via a secure local connection. If this is a break in your Crimes Against Order case, I don't want any chance of the villains finding out we're onto them."

"Nineteen locations across known space, with twenty-two missing people. The chances of that being a statistical coincidence are at the limits of my mathematical ability, and as you know, I'm a genius," Perry said.

"Humble, too. Okay, so we've now got nineteen locations to check out. What are they, anyway? Banks?"

"Banks, scummy loans outfits, trust companies, and I think there was a posh investment house in there somewhere. One place was even a courier depot. Any place that could reliably receive and hold money, and always in amounts small enough to not trigger an alert, of course," Gerhardt said.

I turned to Perry. "Looks like we've got some legwork to do."

"We do. And I can even recommend where we start."

"Where's that?"

"The First Trust Bank of Mendocino, in good ol' California, US of A."

"Mendocino? I've *been* there." I glanced at Gerhardt. "Great wine."

He smiled. "Bring me back a few bottles."

"I will."

I stood and turned to leave, but Gerhardt spoke up.

"Tudor?"

I turned back.

"Go get these bastards," he said, his smile gone, his eyes hard as crystal. "And if you need anything, let me know."

I nodded. "That's most definitely the plan. And… thank you. I really do appreciate it."

"Don't ask for anything unless you're bringing the wine, by the way. I prefer bold reds, in case you're feeling generous," Gerhardt said.

"I'm sensing cabernet sauvignon in your future, sir," I predicted.

"In that case, the guild stands ready to help. *Generously.*"

13

WE ELECTED to return to the farm in Iowa right away, partly because our last few repairs could be done there as readily as Anvil Dark, but mainly because I wanted to arrange for Miryam's help. While Zeno and Icky puttered about the *Fafnir* in the barn, Torina, Perry, and I convened around the kitchen table and spoke to both her and Tony, who we'd picked up from Appleton along the way.

Tony had brought along his secure, ruggedized laptop, the one that was super encrypted and full of his *truth is out there* screeds and manifestos. He brought up a map that he and his fellow UFO-ologists had painstakingly assembled, depicting unusual missing persons cases around the world that were coincident with UFO reports. The trouble was that there were lots of missing persons and supposed UFO sightings, so there were lots of matches. Most of them were in the United States and Europe, with a few on other continents—including one that really stuck out.

"How the hell does someone go missing in *Antarctica?*" Miryam asked, pointing at the sole dot on the frozen continent's coast.

Tony shrugged. "I'm sure there's a story there."

"Yeah, a story that probably comes down to some sort of bureaucratic screw-up," I replied and frowned at the map. "Tony, there are dozens of cases on this. Dozens and dozens. We don't have any evidence that our identity thieves have been that active here on Earth."

"A pre-spaceflight planet wouldn't make a bad hunting ground," Torina offered.

Miryam sighed. "As if I wasn't spending enough time looking over my shoulder."

"Hey, the data is what it is," Tony said, shrugging again.

But I shook my head. "Let's try this. Tony, pick the ten cases from this map that correspond to what you think are the ten best, most reliable UFO sightings, and let's see them."

"You got it," he said, turning his computer back toward him and working the keyboard and mouse.

"Van, I looked into that case you asked about, the one in—" Miryam began, but I raised a finger.

"We've avoided mentioning the place in question in Tony's presence to avoid him picking up any bias. I want to see if he comes up with it independently," I said.

"Smart move. Okay, so I dug into that location. Nothing really stands out. It's a small, local institution, up to date on all its permitting and regulatory requirements, with a solid reputation. I can't really tell you much more just based on the background stuff I can do from here in the middle of the corn belt."

Tony turned the computer around. "Here you go, my top ten."

I saw all of the dots, four in the United States and six in Europe, including three in Sweden. But one of the dots in the States immediately caught my eye. It was in Mendocino, California.

"Well, hello there, Northern California. Looks like we're going to be paying you a visit."

Tony immediately did a fist pump. "Yes! I was *hoping* you'd pick that one!"

"Why?"

"You're not the only one who's been holding back information to see if you gave me an independent hit. That case in Mendocino is actually six cases, at least as far as UFO activity is concerned. And they're all rated category A, the most reliable, mainly because they involve independent reports of a similar spacecraft, but at different times. A bunch of reports at the same time means many people seeing the same thing, whether it's a genuine contact or not. But separate, similar reports at different times?"

"Yeah. So unless the people of Mendocino are conspiring to convince the world they're being visited by UFOs—"

"They're actually being visited by UFOs—either one, or several of the same type," Perry said. "Are there any photos?"

Tony grinned. "Are there any photos? Please," he said, moving and clicking the mouse. He brought up three images, each of a fuzzy, roughly cylindrical shape in the night sky. They did indeed all look approximately the same.

Netty spoke up over the comm. "Perry shared these images with me. I make that out to be a class 6 workboat of a type built by a shipyard at Sunward, in the Procyon system. It was meant to be a competitor to the other standard versions of the class 6 but never took off."

"Looks like it's flying here, in these images," Tony said.

"I—no, I mean, *never took off*, as in, never caught on in the market."

"Ah, gotcha." Tony shook his head. "So you guys recognize this thing and know where it was built and its history? Like it's… a car or something?"

"Netty recognizes it. I just go by what she says," I replied, staring at the image. "Okay, this is about as firm as firm gets. Guys, I need to know everything you can tell me about Mendocino, the bank there, this UFO, and the missing persons. I want to know all the details before we go sticking our nose into this. This is the biggest break we've had in our identity theft case in—ah, ever, prob-ably. So I don't want to go off half-cocked and tip off the bad guys we're on to them."

Everyone turned to get to work, while Icky and Zeno slipped away to tinker with the *Fafnir*.

For this mission, we needed the ship tuned like never before. It wouldn't do to go to California and *pollute*.

"Hɪ, and welcome aboard *Fafnir* airlines. This is your Captain, Van Tudor, and I'll—"

"Van, you did this the last time I was aboard, too. This isn't my first interstellar rodeo, remember," Miryam called from the back.

I laughed as Netty opened the barn's roof and the *Fafnir* began to lift. I heard Tony, who was back in the galley with Miryam, speak up.

"This never gets old for me. Hey, Van, when do I get a trip out into the wild black yonder? You told me you'd buy me a drink at this Dark Anvil place sometime."

"And I will. I'd rather wait until the chances of us ending up in a space battle are something less than pant-shittingly likely. I'd hate for you to get vaporized by a mass-driver slug or something while en route to the bar," I called back. "Ruins the evening."

"Not as much as I'd hate it," I heard Tony mutter. Miryam laughed.

We crossed the darkened western US in short order, Netty lifting us only a little higher than commercial airline traffic normally flew. Sure enough, the tactical overlay sparkled with icons, overnight flights and red eyes traveling from Somewhere, USA to Somewhere Else, USA We had a United flight pass directly under us, zipping by less than a thousand meters below.

"Hey, Van, have you ever been tempted to turn off your stealth rig and let some of these people see you, just for the hell of it?" Tony called.

"Nope. That's the last thing we—" I stopped.

Torina raised an eyebrow. "Something wrong?"

"I don't know. Perry, why were we able to see any pictures of that class 6 flying around Mendocino? Shouldn't it have been fully stealthed up like we are?"

"Good question, and the answer is yes, but only if the ship's suppressor system was actually working."

"You'd think that'd be considered a critical system if you're going to be flying around here on Earth," I replied. The suppressor system would do nothing to obfuscate the scanners of any ship like the *Fafnir*, or any of thousands of others in known space. It wasn't intended to, which is why the system was normally deactivated when detection by a pre-spaceflight race wasn't likely. It consumed a fair bit of power, for no benefit away from places like Earth.

"There are two possibilities. Either that class 6 *couldn't* use it, because it was defective or not even installed, or the crew chose not to," Netty said.

I watched the dark, empty sprawl of Nevada slide beneath us. Ahead of us and to the left, beyond the Sierra Nevada mountains, the glow of San Francisco was just breaking the horizon.

"Hey, Tony, we're passing not too far north of Groom Lake Air Force Base, aka Area 51—want to pop in for a visit?" Perry called back.

"Okay, straight up—do they have alien tech there that they're using to build, like, secret airplanes and stuff like that?"

"Yup. They've got the remains of an old class 2 shuttle that lost power and crashed near Roswell in 1947. No twist drive or anything like that, just an orbit-to-surface boat—basically a flying delivery van."

"Way to take all the mystique out of it. Kinda wish I hadn't asked now."

"Then I won't tell you it was here delivering groceries and stuff to a cultural survey team and hauling their garbage back up to orbit."

"Well, shit."

I smiled at the exchange, but I voiced the question that came to me. "Why would someone choose not to use their suppressor system while anywhere near Earth? If you're in the identity theft business, that would seem to be exactly what you don't want to do, attract attention to yourself—and end up attracting the attention of the Peacemakers as a result."

"You probably wouldn't," Zeno offered.

"No, you probably wouldn't. So that only leaves a ship that couldn't use it, because it was broken or not installed. So why would someone risk flying around Earth without it?"

"They had no choice maybe?" Icky offered.

"Yeah. So the next logical question is, why? What reason could someone have to fly to and from Earth, despite not having a working suppressor system?"

Tony poked his head into the cockpit. "There's a concentration of sightings in Northern California. Maybe whoever it was figured they'd just get lost in all the background noise or all the other UFO incidents? I mean, if Earth is a backwater like you say, and someone was trying to hide out…"

I glanced back. "Tony, you're brilliant. I think we've got an alien down there—alien to Earth, anyway—hiding from *something*."

"Or someone," Torina said.

"Exactly. Now we just need to figure out where in Mendocino they're holed up."

"I think I can help with that," Miryam said, displacing Tony at the cockpit hatch. "With Perry's help, we've accessed the client list of the First Trust of Mendocino—"

"You hacked it, you mean."

"What an unsavory term. I prefer *accessed*. Anyway, I've been going through the list, comparing it to transactions that match the ones your people back in the Guild uncovered. I've got three hits on the same client, each later in the same day that the funds were received by the bank."

"How the hell does an interstellar transaction in bonds get

converted to US dollars anyway? I don't think the currency exchange at the airport deals much in alien money."

"At the digital level. It's a glorified hacking-laundering that makes money out of thin air, but doesn't garner any attention because *some* kind of currency is being deposited. As to the bonds' route, that's interesting too. It seems that they arrived on Earth somewhere in Croatia and were bounced around the globe a few times, to Macao, then Chile, then up to Montreal, and finally back down to Mendocino."

"You and Perry were able to hack all that?"

Miryam smiled. "I didn't need Perry's help for this little issue. I'm not entirely without resources of my own, shall we say."

"Okay, Miryam, fess up—what'd Gramps set you up with?"

She shook her head. "This is a case where you don't need to know, Van. Because if you don't—"

"I can't compromise it, right. Can I at least assume that if I need to know something about Earthly finances, you're the person to come and see?"

"Let's put it this way—if you buy a pint of beer in Munich during Oktoberfest, I can eventually find out about it."

"Really?"

Miryam just smiled.

"I'll get Netty the address of that bank's client."

———

"Netty, I don't see anything down there except darkness," I said as we circled five hundred meters above the address Miryam had provided to Netty. Whoever lived down there had apparently withdrawn the funds each time in US dollars, which Perry and Miryam speculated were then used to purchase some commodity valuable back in known space, like platinum.

"So if this guy was a waystop in an intergalactic money-laundering scheme, why was he so casual about flying around in his spaceship that everyone could see?" Zeno asked.

"Good question. The only answer that comes to mind is that he was desperate—"

Netty cut in. "Van, we're not seeing anything down there because there is nothing down there, except for the remains of a landslide. Seems the whole side of that hill currently off to our right gave way and rolled right down over top of that neighborhood."

"*Really.* Now wasn't that convenient."

"This region is prone to landslides, Van. You've got a combination of unconsolidated soil, rough topography, recent fires that burned away the vegetation, high amounts of rainfall and earthquakes to set it all in motion," Perry said.

"Why the hell would anyone want to live where all that shit's going on?" Icky asked.

"The weather's nice, and the wine's even nicer. Also, a lot of fusion cuisine. Don't knock it until you've had Korean tacos," I replied. "Can we at least scan through the slide, see what's underneath?"

"Unfortunately, no. The *Fafnir*'s scanners are very good at what they do, but what they do isn't trying to see through ten meters or more of mud, gravel, and boulders."

I took a slow breath. "Shit. All this and it's, what, another dead end—?"

"Not necessarily," Perry said.

We all looked at him. "What do you mean?" I asked him.

"I've got a… feature installed. One I've only used once before, to try it out."

"What kind of *feature?*"

"I can dig."

"You can… dig? But you're a bird."

"No, I'm a bird-shaped mechanical construct. If I was a bird, I'd be dumb and loud, and I'd spend all my time shitting on things."

"That describes you perfectly—*bird*," Icky said with a feral grin.

Perry shot her a glance. "Just like *a bag of carpet shavings* is a perfect description of you, you—"

"Okay, children, let's play nice. Perry, are you serious about being able to dig?"

"I am."

I shrugged. "Alright, let's set down then and give it a try. Better than coming all this way for nothing."

To ME, it was nothing but a bleak expanse of damp soil, small rocks, and broken stumps of tree branches and roots. The night air hung heavy with the rich, loamy odor of newly turned earth and a hint of salt tang from the distant sea.

"Hard to believe there's part of a neighborhood under here," I said, turning in place.

"Looks like half that hillside up there let go and came slumping down," Torina said, then abruptly stiffened. "There's not a risk of the rest of it coming down, as in right on top of us while we're standing here, is there?"

Netty answered. "While the *Fafnir*'s scanners can't really pene-
trate very far into solid ground, the data I am getting seems to
suggest that the slope above you is stable."

Torina crossed her arms. "*Seems to suggest*, huh?"

"Sorry, my geophysical survey module's pretty basic, so that's the
best I can tell you."

Torina looked at me. "Might want to upgrade that sometime."

"How likely are we to need Netty to do detailed geophysical
work?"

"Asking me that question now, standing under that damned
slope up there, I'd say one hundred percent likely."

I smiled. Zeno and Miryam circled a thousand meters above us
in the *Fafnir*, keeping watch from on high, and not just downward.
Since there were advanced aliens implicated in whatever had been
happening here, we couldn't rule out them coming back or necessarily expect them to be friendly if they did. The rest of us had
disembarked and were standing on the vast mound of earth that
had decided to give up hanging onto the hillside above us and just
came slumping down here in a raucous tumble. A hint of violence
clung to the debris, though the hulking slope was quiet and still.

It was damned impressive, in an unnerving way, so I got Torina's
unease. Parts of the earth weren't supposed to up and move all by
themselves like this. I knew it wasn't uncommon in California, not
to mention many other parts of the world, but you didn't tend to
worry about landslides much in Iowa. Not where I lived, anyway.

"Okay, Perry, I'd like to get this over with before sunrise. What
do you need us to do?" I asked him.

"Just stand back. I'll do the rest."

Icky snorted. "So, what? Do you make like a drill bit and spin?"

I saw Perry's amber gaze snap in her direction in the gloom. "Why don't *you* spin—"

"Perry, Icky, you two play nice now. We've got guests, remember?" I snapped, my nerves frayed by our exposed position and bickering crew.

Tony, who we'd brought along in case we found anything that could benefit from his particular UFO-ish expertise, rubbed the back of his neck and shook his head. "I don't know, I always thought that when I finally met aliens, they'd be more… majestic, more inscrutable and awe-inspiring, and not so—"

"Immature?" Torina offered.

"Yeah. Those two are kinda like my niece and nephew in Milwaukee. No stains on their face from juice boxes, but other than that. . . ."

"I feel sorry for your brother or sister," I said but cut both Icky and Perry off when they started to object. "Okay, Perry, let's get this show on the road. How *do* you do this, exactly?"

"Ultrasonic vibrations. They let me move through soil of this consistency at about a meter a minute. In theory, I could vibrate my way through solid rock, but it would take longer."

"Okay, why do you have this capability anyway?" Torina asked. "It seems kind of offbeat for a combat AI, doesn't it?"

"In theory? It's to allow me to collect buried evidence."

"Oh. Okay, well, that makes sense. Why haven't you mentioned it before?"

Perry muttered something.

"Sorry, what was that?" I asked him.

"I said it's because of Hosurc'a, okay?"

"K'losk's combat AI?"

"Yeah. Him."

"What the hell does you being able to dig through soil have to do with him?"

"Because when the asshole found out about it, he started calling me by a nickname I hate."

I could feel Torina starting to smile through the darkness, even if I couldn't see. "What nickname was that?"

"Yeah, like I'm going to say it where Icky can hear it."

I turned to Icky. "You are never to use this nickname Perry's about to tell us, Icky, and that's a direct order, got it?"

"Just once? *Please*—"

"No." I turned to Perry. "Well?"

"When he found out about it, he started calling me... ground pig. And he didn't even get it right, he meant groundhog, but he's so willfully ignorant—"

I bit back a chuckle. I saw Torina bow her head. Icky laughed out loud but cut it off when Perry turned on her.

Tony held up a hand. "Wait, you're saying one AI gave another AI an insulting nickname, and now they have some sort of, what, grudge?"

"It's more than that. Hosurc'a's such a primping, preening ass, with that tail of his. He thinks he's *special*."

Tony put his hands on his hips. "Holy shit. Space is *so* weird."

I clapped him on the shoulder. "You have no idea, Tony. You have no idea."

NICKNAMES ASIDE, Perry's ability to dig ultrasonically was actually impressive. In less than thirty seconds, he'd sunk into the ground and vanished. I got nervous at that point, and more so as the minutes wore on. I was keenly aware that if he got stuck, we'd face a major problem getting him out. He trailed a safety tether behind him, but we wouldn't just be able to pull him out with it. It was more to help us locate him if we had to, as well as enable effective comms through the ten meters of mucky debris. No, recovering him would involve a lot of digging, probably over the course of several nights, with all the risk that entailed.

"Shitty luck, this landslide just happening to bury the house we're interested in," Tony said.

I nodded and grunted my assent. It was very shitty luck indeed. Maybe too shitty. But I'd reserve judgment until Perry returned and presented whatever he'd found.

"So eleven people died here? That's horrific," Torina said, then turned and stared across the rest of the subdivision, all darkened houses and streetlights. A part of it around the slide had been evacuated, but we still had several thousand people within a few hundred meters of us, and they'd be waking up and starting their day in the next hour or so.

I checked the time. He should have reached the buried house by now. "Perry, how's it going down there?"

"I just reached the house, or what's left of it. It's smashed up and crunched down. Catastrophic damage. The rescuers might have found the human victims, but anyone in the western section of this house is in their permanent resting place. The debris isn't talus or scree. It's boulders the size of, ah… houses. Massive stuff. Doesn't look like any human devices or digging has shifted anything at all."

"Shit. So you can't get inside?"

"I didn't say that. There are lots of void spaces down here. Just gimme a few minutes."

We resumed waiting.

Icky turned to Tony. "So what is it with all that probing stuff you guys think aliens do, anyway? I mean, that's kind of... weird."

He chuckled. "That's more a trope than something serious UFO-ologists believe. Medical scans and such, sure. But if there's more to it than that—well, I guess you guys would have to tell me, right? You're the aliens."

"If there's one thing I can guarantee you I've got zero interest in doing, it's that. It's... gross."

Tony nodded. "Actually, Icky, I think it says more about us than it does about you—"

"Found something," Perry said.

We all stiffened. "What?"

"Well, I've got good and bad news. There's definitely an alien here. Looks like it was some kind of humanoid, and a male. I think."

"What's the bad news?" I asked.

"He's dead."

"Yeah, I sort of assumed that, Perry, but thank you for the autopsy."

"No, the autopsy is the bad news. This guy wasn't crushed by California mud. Or he was, but it's not what killed him. It was either the laser to his face, the slug that blew out about a foot of his spine, or his missing fingers. As in all twelve of his missing fingers. This guy was, ah, questioned. I'll look around a little more."

"Questioned? By whom?" Torina asked.

"Now that *is* a good question," I replied while we resumed waiting for Perry to look around. I resolved to give him another ten minutes, then have him extract himself and return to the surface. That should leave us twenty minutes before sunrise, which was cutting it close, but if we needed to spend more time poking around, I'd rather come back another night and do it properly.

"Nah, there's not much down here aside from what you'd expect to find in a typical suburban house."

"How the hell does a twelve-fingered alien get away with living in a middle-class California subdivision?" Tony asked.

I shrugged. "He couldn't afford something more upscale, I guess, what with the current market."

"I no, that's not what I mean—"

I smiled. "I know what you mean. He probably had some sort of disguise tech, or maybe some shapeshifting ability, or maybe he was just a complete recluse—"

"I wonder who Jakob Novak is," Perry said.

I looked at the tether protruding from the ground. "No idea. Why?"

"Because that name is on a sticky note still stuck to this guy's computer. Jakob Novak, and an email address—"

"Is this Jakob Novak in Croatia?" Tony asked.

"Uh—well, this email address is. Why, do you know him?"

"If it's the Jakob Novak I know, he's a prominent UFO-ologist in Johannesburg. A real full-of-himself asshole. I've met him twice, at two different cons. He led bullshit panel discussions at one, and was the UFO-ologist guest of *honor* at the other one, in Miami, about... oh, four years ago."

"Cons?" Torina asked.

"Conventions."

"You UFO people have conventions?"

"Hey, there's a whole industry built around UFOs, Torina. There are towns around the world who run booming tourism economies on it." He adjusted his ever-present fedora. "Guess that sounds kinda dumb to you guys, though, huh?

"No, not at all," Torina said, and although I couldn't see it, I could feel her rolling her eyes. But I turned to Tony.

"Why am I getting a Perry versus Hosurc'a vibe from you and this Jakob Novak?"

"Because he's got money, and he's not afraid to throw it around. That's made him prominent in the global UFO scene—you know, kind of a rock star. But he's got an ego to match."

Miryam's voice came over the comm. "Van, the landing site for those financial transactions on Earth was in Croatia, a bank in Zagreb."

"Yeah, I know. Perry, come on back up." I looked around. "So we've got an alien living here and, we're assuming, hiding out. But he's got a direct connection to a UFO guy in Croatia, which is where off-planet money is being injected into the global banking system."

"And that money is ending up in a bank just a few klicks from here," Miryam said.

"And now our alien friend here is dead, apparently tortured in a really nasty way, and—holy shit, this landslide wasn't an accident," I said.

"Wait. Are you saying that whoever did this to that poor bastard down there deliberately caused this landslide to cover up their crime? And killed ten other people in the process?" Tony asked, his voice tautly quiet.

"Sure seems that way." I chewed on it for a moment. We were close to something big here. I could feel it. We just—

I turned to Tony. "Do you remember those sketches you sent us? The ones made by people who'd claimed to see aliens? Wasn't one of them from Croatia?"

"Yeah. It was. From just outside Zagreb—" He stopped, frowning through his scruffy beard. "Holy shit. Yeah, it didn't mean much at the time, but I guess now it's important."

"What is?"

"Jakob made a big deal about how that sketch was just someone trying to perpetrate a hoax, about how he'd checked it out and found nothing to it. And because he's Jakob freakin' Novak, everyone believed him."

I looked at Torina. She was looking right back at me. We each knew what the other was thinking.

"That picture was of a Trinduk, a Sorcerer. This Novak was covering up for them. He's working with them," I said, and Torina nodded.

Icky clapped Tony on the shoulder hard enough to stagger him. "Looks like you're not the only UFO-probing guy to be working with some aliens, huh?"

The dirt a few meters away suddenly churned, and Perry reappeared, slathered in gritty mud. He looked around. "What, no smug comments?"

"Now is not the time, Perry. We've just worked out that this was a hit perpetrated by the Sorcerers that killed that poor guy down there and, oh yeah, ten other people to cover it up."

"Oh. Ouch."

"Yeah, ouch indeed." I looked at Torina again. "We aren't dealing with some moron like High Doctor Markov here, not this time."

"No, we're not. This just got a whole lot more complicated—and dangerous."

I nodded. "We need help. It's time to call Petyr."

14

WE AGREED to meet with Petyr Groshenko aboard the *Iowa*, so after dropping Miryam back in Iowa and Tony in Wisconsin, we broke Earth orbit and made our way out to the Kuiper Belt. We found Groshenko already there, waiting for us aboard a sleek, venomous-looking class 12 corvette he'd named the *Poltava*.

"July 8, 1709, the Battle of Poltava, where Peter the Great delivered a crushing defeat to the Swedes and put an end to their territorial ambitions in Russia," he replied, when I asked him about the significance of the name. "It was one of my country's finest moments."

"Well, she's a beauty. Retired Masters must get one hell of a pension."

"Nah, it was all that stolen money I socked away in hidden accounts."

I glanced at him, and he laughed. "You really do believe Masters are inherently corrupt, don't you? You even thought I was, at least for a while."

"Seems that most of them are—present company excepted, of course. And Gerhardt. I swear the guy would give himself a ticket if he parked wrong."

We'd convened aboard the *Iowa*, sitting around the table in our barren crew lounge. I brought the vodka this time, the best I could get in the short time we had available in Appleton. I wasn't sure how good it really was, because to me, vodka just tasted like nail polish and despair. Groshenko uttered a contented sigh and licked his lips after taking a sip, though, which I took to be his seal of approval.

We filled him in on what we'd learned on Earth. He listened with grave attention, nodding along.

"So I want to do the same thing to these damned Sorcerers that we did to the Fade at 109—hit them and hurt them, and hurt them badly," I finished.

He sipped his vodka. "I'm a hundred percent behind that, believe me. I've faced opponents I respected because they did what they did out of a genuine sense of duty and morality and were fighting for something they believed in. These Sorcerers—there's no honor or nobility there, no sense of purpose beyond making money."

"And hurting people. They seem to take perverse delight in inflicting pain and humiliation, and they have no qualms about killing. That landslide they triggered led to the deaths of ten innocent people, just as part of a cover-up," Torina said. Her voice had a hard edge, like a scraper on an icy windshield. Just thinking about the Sorcerers pissed her off, and I didn't blame her one bit. The Fade had just been cynical opportunists, doing what they did to make a buck. The Sorcerers were that, but they were also cruel and sadistic to the point of psychopathy.

Groshenko nodded. "Indeed. And that's why there are now a number of retired Peacemakers paying attention to this case and looking for ways to help."

I sat up. "Really? Who?"

"Better if that knowledge isn't widely shared. If they learn anything, though, they will feed it back to you, mainly through me. In the meantime, I have a suggestion."

"I'm all ears," I said.

"Well, you're a fan of taking the fight to the bad guys, so let's do that. I think we should grab a Trinduk, a high-profile one with possible connections to a wide array of wealthy, influential people."

"Huh. Ballsy. How would we know that it's also a Sorcerer, though? Because, correct me if I'm wrong, Trinduk is a race, but Sorcerers are a... a title, or a job. And that means not all Trinduk are Sorcerers, right?"

Groshenko shrugged. "So? If they turn out not to be a Sorcerer, we apologize and let them go. Bad intelligence leads to lots of mistaken arrests. But we hold them in the meantime, well out of the public eye, and see what they have to say." Groshenko grinned around his vodka glass. "More to the point, we let all those wealthy and powerful connected to them stew, wondering what they might be giving up. And while that's going on, we watch to see who does what. After all, people who are afraid they're being implicated in something often don't make very good decisions, do they?"

"The Trinduk will just lawyer up, though, and any of their contacts will know that," Perry said.

Groshenko's grin didn't waver. "Back when I was a Peacemaker,

I picked up a Yonnox on Spindrift who was the spider at the center of a smuggling web I was trying to break. While I was bringing him back to Anvil Dark, my twist drive failed and he was stuck aboard my ship for a couple of days while we fixed it. And there are very, very few lawyers in deep space."

I smiled. "Surprised he didn't demand to have one brought to him."

"Eh, my twist drive was offline, so my twist comms were, too. We were isolated."

"And his lawyers didn't see right through that? Get anything he told you declared inadmissible since he had no access to legal counsel?"

"I didn't need anything he told me to be admissible. I just needed him to understand that his smuggling days were over. And he did, because after two days alone on a stranded ship with a Peacemaker, none of his evil buddies knew what he might have spilled and would never trust him again. He was a poisoned well as far as those bastards were concerned."

Groshenko sipped vodka. "Oh, and he did do time, actually, thanks to some legal advice I got from one hot-shot young Peacemaker named Gerhardt."

I laughed. "Really."

"Do you know the real reason why Gerhardt has memorized not just every line of existing law, but even stuff that's been rescinded or repealed? It's not just so he can be an obstructive asshole."

"Why, then?"

"So he knows how to get around it. He found some obscure case revolving around what on Earth would be called *force majeure*, an act of God, that he claimed was a legal precedent. It was a combination of my unforeseeably broken drive, the fact we faced the very real risk of dying as a result, and the concept of death-bed confessions—"

He shrugged. "Anyway, Gerhardt managed to convince an adjudicator that the Yonnox's statements should remain admissible. So he not only gave up his fellow smugglers but went to jail as well."

"I have a question," Icky put in.

Groshenko turned to her.

"What was wrong with your twist drive?"

Groshenko looked back at me, and we both laughed. But I quickly turned to Icky, shaking my head.

"Icky, don't ever stop being you."

AFTER PORING OVER INTELLIGENCE DATA, both from official Peacemaker sources and Groshenko's less official ones, we settled on heading for Dregs. There was strong evidence that the Sorcerers had a frequent, and maybe even permanent presence there. It was even possible that they used the scummy spaceport as a sort of headquarters, or at least a staging base for their nefarious operations. That was about all the detail we had, so our first job when we got there was getting some more granular, higher-quality, and up-to-date intel.

"I've got a few sources there who might be able to help. How about you?" Groshenko asked as we packed up our planning session in the *Iowa*'s lounge. I was surprised how long we'd been at it—long enough for repeated refills of coffee to take over from the vodka.

"A couple. One of them's a street medic who helped us out after someone tried to car bomb us. He seems to know what's going on in the underbelly there pretty well," I replied.

"That sort of contact is gold," Groshenko agreed. "So that's the two of us, plus Lunzy. I don't think we want to pull anyone else into the circle of knowledge about this, at least not yet—"

"I have a suggestion," Torina said in a tone that meant she'd been thinking, and we both turned to her.

"You should bring in Carter Yost. I think he's proven himself, plus he seems to have a facility for dealing with unsavory types."

I inhaled, then let the breath trickle out as I chose my words. "You mean the various times he was kidnapped or held for ransom? His track record is, ah, *spotty* at best."

Torina smiled. "Okay, he has a facility for *finding* unsavory types, how's that? But there's another reason. You and Carter gained a lot of mutual goodwill. And it's not like allies you can trust are easy to come by. If you keep him engaged, you'll also likely keep him in the trusted ally column. Let him wander too long on his own, though —" She shrugged.

"It's a good point. You don't want him falling in with a bad crowd," Perry put in.

I glanced from one to the other, then sighed. "See, now *this* is why I surround myself with quality people. They come up with good ideas and have excellent answers—even if it means I have to spend more time with Carter."

"Oh, he's not that bad, Van," Torina said.

I sighed again, with gusto. "No, you're right, not anymore he isn't." I glanced at Groshenko. "And it only took the two of us leaving planet Earth and becoming intergalactic cops together to patch up family differences."

"Interstellar, Van. The Guild's jurisdiction isn't intergalactic," Perry said.

"Pedant," I growled.

Groshenko laughed. "When I see a crew bitching and snarking at one another, I know it's a good one. It's the quiet, sullen ones you have to watch out for."

"Well, in that case, we're a well-oiled machine."

Groshenko laughed again, then snapped his fingers, remembering something. "Right. I brought a present for you." He looked pointedly around. "Van, you need to think about crewing this big old beast. Good Peacemakers have allies they can trust to back them up. Great ones are their own backup."

He accessed a terminal and inserted a data module. A few taps at the screen, and he pulled up a schematic. At first glance, I thought it was the *Iowa*. Studying it, I could tell it was the *Iowa's* class of battlecruiser but substantially different, especially in its lower compartments along its keel.

"Are those—what, some sort of smaller ship, workboats or something, down here below deck three?" I asked.

"Not workboats—fighters. SupraDyne FT-100's, in fact."

That piqued Zeno's and Icky's interest. They'd spent most of our planning meeting focused mainly on various technical bits and pieces, and this was another one for them to chew on.

"Oh wow. This is a class 20 military schematic—and one labeled Clearance Alpha-2, at that. This should be locked away in some secure facility somewhere," Zeno said.

"It was," Groshenko replied. "And now it's not."

"How did you get this? I mean—damn. I tried for years to get my hands on anything rated higher than Alpha-5, with no luck."

She traced a finger along the schematic. "And never mind those fighters. This data bus for the fire controller is high-end military grade. I mean, look at these specs. Where would you even get something like this?"

Groshenko smiled and tapped the screen. A new schematic opened, depicting the data bus in more detail.

"Holy shit! *Complete* specs, right down to the tiniest component—in fact, these are *manufacturing* specs." She tapped the screen, scrolling through page after page of data. "We could use this to build our own system from *scratch*. I mean, some of this must be proprietary data right from the individual subcontractors' own files." She looked at Groshenko. "I'll ask it again—how did you get this? How could all of this even be together in one package?"

"I take it this is a big deal," I said.

Perry nodded. "Think if you not only had the complete builders' plans for your father's aircraft carrier, but also the complete plans for every component from every contractor and from *their* subcontractors and… well, the complete metallurgy from the companies that made the steel for her hull. The only things missing would be like the detailed production plans from the mines that produced the ore that was made into that steel."

"So it's a big deal."

"Uh, yeah."

I turned back to the screen. "This is… amazing? But all I can see is dollar signs. Or bond signs. Many, many of them."

Groshenko chuckled. "Pfft. You're at least ten years away from being able to realize all this, Van. But I think Zeno and Icky and the rest of your crew can figure out what's worth pursuing sooner and what stuff is better left until later."

He looked around again. "You've got a good ship here, Van. But even with the guns you've given her, she's still just a shell, just a shadow of what she could be."

"I'd figured that with the automation that Icky and her dad installed, plus the guns, she'd be more or less ready for use now."

"And she is, but in a limited way. If I understand how you've got her rigged, you could basically fly her somewhere for use as a gun platform, and that's about it. Right now, she's more a mobile bunker than an actual ship."

"He's right, Van. The automation's good enough for a couple of people to get her from point A to point B, but that's about it. My dad's ship, the Nemesis, is the same. He can get it from place to place and shoot at whatever comes in range, but that's all," Icky said, then shrugged. "That's all he wants from her. But Petyr here is right. With this"—she waved a hand at the screen—"we could turn her into a genuine, kickass warship. Force projection, not just a standoff battery with some movement."

I pulled up the specs for the fighters, which were also included, of course. We could build our own versions from scratch as well, if we wanted. They were class 6, loaded with front armor at the expense of her flanks and rear, and seemingly built around a pair of mass-drivers the same way the storied A-10 ground attack aircraft used by the US Air Force, the Thunderbolt II, aka the Warthog, was built around its GAU-8 30 mm cannon. Like the Warthog, these FT-100 fighters were fast, nimble flying guns and little else.

"Those fighters need a real name. FT-100 sucks," Icky said.

"Okay, what would you suggest?" I asked her.

She gave me a sly grin. "I was hoping you'd ask that. There's a

Wu'tzur word, and hey, translator AI, don't translate it. It's *canil-strukke*."

"Nice," Perry muttered.

"Thanks, bird."

"Uh, okay. What does it mean?" I asked.

"Literally something like impermanent or transient phenomenon," Perry said.

"Quick, let's scramble *our impermanent or transient phenomena?* Doesn't really roll off the tongue, does it?"

Icky shook her head. "The meaning I'm thinking is *falling star*."

"Falling star, eh?"

Torina smiled. "I like it."

I pursed my lips for a moment, then nodded. "So do I. And now we have a name for our new fighters we won't be able to afford to build for another decade. Goals, friends. It's what we have here on Team Fafnir."

Icky looked hopeful. "Does this mean we're getting airbrushed t-shirts? You know, that match? Like a team?"

I turned to Torina with an accusing stare. "Did you tell her about—"

"I saw it on a YouTube video about bachelorette parties in Nashville," Icky said, warming to her story. "They wear matching t-shirts and tiaras, which seem like a waste of perfectly good metal and crystals and they also yell *WOOOOOO* a lot and do shots of something called Fireball? Is that even legal, to drink atmospheric fighter fuel?"

I stood, hands on hips, looking down as a long sigh trickled out. Icky's face was *beaming* with excitement. "I cannot believe I'm going to ask this, but... Icky, what size shirt do you wear?"

WE BID Groshenko goodbye at the airlock, with an agreement to meet with him and Lunzy at Dregs in three days. Shortly after the *Poltava* undocked and pulled away from the *Iowa*, Netty managed to get Carter on the twist comm. I explained the situation to him.

"Yeah, I'd be glad to help, Van," he replied, hesitated, then seemed to gather himself and went on.

"I really appreciate you asking me, Van. I mean... really."

"Yeah, well, every time we work together, Carter, you prove to be less and less of an asshole," I replied, smiling.

He grinned back at me. "Well, I don't *completely* hate you anymore, either. I'll see you at Dregs," he said and signed off.

We boarded the *Fafnir* and departed the *Iowa*. There was no current evidence of illegal mining activity on Pluto, but we still gave the little planet a wide berth. There might be sensors on the surface or in orbit, and I didn't want to scare the illicit miners off. If anything, I wanted them to feel comfortable about coming back to Pluto, so *we* could observe *them*. To that end, Netty focused a large part of the *Iowa*'s passive scanner resources on the dwarf planet. We then deployed a pair of sensor buoys a million klicks in opposite directions, connected to the battlecruiser by discreet comm beams. This would give her the ability to triangulate emissions and get even better data if our illegal miners did come back.

We then set course for Dregs. I wanted to arrive a day or so early to get the lay of the criminal landscape, as it were.

LESS THAN AN HOUR after we'd twisted into the Dregs system, our comm lit up with a Flash Priority message broadcast across a dedicated and encrypted Peacemaker channel. It could mean only one thing—someone was in trouble.

Sure enough, the message was a distress call from a pair of Peacemakers I recognized by name, although I don't think I'd ever actually spoken to them. They were Akansi, genderless aliens who were always pair-bonded, although in ways that transcended any simple concept of mating or matrimony. The species either couldn't, or simply wouldn't explain the nature of their bonding—which was fine. All I needed to know is that they were Peacemakers, and in distress, apparently under attack.

"They're calling from the Wolf 424 system, our favorite spot for clandestine meetings, I see. Netty, can we twist from here, or do we need to reverse course?"

"If we twist right now, we should be fine."

"Alright, let's do it. Everyone else, suit up and get yourselves ready for a fight."

WE ARRIVED to find the two Peacemakers, Koneese and Bulfir, under attack by a pair of class 10-equivalent ships of a design I didn't immediately recognize. Netty did, though.

"Those are both Trinduk designs," she said.

That made me blink in surprise. "Trinduk? Sorcerers? Really?"

"Not all Trinduk are Sorcerers, Van," Perry said, but I waved a hand at him.

"For our purposes, they might as well be. At the very least, they're Sorcerers until we're satisfied they're not."

Torina checked her helmet, making sure it was clamped in place on the side of her seat and in easy reach. "Now, what are the odds of that, running into Trinduk attacking Peacemakers right after we start digging into their nasty little affairs?"

"My thoughts exactly——" I started, then cut myself off as a new contact appeared on the tactical overlay. I pointed at it. "And what are the odds of that? That's the *Poltava*. Groshenko is here, too."

"A big ol' reunion happening here," Zeno muttered.

I snorted. "No shit." I activated the comm. "Petyr, what the hell's going on here? How did you just happen to show up where these Peacemakers are being attacked by Sorcerers?"

"Koneese and Bulfir are two of my key contacts in the Guild. How or why the Trinduk are attacking them, I have no idea. I doubt it's all just a big coincidence, though."

"My conclusion as well."

Someone spoke to Groshenko from offscreen. He listened, then turned back. "We can't raise Koneese and Bulfir on the comm. Can you?"

"Netty?"

"That's a no. There's some sort of modulated interference preventing it, presumably being generated by the Trinduk."

"Can you clear it? Burn through it?"

"It exceeds the transmission power threshold I could simply burn through. I wouldn't recommend interacting with it, though."

"Why not?"

"Like I said, it's modulated. It's like they're continuously broadcasting something specific that seems like random noise but I suspect isn't. If you give me some time, I can do some pattern hunting—"

"We don't have time to spare, or those Peacemakers out there don't, anyway. And we need to be able to coordinate with them. Whatever it takes, get a line through to them. Icky, Zeno, help her out."

We accelerated to intercept the running battle. So did Groshenko. We could coordinate with him, but without being able to do the same with the targeted Peacemakers, we could only guess at their intentions.

Another new contact popped up, entering the field. I tensed, but it was a Peacemaker, relatively new to the uniform, named Dugrop'che. Again, I only knew them by reputation, but it was a good one—they were one of the new crop of Peacemakers making a good name for themselves.

We powered on, the range ticking steadily down. Groshenko's *Poltava* was the most combat-capable ship, so he moved for a direct intercept, while we and Dugrop'che stayed to his flanks, offering support and each being prepared to cut off the battle if it came our way.

"The targeted Peacemaker ship has been damaged and… and her drive just cut out," Netty announced.

The two Trinduk ships raced in, closing for the kill.

"Van, I've found a way through that damned Trinduk noise," Icky announced.

"Good. Let's get a message through to Koneese and Bulfir. Netty, open a comm channel to them—"

"Van, I'm not convinced that's a good idea. We still don't fully understand the nature of the Trinduk jamming—"

"Netty, there's no time! Just do it, before those Peacemakers get overrun!"

I saw the channel flick open and drew a breath to speak.

Then the lights went out.

15

I'd had a bad experience with some malware once, while doing a routine security audit for a big oil company who had facilities in a particularly unstable part of the world. I'd been doing my white-hat hacker thing long enough to get really good at it but, as it turned out, not long enough to know and accept my limits. In other words, I got cocky, and not only accidentally triggered a piece of ransomware I'd found lurking in the oil company's enterprise intranet, but also managed to get my own system infected with it.

It was a humbling experience, and I resolved then and there to never let my confidence get ahead of my judgment.

But that's exactly what I'd done here. Netty had tried to warn me about trying to engage with the Trinduk jamming emissions. But I let a determination to save Koneese and Bulfir trump my tactical prudence. Worse, I'd started to believe—what with Torina's Declaration, the Guild promoting me, Gerhardt's faith in me, and our general path of success—my own press. I'd screwed up, and now the *Fafnir* was entirely offline. The reactor had shut down, as had the auxiliary generator, and we couldn't even get the final fail-safe, the power cells, to come online and bring the ship back to some semblance of life.

"Icky, Zeno, get us back up and running!"

"Working on it, Van!" Icky called back as she flicked on her helmet lamp and, using it like a flashlight, scrambled aft. Zeno snapped some switches, then cursed and followed her.

Torina, Perry, and I sat in utter silence. And by utter, I mean *total*. I'd never heard the *Fafnir* so quiet. Even when she was at rest, in the barn, there was a faint background hum, her air circulators and reclamators doing their nearly inaudible thing. But this was dead silence, the silence of a tomb. Even the status board, which would have given at least some hint of the problem, was dark.

I leaned my head back and snapped the vilest curse I could at myself.

I turned to Perry. "Can you hear anything from Groshenko or anyone else?"

"Sorry, Van. If I was outside, I might be able to, but the *Fafnir*'s structure and armor degrades the signal. And before you ask, no, I can't transmit anything they'd be able to hear more than a couple of hundred klicks away."

"Shit." We'd literally been reduced to what we could see out the windows.

"Do you want me to go outside?"

I rubbed my eyes. "No, because if we do manage to get back online, I don't want to take the time to retrieve you."

"What about Evan?" Torina asked, referring to the EVAMS, our external repair bot.

I sat up. "He's independently powered, right? So he'd still be online?"

"He is. I've got a link with him and am deploying him now," Perry said.

A moment passed, then our suit comms hummed with faint, garbled voice traffic. Evan was receiving it and passing it to Perry, who'd then relayed it to our suits. I heard only snippets, though, including the words *boarding* and *urgent*, both uttered in a desperate tone that rang as clear as a bell through the static.

"Damn it! Icky, Zeno, what's going on back there?"

Icky poked her head into the cockpit. "Looks like everything's been switched off."

"No shit—!"

"No, Van, I mean literally toggled off. Every single system has been powered completely down. The only thing working is anti-matter containment, because it's an independent system not hooked into the *Fafnir*'s power or data buses at all."

"Can you switch any of it back on?"

"Working on it."

"Faster, Ick. We're sinking here."

"We're doing our best, Van."

I looked back and met Icky's eyes. She looked as stricken as I felt. But she had no reason to. She hadn't failed. I had.

"Van, Evan's scanners are good out to a few klicks. If there's a missile on the way—" Perry said, but left it at that.

Torina reached over and took my hand. "If there is a missile inbound, I want to be holding your hand when it hits," she simply said.

I squeezed her hand and stared past the blank instrument panel at the stars. There was nothing else I could do.

"Okay, Icky, try hooking that cable to the backup bus and see if you can get that flow controller to light up," Zeno said. We could hear her and Icky working away, trying anything they could think of to coax signs of life from the *Fafnir*. I just sat, holding Torina's hand, waiting. Me urging them to work harder or faster wasn't just pointless, it was counterproductive. I reminded myself that I assembled good people, and that my role now was to step back and let them do their jobs.

"Nothing," Icky called back.

"Shit." A pause, then Zeno called out again. "Okay, try it now—"

The emergency lights popped on, relieving the deep gloom. I sat up, and Torina and I released our mutual grip. It wasn't much, but it was progress.

"Okay, now run that second cable into the flow controller's external power port—"

"Done, fire it up!" Icky called.

More of the *Fafnir* came back to life. The air circulators began to whisper, and the status board lit up. It was entirely red, but at least it was now able to tell us nothing was working.

Zeno appeared. "We've managed to cobble the power cells into the main bus. It's not much, but it's enough to let us access more systems."

"Can you give us scanners?"

"Uh… passive, yes. Active, no way."

"Do it, please."

She looked like she was going to balk but finally nodded. "Give us a minute."

That minute seemed to last at least an hour. It ended up being about five—time during which we could only sit in the crippled, drifting *Fafnir* and await whatever fate was delivered to us. We had no control. None. We were as defenseless as a floating rock, and it made me want to weep, to hit things, to scream at the top of my lungs.

Because it was all my fault. Netty had tried to warn me—

What had I said so airily to Groshenko? *…this is why I surround myself with good people. They come up with good ideas and have good answers…*

Yeah. Sure. But that only means anything if you actually *listen* to them.

I could feel Torina beside me, wanting to talk, if only to let me know she was there—and on my side. She knew better than to try, though. So did Perry. The moment stretched, gravid and tense.

The passive scanners finally came back online. After that, Icky and Zeno were able to quickly restore more systems. Finally, nearly thirty minutes after she'd gone abruptly dark, they'd coaxed the *Fafnir* back to life. That included Netty, who announced herself.

"Dragon-class ship control AI serial number 44503895-A-T678-B online, all functions at baseline values or better."

"Netty? Shit—she hasn't been completely wiped, has she?" I asked Perry. I envisioned a blank, fresh-out-of-the-box version of Netty who had no idea who we were. Maybe we could restore her from the second instance of her running the *Iowa*—

"Hey, give a girl a few seconds to wake up. What'd I miss?" she asked.

"The aftermath of me being a smug, overconfident asshole. I should have listened to you, Netty, I'm sorry."

"Van, there's still a space battle going on out there," Perry said.

"Right, let's get back to brawling, shall we?" I studied the overlay, which was refilling with data. But a sudden explosion of noise from the comm truncated my thoughts.

"Don't stay and fight! Go get the other Trinduk, the one that took my pair!"

It was Koneese. Their ship was disabled and drifting due to severe battle damage and multiple hits to their fuel tanks. Groshenko in the *Poltava* kept station nearby, a wrecked Trinduk ship lazily tumbling and trailing debris a few thousand klicks away. The second Trinduk was accelerating furiously toward the ecliptic, while the other Peacemaker, Dugrop'che, burned hard to follow.

The overlay told the grim story. The *Poltava* had obviously maneuvered to take on and defeat the derelict Trinduk ship. Dugrop'che, who'd arrived to the battle later, was struggling to bleed off velocity and essentially reverse course but would never succeed before the second Trinduk ship—the one that had apparently boarded and captured Bulfir—managed to twist away.

"Netty, can we catch that Trinduk bastard?"

"Ironically, because we've done no maneuvering for the past thirty-seven minutes and still have the same velocity we did then, yes. It won't be much of an engagement window, though."

"How far can you push the drive?"

"Emergency overpower of one hundred and ten percent is

authorized for short burns, no more than five minutes duration with fifteen minute cool-downs—"

"I didn't ask what was authorized, Netty. Tell me what's possible."

"One hundred and ten, maybe one hundred and twelve percent for twenty minutes is the most I'd want to push it, and that's risking both damage to the drive core and a small chance of catastrophic failure."

I opened my mouth to tell her to do it but caught myself.

"What do you think? Is it worth the risk?"

"To save a Peacemaker from those Trinduk? Yes, it is."

I glanced back at Icky. I could tell she wanted to object because of the risk of damage to the drive, but she didn't.

"Let's do it, Netty. Every gram of acceleration you can manage."

Without preamble, the *Fafnir's* drive lit, and we shot off in pursuit of the fleeing Trinduk.

"MISSILE RANGE IN THIRTY SECONDS. That will open an engagement window of about eight minutes duration before the Trinduk can twist," Netty said.

Torina turned to me. "Van, missiles are—"

"Blunt objects, hammers, I know. Is there any chance we can disable them with the lasers, Netty?"

"There's always a chance."

"Don't like that at all," I groused.

"Same, boss," Perry murmured.

We could severely damage or destroy the Trinduk ship, and likely injure or kill anyone on board. Our only other option was to let it go and hope we could manage to rescue Bulfir at some future time and place.

I could feel my crew glancing at me. They were waiting for me to make a decision. That implied answers, though, and I didn't have any. So I threw it back to them, these *good people*.

"Ideas, anyone? Some way we can stop those Trinduk without killing Bulfir?"

No one spoke for a moment. Perry finally broke the silence.

"We can't, Van. But we should open fire anyway."

"What, and kill a fellow Peacemaker?"

"Yes."

I stared at him for a long moment. "Seriously?"

"Van, what are the Trinduk likely to do to Bulfir?"

I said nothing but found myself sifting memories that brought back a pain so intense it felt real all over again.

"You experienced a few seconds of what happens to one of their victims in that Cusp machine. Which is the better outcome for Bulfir?" he said.

I stared into that amber gaze of his, because he'd read my mind. For a heartbeat or two, I knew true anger, some of it directed at Perry for being a dispassionate machine that only simulated a personality.

But that anger faded like smoke on the breeze because it wasn't true—Perry *was* real, and more importantly, he was right. With that admission, my rage kicked into high gear—a pure, cold anger fueled by the understanding that Perry was thinking about one hideous fact.

What might Bulfir endure?

It wasn't the calculations of a machine. Perry was employing empathy in its truest form, and I knew it.

With a feeling of desolation, I sank back, then looked at Torina as the decision hove into sight, whether I wanted it or not. *Welcome to command, Van. You wanted it, you got it.*

"Weapons hot," I said.

She stared back. "Van, are you sure?"

"No, but do it anyway. Then transfer the firing control to me. This is one trigger I have to pull myself."

Torina stared a few seconds longer, then tapped at her weapons console. "The missiles are online."

I took a breath and turned to my own panel—

"Van, the Trinduk have released something from their ship," Netty said.

"They're shooting?"

"No," she said and lit the central display with a zoomed image. Something had come tumbling out of the Trinduk ship. It was a body, distinctively clad in a b-suit.

"No."

I wasn't sure who had said it. It might even have been me.

The Trinduk ship rapidly pulled away from the corpse. As it did, it veered, swinging its fusion exhaust plume like a colossal torch. The flare engulfed Bulfir's body, instantly rendering it down to ionized atoms.

The *Fafnir* shuddered as two missiles leapt away, then two more, then two more after that. I thought I hit the firing control again, but Torina had taken the missiles offline so I didn't fire them all.

None of us said anything while the missiles tracked. The

Trinduk destroyed two with lasers, and two more with a barrage of point-defense fire. A fifth lost its tracking and sailed off into oblivion. The one that did detonate may have damaged them but not critically enough to stop them from twisting away.

If I was angry before, then there weren't words for what descended over me in the aftermath of Bulfir's execution. No one spoke. No one *moved*.

Outside, what had been Bulfir spread among the stars, another victim in a galaxy filled with things that were sacred and profane.

Today, we had seen the profane.

DUGROP'CHE DECLARED that he would immediately get to work trying to track the Trinduk. I thanked them, and meant it, but I also knew it was probably a wasted effort. It wasn't likely they'd be heading for Spindrift or Crossroads or some obvious place. They'd go to some hidden lair in some isolated place off the well-traveled space lanes where we'd never find them.

We joined the *Poltava* and the damaged Peacemaker Dragon. Groshenko gave us a terse account of what had happened.

"The Trinduk disabled them the same way they got you— through their comm. Then they boarded, and both Koneese and Bulfir put up a hell of a fight, but it wasn't enough. Bulfir was wounded, and Koneese wasn't able to reach them, which is when we arrived. The other Trinduk ship held us up long enough for their comrades to escape. You know what happened after that."

"Yeah."

Groshenko stared out of the comm at me for a moment. I

braced myself for him to say something meant to be comforting or inspirational. I was surprised, then, when he merely nodded.

"*Poltava* out," he said, and the comm flicked off.

That left me staring at the Peacemaker logo on the screen. "I... was expecting a pep talk," I said.

"Disappointed?" Perry asked.

"No. Grateful, actually."

"And Groshenko knows that."

I gave a slow nod. Groshenko was an old soldier. He knew when an inspirational speech was going to be effective, but more importantly, he knew when it wouldn't.

"Van, between the stress on the drive from our pursuit and the ship's power failure, I strongly recommend we return to Anvil Dark. We may need access to heavy repair facilities," Netty said.

"We *will* need access to heavy repair facilities," Zeno put in, gesturing at her panel. "Based on these performance numbers, the drive core needs to be pulled and given a complete inspection and overhaul, or maybe even replaced."

Icky sighed. "I'll get to work back there—"

But Zeno put out a hand. "No, Icky, don't bother. There's nothing you can do to access the core out here in deep space, and without it properly in tune, any tweaks you make might cause more problems than they solve."

"But—"

"But you already know that, don't you?"

Icky glared for a moment, then deflated and sat back down.

I turned back to the instruments. "Okay, Netty, take us back to Anvil Dark." I glanced around. "The *Fafnir* needs some time in the shop, and I think we do, too."

16

News of the battle and the loss of Bulfir had preceded us to Anvil Dark. We were greeted by a handful of Peacemakers who wanted to know what had happened. I wanted to tell them to go to hell, but Perry spoke in my ear bug, urging me not to. So instead I gave a blandly bureaucratic answer that I had to file my report before making any comments. I caught the glances of recrimination as the group broke up. They wanted answers, but I had no good ones to give them.

Gerhardt, on the other hand, wasn't so willing to relent. He didn't ask what had happened though, and simply made a flat, brusque statement.

"I want your report filed by the end of today. You'll then plan to spend the next three days minimum on Anvil Dark, in case there's any follow-up required."

He didn't say, *such as a Board of Inquiry*, but he didn't have to.

The *Poltava* arrived a few hours after we did. Groshenko

offloaded Koneese, who was under heavy sedation. It wasn't because of injuries, though, or at least not physical ones. The trauma of being separated from Bulfir, followed by their horrific death, was a mental and emotional injury of the highest severity.

Groshenko showed up at the *Fafnir* about an hour after the *Poltava* docked. He said he wanted to check in on the state of our ship and how much work she required, but I knew the real reason. He apparently again decided that a heartfelt, encouraging speech wasn't going to work and departed soon after, promising to be in touch in a few days.

In the meantime, the *Fafnir* was hauled into a pressurized hangar for a complete tear down of her drive. At the same time, every one one of her systems had to be checked, every component that could harbor some sort of residual Trinduk malware painstakingly scanned, and replaced if there was any doubt. Netty herself had to be evaluated right down to her individual bits. Even Perry wasn't immune, being called in to the AI support shop for a scan and evaluation.

It left me seething but still stuck writing my damned report. I sealed myself in one of the spartan transient offices kept available for use by Peacemakers who couldn't or didn't want to work aboard their ships and worked at it. I made three false starts, my narrative description rapidly spinning off each time into bitterness and self-recrimination. The AI assistant stopped me after the third time.

"Why don't you take a break, Peacemaker Tudor?"

It was good advice, but Gerhardt's deadline was rapidly approaching. So I took a few minutes and, for the fourth time, started in. I forced myself to pretend I was just an external observer to it and not a participant in the stress, fear, anxiety, and horror of it all. It wasn't easy, and I had to restart several sections more than once, but I finally got through it with a couple of hours to spare.

I told the AI to file it, then stood and strode out of the office. I was heading for *The Black Hole* and a deep pool of liquor. It was stupid, I knew—getting drunk when in this sort of mental place was never a good idea. But I was going to do it anyway, and if Gerhardt or anyone else didn't like it, to hell with them.

Before I could enter the bar, though, Perry sailed down from somewhere above me and landed on the deck, blocking my way.

"Van, we need to talk."

"No, Perry, we don't. At least, not now."

But Perry just returned his flat gaze. "No, Van, we really do need to talk."

"I do *not* need some sort of glib pep talk—"

"I know that, duh. That's not what we need to talk about. I know why the *Fafnir*'s power failed, why every system went down."

That stopped me. "Why?"

"Not here, in the middle of the concourse. Follow me," he said and sailed off.

I glanced at the bar, then sighed and turned to follow him.

HE LED me to a small greenspace, a park-like compartment laid out with flowers and shrubs and plants from a dozen different worlds, all selected for being able to thrive in the same environment and in relative harmony. I recognized one Earthly plant, a hibiscus. There were probably others, but I was no botanist.

Perry landed on a bench beside a small pond. A thin stream of water tumbled into it from above, then drained out and flowed away in a system that was cleverly hidden. I'd been told that these little parks, of which there were a half-dozen or so scattered around the station, were actually part of the environmental system helping to clean both the water and the air. I believed it, but I suspected they were as much about places to find a bit of serenity amid the madness of being a Peacemaker, and that had a value all its own.

I sat on the bench. "The *Fafnir* lost power because I was an arrogant, overconfident asshole. I should have listened to Netty, and I didn't, so I almost got us killed, and I *did* get Bulfir killed."

"No you didn't, Van."

"Perry, I appreciate the sentiment, but yeah, I did, and now I have to live with—"

"No, Van, you didn't, and I mean that literally. Netty counseled caution, sure, and based on that you knew there was a risk. And you accepted that risk anyway, because that's what commanders and leaders do—they manage risk. Note I say *manage*. The only way to eliminate risk is by laying up the *Fafnir* in a mothball orbit and going home."

"Yeah, well, maybe that'd be best for everyone—"

Perry leapt onto the bench, his wings unfurled and spread like a raptor's on the hunt. He suddenly wasn't the smart-assed sidekick. He was a purpose-built combat AI, a machine designed to deliver lethal force with pinpoint accuracy. He could process hundreds, maybe thousands of pieces of information in the time it took me to deal with one, and use them to drive reflexes measured in milliseconds.

"Would you ease up on the self-flagellation, Van? Bitching like this doesn't become you, and it flies in the face of who I know you to be. Also, it's annoying and beneath you. Yes, you knowingly incurred a risk, but you did it to try and save a fellow Peacemaker. Now smarten the hell up and listen to what we're going to say."

I closed my mouth.

He folded his wings. "Netty, over to you."

Her voice sounded from the comm. "Van, when I counseled caution, I was concerned about a Trinduk cyberattack, absolutely. There are viruses and types of malware that can affect a ship's functions. The Trinduk are known for employing them. They employed a similar attack on Koneese and Bulfir, using their own comm to inject a piece of malware while they were calling for help. It temporarily knocked their nav offline and cut their drive—for about twenty seconds, then their ship's AI restored all functions. That loss of twenty seconds of acceleration was enough to let the Trinduk overtake and board them, so it was still critical. But that's *all* that happened."

"They lost just a few functions for twenty seconds? But we lost everything for over half an hour? What made the *Fafnir* so vulnerable?"

"An excellent question, and one that Perry and I have been chewing on since the battle. It took us a while to figure it out, but we have," she replied.

"There's no way the *Fafnir* should have been so fragile. She was designed with systems hardened to near-military specs against intrusion by hostile software," Perry added.

"So what went wrong? Why didn't the firewalls or any of the countermeasures work? How did the Trinduk manage to knock *everything* offline?"

"They had help," Netty said.

I stiffened. "From whom?"

Perry lifted his gaze to mine.

"From Icky."

I HEARD WHAT HE SAID, but it didn't register. It was as though he'd just accused Netty of being part of a conspiracy with the Trinduk. Or Miryam. Or... hell, Mother Teresa, for that matter.

I finally found my voice.

"What?"

"Icky was responsible for introducing a critical flaw into the *Fafnir*'s systems security. I don't doubt for an instant it was inadvertent, that she never intended it to happen, but there it is."

I stared. Blinked.

"Perry, what the hell are you talking about? How the hell was *Icky* responsible for this?"

"Netty, you want to answer this?"

Netty spoke up. "It seems that in her never-ending quest for drive efficiency, she bypassed a regulator that monitored power flow from the main bus into the drive's fuel feed system. It allowed the feed system to get a slightly faster response to its power demands from the bus. And that improved response time let the feed system do a better job of changing the fuel flow in accordance with shifting harmonics in the drive's fusion core at different power settings—"

"Netty, can you be *less* specific, please?"

"The Trinduk malware was designed to break out of the comm and into the ship's main bus through the comm's power supply. It did that. It was then intended to use the bus to access and break through into the drive's fuel feed system and shut the drive down temporarily, like it did with Koneese and Bulfir's ship. But when it got to the regulator that would have at least attempted to firewall it off and stop it, it instead found an open, unprotected circuit right into the drive. That was bad enough, but what made it so much worse was that that regulator protected some other systems, too. We don't know if the malware would have tried to infect them at the same time it did the drive, but with nothing stopping it, it did anyway. Once that happened, it just spread to the rest of the ship."

"It was like taking out part of a dam to let some water trickle through for your garden. That was fine until the water rose, then the trickle became a torrent and flooded your garden, along with everything else behind the dam," Perry said.

I sank back on the bench. "Why the hell would she do that?"

"Like Netty said, to improve the efficiency of the drive. She got another 0.08 percent performance improvement by taking the regulator out of the loop."

I leaned forward and rested my elbows on my knees. I couldn't rein in my racing thoughts. They whip-sawed from thinking that Icky had made a well-intentioned mistake, to her being egregiously negligent or outright reckless. I even had a hideous flash of her being compromised by the Trinduk, who were so creatively evil that even the noble, goofy Icky was susceptible to their nefarious plans.

In the end, none of these things could be possible. Or they all could.

My tumbling thoughts finally found a grip on something. "Netty, Perry, how come we didn't detect this? Shouldn't there be… I don't know, systems of some sort to alert us to shit like this?"

"There are. When the regulator stopped receiving power to send

235

to the drive's fuel feed, it should have triggered a fault warning. But it would seem Icky disabled that function, too—probably because the constant fault alert would have been annoying," Netty replied.

"Think having the check engine light in your car come on, so you put tape over it so you can't see it. There's still a fault, you've just blinded yourself to it," Perry added.

"For that matter, in the absence of a cyber attack on the *Fafnir* much like this one, the flaw never would have come to light—at least not until someone else happened to work on those particular components and discovered what she had done," Netty said.

I let my head drop back and stared at the top of the compartment. Whatever her motivation, Icky had introduced a critical flaw into the *Fafnir* that happened to trigger at the worst possible moment. It had disabled the ship for more than thirty crucial minutes, taking her out of battle—a battle that had resulted in the death, or worse, of a Peacemaker.

I stood and started back to the *Fafnir*.

"Van, where are you going?" Perry called.

"To think. I need to sort this shit out and figure out how to approach it." I also had to calm myself down.

17

When I arrived back at the *Fafnir*, I felt like I had lead weights on my feet the last few steps into the hangar. I didn't want to lose Icky, but there might be no choice. Before any decisions could be made, though, I had to know for sure what her motivations were.

I braced myself as I approached the ship. Netty had told Torina everything she'd told me, but I didn't know if she'd spoken to Icky yet. As soon as Torina, who was talking to one of Anvil Dark's techs near the *Fafnir*'s port main landing strut, saw me, she hurried my way.

I stopped. "Have you talked to her?"

Torina nodded. "I felt I had to. Otherwise, it would be—" She seemed to struggle for a moment. "It would be a… a security issue, wouldn't it? Anyway, I sent her and Zeno to wait at the transient office you booked for yourself. So let me ask you, Van. What do you intend to do?" Torina asked.

I crossed my arms. "I don't know yet.

I turned to Perry. "What's the normal procedure for something like this?"

His answer was deliberate, if grim. "Since it affected multiple Peacemakers, a Board of Inquiry convened by a Master is the usual thing. Its findings could lead to further action, including criminal charges"

I looked back at Torina. She looked at me, waiting for me to decide. I knew whatever it was, she'd support it.

I sighed. "Perry, set up an appointment with Gerhardt. I'm going to ask him to convene that Board of Inquiry."

Torina cocked her head. "Gerhardt? Are you sure?"

"Can you think of anyone who'd be more impartial or give Icky a fairer hearing?"

She shook her head.

I sighed again. "No, neither can I."

I'D PREPARED myself for a wait of several days while statements were collected and evidence gathered, but Gerhardt ordered all of that done in a single day. I saw Icky during that time, accompanied by Zeno, looking like the picture that would accompany the phrase *abject misery*. She did come right to me, once, her head hanging.

"Van, I… I'm sorry."

I regarded her with a look that fell as close to neutrality as I could muster. "I know you are, Icky."

It was all I said. I was trying to remain as detached and clinical about all of this as possible. I was keenly aware that the *Fafnir* was my ship and Icky was my crew, which meant that the ultimate responsibility was mine. I remembered my father telling me about a friend of his who had been made captain of a logistics support ship as his first US Navy command. One night, while he was asleep, the Officer of the Watch somehow ran the ship aground. My father's friend, despite being legitimately off-duty and asleep, was court-martialed and held responsible because it was his ship, and he had "allowed the conditions to exist that had led to the accident." He wasn't discharged, but it did end his command career, ensuring he spent the rest of his time in the Navy sailing a desk.

Wasn't I guilty of the same thing? I'd allowed the conditions to exist that had led to the Trinduk's thorough takedown of the *Fafnir* by not watching Icky and her tweaks to the ship closely enough and not making her accountable for them. So yes, Icky might have pulled the trigger, but I'd watched her pick up the gun and start fooling around with it and made no attempt to stop her.

In short, it was on me.

We convened the next morning in a conference room in The Keel. Everyone who had formal uniforms wore them, and although the damned collar still bugged the hell out of me, it seemed like awfully minor shit. Gerhardt sat at the head of the table, with me and Torina on one side, and Zeno on the other. Icky sat at the end opposite Gerhardt, facing him directly, while Perry remained off to one side. Max, the several-people-in-one administrative overseers of the Masters' affairs, sat at a separate table, making a transcript of the proceedings and taking notes. The notes were copious, I assumed, based on the amount of tentacle movement I watched out of the corner of my eye.

I glanced at Koneese. They were hard to read, simply sitting motionless, their big, dark eyes focused on some random point on the table. Icky sat much the same down at her place of… dishonor.

"This Board of Inquiry is now convened. Max, please note the time," Gerhardt said.

The next half-hour or so was all process—informing Icky and everyone else of their rights and obligations, then reading the particulars of the case being examined into the record, followed by statements already provided by everyone at the table. Koneese's statement was especially poignant, ending with *and just like that, Bulfir was gone and I couldn't save them.* I saw Icky flinch a little when Max read it aloud.

Gerhardt then went around and asked some questions based on the statements, mainly for clarification. He was dispassionate and to the point. It struck me that all the bitching and moaning I'd done about his slavish dedication to process had belied the fact that it gave the man not just credibility as an impartial judge, but also the moral authority to embrace the role and give it the gravitas it deserved. We may not end up liking the outcome of this trial, but I knew that at least it would be a fair one, based on the facts and not emotion.

The proceedings wore on for another hour. Gerhardt's questions were incisive and penetrating. He established the facts regarding what had happened, the things that everyone agreed on. He further teased out each individual's perspective and quickly determined which parts of it were relevant and which were not, or were even just unfounded opinion.

Perry and Netty were particularly compelling, their testimony being based on the flawless, factual recollection of a machine. I'd seen them in action before, testifying at trials for various cases we'd been involved in, but I'd never really appreciated just how credible their statements were until now. They told the objective truth as they had recorded it—no more, no less. Despite this, Gerhardt *still* managed to extract observations and conclusions from them that they clearly hadn't considered themselves.

By the time he called a recess, I had to admit to being a little in awe of the man's mastery of getting at the truth and establishing a firm foundation for some decision-making. Without a word, Gerhardt withdrew, leaving us in the room in silence.

Icky abruptly stood up and walked around the table, to Koneese. "I—"

It was all she managed before she burst into braying sobs, which was quite a sight given her size and hirsute nature. I moved to intervene, but Zeno intercepted me with a hand and shook her head.

Koneese stood, facing Icky. It was a strange sight, since Icky had nearly twice the height and probably three times the mass of the smaller alien. The rest of us just waited, holding our breath.

A moment passed, then Koneese reached out and embraced Icky.

"I forgive you."

Icky collapsed entirely at that. Torina bit back a sob. I had to blink fast and wipe my eyes.

Koneese pulled back. "But my forgiveness comes at a price, Icrul. I need... I need Bulfir to be... okay." They turned to me. "I need to know that Bulfir is at peace, no matter what that means."

I raised my hand and held it next to me, palm out. "I won't rest until that happens. I promise you that."

We all took a few minutes to collect ourselves, then Gerhardt returned and reconvened the Board.

He gave a bit of preamble, essentially summarizing the situation for the sake of the record being assembled by Max. He then asked Icky to stand. A thrill of tension rippled through the room as she did.

"Icrul, I can find no evidence of deliberate collusion or intent to interfere with Peacemaker operations on your part. Accordingly, your behavior does not reach the bar of sabotage or conspiracy to commit the same. There is, therefore, no reason to proceed with any criminal charges."

I relaxed but only a fraction because I knew Gerhardt wasn't done.

"However, I do find that your actions constitute negligence, which is failure to use reasonable care, resulting in damage or injury to another. While not criminal, these negligent actions are still egregious and require an answer."

He turned to me. "Peacemaker Tudor, I am leaving the decision as to retaining Icrul as a Peacemaker Guild Auxiliary to you. Do you intend to retain her or not?"

I looked at Icky. She'd screwed up, yes, and big time. But set against that were all the times she'd risked her life for the *Fafnir* and its crew. So I gave a single, decisive nod.

"I do."

"Very well. In that case, Icrul, you will spend the next fourteen days in administrative detention here at Anvil Dark, during which time you will complete a suite of courses and examinations regarding the operation and maintenance of the critical systems of a Dragon-type spacecraft. Failure to satisfactorily complete those examinations within that time will result in your dismissal from the Guild with prejudice. Do you understand?"

She deflated, but only a bit, and then she too gave a deliberate nod.

Gerhardt then turned to me, just as I knew he would. "Peacemaker Tudor, this unfortunate incident occurred because you did not exercise adequate command and control over your crew. The *Fafnir* may be your ship, but she flies bearing the Guild insignia. Therefore, effective immediately, you will maintain a detailed log of every repair or alteration to the *Fafnir*. I don't care if you buff out a scratch on a bulkhead, I expect there to be a detailed and duly authorized log entry describing it."

"I understand."

"Furthermore, you will bring the *Fafnir* to Anvil Dark once every two calendar months for the next standard year for a Level 2 inspection of her systems by Guild technicians. If there are any disagreements between what they find and what you have logged, you will be accountable for it."

"Absolutely."

"Finally, I am censuring you with a formal reprimand that will be placed on your personnel file for two standard years. During that time, you will not be eligible for promotion and will be subjected to a performance review conducted every six months by me and anyone else I see fit to include."

Inwardly, I winced, but I repeated my earlier words. "I understand."

"Finally, under the terms of ancient Galactic Knights and Guild custom best described by the Earthly term wergild, you will pay five hundred thousand bonds to Koneese as reparations." He stood. "These are my findings. This Board of Inquiry is adjourned."

I MADE TO LEAVE, but Koneese stopped me. "Van, I want you to give me that five hundred thousand bonds."

"I… will, Koneese. As soon as I can draw it and transfer it to you—"

"No. I want you to say to me, right now, that you are giving me that money."

I frowned. Was I being accused of being untrustworthy? Did Koneese consider me such a villain that they needed me to commit to this in front of witnesses?

I finally just nodded. "I am giving you the five hundred thousand bonds, as ordered by Master Gerhardt."

"Good. Thank you. I am now giving them back to you, the full amount."

"You—what?"

"I don't want your money, Van. It means nothing to me. What I do want from you is the fulfillment of that promise you made to me, that you'll ensure that Bulfir is properly at peace. Use the money for that."

I had a speechless moment, then nodded. "Like I said, I won't rest until it's done. I will use any and all of my—and my crew's—resources and abilities to do so."

"I believe you. I also believe you're the best Peacemaker in the Guild, and that if anyone *can* do it, it's you."

I shook my head. "If I was the *best* Peacemaker, we wouldn't be standing here having this conversation."

Koneese touched my shoulder with a long-fingered hand. "The

best Peacemaker is the one that makes mistakes, then goes out and fixes them."

They patted my shoulder, then turned and walked away.

"Van?"

I turned. It was Icky.

"We haven't really, you know, talked. I just——"

I held up a hand. "Icky, Gerhardt was right. This was my fault as much as yours. What we *must* do now is regain that trust we need to work as a crew. You can't act like you're on an island, fiddling around with stuff on your own because... I don't know, it's a fascinating problem for you. The *Fafnir* isn't just a machine to be tweaked. She's... part of the crew. We both need to remember that."

Icky bowed her head slightly.

"So, the first step—you have to do the things Gerhardt laid out, so do them. And once you're done, you'll rejoin the *Fafnir* and we'll carry on. I'm choosing to trust you. As for everyone else, that has to be *their* decision." I took a step closer and looked up into her face. It was a gut punch to see those eyes, usually twinkling, clouded with guilt and sadness.

"I can't do this alone. I won't do this alone."

She nodded. "I won't let you down again."

"I believe you. And I want to say the same to everyone else," I said, turning to look at the rest of the crew. "I won't let you guys down again either."

IT TOOK another two days before the *Fafnir* had been thoroughly scoured of any lingering effects of the Trinduk cyberattack and was declared flightworthy again. Icky got to work on her remedial training, throwing herself into it with an enthusiasm that impressed even the dour AI running it. I learned that from Gerhardt, who summoned me into his office the day after the Board of Inquiry.

"Boffin tells me that your Icrul is well above the performance curve on her makeup training already," Gerhardt said after he'd gestured for me to sit down.

Boffin, the training AI, was on Gerhardt's comm. "She is. She's not just enthusiastic, she seems to have an almost innate understanding of systems. When I've given her a problem to diagnose, she not only comes up with the correct answer very quickly, but she also goes on to suggest potential positive effects on other systems. Some of her thinking is quite lateral. I hate to admit it, in fact, but she's pointed out a couple of things that aren't even in the manuals and that I've never even considered."

"I suspect that's part of the problem. She's a savant when it comes to the machinery and sees every little imperfection as something to be fixed. Unfortunately, her interest seems to stop where the mechanisms do, so she doesn't think through the real-world implications of what she's doing," Gerhardt said, nodding along.

I nodded, too. "Icky is happy as a pig in shit when she's elbows deep in the reactor or drive. When it comes to the rest of the universe, though, she's a little, um… unrefined."

Gerhardt smiled. "Thank you, Boffin. Keep us apprised regarding her progress," he said, then leveled his gaze on me.

"Now that a day has passed since the Board, what are your thoughts, Tudor?"

"That I screwed up."

Gerhardt steepled his fingers but said nothing.

I sighed. "I told Groshenko I surrounded myself with good people. I still believe that. But looking back, I think I leaned too heavily on that *good people* part and let myself forget that I'm still the one in charge."

"And the one ultimately responsible."

"Exactly that."

The Master smiled again. "Humility looks good on you, Tudor. You should wear it more often."

I offered a thin smile back to him. "I think this whole affair has brought it to the front of my closet. Hard to feel anything *but* humble these days."

"Too much of anything is unhealthy. Keeping with the metaphor, humility has to be one of the things you wear. The whole outfit has to include a lot more, including some of that cocky, pushing-the-rules attitude you obviously inherited from your grandfather. You didn't become a First Veteran Peacemaker in near-record time by accident, after all. The Guild doesn't want to lose that from you. *I* don't want to lose that from you."

He sat back. "Now, what's your next move?"

"Well, once the *Fafnir*'s cleared for flight ops, I intend to get back out there and try to earn that rank. I'm hoping that Koneese can shed... I don't know, some sort of light on those Trinduk. Maybe a past encounter, or maybe a few bits of scanner data from their ship."

"No need," he replied, tossing a data slate across his desk to me. "While all of this drama has been playing out here, Dugrop'che has been out there nosing around, and he has a lead."

Dugrop'che. Right. Amid all the drama, as Gerhardt put it, I'd entirely forgotten about the other participant in the recent battle. I scanned Dugrop'che's report, which was itself concise and yet detailed, and obviously the result of some good, methodical investigative work. I added a mental note to consider adding him to the short list of Peacemakers I trusted, which was currently Lunzy, Lucky, Alic, K'losk, and—and this still surprised me—Gerhardt himself.

"The Trinduk seem to have headed for the Cross of Novae? Where's that?" I asked, looking up from the slate.

"It's a dusty nebula about ten light-years spinward of the first of the star systems claimed by Unity."

"Ah. Not the first time *they've* come up in all this."

"Tread carefully around them. They've made it abundantly clear that they want little to do with the rest of known space, and if that's ever going to change, we need to keep the number of diplomatic incidents as close to zero as we can."

I sent Dugrop'che's report to Netty to disseminate to the rest of the crew and nodded. "No diplomatic incidents, I promise."

I stood to go.

"Oh, by the way, Tudor—you mentioned a moment ago that your Icrul isn't exactly refined, in pretty much the same breath you described her *as happy as a pig in shit.* The irony aside, your grandfather used to use that phrase. I finally looked up what a *pig* is. They sound like unpleasant creatures, so I gather they have some value other than, well, aesthetics?"

I grinned. "You mean you've never had bacon?"

"No. What is that? A commodity of some sort? An activity?"

"A little of both but so much more. I'm surprised Gramps never introduced you to it. Next time I'm on Earth, I'll grab some and bring it back to fry up for you."

"I'll assume I should look forward to it."

"I'll put it this way—if the Earth blew up tomorrow and the only thing that survived was bacon, it would still be a huge contribution to known space."

"Does this bacon arrive in kilos?"

"It can."

Gerhardt held up fingers. "In that case, I'll take two."

18

"THE PROBLEM, Van, is that we don't know what's in there. The Cross of Novae isn't a very big nebula, but it's unusually dense—enough that existing scanner data only penetrates about ten percent of the way into it," Netty said.

We sat around the *Fafnir's* galley, studying the data describing the Cross of Novae. It was a pillar-shaped pall of dust and gas about twelve light-years long, with a thickening at its mid-point vaguely suggestive of two shorter, perpendicular arms—hence its name. It glowed with the emissions from some young, hot, blue stars buried deep inside it, but little was known about it otherwise. The fact that Unity's claimed territory sat partly between it and known space made it an awkward place to get to, necessitating at least two twists with a mid-course nav fix to avoid that diplomatic incident Gerhardt had mentioned. And with literally infinite amounts of empty space to spread in every other direction, it was little wonder that it had generally been viewed as nothing more than an interesting cosmo-logical phenomenon.

That relative anonymity was likely what had attracted the Trinduk to it in the first place. Far away, hard to get at, and largely unknown, it was perfect for hiding out even a sophisticated operation.

Dugrop'che, on the twist comm, spoke up. "I got as close as I dared and only used passive scanners. That didn't add much to what we know. If we're going in there, we either need to find some way to get better data, or just go in blind and hope for the best."

"Yeah, hope for the best isn't a very good plan," I said, glancing around. "Ideas?"

"Flush them out. Do a high-speed run right along the length of the thing. Maybe four twists, about three light-years each, and hammer away with active scanners every time," Zeno suggested.

I nodded at the screen, which was currently depicting the Cross in false-color glory. "I like it. Make sure the bad guys know we're onto them, and gather some useful data while we're at it."

"If they're smart, they won't take the bait. At best, we'll still only get scan data from about ten percent of the nebula during that pass. That leaves ninety percent perfectly good for hiding."

I rubbed my chin, calculating odds. "Yeah, but it's still probably our best bet. Back in my army days, when I was learning squad-level tactics and we had trouble finding who'd just shot at us, we used speculative fire into likely enemy positions to try to provoke them into shooting back and showing themselves. Even during training, it worked more than it didn't."

"You shot at one another during training? That's pretty hard-core," Zeno said.

"Uh, well, we did, but not with bullets. We had laser emitters on our rifles and receivers on our bodies to record hits."

"Still—lasers."

I laughed. "Lasers about as intense as flashlights, actually."

"Okay, that's considerably less hardcore."

We didn't end up with a better plan, so we settled on the one Zeno had pitched. Perry, though, suggested a twist.

"Groshenko said he was eager to help out any way he could. I think he's feeling like he failed Koneese and Bulfir, too. So if we're gonna do this, and if we do end up with the Trinduk hot on our tail, why not prepare a fun little surprise for them while we're at it?"

I contacted Groshenko, and he was immediately all-in. Gerhardt liked the idea, too, and assigned three class 10 corvettes from the Guild's quick reaction force to help out. It was a substantial chunk of combat power, particularly since the Guild only maintained a half-dozen ships in the QRF, mainly to deal with possible threats to Anvil Dark.

Which meant we were all set. Dugrop'che stayed in place to keep an eye on the Cross of Novae—or as much of an eye as a single ship could keep on something twelve light-years long, anyway —while Groshenko in the *Poltava* and the three ships of the QRF agreed to rendezvous with us at a designated staging point two days from now.

Unfortunately, though, we were flying without Icky. Per Gerhardt's orders, she was stuck on Anvil Dark completing her remedial training. It wasn't intended as punishment but as a sort of personal development. Icky took it as punishment, though.

"You guys be *extra* careful. You don't have me around to look after you," she said, her tone crestfallen.

I patted her arm. "Don't worry, Icky. I have a feeling there are going to be lots of Trinduk heads to bust in the coming days."

With a gusty sigh, she managed a smile. "You're just trying to make me feel better."

TWO DAYS LATER, we'd marshaled our small fleet. Groshenko had brought the *Poltava*, the only ship his mercenary company didn't have otherwise tied up on contracts. She joined the three Guild class 10s, plus Dugrop'che and Lucky, who'd shown up as a last-minute addition. She and Koneese and Bulfir were apparently close, so she was not only willing when I saw her at Anvil Dark and pitched it to her, she insisted.

"I want a piece of this, Van," she said, almost as though she was daring me to refuse. I didn't, of course, and here she was.

The plan was simple. The *Fafnir*, accompanied by Dugrop'che for added firepower, would do a high-speed run through the Cross following its long axis. The *Poltava*, Lucky, and the Guild ships would hold position at the coreward end of the nebula, closest to known space. Hopefully, we'd draw some Trinduk out and provoke them into chasing us, whereupon we'd lead them right into the waiting guns of Groshenko and the others. Or if they chose to respond in more force than we could handle, we'd all withdraw under the cover of our own fire. And if the Trinduk didn't respond at all, as Perry hinted might happen—well, that left us no further behind than we were now, did it?

We only had one problem.

"Fuel, as in, the *Fafnir* isn't equipped to carry enough to twist to the far end of the Cross. We have a stop, then three more twists through the nebula, but it's the last stage where things get spicy because we might need a *fourth* twist at the end just to save our skin," Netty announced. "Or circuits, as in my case."

"And mine," Perry added.

I'd assumed as much. And the trouble with antimatter was that you couldn't just lug it along in spare fuel cans.

"What's the best we can manage without refueling, Netty?" I asked her.

"We pretty much need to refuel after our second twist inside the nebula."

Zeno sniffed. "Right in the heart of enemy territory, huh? Ouch."

"What if we carry along one of those refueling pods like we saw being used to refuel those class 3 workboats out in the middle of nowhere? Right after I was recruited by Group 41?"

"That will work, but the added mass will substantially reduce the *Fafnir*'s performance in normal space maneuvers. We would also have to take the time to refuel Dugrop'che."

I sat back in the galley seat, then stuck out and crossed my legs. "Okay, then. Change of plans. Tell Dugrop'che he's going to chill and wait with the *Poltava* and the rest of them. Looks like we're flying this mission solo."

Torina raised her index finger, along with a brow. "To clarify— all alone, our performance degraded by a spare fuel pod, right in the middle of unknown space potentially full of enemies intent on doing worse things than killing us?" Torina asked, her eyes glittering with mischief.

I tried a modest leer. "Are you telling me all the excitement and danger does something for you, my dear?"

"Yeah, makes me feel a little nauseated, actually."

"That was not what I was going for, not at all."

———

NETTY WAS RIGHT. Having the bulky fuel pod strapped to her belly turned the *Fafnir* into a glorified grocery-getter. It wasn't that she couldn't fight, but she had lost her edge. I gave her a thorough work-out, and while she wasn't exactly wallowing, her performance was nothing special. Moreover, the pod was *massive* and threw the ship's center of gravity off, meaning her thrust was now delivered off-center. She required constant thruster corrections just to keep her traveling in a straight line, sort of like driving a bike with handlebars that were twisted just enough to make things interesting.

Still, it couldn't be helped. Without the extra fuel for the twist drive, this show was over before it had even begun.

I glanced back into the cockpit behind me. "Does anybody have to use the restroom before we go?"

"I don't," Perry said. "Achieving existential perfection and all that, yanno."

"Those feathers *are* impressive."

He dipped his beak. "Thanks, boss. You never know when it's your moment to shine."

I smiled and instructed Netty to activate the flight plan. We'd already checked in with Groshenko, who was on his way to his station at the coreward end of the Cross of Novae, along with the other ships. They would experience less time dilation from twisting than we would, meaning that while we estimated we'd see them in another three days, for them, it would be about five.

"I wonder how Gramps felt, knowing he was shifting further and further out of his now and into his future each time he twisted." I turned to Perry. "He ever say much about it?"

"Not really. He had Valint, your grandmother, traveling through time right along with him, and that seemed to be good enough for him."

I glanced at Torina. "Yeah, I get that."

"Keep your mind on the job, you," she shot back, but her look was more challenging than annoyed.

We made our first twist. It put us about halfway along the length of the Cross, in a narrow region of space between it and Unity territory to spinward. We spent only long enough at our waypoint—a lonely red dwarf with a solitary planet and just a number, no name —to get a nav fix, then twisted again.

We were now officially closer to the galactic rim than I'd ever been before, but only by about twenty-five light-years, which wasn't much in the greater scheme of the Milky Way. It put us out on the true frontier, beyond Unity space as we understood it, and well outside known space. Looking further rimward, I saw a vast multitude of stars, virtually none of which had ever been visited by anyone we were aware of.

"I wonder how many more civilizations are out there?" I mused, looking out our canopy at the celestial wild west. I shivered a little at the terrifying splendor of so much unknown—and unknowable.

"Maybe none," Perry offered.

I scoffed. "Sorry, but speaking as a guy who until just a few years ago assumed that humans were alone in the universe, you'll excuse my skepticism."

"Quite a change, isn't it, going from believing there's no one out there to believing there's no way there's no one out there?" Zeno said.

"Tell me about it." I looked the other way, back toward the galactic core. "But our travels don't take us out there today. Netty, please make our first twist into the Cross of Novae at your convenience. As to the rest of those stars—we'll be seeing you."

"Twisting in ten seconds…"

OUR FIRST STOP was a searingly hot blue star only about a million years old, by Netty's estimation. Like many nebulae, the Cross was a stellar nursery, dust and gas gravitationally clumping into ever larger and denser blobs of matter that eventually compressed enough to ignite as stars. This particular star was surrounded by a thick halo of yet more dust and gas, shot through with rocky masses that would continue to coalesce and someday form planets.

It was *stunning* but also made for some significant nav hazards. We had to stay well clear, further from the star than Pluto is from the Sun, just to keep an adequate safety margin between us and all that whirling, cosmic material that clashed and coalesced in an eternal dance.

Looking away from the star was no less disconcerting, though. Immersed in the vast envelope of dust and gas that was the nebula, we could only see the nearest stars as somewhat fuzzy patches of light. The universe looked very different when most of it was obscured from view. It meant the *Fafnir* hung in an utter blackness relieved only by the light of maybe a half-dozen stars.

"Lonely out here," I muttered.

"Even I feel it, boss," Perry agreed.

We hammered away with our active scanners for a couple of hours, while happily transmitting it back to Anvil Dark via twist comm. That last bit wasn't really necessary. While our research shop certainly wasn't going to turn down the data feed, they weren't particularly interested in it, either. It was really just a way of making ourselves even more visible to anyone who might be watching.

"Van, Netty and I have been doing some calculating. We estimate that, at best, we'll be able to make our presence known to about thirty percent of this nebula, under the current plan," Perry said.

"Which means that if the Trinduk are hiding out somewhere in that other seventy percent, they may not even realize we're here," Netty added.

"Okay, so how do we increase that?" I asked.

Perry shrugged. "The only thing we really can do is just spend more time at each waypoint in the nebula, starting with this one. If we bang away with the active scanners long enough and at high enough twist-power settings, we can realistically get that up to about fifty percent of the nebula's volume."

"Why do I sense a *but* dangling off the end of that."

"Yeah, gotta hate those dangling buts," Perry said, earning simultaneous eyerolls from Torina, Zeno, and me. "Anyway, yeah, isn't there always? The comm and scanner burn antimatter fuel when they're running in twist mode, which is going to leave us with a really thin margin when we reach Groshenko and the others."

"And by really thin, we mean that it's by no means certain we'll have enough to twist again. So if we do manage to draw a bunch of Trinduk out—"

"We may not be able to get away from them."

"Not without refueling again. And I'd really hate to try and refuel with a flotilla of Trinduk ships breathing down our necks," Netty went on.

I drummed my fingers on the armrest and stared out at the obscured universe. Okay, it actually wasn't quite as obscured as I'd first thought. I still couldn't see as many stars as I was used to, but there were still hundreds, maybe thousands, their light attenuated by the nebula.

I sighed. "There's no point in being bait if your quarry doesn't even know you exist. Let's do it. Netty, replot our course and waypoints to give us enough time at twist-power settings to... let me think here. Okay, calling it at the following number. We need enough juice to beat at least half of these nebular bushes, please and thank you."

"And if that leaves us without enough fuel to twist away at the other end?" Torina asked.

Perry cut me off. "Then we activate our contingency plan."

Torina gave him a lifted eyebrow. "Which is?"

"Cursing, blaming Van. The usual."

"I like it—nice and simple, the way all the best plans are."

OUR SCANNERS DIDN'T REGISTER EVEN a glimmer of response at our first waypoint, nor at our second. Netty ended up collecting a pile of interesting astronomical data about the nebula, which was great for advancing known space's understanding of the Cross itself but didn't really help us at all. We twisted to our third waypoint and started banging away with active scanners, and—

Nothing.

"Maybe we're making ourselves too obvious. I mean, it is kind of standing in the middle of an open clearing screaming at the top of your lungs, hoping it will attract some game," Zeno said.

"That's only a problem if you're the apex predator, though. If you're soft, squishy, and tasty and you do that, you might pique the interest of some things with fangs, right?"

"Well, yeah, but if everyone in earshot *thinks* you're the apex predator, even if you're not, it amounts to the same thing, right?"

I sat up. "Zeno, you're brilliant."

"I am—? I mean, of course I am. But pretend I'm not and explain why."

I smiled at Zeno. "Netty, what kind of comm traffic are you generating from us?"

"Routine nav data, scan results, that sort of thing."

"Does that include any information about who we actually are?"

"No. Per Guild protocol, we use prearranged alphanumeric call signs in every message header, for operational security."

"Yeah, maybe that's the problem." We'd agreed to transmit regular twist-comm messages to Dugrop'che, who was sitting at the coreward end of the nebula waiting for us. The *Poltava* and the other ships were powered down and lurking in the fringe of a nearby star system's Oort Cloud. We'd intended that it look like Dugrop'che had tracked the Trinduk to the Cross—which he had—and had alerted us, and that the two of us were checking it out.

But there was a piece missing from that, one that was probably crucial for convincing the Trinduk to come after us.

Torina voiced it. "The Trinduk don't know that we are who we are."

"Exactly. As far as we know, there's still a bounty hanging over us. And between knocking down the Fade and generally disrupting their whole identity theft thing, we've been a major pain in their ass." I reached for the comm. "So let's make ourselves even softer, squishier, and tastier, shall we?"

I opened a comm channel to Dugrop'che, with both audio and imagery.

"Dugrop'che, I'm ready to give up. I don't think there's anything out here. Your information is just plain bad."

Dugrop'che stared. "I—no, the Trinduk came out here, I'm sure of it—"

"Bullshit. This is a waste of time—time I could have spent looking for Bulfir. We're done here," I said, then snapped off the comm.

"Can we assume that was a little one-man show?" Perry asked.

I glanced at him. "What do you think?"

"Shouldn't you let Dugrop'che in on it so he can play along?"

"Nope, because the best way for him to play along is for his responses to be genuine, right?"

"Kinda hard on the guy. You're a senior Peacemaker, after all," Zeno said.

"He'll get over it."

I exchanged another few messages with Dugrop'che, each time making him more miserable while portraying myself as a frustrated, revenge-bent asshole who was blaming himself for what had happened to Bulfir. It didn't hurt that that wasn't entirely an act, either. Self-flagellation is a specialty for me, although my midwestern roots demand that I generally do so in private.

Like eye contact, emotions, and forgetting to bring a covered dish to church, there were certain things my family simply didn't *do.*

It turned out that making myself out to be an angry asshole desperate for revenge was just what we needed to make ourselves *truly* attractive bait. A half-hour after I'd first snapped at Dugrop'che, a trio of icons popped up on the tactical overlay. It took only a moment for Netty to work up a positive ID after they'd twisted into the system.

"Three Trinduk ships, two class 8s, and a class 9. They're accelerating toward us and will be in missile range in two minutes, give or take," she announced.

"Well, that worked," I said.

"It did, and all you had to do was make a rookie Peacemaker feel like a complete piece of shit," Perry replied.

"I'll buy Dugrop'che a drink." I sized up the situation on the overlay. "Netty, is it safe to assume that the Trinduk know where Dugrop'che is?"

"It's unlikely they don't. Unless they're blind, they'll have been able to detect the origin of Dugrop'che's transmissions."

"Perfect. Torina, get him on the comm and tell him we're on our way. Make it clear that you're doing this over my strenuous objections, that I just want to stay and fight, blah, blah. Bonus points if you can make it seem like we're in the midst of an almost mutiny." I shot her a grin. "Let's see how good an actor you are."

She grinned. "I've got some community theater experience. Be a lot better if I could sing, but I can pull this off almost as well as you have. You make it seem so natural."

I shrugged. "Long practice pretending I'm people I'm not in cyberspace, I guess. But, thank you anyway. And, ah… you sing?"

"Badly."

"Huh. Then hold off on the showtunes and give us your best performance," I said.

"I won't be as good as you, but I'll try."

"Really? You thought I was a natural?"

A sly grin curled her lips. "See, you believed that. Now *that's* acting."

19

DUGROP'CHE MUST HAVE THOUGHT we were insane, or at least that I was. We even made a show of Torina effectively taking charge, with me shouting in the background about *insubordination* and *betrayal*. His reaction was suitably horrified because, as far as he knew, it was all real.

The Trinduk bought it, which gave us our first piece of hard data about their presence in the Cross. By combining all of the various factors, including the power of our twist-comm emissions and the assumed maximum time dilation that would limit the distance the Trinduk could have twisted to reach us, we were able to narrow down the location of their base to a spherical volume of space. And given the relative paucity of stars inside the nebula, it left only three possible candidate systems. We still weren't sure which, but three systems was a cosmological far cry from the potentially dozens, perhaps hundreds of possibilities we'd started with.

"I am going to see all of you locked up, you miserable, treacherous assholes!" I shouted into the cockpit from the galley, where I was supposedly being restrained. Perry hopped into the hatchway.

"We're about to twist, Van. You're not on the air anymore."

"Oh. Damn. I was really getting at the core of my role."

"Cursing your crew?"

"It was cathartic, and I'm a method actor."

"If you start referring to yourself in the third—"

"Sorry, Perry. Van is the only crew member allowed to use that acting method, and Van is pleased with the results."

Zeno sighed in disgust. "Artists."

I winced as we twisted. When the momentary wrench of space-time distortion faded, I clambered back into the cockpit. The view out the canopy was back to its usual starscape, meaning we'd cleared the nebula. The misty glow of the Milky Way's distant core sprawled across the field of view.

I pulled my gaze back inside and put in on the tactical overlay. It held only one icon—blue—Dugrop'che's ship, just a few light-seconds away. A few more returns speckled one edge of the display, depicting rocks and chunks of ice at the very margin of the nearby system's Oort Cloud. The *Poltava*, along with Lucky and the other ships of our small flotilla, would be sheltered among them.

That was all.

"The table's set, now we just need the guests to arrive," I said, watching the overlay intently. The Trinduk had taken the bait in the nebula, but that was no guarantee they'd chase us beyond it. It all depended on them wanting me, the *Fafnir*, and the various bounties attached to us badly enough to come after us.

"Van, we don't have enough fuel to twist again. I'd recommend we remedy that while we have the chance," Netty said.

I kept watching the overlay. Nothing.

"Not yet. The last thing I want is to be fiddling around transferring antimatter between ships when the Sorcerers show up."

"Alright, but if we have to run, it's going to take us a long time to get anywhere."

"So I guess we aren't going to run then, are we?" I glanced at the others. "Sorry, guys."

Zeno shrugged. "I had nothing on my calendar today."

There was still nothing on the overlay. Maybe they weren't going to make chase after all. Or maybe they'd failed to detect Dugrop'che's location and couldn't come after us, not knowing our twist destination. Or maybe—

A warning chime sounded. The three Trinduk ships had popped into existence an alarmingly short distance away. Without preamble, they cut loose with a barrage of missiles that were backed up by a fusillade of long-range laser fire.

"Holy shit! Netty, dump that fuel pod and burn like hell. Get us some maneuvering room!"

Fourteen missiles streaked in, and our quick math told us we had three minutes and change to impact. I spat a curse. The Trinduk had either gotten phenomenally lucky or someone had been able to pin down our location with fearsome accuracy. Either way, all we and Dugrop'che could do was burn as hard as we could to get some distance. We weren't just outnumbered by the Trinduk, but outgunned by a wide margin. Their ships were *bristling* with weapons.

Torina and Zeno were already on our defenses, engaging the incoming missiles. Dugrop'che did the same, his AI and Netty cooperating by sharing our firing solutions. Thanks to Gerhardt, we had a better fire-control system, and it showed, as our two ships blasted missile after missile to glowing fragments. That was great, but it meant we were fighting a defensive battle while the Trinduk could concentrate on us with their remaining weapons. I saw Dugrop'che's ship take two solid hits, one of which blasted apart a laser battery, further widening the firepower gap. We were hit twice ourselves. Neither was critical, but we lost two REAB modules and some of our passive ablative armor.

I cursed again, my eyes flickering over any and all scans we could get a return on. Where the hell was Groshenko? I didn't want to call him for help because that had kind of been the point of this —he'd be the unexpected hammer against the anvil of the *Fafnir* and Dugrop'che. But the anvil was looking pretty feeble, more aluminum foil than obdurate steel.

Torina finally scored a solid hit on one of the Trinduk ships, causing it to spall off incandescent debris and fall back. That was good. Unfortunately, the surviving Trinduk missiles reached their detonation points, two on each of us, and Dugrop'che. Explosions showered both ships with depleted uranium shrapnel, inflicting a rapid succession of damaging hits. None were critical, but they added up to more gaps in the REAB protection, more hull and systems damage. We started a slow decompression from somewhere aft, the mosquito whine of atmospheric loss dancing just at the edge of my hearing. Netty got Waldo to work fixing it, but I missed Icky. She had a knack for dealing with stuff like this swiftly and decisively, and not having her aboard was costing us.

Systems flickered to yellow, and a few non-critical ones to red. We'd fired a spread of missiles back at the Trinduk, but none made it through their envelope of defensive fire.

Screw it, I thought, and hit the comm.

"Groshenko, if you're out there, now would be a nice time to——"

"To appear in the nick of time and save your sorry ass?" Groshenko replied just as the *Poltava*, Lucky, and the Guild's class 10s twisted into being almost on top of us. I actually winced as Groshenko's ship seemed to fill the view out the left side of the canopy. It was actually more than a klick away, but in celestial terms that was *touching*.

It was a daring strategy, twisting right into the middle of a battle. Dangerous, even. The empty space filled by a twisting ship typically contained only a handful of stray atoms and motes of dust. These were seamlessly incorporated into the ship, its contents and crew with only microscopic harm. Even the nebula had only been denser in a strict relative sense—more atoms of gas and motes of dust for every unit of volume, sure, but still not enough to present a measurable problem.

When things got tight enough for significant amounts of matter to overlap, trouble could arise, leading to everything from minor issues to catastrophic explosions as two hunks of matter mutually shredded one another into atoms. It was part of the reason ships generally twisted into remote parts of star systems, to lessen the chances of collisions. The effects of gravitation were more critical, but no one wanted to find themselves occupying the same space as a rock.

So it was jarring to see the *Poltava* twist into existence close enough to see her deck plate connections. The actual risk had been small, but it still made my stomach do a twist of its own.

The *Poltava* abruptly vanished again, this time because she and the *Fafnir* were accelerating in different directions. I flipped us over and did a hard braking burn so that we could face and rejoin the battle. The Trinduk ships had abruptly gone from being masters of the battle to very much on a back foot, as the *Poltava*, Lucky, and the other Guild ships poured precision shots into them from stunningly close range. I had to admit, Groshenko had executed the ambush like a true master.

In rapid succession, the two lead Trinduk ships staggered under punishing hits and went dark. The third, the one we'd damaged and that had fallen back, might have twisted away but for a clever move by Lucky. Noticing that our discarded fuel pod wasn't far away, she fired on it, detonating the small amount of antimatter fuel it contained. The blast seared the Trinduk ship, which vanished in its own dazzling flash of destruction just a few seconds later.

"Vicious. I like it," I said.

Lucky's laughter was wicked. "Thank you. I enjoy it when they give me a gift. Their final gift ever, but still."

By the time we'd managed to reverse course, the short, sharp battle was over. Two of the three Guild Class 10s took up a protective stance while Perry and Zeno worked with the Comm Officers on the other ship to jam the Trinduk communications. It should buy us some time, but I had no doubt that the Trinduk would show up in force if they didn't get a check-in soon from their trio of ships.

"Two prizes. How do you want to handle this?" Groshenko asked over the comm.

"These are Sorcerers, a lot more dangerous than your average bad guys. I'd suggest we board both of them in force," I replied. "First, though, we need to refuel the *Fafnir*. Otherwise, it's about eighty years to the nearest star, and I'd have to spend all of that time with Perry."

"Hey!"

Groshenko laughed. "Let's get you gassed up then. But I don't want to wait to board these bastards. Their reactors might be offline, but give them enough time and they might be able to knock out their antimatter containment and scuttle their ships."

I agreed. "I would not put it past these scumbags, not for an instant."

"GRENADE!"

I flung myself aside, which resulted in one of those flukes you could never manage deliberately. As I dove for cover, my foot clipped the grenade the Sorcerer had thrown down the corridor at us, kicking it back in his direction. It detonated with a dazzling blast that made the Trinduk ship ring like a gong under me. Two of the Guild crew from the Class 10 assisting us seized the moment and charged down the corridor, pumping out a hail of flechettes from their boarding shotguns as they drove forward.

I levered myself back up—and was face-to-face with Torina.

"Smooth move with the grenade," she said.

"I meant to do that.'

"Uh-huh."

"Honest. Watched a series of videos titled *Kicking Ass and Using Hand Grenades with Panache: A Starter*, and it did wonders for me."

"You don't use the word *panache*."

"Fair. Luck it is then," I admitted.

We rounded the corridor and followed the two Guild troopers. They stood over the corpse of the last Trinduk, which had been shredded like pulled pork by the cloud of flechettes. It wasn't a pretty sight, but it looked good on a Sorcerer.

"That makes three dead and one in custody," the lead Guild trooper, a grizzled old chief, said. "The intel folks have already taken the live one back aboard our ship. Which means, Peacemaker Tudor, this ship is clear and secure."

The other Guild troop leaned in. "Hear that, Peacemaker Tudor? The ship is secure. We helped secure it."

I grinned. "I'm sensing that you may have possibly assisted, albeit in the most minor way possible—Torina, what's another word for, um—"

"Minuscule."

"Thank you, dear. Your minuscule efforts *may* have led to the securing of a minor asset, which we of course will sell and divide in the true spirit of Guild unity," I finished with a cheesy smile.

"You're gonna give us nothing?" asked the troop, following up with his concern. "With respect, Peacemaker, I, ah—"

"Nope. You're getting your fair share. Just having a laugh."

"A small one," Perry added.

"Excuse me, feedback is not warranted at this time, bird."

"Thought I'd help with your material, boss."

"Okay, that's not unwelcome. Was it my delivery, or my—"

"Um, are we getting paid, or not?" the troop asked.

"Oh, right. Sorry, we take comedy—and battle—seriously. Yes, give your ID to Torina, and you'll get paid every bond you're due," I assured them.

With visible relief, their body language eased.

"Is Torina in charge?" Troop number two asked, giving her a frank look of appraisal.

She lifted a brow. "Yes. Yes I am."

They both returned grins and a thumbs-up. Per Guild regulation —one of the oldest on the books, in fact—every crewman of every Guild ship that participated in taking a prize got a share of the prize money. Those who engaged in boarding actions got more. It could end up diluting the prize pool a whole lot, but the prize reg was considered sacrosanct in a way that most other regulations, policies, and procedures weren't. It had a whiff of the sort of things pirates did, which sometimes made me wonder about the Guild's true origins, but the official histories insisted it was all squeaky clean.

My comm spoke up. "Van, Groshenko."

"Go ahead."

"We're done over here. Two casualties, one Guild, minor injury, and one of mine, more severe."

"We got lucky. No injuries at all over here." I glanced down at the grotesque remains of the Sorcerer. "More or less, anyway."

"We actually have a pleasant surprise over here for you," Groshenko said.

Torina glanced up from her slate, where she was recording the ID info about the Guild boarding party. I narrowed my eyes.

"A pleasant surprise? Do you mean that, or is it something I'm actually not going to like?"

"Oh, I think you're going to like it."

I waited, then puffed out a sigh. "Well don't keep me in suspense, Petyr—"

His laugh cut me off. "It's Bulfir. They're—well, alive and well, or as alive and well as could be expected, anyway."

"Holy shit. I'll be right over."

THE OTHER TRINDUK ship was a charnel house. It had clearly been a *much* harder fight over here. It turned out that there'd been nine Sorcerers aboard this ship, compared to the four we'd had to overcome. Groshenko's people were professional soldiers, though, so the battle had been intense, but the outcome was a forgone conclusion.

Still, the vicious, close-quarters fight had left blood and gore spattered across the decks, laser hits seared into bulkheads, chips of fresh alloy exposed where slugs and flechettes had impacted. A thin haze of smoke hung in the air, and the stench of cooked people—there was no other word for it—left me uncomfortably aware of how barbecue and war shared some sensory elements.

I turned in a circle, looking. "Holy shit, Petyr. When you have a firefight, you don't screw around, do you?"

"Well, I did try sweet-talking them, but it didn't work. They spurned my advances."

Perry, who'd joined us to help scour the Trinduk ship for intel, made a tongue-clicking sound. "Oh, you Russians and your delicate approach to diplomacy."

"We're a complicated people."

I snorted. "Incidentally, that was some ballsy twisting, popping right into the middle of battle that way and at just the right moment. Cutting it a little fine, though, don't you think?"

"Especially considering the Trinduk twisted in almost right on top of us. All this space around us and everyone seems to pop into the same tiny piece of it," Torina said.

Groshenko shook his head. "Neither the Trinduks' twist nor ours were just luck. They actually twisted into that Oort Cloud, apparently for cover while they got an accurate fix on you, then twisted out again to attack you. It was a clever strategy. Too bad we thought of it first, though, and they never noticed. We got to watch exactly what they did and respond accordingly."

"Petard, hoisted, and so forth," I said.

"Just so," Petyr agreed.

Netty reported that the *Fafnir* had been refueled enough to get us to an actual depot. I wanted to get the hell out of dodge as soon as we could, in case the Trinduk showed up in force and tried to take their ships back. But the Guild apparently had other ideas. Two Trinduk ships more or less intact, along with a live Sorcerer as a prisoner, was an intel coup too good to pass up.

Lucky had reported our success back to Anvil Dark, whereupon Gerhardt had dispatched the Guild's mysterious and frankly sinister battlecruiser, the *Righteous Fury*, along with a full intel crew. The *Fury* had enough firepower to ward off all but a truly determined attack, probably more than the Trinduk could muster. Her sleek, dark presence was reassuring but also a little off-putting. No one seemed to be able to explain why the Guild kept such a powerful warship on the books. Even Groshenko, a former Master who'd probably know, was evasive about it. It hinted at some other purpose to the Guild.

A purpose that felt a lot like war.

While the *Fury* took station, Perry and Zeno kept sweeping the two Trinduk ships for immediate intel. I took a deep breath and made myself meet Bulfir, whose identity had been installed in a maintenance bot aboard the ship Groshenko had taken. I immediately launched into an abject apology for screwing up the way we had and getting them killed—ish. Bulfir abruptly cut me off.

"Van, stop it. No one could possibly have foreseen what

happened to your ship. Your engineer was making a good-faith effort to improve its performance, right? To *help* you do your job?"

"She was, but—"

"But nothing. Moreover, Groshenko tells me that this whole operation was essentially your idea, in part to try and rescue me."

"It was, but—"

"Then here we are. Nothing else is necessary. Well—" The bot's imager, extended on an arm, rotated so it could look at itself. "A new body. A new body is necessary. I don't want to spend the rest of my life as a glorified toolbox, thank you."

"Even though it was part of the plan, actually finding you is pretty remarkable," Torina said.

I managed a thin smile. "Lucky barely begins to describe it."

"That's because it wasn't luck. When the Sorcerers realized it was you, they decided to bring me along specifically to use me as some sort of bargaining chip if they needed to. What they really wanted was to take you alive, though, and make sure you knew all about me before doing… whatever it was they were going to do to you."

"Probably *not* throw me a party."

"Probably not."

"You are lucky they didn't just decide to kill you—again—when it all went sideways for them."

Bulfir laughed. "They installed me in a maintenance bot designed to get into all the little nooks and crannies of a ship. They soon regretted that because those same nooks and crannies make great hiding places. I just had to hope you arrived before they finally got me cornered. And, again, here we are."

We took Bulfir aboard the *Fafnir* and, leaving the *Fury* to finish up, started back to Anvil Dark.

I brooded along the way, lost in my own thoughts. Bulfir had said the Sorcerers wanted to take me alive. That was disconcerting, considering the biggest bounty on me only paid out if I was dead. It meant that they weren't motivated by money. I'd play-acted it being personal to suck the Trinduk in—something for which I apologized to Dugrop'che, for making him an unwitting part of the act. To the Trinduk, though, it apparently *was* personal, a thought I found unnerving. The idea of being captured alive by the Trinduk—

I didn't linger on the idea, that's for sure. Some fates are best left unexplored.

20

WHEN WE ARRIVED AT SPINDRIFT, Koneese crowded into the airlock, desperate to find Bulfir. The Guild had paid for a new organic body for them, which had been completed a few days prior. Bulfir was subsequently installed into it, in a process that had apparently been developed at least in part by the mysterious bio-research facility called *Ponte Alus Kyr*. Organic-mechanical interfaces were the focus of their research, which was highly secretive and Perry believed was intended for military applications.

"This whole reinstallation of a person's identity back into their body is damned miraculous, but I suspect it's just a spin-off," he said.

Zeno agreed. "I'm thinking people directly integrated with their ships and weapons, maybe even built right into armored bodies—"

"That all sounds… horrifying," Torina said.

I nodded. It did. But if it also provided a way to undo the

damage being done by the Sorcerers and their evil accomplices, then it at least had a glimmer of a *good* side, didn't it?

Icky had finished her remedial training, passing with more than flying colors. The tech who administered it had just shaken his head in wonder, noting that *he'd* learned some things from *her*. She now stood right behind Koneese in the airlock, just as anxious to finally meet Bulfir.

The reunion in the Spindrift docking port was a touching one. Koneese and Bulfir had said nothing, merely clasped hands and stood for a while in some sort of silent communion. We held Icky back while they had their time together, but when they pulled apart, she yanked free and practically fell to her knees in front of Bulfir.

"I'm sorry, I'm so sorry—"

Bulfir took her hand. "I know you are, Icrul. And that's sufficient. I forgive you and harbor no ill will toward you. As I told Van, I know that you were doing what you thought was right, in good faith. And you and your crew have made it right again."

"More than right. I notice you've lost that limp you had after that boarding fight at Wolf 424," Koneese said.

"You mean Dregs," Bulfir replied.

"No, Wolf 424."

"No, it was Dregs. Wolf 424 was the time I got that nasty cut on my arm, but that healed up fully."

"I don't think—I'm sure it was Wolf 424—"

Bulfir waved airily. "In any case, Van, thanks to both you and your crew. And thank you for teaching me something valuable."

"What's that?" I asked.

"I have no desire to be either immortal or mechanical."

Perry made his tongue-clicking sound.

"Hey, it's not *that* bad."

"So I GUESS we can put Koneese and Bulfir in our trusted column," Torina said as we backed away from Spindrift. We hadn't hung around long after the reunion, mainly because I wanted to get back to Anvil Dark and dig into the intel that had been extracted from the Trinduk ships and our sole live prisoner. I had to admit that part of it, though, was a general unease hanging around the relatively freewheeling and occasionally lawless confines of the station. That was something I was going to have to overcome. If I let the Sorcerers start living rent free inside my head, making me hesitate, they'd already won a sort of victory, hadn't they?

"I guess we can," I agreed, then forced myself to talk, free and easy, as we entered the departure pattern from Spindrift. If I didn't want to let the Sorcerers get to me, then a good start was not closing in on my thoughts. Getting lost in my own head was bad for me.

For my crew, it could be lethal.

"Van, we've got a problem with the number three thruster on the port-rear cluster," Netty said about a half-hour out from Spindrift.

I glanced at the status board. Everything showed green.

"It all looks good to me. You sure there's a problem with that thruster cluster?" I couldn't resist and grinned. "It's not a long poem, but it's a good one."

"It might sound like fun, but yes, while it's functioning properly, there is a problem with it. The number three thruster isn't aligned correctly, so it's exerting a slight push to starboard and forward when it fires. It's forcing me to use additional thruster fuel to compensate."

I wiped away my smile. "How serious is it? Can it wait until we're back in dock?"

"It can, but it's also an easy fix, maybe five minutes with an alignment tool. I'd send Evan to do it, but he's still offline."

I nodded. Evan had been damaged by shrapnel from a Trinduk missile, and we hadn't yet had an opportunity to get him back in action.

Icky sighed. "Okay, I'll go out and fix the damned thing—"

I turned. "Actually, Icky, I'll do it. I haven't done a spacewalk in a while and don't want to get rusty."

Besides, I thought, it would give me something to do besides staring at the instruments and trying to make conversation. There's nothing like the yawning chasm of space to give me a little jolt of fear and joy, all at once.

I unstrapped and clambered out of the pilot's seat.

"If anyone needs me, I'll be outside."

———

IT *HAD* BEEN a while since I'd done a spacewalk—at least a spacewalk that wasn't part of something more dire, like a boarding action. And on those occasions, my attention was laser focused on the immediate situation, leaving no time for anything else.

As I pulled myself along the *Fafnir*'s hull, I thought back to my first, absolutely terrifying spacewalk. I'd clung to the ship with a deathgrip, afraid to even open my eyes for fear of the feeling of falling into an abyss no matter which direction I looked. If I let my eyes rest too long on the starfield, a queasy sense of vertigo would still start tugging at my gut. I'd learned to keep my attention moving, only concentrating on things nearby, like the reassuring flank of the *Fafnir*.

I reached the balky thruster cluster, then smiled. Even in the midst of my new reality, I was still amused by the small details of life.

Like a two word rhyme while the stars beckoned all around me.

I sighed at myself. "Little focus here, Tudor," I muttered, provoking a response from Torina.

"Van, everything okay?"

"What? Oh, yeah, everything's fine. I was just thinking *thruster cluster*—"

"Sometimes you've got an adolescent sense of humor, you know that?"

"Look, fart jokes are an art form, and I'll die on that hill. Anyway, keep your fingers away from those flight controls. I've got my face stuck over that thruster right now."

"Sorry, bad comms, Van. Did you say fire the thruster right now?"

"I'd be medium well if you did," I quipped, then I thought of Bulfir, and suddenly the joke was gone.

Torina worked to that same conclusion. "Sorry. You okay?"

"I am. Thanks."

Sometimes you can use an economy of words with the one who understands you.

I extracted the thruster alignment tool from my harness and used it to loosen the fittings holding the thruster bell in place. When it was free to move around both axes, I planted the tool under the bell, a flaring exhaust nozzle about the size of a basketball, and clamped it in place. All it took was a few turns of two knobs to align the bell. With that small fix, the thrust axis was perpendicular to the cluster assembly, and I could remove the tool and head back onboard.

In theory, anyway.

I aligned the bell with ease—it took two turns—and then tightened everything to specs, the tool's gauge reading green when I hit the optimal torque. When I tried to unclamp the tool, it was stuck. As in frozen in place. Unmoving. Maddeningly still, and I felt that surge of anger that every mechanic and engineer knows and hates, staring down with my eyes narrowed to furious slits.

I exhaled. Twice. "Oh for—"

"Van, what's wrong?" Torina immediately asked.

"This… damned… tool… is stuck."

Netty cut in. "It's a new bell, switched out at Anvil Dark. It might not have had time to properly oxidize, so you might have some vacuum welding going on."

I grunted my understanding. The alloy parts of a ship were designed to develop a non-reactive oxide coating to stop the phenomenon known as vacuum welding. Essentially, in a vacuum, atoms on the surfaces of two pieces of metal brought into contact could lose track of the piece they belonged to, resulting in them effectively bonding together. Parts were supposed to be pre-oxidized for that very reason, but sometimes the oxide coating got scraped off, exposing bare metal. Netty was right, that was probably exactly what had happened here.

I tugged a few times. It seemed stuck fast, confirming my theory that the angrier you get, the more stuck something became. All earthly mechanics know this at a cellular level, along with the fact that 10 mm sockets vanish into thin air if you turn your eyes away from them for a second.

"Shit. Netty, is it a problem if this stupid thing stays clamped here until we get back to Anvil Dark?"

"Not really. Oh—wait. Icky just informed me that's the only alignment tool we have on board. So as long as we don't need to align any other thrusters, we're fine."

I sighed. "Let me get my feet planted here and give a good pull. If it doesn't budge, I'll just leave it."

"Make sure your tether's secure," Torina said.

"Yes, mother. I put on my raincoat and galoshes, too."

"What are *galoshes*?"

With my feet planted on the hull, I gripped the tool, took a breath, and heaved.

"They are—"

An explosion of incandescent pain cut me off.

"Van? Van, what's going on?"

I blinked through tears, hissing inward as lights danced behind my closed eyelids. "My knee. I think it... just blew out."

"I'm on my way—"

"Just... wait for me at the airlock. I—"

I closed my mouth, teeth together in order to stay silent. I didn't want to say what I was thinking. Or feeling.

"—don't need my knee to... get there."

Abandoning the stuck alignment tool, I pulled myself back to the airlock. By relaxing my leg and letting it trail along behind me, the pain faded enough for my vision to return to something like normal. I suspected it was going to hurt like hell when I was back in gravity and tried putting any weight on it, because even in zero-g, I could feel an ominous pulsation in *every* component of my knee.

Flexion deformity, it was called. Essentially, the muscles and bones in my right leg had grown at slightly different rates for whatever reason, and the two had never quite caught up. It limited the range of motion in my right knee slightly—not enough for everyday use, and even then only rarely when I was straining myself. It had been enough to ultimately wash me out of the army, but it also wasn't that difficult to fix, at least not out here in known space. The trouble was that the operation to essentially replace my knee would keep me off my feet for a couple of weeks, down-time that never seemed to be available.

Torina and Icky both waited for me in the open airlock when I reached it. They helped me inside, Icky holding my right side up when I stepped back into the ship's gravitational effect. Down reasserted itself, one g of gravity suddenly pulling hard on my leg. Even without trying to put weight on it, the slight tug slammed a lightning bolt of agony through my leg, and I hissed like a wounded serpent.

"Shiiiiii—" I managed. Given the pain, it was fairly eloquent.

"Icky, let's get him to his bunk," Torina said.

I shook my head as she pulled my helmet off. "I'm not spending the trip back to Anvil Dark in my rack."

"Yes, Van, you are. Netty, switch Waldo into medical mode and send him to Van's cabin."

I started to object again, but the implacable expressions on Torina's and Icky's faces told me not to bother. They weren't going to argue, and honestly, I wasn't really inclined to. Something was horribly wrong with my leg. Something felt *disassembled*.

I peeled off my b-suit with their help, then they moved back to let Waldo, a medical scanner latched to one of his manipulators, get close enough to examine my knee. At the same time, he touched a pneumatic syringe to my thigh, injecting me with a drug cocktail strong enough to make an arthritic hippo think it could dance. The pain immediately subsided from bright, sharp agony to a dull and distant ache, following my heartbeat in an obedient thumping that didn't bode well for my future as a runner.

Not that I like running. Hell, I barely *tolerate* running.

Netty had the verdict less than thirty seconds later. "You've had a tendon separate from the bone in your knee. That's the reason for your flexion problem—it was just a little too short. Seems the anchor point on the bone finally gave way."

"Great. Can you fix it?"

"With the medical resources aboard the *Fafnir*? No, not at all. This requires specialized medical care."

I let my head sink back on my pillow. "Well, that's a kick in the —how about Anvil Dark? Can they do it there?"

"Probably."

"Probably?"

"It depends on what medical resources are available. At any given time, Anvil Dark has a lot of injured Peacemakers and their Auxiliaries in some level of care—"

"Van, we don't have to go to Anvil Dark," Perry said, hopping into my cabin.

"This is not the time to start practicing your surgical skills, Perry. Especially on me."

"As interesting as that sounds, that's not what I was suggesting. I just had a memory unlock."

We all turned to look at him—except for Waldo, who busily strapped a brace around my knee.

"A memory about what?" Torina asked.

I winced. "Please don't tell me you've just remembered that I've got a Yonnox half-brother or something like that."

"How could you have a Yonnox half-brother? I mean, how would that even—?"

"Focus, bird, focus."

"Fine. There's a skilled medical practitioner available who's a lot closer than Anvil Dark. In fact, she's here, in the Spindrift system. Netty confirms that she's on one of those outbound ships ahead of us, about a light-second away, give or take."

"Okay. And what makes her so special?"

"Well, for one, she's a medical specialist—it's what she does. For another, she's close. And, she's a Peacemaker."

"I don't remember seeing any Peacemaker transponder—*owww*, shit, Waldo, or Netty, or whichever one of you is just a little too enthusiastic. Can you loosen that a bit, please and thanks?" I sank back to the pillow. "Anyway, I didn't see any other Peacemakers ahead of us, just two behind us, one at Spindrift and one in the departure pattern."

"Hence the whole *I just had a memory unlocked* thing. I didn't know she was a Peacemaker until that happened. She's not broadcasting Peacemaker credentials, but she's definitely part of the Guild."

I glanced at Torina, who shrugged. Icky narrowed her eyes.

"Since when are there secret Peacemakers?"

"Maybe she's working undercover," Torina suggested. Perry, though, shook his head.

"Why would a medical specialist be undercover?" I asked.

"To… do undercover medical things? I don't know."

"Perry, what's her name?"

"B."

"B, as in… Beatrice?"

"Literally B, as in just that letter."

"Huh. Well, I'm intrigued. The question is, what suddenly unlocked this memory of yours? Me having my knee blow out?"

"Actually, any debilitating injury on your part would have unlocked it. And before you say, *but I've been hurt badly before*, yes, you have—like the time you got shot on that bogus terraforming planet. But these memory registers seem to only unlock in a particular sequence."

I opened my mouth, but Perry cut me off.

"And before you ask *why*, I have no idea. Your grandfather obviously put a lot of thought into this, so whatever the reasons for it, they're his."

Torina gave Perry the side-eye. "So Van gets hurt, that unlocks your memory about this mysterious Peacemaker named B, and it turns out she happens to be only a half-hour away?"

Icky nodded. "Does sound kinda *convenient.*"

I shrugged, awkwardly because I was lying down. "It does, but there's one sure way of finding out just how *convenient* it really is. Perry, call this B, let her know what's going on, and ask her if she can help."

"Way ahead of you, boss. She's already heaved to and is waiting for us."

"Ah. And what if I hadn't wanted to do that?"

"You would."

I stared for a moment, then leaned back and closed my eyes. The pain blocker Waldo had injected was making me feel a little fuzzy.

"Yeah, you're right. Now all of you hit the road. I'm just going to lay here dozing and feeling sorry for myself for a while. Also, not dancing."

"You don't dance," Perry offered, helpful as ever.

"Well, not *now*, bird. Away with you. I'm bracing myself for having a knee bolted on, or whatever."

"That's my boss. So sciency," Perry said, saluting me with one wing.

I didn't doze, though. My mind kept turning back to this enigmatic B. Who was she? Why had Gramps locked any knowledge of her existence away from Perry and, presumably, Netty as well? And why would blowing out my knee unlock it?

I sighed up at the overhead. There was something going on here, something that felt big and important and deep. Something, in fact, that might change everything.

I just hoped that if it did, it was going to change it for the better, because the alternative was something we didn't have time for. Not now, and maybe not ever.

———

BACK IN COLLEGE, I'd briefly owned a car, a middle-of-the-pack, utterly unremarkable automobile so bland I had trouble even now remembering exactly how it looked. The only thing that really stuck with me was the fact that I forgot where I parked it *every time*. I'd step out into the lot and just stand for a while, staring dumbly. The thing was so unexceptional that it just smeared itself into obscurity among all the other parked cars. I remember thinking it would have been the perfect car for an undercover cop, drug dealer, or anyone else who wanted to vanish in plain sight.

B's ship was like that. It was a class 9 cutter so uninteresting that, just like my nearly invisible car, it would just lose itself among everything else docked at Spindrift or Crossroads. Her ship was the equivalent of bringing a silver, four-door sedan into space, although in fairness, I haven't seen mid-size cars with weapons systems that could pummel an armored enemy.

Which brought me back to the idea of an undercover cop. Who was this B, and why was her existence so secretive? Especially if she was a medical professional? You'd think people like that would *want* to be found.

We docked, then the airlocks sealed and opened. Leaning on Icky, I hop-hobbled my way aboard B's ship. The air smelled strangely clean, like fresh cut flowers and rain but without the cloying, artificial back notes of an air freshener. We exited the airlock, and I found myself facing a short, rather curvy woman with striking hazel eyes and a piercing on her upper lip—a flickering red gem. I'd have taken her as fully human if it weren't for the pair of antennae sprouting from the top of her head. They were articulated and seemed to move on their own and independently of each other. I supposed they might have been implants of some sort, but frankly, the pain lancing through my leg kind of blunted my interest in anything else.

"So. You're Van Tudor," she said.

"My upper half, yeah. Below the waist, I'm just in pain."

She grinned. "Typical man, going straight to whatever he's got below the waist."

Torina, following us, spoke up. "I know, right?"

"You know, if I could interrupt this female bonding for a moment, my leg really, really hurts," I said, looking for a soft place to fall.

B directed us forward into a fully equipped medical bay that glittered with technology and purpose. She had Icky lift me onto a treatment table, then told me to unbuckle my pants so she could pull them down.

I tried to offer a wry grin, but I think it came out more *rictus of pain*. "Not going to buy me a drink first?"

"Don't be a dick, Tudor. There are plenty of those out here," B said, pulling my pants down to my ankles, then picking up a small medical scanner.

"I was just, ah—"

"My ship, my rules, Tudor," she said, running the scanner over my knee. Her eyes never left the device, which had a small screen that scrolled data faster than I could read it.

"Oof," B said.

"Oof? That's your professional opinion?"

"For the moment," B said, then began a second scan, this time, from the exterior of my leg.

It didn't take her long to confirm Netty's diagnosis. A tendon in the back of my knee had pulled free of where it should have been anchored on the bone, and it had done so in a spectacular fashion. She shooed Icky and Torina back to the *Fafnir*, adjusted the scanner's settings, then had me flip onto my stomach so she could collect more detailed imagery of the actual injury.

"Hmm. Yup, there's your problem, clean separation of the tendon. No signs of extensive trauma, though—I take it you've had a problem with this knee for a while, now?"

"Since my middle teens, yeah. I had it diagnosed as a flexion deformity."

"Sounds about right. Okay, Rick, you wanna wake up Alice? I'm going to need her to assist."

A new voice replied in a drawl I immediately placed as Kentucky-ish, if not purely Kentucky. "You bet, darlin'. Darik, too?"

"Nah, he can keep working on those sample cultures. That outbreak of whatever the hell it is on that mining colony ain't going to cure itself."

I glanced back. "Uh—outbreak? As in a disease?"

"No, it's an outbreak of happiness and good cheer." She sniffed. "Of course it's a disease outbreak. And yes, before you ask, we've got all the appropriate measures in place to keep the samples nice and secure."

"So who's Rick?" I asked as B studied a strikingly detailed 3D image of my knee on a screen over the bed.

"He's my ship's AI."

"Sounds like he should be drinking bourbon and… doing whatever else people from Kentucky do. That's a place on Earth, by the way."

"Is it really? Wow, tell me more, Mister Earthling. Are your people friendly? Can you take me to their leader?"

"You've been to Earth."

"Once or twice, yeah."

Alice appeared, another human, probably late thirties and attractive in a clinically detached kind of way. She had an attitude of brusque efficiency, though, which I actually found reassuring. I guess I like my medical professionals to be, um, professional—more matter-of-fact and even a little aloof. B's folksy charm actually made me a touch leery of her skill.

Her competence wasn't in question. It was becoming quickly apparent with each passing moment of her complete command. She rattled off a series of instructions to Alice, who began prepping for surgery. That *did* surprise me a little. I'm not sure why, maybe because back on Earth surgery wasn't an immediate thing for any condition that wasn't life-threatening—in my experience, at least. I'd assumed she'd stick me in some sort of brace or cast, give me some drugs, and call it a day. I'd then be on my own to get the full workup at Anvil Dark.

I said as much, and she just grinned. "Back when I first began doing this, that probably would have been how it worked out."

"First began? How long have you been doing this?"

B's eyes went far away for a moment. "Oh, let's see. Well, I met Rick in 43, so it was not long after that—"

"You met your AI in… 43?"

"No, not my AI. The actual Rick. I met him on Earth, in Tunisia, in 1943."

"Wouldn't he have been in Morocco, not Tunisia?"

B blinked at me. "What?"

I smiled. "Rick, North Africa, World War 2? Humphrey Bogart's character in *Casablanca*, Rick Blaine?" I shook my head at her blank look. "Sorry, I used to have a thing for old movies. *Casablanca* is one of the greatest, all about complicated love in wartime North Africa."

"Well then, I lived your *Casablanca*. Anyway, my AI's named after him."

"Let me guess—he was from somewhere in the southern United States."

"Kentucky."

"Huh. I got the accent right, what do you know—"

I stopped, wincing, as Alice injected me with something in the back of my thigh. The waves of pain radiating from my knee immediately subsided.

"Anyway, to answer your question—Van? Can I call you Van?"

"Absolutely."

"So to answer the question you asked me, how long I've been doing this, and the one you haven't, why... let's just say that humans have been busy out here among the stars. I know some of your friends. And some of your enemies, too, I'd bet."

While she spoke, she moved an AI-driven unit on an articulated arm into place over the back of my knee. She studied a small display built into it, manipulating controls. A gleaming blade appeared and descended toward my flesh.

"Uh... no general anesthetic then?"

"Pfft. For this? Not worth the bother." The blade touched my flesh, dimpled it, then penetrated and began to slice. Alice deployed a small suction device to wick away the blood. I felt nothing except a bit of pressure.

When she'd made an incision about two inches long, she lifted the blade and inserted a thin probe through it, into my knee. She then began working the controls, presumably directing the AI that did the actual detail work. I felt something moving around inside my knee, a distinctly strange and uncomfortable feeling.

"Nearly done," she said.

"Already?"

"Like I said, we've come a long way," she replied, her eyes still on the small display, her fingers deftly manipulating the controls. "Believe me, this is a lot less invasive, even less… violent, I guess, than it used to be." She smiled. "That could apply to a lot of things, actually. Like diplomacy. War. Even the law."

She punched one final control and stepped back. "There, all done. I've reattached the tendon and tweaked it a bit to get rid of your flexion problem, too. Surprised you didn't get this done before it had to blow out."

"That's because I was told it will keep me off my feet for a couple of weeks, which is a couple of weeks of downtime I just can't afford." I watched as Alice directed the AI through stitching me back up, then sighed. "Guess I have no choice now, though."

B's antennae waggled, and she shook her head. "You should be as good as new in a day or so."

I looked back at her. "Really? So that two weeks thing was, what, just bullshit?"

"Not at all. If you'd gotten this done on Anvil Dark, you really would have been down and out for a week or two."

I narrowed my eyes at her. "So if your capabilities are so much better than those at Anvil Dark, what are they doing out here, flying around from star to star?"

She shrugged. "It lets me go where I'm needed and can do the most good."

"Yeah, I'd buy that if it wasn't for the fact that I had no idea you existed and that you're not even registered with the Guild—at least, not registered anywhere I can find you. And my AIs had your existence sealed away behind memory locks that only let go when I blew out my knee. My grandfather apparently set up a series of sequential memory locks in Perry and Netty, in fact, with a debilitating injury triggering the one that revealed you."

"Did he, now?"

"Yes, he did. And before you play dumb, I think you knew my grandfather and you're part of... something. Something he was involved in. And in case it isn't obvious by now, I'm not getting off this table until I have an answer that isn't just wide-eyed innocence."

B laughed, silvery and rich.

"What's so funny?" I asked.

"You're right, I did know Mark. And I'm laughing because that little tirade could have come straight out of his mouth. Guess the apple doesn't fall far from the apple that fell from the tree."

"Cool. Now, how about answering my question?"

"Actually, Van, I think this is my department," a new voice said. It was Perry. He'd glided into the medical bay and settled himself on a console.

"Hey hey, watch the talons. That's a brand new tissue analyzer," B snapped.

Perry, though, just looked straight at her.

"Clearance required for Peacemaker Subclass *Galactic Knights Uniformed*, subject Peacemaker Van Tudor—Agent Gerti, am I right?"

B's antennae twitched. "And there it is, the missing piece. So, I guess it's time, huh?"

I rolled on my side and looked from one to the other. "Um… someone care to explain what's going on?"

B gave a thin smile. "Sure. You're about to learn the biggest, deepest secret of the Peacemaker Guild. And you're going to do it while not wearing pants."

I laughed. "Icky is gonna be *pissed*."

B's antennae twitched. "Why? Because of the secrets?"

I waved at my legs. "No, the pants. Or rather, lack thereof. But you were saying?"

I FELT WELL ENOUGH to sit up, so we reconvened to the galley and crew lounge sandwiched between the medical bay and cockpit of B's ship. She dismissed her two assistants, sending them aboard the *Fafnir*, where they'd wait with the rest of my crew.

"Okay, so what's the huge secret? That the Guild is actually a front for the Illuminati? That it's run by the lizard people?" I asked, sitting down and stretching out my leg. "At this point, I'll believe anything."

"Excellent. Let me tell you about a timeshare opportunity on the Gulf Coast. I assume you have a few hours?" B asked.

I barked with laughter. "Finally. The galaxy makes sense."

B smiled, one side of her lips curled higher than the other. "No timeshare, but you're not far off, actually. I assume you've heard of the Galactic Knights Uniformed?"

"I've heard the term, yeah. I gather that they were an older organization, a sort of intergalactic—"

"Interstellar, Van. It's kinda hard to enforce laws thousands or millions of light-years away."

"Well then. An *interstellar* order of... knights, kinda? Like the old Templars back on Earth? I've heard they're defunct—but I suspect you're about to tell me they're not."

B smiled. "They are not. They have changed over time, but they still very much exist."

"Changed in what way?"

"The GKU began as a paramilitary outfit, a collaborative effort to form a neutral force that could deal with threats that spanned multiple star systems and political entities. It was sort of like the UN back on Earth, if the UN had a more militant focus rather than purely international dialogue and cooperation and the like," B said.

Perry spoke up. "Basically, the GKU were the Peacemakers of the time, but much more heavily armed—more like Groshenko's mercenaries, in fact."

B nodded. "Without coming out and saying it, Petyr has essentially fashioned his mercenary company into a modern-day version of the GKU. The real thing was a lot larger and had *way* more combat power, but it's the same idea."

I nodded. "Okay. So this GKU—and why that name, by the way? Aren't *knights* kind of an Earthly thing? I mean, is everyone out here really that enamored of Earth culture?"

B laughed. "Not even a little bit. *Knights* is the closest translation in English because the GKU did have some of the attributes of an old terrestrial knightly order—in particular, a code of honor that was taken to transcend all other laws."

"Which was a distorted version of their original purpose. They *were* meant to enforce a set of agreed-on laws across all of known space. Over time, that morphed into, we are above the law and answerable only to ourselves—and that's where the Honor Code came from. It was supposed to keep the GKU reined in and stop them from becoming worse than whatever problems they were intended to solve," Perry said.

B nodded, her antennae twitching along. "And that's where they got in trouble."

"This really *is* starting to sound like the Templars. Let me guess, they started a power grab?" I asked.

"You guessed it. Power corrupts and all that. Over time, the GKU became more and more a player in their own right in interstellar affairs. It all came to a head about fourteen hundred years ago. The GKU ended up being disbanded in all but name, and a new organization, the Peacemaker Guild, was set up to replace them. Instead of a dedicated paramilitary organization, it was all about law enforcement. And instead of a rigid hierarchy, the Peacemakers were designed to be freewheeling, more a bunch of independent operators than a unified body."

"And that's the situation as you know it," Perry said. "The Guild is the actual thing, and the GKU is just some vague, distant thing with some vague, distant, and probably fluffy ceremonial purpose—a bunch of old people in fancy uniforms sitting around drinking and feasting and having secret handshakes and the like."

I flexed my knee. It ached, but no more so than if I'd just banged it into something. "But they're not."

"No, they definitely are all that," B said. "But that's just the GKU you *see*. For reasons I won't get into right now, at the time it was disbanded for being naughty, a handful of visionaries realized that there was still a need for a body that could deal with the real interstellar troublemakers."

"We like to think of known space as the Eridani Federation, the Seven Stars League, the Ceti Alliance, and parts between, but it's really mostly empty space. And that empty space breeds things like the Stillness, and the Salt Thieves, and the Fade, and a bunch more like them—non-state actors with their tentacles wriggling across multiple political boundaries," Perry said.

B leaned forward. "What it comes down to is that the GKU was never truly disbanded. A small cadre of the Knights went underground, nurturing a secret organization dedicated to its original cause."

"Working outside the law to deal with troublemakers," I said.

"Exactly. Don't get me wrong, the Peacemakers do good work. They keep a lid on smuggling, and gun-running, and a million other mundane little infractions that genuinely need to be stopped. But they're not really suited to deal with the big, complicated, and truly dangerous things."

Perry nodded. "Like the Sorcerers and everyone else involved in this identity theft thing. Yotov was a self-serving piece of shit, but she was right about that. What they're doing is a Crime Against Order."

"And that leads to the underlying truth of the GKU. Sometimes there are things that need to be done that the Guild or anyone else can't do," B said, her gaze boring into mine. "Generally unpleasant things, and often illegal things, but necessary things—things that still need to be done."

I sat back. I suspected I knew where this was going, but I wanted to hear it.

"So this is either a case of *we can tell you about this but then we have to kill you*, or I'm about to be invited to join this plucky little band of secret do-gooders, am I right?"

B laughed. "Oh, Van, you're sweet. You've been part of the GKU for a long time now. You just never knew it."

I SAT FORWARD AGAIN. "So I've been—what? A pawn of some sort?"

"Not at all. In a way, the whole Peacemaker Guild kind of works for the GKU, even though the vast majority of them don't realize it. In fact, all but a handful of Peacemakers understand the Knights to be just that old fossil of a ceremonial outfit, a remnant of a bygone era. Only a few know differently," B said.

"And you're one of them now, thanks to another memory lock clearing when we rendezvoused with B," Perry said.

I shook my head. "Okay. So, who knows? The Masters, I assume—"

"Some of them," B put in. "In case you hadn't noticed, the Masters are some of the Guild's biggest headaches. To most of them, Master is a cushy political appointment, sort of a combination of retirement posting and status symbol."

"And a great opportunity to make money," Perry added.

"Yeah, I've kinda noticed that Masters keep turning out to be corrupt as sin. So which ones are in the know?"

B smiled. "I'll let slip that Groshenko was one, but that's all. One of the ways the GKU is able to keep operating is by keeping the circle of knowledge very, very small and very, very compartmentalized."

I sat back again and blew out a breath. "Okay. So, if I'm already effectively part of these Galactic Knights Uniformed, and I'm already working on the sort of case that they're apparently intended to deal with, then—well, so what? What's changed? Do I get the secret decoder ring or something?"

B laughed. "What changes is that you know the organization exists and that you're part of it. For now, that's all you need to know."

"Aside from the fact it's a secret that can't be shared with anyone, not even your own crew. Not even Torina," Perry said.

"Isn't this kind of closing the proverbial barn door after the horse has bolted? I mean, you pulled back the curtain to give me a peek behind it, and now you're telling me it's all hush-hush?"

B nodded. "Yup. That's exactly right. But we have it on good authority that you can be trusted."

I frowned. "Groshenko?"

"Him too."

Now I nodded. "My grandfather. He was part of this, too, wasn't he?"

"He trusted you enough to let you have that look behind the curtain when the time was right. And if it's good enough for him, it's good enough for us," B said.

I made a sound of agreement. I'd been a free agent, as B put it, pretty much all my life. My one departure from it was my abbreviated Army career, but I'd been a loner as a teenager before that and a freelance cyber warrior, and now a Peacemaker since. I'd never felt any particular loyalty to anyone, at least until I met Perry and Netty and the rest of the crew—and Torina, of course.

But there had been one other person I considered myself loyal to, and that was Gramps. So if he trusted me enough to bring me into the circle of knowledge—even if it *was* after he was dead and it *had* only been through a convoluted sequence of events—then he trusted me to keep that circle closed.

Which meant B was right. If it was good enough for Gramps, then it was good enough for me.

My sudden conviction must have shown on my face because B smiled.

"Congratulations," she said.

"For what?"

"For becoming the newest member of the Galactic Knights Uniformed." She stuck out her hand.

"Let me be the first to welcome you aboard, Knight Tudor."

21

B HAD BEEN RIGHT about my knee. An hour or so after leaving her ship, it felt mostly fine. She cautioned me that it might ache from time to time over the next several days and gave me some mild painkillers to deal with it. If I'd had this done on Earth, I'd have been in a hospital bed for a long spell, followed by a bunch of physiotherapy.

I didn't reflect on my knee too long, though, my thoughts quickly spinning back to what I'd learned from B. I still didn't really have any appreciation for what the Galactic Knights Uniformed were, or what they did, or even what they meant. She and Perry assured me that when the time was right, I'd learn the things I needed to learn, no more and no less. They emphasized that aside from them, the only other person I could even bring the subject up to was Groshenko, and then only behind firmly closed doors.

I was still chewing on the implications of all this when Netty interrupted.

"Van, I've just got a general distress call from a ship outbound from Crossroads. Her transponder data shows her to be the luxury liner *Parallax*, registered with the Seven Stars League. She says she's under attack."

I frowned at that. "Seven Stars League, huh?" I glanced at Torina. "Kind of find it hard to trust those guys, considering that Satrap told the universe he wants to arrest me."

Torina made a sour face. "Using a phony distress call to set up an ambush is exactly the sort of shady, scummy thing the League would do."

"What if it's genuine, though? Aren't we obligated to respond to distress calls?" Zeno asked.

I glanced at Perry, who dipped his beak. "We are, unless circumstances are so dire that it's not practical—like, we're already involved in a fight or rescue operation of our own."

I sighed. "Which we are not. Okay, then—Netty, take us to Crossroads, if you please. But try to twist us in with some distance between us and this *Parallax* so we can look over the situation before we dive headlong into it."

———

"Well, that's either a real pirate attack on a liner, or the League has put on an Oscar-winning performance just to try and nab me," I said, eyeing the tactical overlay.

The Parallax was indeed a big liner, probably class 16 or so. And she was obviously carrying someone or *something* awfully important, since she had two class 7 cutters escorting her. Had, because one of the cutters was a battered, lifeless wreck, while the other had been disabled and now limped along far behind her charge. The liner was fast, I had to hand her that, and would probably be able to twist out of the system in another thirty minutes or so. The trouble was that Netty's projections saw her pursuers—two more class 7s and a class 4—catching up and being able to rake her with fire in about fifteen minutes.

The rest of the tactical overlay was blank. There were two Peacemakers at Crossroads, but they were at least three hours away. There hadn't been any other Peacemakers available to help either, aside from B. And she'd made it clear that this wasn't her thing.

"Sorry, Van, this isn't a warship. If you need medical support, let me know. But if you can't subdue pirates dumb enough to attack in-system, then I'd suggest you go back to runway modeling."

"Uh… I was never a model."

B flashed a wicked grin over the comm, her antennae twitching. "That's a shame. Anyway, I guess you better not miss, then. See you around, handsome." She winked.

I heard Torina mutter, "Not if I can help it," then she shot her a bemused glance. She studiously ignored me in a way that told me everything I needed to know—she didn't like anyone flirting with me or vice-versa. That made me smile but also realize that I'd have to watch myself a little more rigorously. She had Declared for me, after all. I guess I just wasn't yet used to being *attached*.

"Van, we can intercept in a little under twelve minutes, which means we'll have about a three minute window before those bad guys can bring the *Parallax* under effective fire."

"Three minutes to take on three ships, huh? And their combined firepower is"—I glanced at the data on the overlay—"at least twenty percent greater than ours? That's a little less certain than I like things to be."

"All we really need to do here, Van, is buy some time for the liner to make a getaway, then we can twist away, too," Perry said.

"What about the crews of those two escort cutters? They kind of need help," Zeno added.

"Yeah, but I don't think these pirates are interested in them. They want whatever's on that liner." I nodded. "Okay then. Netty, spark up the drive. Torina, weapons hot—and feel free to light those assholes up with our fire control scanners. Pirates generally don't want to fight, so maybe we can just spook them."

I hoped so, anyway. I still couldn't get past the idea that this might be a Seven Stars League ploy. If the pirates decided to give up and run, that would be great. If they wanted to fight, though—

Well, then I had some tough decisions to make. And those decisions were going to end in a cloud of plasma.

The only question was, who would be gas, and who would be toasting victory.

THEY CHOSE TO FIGHT.

Rather than breaking off when we made our presence and intention to intervene clear, one of the class 7s turned directly toward us and charged. Its two companions, the other class 7 and the class 4, kept pursuing the *Parallax*.

It was a tactical mistake. The three pirate ships combined had us outgunned. Even the two class 7s had a slight edge on us. But just one of them couldn't match our weight of fire, especially when the firing solutions were coming from our kickass fire control system. Torina loosed a spread of missiles at the other two ships to force them to maneuver, which would cause them to lose ground on the liner. Then she opened up with the lasers as soon as they came in range and immediately landed punishing hits on the oncoming class 7. Chunks of glowing debris, armor, and hull plating tumbled off in its wake.

We took a few hits in return, including one that must have struck the *Fafnir's* canopy square on. The canopy was designed to take it, though, and instantly turned mirror-bright silver, deflecting much of the hit. The rest of the energy was wicked off by the superconductive effect built into the tough, transparent aluminum alloy. Ironically, next to the drive bells and exhaust shielding, the canopy was probably the most resistant part of the ship to laser hits.

"If we built the entire ship outta that stuff, we'd be indestructible," Icky observed.

It would also make the ship ruinously expensive, but Torina had a more practical objection.

"I'd like to be able to take a shower without every other ship docked in Spindrift watching me, thanks."

Icky shrugged. "Wouldn't bother me."

"You don't wear pants, Icky."

Icky sniffed indignantly. "Just saying if you've got it, flaunt it."

I pointed back to the screens. "I appreciate your confidence. However, let's toast some villains, shall we?"

Icky saluted with two arms, and we began to pour fire into the enemy with renewed vigor. The exchange lasted thirty seconds, and then we reached particle cannon range.

With that, it was game over.

The punishing beam slashed apart the class 7, leaving it a battered wreck. It ejected an escape pod, then flashed past us on its way to the galactic core.

We focused our attention on the other pirates. The class 7's attack had delayed us a little, stopping us from altering to a more direct intercept course. Netty estimated the two of them to have a similar weight of firepower to ours, so even odds—but that was still more than I liked. It made the outcome of the battle feel like a coin flip.

But we'd come here to do a job, and even odds were better than being outright outgunned. I angled the *Fafnir* onto a course that would force the pirates to either continue pursuing the liner or maneuver to engage us—I hoped.

Torina fired a spread of missiles to try and poke them into taking their focus off the *Parallax*. Every second we could buy the big ship was a second closer to it escaping. She was sleek and elegant and fast but also only lightly armored over critical sections. As to offensive punch, she only had a single laser and a trio of point-defense batteries. We did spook the class 4 into starting to maneuver to present a more favorable aspect to our missiles, but the class 7 just drove on. Her pirate crew clearly wanted to get close to the liner, probably to take out her drive before turning to engage us, which revealed a level of tactical acumen I wasn't comfortable with, especially for common pirates.

I glared at the tactical overlay. Unfortunately, the immutable laws of physics meant they'd have at least a thirty second window to do just that, which would leave the big ship disabled while the battle was far from decided.

At least, that was true until Netty pointed out something

happening on the *Parallax*. She zoomed in the view on the center display.

"Someone's emerging from a hatch on her dorsal stern, just ahead of her drive section," Netty said.

Sure enough, we saw a small figure push out of an open airlock and drift to the end of a short tether. Two things immediately jumped out at me. One, the figure cradled a bulky device of some sort, a tube maybe a meter and a half long. And two, whoever this was, they were wearing a b-suit.

"Is that a Peacemaker?" I asked.

Netty zoomed the image a little more. It lost some resolution, so we couldn't tell for sure if it was a Peacemaker or not. Other groups and agencies wore similar gear.

The figure lifted the tube onto their shoulder and aimed it like one of the anti-tank weapons I'd trained with in my Army days, an AT-4 or a Javelin guided missile. After lining up on the class 7, they fired. A launch motor accelerated the projectile to about a hundred meters distance, then the flight motor kicked in and it streaked toward the class 7 in a blur. Whatever the power source, that missile was *fast*.

"Ballsy, but more a last act of defiance," Perry said, and I nodded. The class 7's point-defenses opened up, fingers of tracer rounds reaching out for the little projectile. But it proved too small and elusive a target, and they just groped blindly. Not that it would matter, because the tiny warhead might, at best, poke a hole through something—

The class 7 vanished in a searing flash. When it cleared, there was nothing left but cooling gas and fragments of debris.

We stared in silence for a moment. Perry finally spoke up.

"Or that could happen."

"Holy shit. That had to be an antimatter charge. In a shoulder-launched weapon," Zeno said.

I sat back. "I think we need to do some thanking. Is the class 4 bugging out?"

"Very much so. Their enthusiasm for the chase seems to have waned, what with seeing their buddies get turned to vapor and all. Tag them?" Netty asked.

I nodded. "Please do, then broadcast the tracker ID to all Peacemaker ships. We, or someone else, can catch up with them later."

The deck thumped under my feet as one of our tracker missiles launched. The figure on the display pulled themselves back into the airlock, which sealed behind them.

"Alrighty then. Netty, please tell the Parallax we're going to need to delay them a little longer while we come aboard and get some statements."

"You just want to know what this was all about," Torina said.

"Don't you?"

WE DOCKED with the Parallax and stepped through the airlock into a small, self-contained universe of opulent luxury. My feet sank into a thick carpet that made me want to yank off my boots and pad around barefoot. Flowering shrubs erupted from planters in alcoves, while elaborate artwork scrolled across the bulkheads. Unlike most ships, there was absolutely no machinery in sight—not a conduit, not a cable run, not a power transfer. It had all been hidden away, leaving us walking through a space-borne resort of sumptuous detail and understated elegance. It was as though a high-end hotel in Monte Carlo had been wrapped in a hull and launched into the stars, but without the annoyance of gravity or provincial tourists.

In fact, the clientele were just as brusque and snobbish as you'd expect to find in such rarified air. We were escorted to the bridge by a nattily dressed crewman, the first Yonnox I'd ever seen that didn't appear shopworn or scruffy.. Along the way, we were stopped a half-dozen times by passengers in various stages of entitled impatience, all dressed as though heading to Cinderella's ball.

"What a waste of fabric," Icky muttered.

Perry glanced at her. "Wasted on what?"

"On pants."

Perry made a scoffing sound, and Icky shrugged. "You guys are the ones who keep making cracks about that."

One of the haughty passengers crowded in. "You Peacemakers aren't supposed to allow things like this to happen! Why am I even paying taxes?"

Another managed to braid sneering and a patronizing grin. "This had better not take too long. My daughter has an affair to attend at Tau Ceti—no, I won't name it because you've not heard of it, and it will be a reputational *disaster* if she's late."

"I want your name. I'm going to sue!"

I stopped at the last one, a frumpy old man with a female companion *maybe* old enough to be his daughter. "I'm sorry, you're going to sue… who, exactly?"

"Why, you, of course."

I glanced at Torina. "Okay, I'll bite—why, considering we just saved your posh, indolent asses?"

"Well, if you had been doing your job—"

I stopped him. "You're right. I definitely must do my job. Accordingly, I'm going to get a statement from you, as part of our ongoing investigation. Icky, would you take his statement, please?"

She grinned. "You bet." She pulled out a data slate. "What's your name?"

"Alban Rothstay. The Fourth."

She started pecking at the slate. "Okay, so—A. L. Damn, where's the E on this thing?"

"There is no E in my name, you *oaf.*"

"There is so. Allen Ropstay. I bet there are three Es, now that I think of it. I was good at spelling both years I was in school," Icky beamed, earning a look of furious disgust from the blowhard and his *special friend.*

Grinning, I left Icky *slowly* dealing with Master Rothstay the Fourth, who was imitating a dying star and turning ever more lurid shades of red.

We met the captain in a lounge behind the bridge, apparently his personal meeting space. By the time we got there, a small crowd had gathered. The captain, a Gajur, waved them all back.

"Please, everyone, this is all under control. The Peacemaker—"

"I'm going to sue!"

"Me as well. I'm thinking class action."

"I've already contacted my attorney—"

The captain just maintained a dignified smile and sought to calm everyone down. I glanced at Torina.

"Everyone wants to sue someone."

She smiled. "That's the go-to for the rich and outraged."

A sudden cackle cut us all off. A creature like a giant bat draped in a flowing gown of shimmering green-gold fabric shook her elderly head.

"You people are a bunch of primping, preening assholes," she snapped, then puffed on a small pipe and blew smoke that smelled like lavender with a hint of—motor oil? "All this talk about lawsuits, when the brave Peacemaker who saved us is right here, trying to do his job!"

Surprisingly, everyone went quiet and moved back. A few people even left. Whoever this was, they obviously commanded some respect—or just had more money than everyone else.

I smiled at her. "I like your style, Ms.—"

"Rinwex, of Beta Gris. But you can call me Rin." She leered. "Do you want to pat me down? Maybe a strip search?"

I heard Torina snicker.

"I… don't think that will be necessary."

"Are you sure? I could be armed, you know."

"I'm willing to take that chance."

We spoke to the captain, Perry recording his statement, then Rinwex invited us to the first-class lounge for a drink. I hesitated, caught between not wanting to offend the lecherous old crone and curious about what *first class* would be like aboard a ship already fitted-out like some oligarch's superyacht. Torina answered for me.

"We'd be happy to join you for a drink. Wouldn't we, Van?" she said, smiling sweetly.

"Yes, absolutely," I said, tossing her a quick glare. I didn't offer my arm to Rinwex, but she took it anyway.

The first class lounge struggled mightily to be even more ostentatious than the rest of the ship, but really, you could only get so sumptuous. As we ordered our drinks, though, I saw a solitary figure sitting at a table off to one side. They were wearing a b-suit.

I excused myself from Rinwex's little impromptu court, leaving Torina, Zeno, and Perry to hang on her words. The b-suited figure looked up with a thin smile as I approached. She was another Gajur, obviously older, with a lean, hard face.

"Peacemaker," she said, raising her drink to me, then gesturing to a chair at her table.

"Van Tudor. And you are—?" I asked, sitting down.

"Maxelus Croon. You can call me Max."

"Well, Max, you're doing a good job of being that thing that's not like the others. For instance, I don't see any of the other passengers wielding ship-destroying, shoulder-launched weapons."

She shrugged. "I'm a former Commandant in the Civil Defense Force on Gajur Prime. This is my retirement job, security aboard this platinum-plated, jewel-inlaid tub."

"So you brought along some souvenirs from your old job?"

"Nah. We sure as hell didn't have that sort of firepower available to us. The owners of this thing give me a generous security budget, so what the hell, figured I'd go on a shopping spree." She sipped her drink. "We've got the necessary permits for all of it."

"I'm sure you do. I'm really more interested in what you know about whoever was attacking you."

"Pirates? After a few shovelfuls of the mountains of money aboard? Is there anything more to say, really?"

I narrowed my eyes. "So this ship always flies with escorts?"

Max sat forward. "Actually, she does. The owners don't want to kit her out with any decent weaponry because it's *unsightly*—"

She cut herself off with a frown and pulled out a data slate.

"Well well. Looks like we've got a couple of passengers looking to disembark early. Two of them, down in the shuttle bay—shit. Whoever they are, they've bypassed the security lockouts."

We both stood. "This is starting to sound like an inside job," I suggested.

Max nodded.

"I'd bet my generous pay—far more than my pension, by the way—on it," she said. "Care to help me deal with some miscreants since you're here and being all Peacemaker?"

"Delighted. A criminal brawl sounds better than moderate harassment by an actual old bat." I gestured to the others. They disengaged from Renwix, who made disappointed sounds.

"We need to hurry," Max said. "These assholes have managed to get around every lockout. The only thing stopping them from launching is the time it's going to take them to depressurize the shuttle bay and open the outer doors."

She hurried off.

I turned to Perry. "See if you can flank these guys getting around the security lockouts."

"On it, boss," he replied and sailed off toward a terminal with an open data port behind the bar.

We followed Max and picked up Icky on the way. She was unarmed, since carting around a sledgehammer seemed a little aggressive. The rest of us had sidearms, and I'd strapped on the Moonsword. Max led us through a maze of corridors, down a gangway, and into a part of the *Parallax* that actually looked like a ship and not a high-end shopping mall. It was still far tidier, all white paint and color-coded stencils marking systems. She took us to a set of heavy blast doors, which were closed.

"Perry, how are you doing?" I asked.

His voice hummed out of the comm. "These guys are good, whoever they are."

"Does that mean you can't stop them?"

"Pfft. Please. They're good, but I'm *Perry*. I've got the outer doors locked down, and if you wait about five minutes, I'll get the hangar repressurized."

We waited. It gave time for reinforcements to arrive, a pair of heavily armed security guards in b-suits and over-armor brandishing boarding shotguns.

The pressure indicator turned green. "Okay, Perry, open the doors in ten seconds."

We readied ourselves, the two guards taking point, the rest of us dispersed along the corridor behind them, taking what cover we could from conduits and hatchways.

The doors rolled open with a soft rumble. Max and the guards rushed in. The rest of us followed, armed and ready.

Two figures were just in the process of disembarking from one of the three shuttles hunkered in the bay. One of them was a humanoid race I didn't recognize. The other one—

Was a Sorcerer.

THE SORCERER SNAPPED out a shot from a wicked little handheld laser, the bolt sizzling between Max and one of her guards. The shot passed overhead and smacked into the bulkhead above the blast doors, sending a flare of brilliant light and metal shavings in every direction. Their companion simply cringed, then tried to clamber back into the shuttle.

Both of the guards raised their shotguns at the Sorcerer. I shouted for them to hold their fire, swept out the Moonsword, and charged. Sure enough, the Sorcerer aimed and fired directly at me at almost point-blank range. It was a kill shot, or would have been if the Moonsword hadn't deflected it into the deck. Before the Sorcerer could fire again, I was on them, the Moonsword poised to decapitate —him, I figured, though it was hard to be sure of anything but *evil*.

"I'd prefer you alive, but if that's not going to work out, I'll settle for your simpering little friend in there," I spat into the Sorcerer's face. The look I got in return was sheer venom. I actually expected them to keep fighting, which might have been awkward because I wasn't sure if the Moonsword would protect me from a weapon effectively shoved right in my face. Before either of us could twitch a further muscle, though, Icky's massive hand swept down and grabbed the Sorcerer's wrist, then yanked it back. I heard something snap, and the Sorcerer loosed a thin, shrill hiss.

"Oops."

"Icky. That was very bad customer service. I am disappointed and upset," I said in a flat tone.

"I feel shame," Icky said, eyes shining with laughter.

"You're forgiven. Glad we had this talk."

I pulled away from the Sorcerer, who dropped to their knees. Torina and Zeno had the other alien under control by then.

I sheathed the Moonsword and turned to Max. "This is your jurisdiction, but I really want these two. Our current investigation involves these assholes"—I nodded at the Sorcerer—"in a big way."

Max shrugged. "Last thing I want to do is babysit a couple of prisoners. They're all yours."

I turned back to our two prisoners, who couldn't decide what scared them more—the Moonsword or Icky. "Alright. Let's get acquainted, shall we?"

22

THE SORCERER WAS PRETTY MUCH what I expected—surly, uncommunicative, and a venomous pain in the ass. Perry and I tried to get something more useful than curses and seething hatred out of him for a while, then gave up. We stuck him in the *Fafnir*'s brig just to get him out of our faces.

The other alien was *much* more interesting. Torina and Icky interrogated him, their extreme good cop-bad cop routine barely underway before he broke like spun glass.

"A Grendu? Who the hell are they?" I asked, eyeing the prisoner. He vaguely reminded me of The Grinch from the Earthly Christmas story, but with a little more poise.

"They are one of the three races that make up Unity," Perry said.

"Oh. I don't think I've met—"

I stopped as the implications of it dawned on me.

"So, let's see if I've got this straight. We've got a Grendu, a member of one of the Unity races, sucking up to a Sorcerer. In the meantime, Retta the Francophile slug-on-a-ball tells us that Group 41 was nosing around Unity, until they weren't. So that means we've got a straight-line connection between Group 41 and the Sorcerers that passed through Unity. Does that about sum it up?"

"Sounds about right," Perry said.

"On top of that, we've got another Sorcerer in custody, too. Maybe we can learn even more from him," Torina said.

I nodded, but absently. "Trouble is that once we hand him over to Guild intel, we'll only get back whatever they manage to get out of him and put in their report."

"Is that… a problem?" Torina asked.

I shrugged. "It might be, yeah. Call me paranoid—"

"You're paranoid," Perry said.

I shrugged again. "Yeah, I am. Anyway, because I'm paranoid, I'm not convinced that our friend in the holding cell back there is going to be asked the right questions, or that he's necessarily going to survive in custody at all."

Torina frowned. "Do you really think the Guild is that compromised, that a prisoner could end up dead before they can reveal anything damning?"

"I honestly don't know. And that's the problem. I can't just say *no* to that question, which leaves me with a choice. Do we take him back to Anvil Dark and hand him over to the Guild, or do we interrogate him ourselves?"

"Regs say you have to hand him over," Perry said.

"Yeah. I know they do." I sighed. "But we might never get another chance like this to get the word from the evil horse's mouth."

I stared out the canopy for a moment, looking at the starscape without seeing it. Instead, B's words rang in my mind.

Sometimes there are things that need to be done that the Guild or anyone else can't do. Generally unpleasant things, and often illegal things, but necessary things—things that need doin'.

Sure, but who decided what those unpleasant, illegal but necessary things were? Could any member of the GKU make that call? Wasn't that just a blank check for corruption and abuse, a more elaborate way of saying that what really defined a Knight is that they could do whatever they hell they wanted, in the name of— what, *maintaining galactic order*? Is that why they were called *Crimes Against Order* in the first place?

"You're really struggling with this, Van, aren't you?" Torina asked.

I looked at her.

Things that still need to be done.

Because if they weren't—

I shook my head, having already made a decision but only just realizing it.

"Actually, no, I'm not. Netty, set course for Dregs."

"So… not Anvil Dark, then?" Torina asked.

I shook my head again. "Nope. Dregs. And Netty, get hold of Lucky and Carter, and see if one or both of them can meet us there. Oh, and tell them not to forget their handcuffs."

"Fuzzy, or metal?"

I gave her my best leer. "Spicy girl. Metal, if you please. For this interrogation, we want to put our worst foot forward."

WHEN WE ARRIVED in the Dregs system, I asked Netty to arrange for someplace we could dock that would be *discreet*. When she asked for clarification, I told her that, ideally, it would be a place where we could dock and disembark from the *Fafnir* immediately into a private space with controlled access.

"There's an orbital that's essentially just self storage. Each dock opens into a pressurized, temperature-controlled storage unit with a single internal access door, and that's only used for maintenance."

"Sounds perfect. Line us up to dock there for... let's say two days, to be on the safe side."

"Units are rented on a standard weekly or monthly basis," Netty replied.

"Okay, make it a week."

I felt Torina looking at me. "Van, isn't this kind of—?"

"Unusual?"

"I was going to say sketchy, maybe even borderline illegal, but sure, let's go with unusual."

I turned and faced her squarely. "It's sketchy as hell, actually. I'm going to interrogate that Sorcerer here, get whatever information I can from him, then hand him over to Lucky or Carter, whoever gets here first. They can haul his ass back to Anvil Dark while we act on whatever intel we manage to extract."

Torina simply nodded.

I spoke up, to the cockpit at large. "If you don't want to be part of this, I understand. You can stay aboard the *Fafnir* if you'd prefer. I know that this isn't the way things are supposed to be done, but we've got a Sorcerer in custody and an opportunity to get valuable information out of him before he disappears into the Anvil Dark legal system. And I intend to avail myself of it."

Icky just shrugged. "I'm cool with it."

Zeno gave me a hard stare, but it didn't feel like disapproval. It felt more like curiosity. She finally just shook her head. "Works for me. I'd rather not pass up the chance if we've got it."

I looked at Torina. Like Zeno, her look was keen and searching, as if she was trying to read me. Finally, she gave a small nod, her eyes bright with the weight of a decision.

"I'll be honest—it makes me a little uneasy. On the other hand, I've seen what these bastards do to decent people like the Schegith, and Rolis, and Bulfir. If this will help stop them from doing that to anyone else, then I can live with *uneasy*."

Van, I'm about to object to this for being against regs, and so on and so on. In light of your recent conversation with B, though, I'm doing it for more for show, Perry said in my ear bug.

I turned to him.

"Van, Peacemaker regulations require you to deliver these prisoners to Guild custody with all expediency. You can interrogate them on the way to Anvil Dark, but in accordance with Guild Regulation 14, Protocol 3, Section—"

I gave my gravest nod. "So noted. Please record your objection —and presumably Netty's, as well—and my acknowledgement of it."

"Done."

Netty put us into the appropriate traffic pattern for arrival at the storage orbital. As she did, I found myself brooding over what had just happened. In essence, I was choosing to ignore Guild regulations in favor of expediency—

Sometimes there are things that need to be done that the Guild or anyone else can't do.

—and I was giving myself permission to do it based on a conversation with a complete stranger just a few hours before. Perry was clearly on board with it, and I had no doubt Netty was fully aware, too. But the others were following me blind to even the existence of the GKU. I knew that wouldn't bother Icky, and I suspected Zeno wouldn't lose much sleep over it, either. But Torina had a moral compass that tended to point firmly north, toward what was right.

It was one thing for me to start traversing a narrow, winding path toward the ends justifying the means. But it was quite another to bring the others—especially Torina—along it with me.

And doubly so when they had no idea they were even walking it.

WE DOCKED at our assigned unit, number 23. The orbital consisted of one hundred units in two rows of fifty, with a central shaft connecting them and a control and engineering module in the middle. Ships could dock with their assigned storage unit and load and unload goods. It reminded me of the plethora of self-storage units that seemed to keep springing up back on Earth. No matter how many were built, there always seemed to be a demand for more of them.

Most contained miscellaneous crap, I'm sure—old clothes, housewares, disused barbecues, and exercise machines, that sort of thing. Some apparently contained rare, exotic, and valuable artifacts like unique baseball cards and signed, vintage photos of Elvis, if you believed the various reality shows about amazing finds in old storage units—which I didn't. What I *did* believe was that a lot of them were exploited for their bland anonymity for hiding all sorts of nefarious things, from stolen goods to drug labs.

Which brought us back to this orbital version high above Dregs. The unit we'd rented was empty, but I couldn't help wondering what we'd find in the other ninety-nine, assuming, that is, we even wanted to know.

I stepped through the airlock and into our assigned storage unit. It was about the size of a single-car garage, dimly lit and—

Something slammed into my gut hard enough to drive the breath out of me. I had a vague impression of figures, then snaps of gunfire, ricochets, noise, confusion. Something shoved past me with a ferocious howl and jammed against the storage unit's bulkhead.

"Van! Van, are you—?"

I nodded to Torina. "Fine. What's going on—?"

"An ambush."

"You"—I dragged in a breath—"don't say!" I swept out the Moonsword and made to charge into the fray, but something blocked my way.

Icky.

I'd never seen her brandishing her sledgehammer in such inti-mate detail. She swung in flat, whistling sweeps, switching with preternatural abruptness to vicious, overhand swings. Each blow connected with something, raising a staccato succession of wet, sickening cracks, like someone smashing crockery wrapped in wet rags. All the while she howled like a feral beast, making the storage unit thrum like a drum one second, ring like a bell the next.

And then it was done. Three broken figures sprawled on the deck amid pools of blood and gore. More spattered us and the bulkheads overhead, in both flecks and the odd fat droplet, a grotesque souvenir of the violence.

Sucking in another breath, I called out to her.

"Icky?"

She spun, her eyes blazing. "What?"

I waved her off while making direct eye contact. "Stand down, okay? Battle's over."

She blinked at me, then looked around. Slowly, she lowered her sledgehammer. "Over? Shit." She grinned a toothy grin. "I was just getting warmed up."

Zeno poked her head through the airlock. "Is the screaming and beating and killing done now?"

I nodded, wincing at a dull burst of pain in my stomach. I'd obviously been shot and saved by my b-suit. The impact had still winded me.

"Yeah, I—damn, that stings! Anyway, yeah. Who *were* these assholes?"

While Torina stuck me with a first aid hypo, Zeno checked the remains. "One human, two Yonnox. They look like pretty typical hired thugs—I think, although it's kinda hard to tell with all the blood and broken bones."

I leaned against the wall and nodded. "Not surprising. Any ID?"

She checked but found none. "Wishful thinking. This sort doesn't tend to carry around their library card with them."

Perry tried doing facial recognition on them, but Icky's hammer work had rearranged their features enough that he came up with dozens of possible matches, including, but not limited to, no less than ten races and a predatory mammalian that resembled a plump otter.

"If they were here to rescue the Sorcerer, or kill him before he could talk, how—well, could they? How could they possibly know? We didn't tell anyone except Carter and Lucky we were coming here—and before that makes you start suspecting them, we never told them why," Torina said.

I shrugged. "No idea. Maybe they recognized the *Fafnir* and were after us, or me—trying to collect on one of those seemingly many bounties on my head. Or maybe they were just opportunists, hoping to jump us and steal us blind."

"Maybe it was just a case of wrong place, wrong time," Zeno said. "We could ask them, but"—she nudged a body with her foot—"we'd need to find this one's lower jaw before he'd even be able to talk. Well, that, and he's, you know, really, really dead."

Icky deflated. "Sorry, Van. I guess I should have tried to take at least one of them alive."

I nodded. "Yeah, you should have. But—" I glanced back into the *Fafnir*. "Lemons and lemonade, am I right?"

Torina gave a puzzled frown. "What *are* you talking about?"

The first aid she'd administered was taking effect. I straightened and cleared my throat, provoking only a slight twinge in my gut.

"Torina, Zeno, go get our prisoners and bring them in here."

"What about me, boss?" Icky asked. I could tell she expected to be dismissed and told to wait on the ship, but I smiled at her.

"I want you to just stand there, just the way you are, with your hammer."

"And?"

"And play along. We'll let our prisoners' imaginations do the rest."

329

THE SORCERER AND his Grendu sycophant slammed to a halt as soon as they stepped through the airlock. Icky stood amid the three smashed bodies of our would-be ambushers, spattered with gore, her bloody hammer propped on her shoulder.

Grinning.

The Grendu stared around with a wide-eyed, horrified gaze. The Sorcerer shot me a hard look and shrugged. "So?" he snapped.

I glanced at the bodies. "This was your rescue party. I just figured you should have a chance to meet them since, you know, they went to all this trouble."

He shrugged again. "Alright. Now I demand to be taken to wherever I can have legal counsel."

I smiled. "All in good time."

The Sorcerer's face hardened another notch. "You're obligated, Peacemaker, to allow us to have legal counsel—"

I stepped and glared into his face. "I'm not feeling especially *obligated* to do anything right now. I get like that right after someone tries to kill me. It's a character flaw I'm trying hard to shake."

"I'm ashamed by your lack of control, boss," Icky remarked, letting her hammer thump against one meaty thigh.

"Apologies, Icky. I know how much you value self control."

Icky inclined her head with great dignity, but her eyes never left our guests.

The Grendu puffed himself up and tried to level a hard stare on me. The sidelong glances at the Sorcerer told me this was going to be for his vile patron's benefit, not mine.

"Rest assured, Peacemaker, that I shall give a full accounting of your actions here once you've delivered us to the *proper* authorities."

I opened my mouth to confirm that I was the *proper authorities*, but a wicked desire to make this guy squirm took over.

So I changed tactics.

"You're from Unity, right?"

The Grendu would have blinked in surprise, except he didn't seem to have eyelids, which resulted in a creepy, doll-like stare. "I... am. So what?"

"Well, it strikes me that you and your people fall outside the Peacemaker Guild's jurisdiction. That means you might have diplomatic immunity."

Perry immediately spoke up in my ear bug. *Van, he'd only qualify for diplomatic immunity if he was part of a duly constituted and recognized delegation of—*

I clasped my hands behind my back and waggled my fingers where Perry could see them.

Oh. You're gonna bullshit him. Well, carry on, then.

The Grendu stared at me like an owl. "Diplomatic—"

"Yeah. I guess that means I could just release you, then you could be on your way. There'd really be no need for you to stick around for"—I glanced back at the shattered corpses and Icky standing over them, spattered with blood and still holding her hammer—"the interrogation."

The Grendu's gaze flicked from me, to the Sorcerer, then back again. The Sorcerer just looked venomous, but since it seemed to be the only expression he could muster, that didn't mean much.

"I—are you sure? Diplomatic immunity?"

I nodded.

"I—" He hesitated, tossed another glance at the Sorcerer, then nodded. "What do I need to do?"

I smiled. "Nothing, because I'm just yanking your chain. Of course you don't qualify for diplomatic immunity, you slimy piece of shit."

"But you said—"

"I said you *might* qualify for diplomatic immunity, I *could* release you, you *could* be on your way." I shrugged. "I was mistaken."

Now the Grendu's face turned venomous. "You lying filth. I'm going to—"

"You're going to what? Complain to your boss here? I'm sure he'd love to hear it, considering you just leapt at the first possible chance I dangled in front of you to bail out on him."

I looked sidelong at the Sorcerer. "Good help—it's hard to find, isn't it?"

The Grendu launched into a string of profanity interspersed with pathetic pleas to the Sorcerer to ignore the diplomatic immunity thing. He switched from ploy to ploy—each one more pathetic than the last—in about as many breaths as it took to say it. By the time he was done, even the Sorcerer looked about ready to roll his eyes.

"Okay, then. Time for the interrogation to start. Icky, you've got that list of questions, right?"

"I—yeah. Yeah, of course I do."

"We'll leave you to it, then." I turned to the others. "Who's hungry? My treat."

Perry dipped his beak and shook his head sadly at the prisoners. "I'm sorry. I tried to talk Peacemaker Tudor out of this after Icky finished, ah, questioning these guys. I only hope Zeno enjoys her toast and spice jelly while she's—" He cut himself off. "Sorry, Zeno, didn't want to spoil your appetite."

Zeno sighed. "I know. If my toast and spice jelly experience gets ruined, my day just isn't the same." Together with Perry, she turned toward the airlock.

Icky spoke up. "Toast? I want toast. Make mine with the… the shrimp things I like."

I glanced at her. "You mean trakanite lobster?"

"Yeah, and don't skimp on the blue ones."

"Well, okay—but you're going to be busy here for a while, so we'll wait a bit before we make it. You don't want it cold," I said, turning away.

Torina watched the exchange without comment. I saw the concern in her eyes. Nothing we were doing here was illegal, per se. So far, the only thing we were guilty of was violating a Guild policy regarding prisoner transport. But I could tell what she was thinking —*you meet this mysterious B, a secret Peacemaker doctor, then spend a chunk of the flight afterward in brooding silence, and now you're breaking Guild rules and using this extraordinary rendition pantomime to try and coerce information from the prisoners.*

Van, what the hell is going on?

I kept up the act, looking at Icky instead.

"The blue ones." I rolled my eyes. "I work with barbarians. Well then. Off to lunch."

I turned and walked away, Torina following.

We actually made it back aboard the *Fafnir*, spawning my first doubt that maybe this wasn't going to work. If it didn't, then our only recourse would be doing things the right way, which would make Torina happy, I guess, but—

"Wait!"

It was the Grendu. I exchanged a look with the others, then turned back and reentered the gore-splattered storage unit. I found Icky looming over the Grendu, her sledgehammer raised.

Shit.

The Grendu shook his head. "This is barbaric—"

"I told you I worked with barbarians," I said. "I felt my lips moving. I know I said it. Is it me, Perry? Am I the problem here?"

"Nope. Loud and clear, boss."

Icky lowered her hammer, and the Grendu began babbling so fast I could barely keep up, and each phrase was another version of *I'll tell you everything.*

That didn't surprise me at all. I knew nothing about his people, so I couldn't start generalizing from this one guy, but he was clearly the sycophant type with a spine—and morality—that was quite flexible. I'd encountered his ilk often enough in cyberspace, the desperate hangers-on and fanboys of more accomplished hackers, always pathetically eager to please.

What *did* surprise me was the Sorcerer. With a deep scowl hardening his face—which I hadn't thought could actually *get* any harder —he looked at me, then made a decision. "I want to cut a deal. I tell you what you want to know, you give me full immunity."

I didn't bother hiding a contemptuous sneer, because the cowardly son of a bitch made his bonds from the pain of others, but at the first threat, he folded like a house of cards.

Two years ago, I would have said those exact words. But today, I had a more practical reason to scoff at him to his face.

"Not happening. You're implicated in piracy, as well as depraved indifference, since you obviously didn't give a shit what happened to those people aboard that liner. Try again—or I take your friend here back aboard my ship for a cup of coffee and a chat, and leave you here with Icky since—well, I'll be blunt. You're a murderous piece of shit, and the universe would be better without you in it."

The Sorcerer looked away, then back. "Fine. A reduced charge. I'll cop to Accessory to Piracy. But I want protection."

I glanced at Perry, who'd returned to stand in the airlock. He shrugged his wings.

"Up to you, Van."

I turned back to the Sorcerer. "Fine, deal—but only if whatever you tell us turns out to be true. You lie to us, and I'll bring you, Icky, and her sledgehammer right back here, understand?"

The Sorcerer glared daggers at me for a moment, then sagged a bit, nodded, and began to talk.

Icky interrupted him. "Hey, boss, a question?"

"Yes?" I asked.

"Does this mean no toast?"

23

"WELL, that was quite the treasure trove," I said, putting the data slate down on the galley table. It held our final report on the Sorcerer's and Grendu's statements, which had been dutifully recorded by Perry. It made for a *major* intelligence haul.

In short, the Sorcerers had begun collaborating with Group 41 against Unity. Unity, they believed, was fertile hunting ground for their despicable little ventures. Since Unity was outside known space or Guild jurisdiction, there weren't even any diplomatic ties to speak of. Those two solitudes would, they believed, make any sort of coordinated investigations or response difficult, if not impossible.

But there was a *lot* more.

The Sorcerer claimed that they had tacit support from another party in known space—none other than the Seven Stars League. The Sorcerers were infiltrating Unity's governmental and military structures to start waging a covert war within, while from the outside, they'd take more direct action. The Sorcerers, backed up by their own people, the Trinduk, plus Group 41 and the Seven Stars League, would launch a series of increasingly aggressive incursions into Unity space. Between the two prongs of the attack, internal espionage, and external military offensives, the objective was to destabilize Unity and ultimately allow the Trinduk and the League to seize territory—territory the Sorcerers would be free to plunder for their vile trade in stolen identities.

But even that wasn't the end of their machinations. The Sorcerer didn't know the details, but the Sorcerers—Group 41— League alliance was courting our old friends, the Victory Supernal, another isolationist group of three races, the Hus, the Cotzei, and the Tonaat. Getting them to join the cause would bring the added fun of intolerant religious fundamentalism into the picture, because you can't have a real crime ring without eugenicists and their ghoulish minions.

"And the best part about it all?" the Sorcerer had spat. "No one in known space is going to care. This wouldn't affect Ceti, the Eridani, or anyone else. Even your precious Guild wouldn't have any incentive to try and stop us, much less the jurisdiction."

Then he grinned and made me believe, if I didn't already, that genuine, pure evil really *did* exist. "Nobody in known space is going to try to stop us, because no one in known space will give a shit. Well, except for you, of course—you and your hired thug here with her big hammer. It's going to be an awfully lonely fight, though, Peacemaker. So why don't you make things easier on yourself and just go back to stopping bad guys from smuggling a few hits of dope to some mining colony, writing docking tickets, and… whatever other do-gooding you do to pass the time."

It had taken every gram of control I had to not swing on that smug, leering face or just hand him over to Icky to use for hammer practice. But the Sorcerer had been careful to drop hints that he knew much more than he'd revealed, meaning he might still be of value to us. So instead, I just stayed silent, because nothing I could say would come close to expressing my rage and disgust at what I was feeling.

In that moment of incandescent anger, I did something smart. I looked at Torina, saw her expression, and took the wordless counsel she was offering. For several breaths, I said nothing, the gravid moment hanging between me and the Sorcerer until I waved a hand in dismissal.

Exhaling slowly, I made myself smile wintry and desolate, but it was a smile nonetheless. "Icky? Take this… person… to his cell. If he attempts to harm you, break every one of his limbs. Then at your convenience, come get me."

"Got it, boss. What about the Grendu?" Icky asked.

"They both go to the cell. But as to the Grendu, if he violates our hospitality, then see to it he never leaves the hall. Am I clear?"

The Grendu stood, stunned. The Sorcerer stopped sneering, and even Zeno gave me a measured look.

"You heard him, boys. Move, and if you get the urge to misbehave, you might not have the boss' blessing, but you sure as hell have mine." She hefted the hammer, then pointed to the hatch. "You first."

Like the march of the damned, both prisoners moved off at a slow, hesitant pace.

"Good. I got their attention. Think we can use it?" I asked Torina.

She frowned at the data slate, then crossed her arms.

"It's beyond anything we hoped for. Let's just hope it's admissible," she said.

"Why wouldn't it be?"

She gave me a hard look. "Because it's coerced? Because you told him that you'd let Icky beat him to death if he didn't open up?"

"Did I ever actually say, Icky's going to beat you to death—?"

"Van, you're splitting hairs that have already been split. It was one thing to dangle that possibility of diplomatic immunity in front of the Grendu. But any reasonable person would believe you intended to let Icky kill those two if they didn't talk."

Perry turned to Zeno. "Maybe there's some routine maintenance you, Icky, and I can do back in engineering—"

"No, this involves all of us," Torina snapped. "Van, what happened aboard that ship, the one owned by whoever the hell this mystery Peacemaker *B* is?"

"I got my leg fixed up."

"Is that all?"

I opened my mouth to lie and say *yes, it was.* But my subconscious was obviously smarter than that because Torina would *know* I was lying almost instantly, and that wasn't going to lead anywhere good. Instead, what came out of my mind was a half-truth.

"No, it wasn't. She also told me some things about my grandfather that I'm… still processing. So if it seems like I'm playing a little fast and loose with the rules—yeah, I am. But let's not lose sight of the fact that we've got a *Sorcerer* back there. They kill people and implant their identities into nightmarish video games. They're beyond ghouls. They've gone over the horizon into quantifiable evil."

"So the ends justify the means?"

I was keenly aware that Icky, Zeno, Perry, and Netty were watching. I couldn't just dismiss Torina's concerns, because if they perceived a fracture between her and me, that wouldn't help anyone. And Torina deserved better.

"Sometimes they do. So if this bastard decides to renege on his deal and claim his testimony was coerced, we'll deal with that. And even if it works and he gets off, I think even *that* would be worth uncovering a monstrous conspiracy to seize control of Unity, or parts of it."

I took a deep breath, then continued. "The Seven Stars League is allegedly involved. Remember Mister Charisma who put out the call for me to be arrested? He intends to seize territory from Unity. And I don't think he, or the Trinduk, or those Victory Supernal assholes are going to be happy to stop there. For that matter, Helso was one of his Protectorates, and he's in the midst of losing it. And we can rest assured, there are consequences to his actions that go beyond anything a Peacemaker would do."

Torina glanced down, then up, her eyes flaring with intensity. "Like what, Van? Tell me. Be clear. I deserve that kind of clarity. We *all* do."

"You do. You… you all do. You're right. If he does get Helso back, then your family's *protectors* are going to be people who have allied themselves with the sort of murderous scum we have in our brig back there. They'll be opposed to us in all things, but more importantly, they're willing to use force without limit, if I'm guessing. I can tolerate people coming after me. I'm a big boy. It's part of this gig. But there are things I *won't* tolerate. In fact, there are things that will set me on a path that I don't want to walk. I have too much invested."

"Invested in what, exactly, Van? You strive for clarity, yes? Well, here's an opportunity to show us," Perry said.

I said nothing but pointed to my crew, and lastly, at Torina.

Torina's beautiful face was a map of fugitive emotions, each expression chasing another away until she settled on sad. "Van."

"Yes?"

"Did it occur that *we're* invested in *you*?"

"You commuted my sentence, but I chose to be here," Zeno said.

"You are my family," Icky muttered, looking down.

"And mine," Perry added. "We don't want to lose our family because you decide to break rules in the pursuit of justice."

Torina stepped to me and put her hand on my face, her eyes searching mine. "You're angry, and you're not entirely wrong. But I didn't come this far to lose you because your sense of justice morphs into… revenge. Or rage."

Perry tapped his talons, and I cut my eyes to see him regarding me with an inorganic stillness. "It isn't fair to Icky that she be used as something to fear."

"I kinda like it, actually," Icky said with a shrug.

Torina sighed. "Play along, Ick. Okay?"

Icky sketched a small salute. I returned it, then looked at Torina again. We weren't done with whatever was happening, and the Seven Stars' League was, I knew, a condition, not a cause for the entire issue at hand.

That issue was more than just my feelings for Torina and the welfare of my crew.

"We have to stop these people, Torina. I… I know what it's like to lose one person to an unfair, vile death. But thousands?

Millions?" I shook my head slowly, then let some of the tension drain away from my shoulders. "I can't ask you to be my moral compass, because I should have one of my own. I *do* have one of my own, and I'll use it. You have my word."

Torina's eyes never left mine as she pursed her lips, then quirked a brow before coming forward to kiss me. "I believe you."

"Thank you. If there's a line, I'll ask before I jump. I owe it to all of you."

"You owe it to yourself most of all, Van," Perry said.

"And Mark. And Valint," Zeno added.

And as for Icky—

When I looked at her as she leaned against the bulkhead, she shrugged with the insouciance of an aging maitre'd. "Tell me what needs to be fixed on the *Fafnir*, and I'll fix it. Tell me what heads need to be smashed, and I'll smash it."

"Ladies and gentlemen, Icky's job description," Perry said, taking an avian bow.

I felt more of the tension drain away, but there was a final point to make. For clarity. For my crew.

"The Seven Stars' League is—"

"Under the control of a vicious criminal element, yes, we know that. Can you roll them up in one step?" Torina asked.

My answer was easy. "No."

Torina continued. "Then we do it one step at a time, and we do it with the cold certainty that we're morally *and* legally right. We beat them and bring them to justice, and they live the rest of their miserable existence knowing they lost everything because we had the truth on our side."

Icky smiled wide, then brandished her hammer. "You hear that, girl? You've got a new name. *The Truth*."

Perry lifted a wing, then folded it away with a flick. He pierced me with his gaze, and I understood we, as a crew, had passed a test.

"The truth hurts," Torina said. "But not as much as losing our way, Van. Remember that?"

I answered in the only way possible. "You have my word."

Torina gave a small, decisive nod. "I'll take it. Now... let's go to work."

SHORTLY AFTER WE transmitted our report to Anvil Dark, locked away behind the heaviest encryption Perry and Netty could muster, we got a response. It was Gerhardt.

"Peacemaker Tudor, we need to talk," he said, voice cracking with authority.

I suppressed a sigh, then steeled myself. "Sir, I—"

"Not via comm. I'm sending you a set of coordinates in the L1159-16 system, where our prisoner barge, The Hole, is located. When we've finished meeting, you will be transferring your prisoners directly into custody there, pending their further disposition."

The channel flicked closed.

"I'd make another crack about the principal's office, but I suspect your sense of humor is a little depleted right now," Perry said.

"Good call, bird. Is this one of those teachable moments, do you think?"

Torina grimaced. "I'm afraid so. The real question is this—what are we going to learn?"

—

It wasn't Gerhardt waiting for us, though. It was Lunzy's ship, the *Foregone Conclusion.*

"That's… odd," I mentioned as Netty started maneuvering the *Fafnir* to dock.

"Maybe Gerhardt couldn't make it, so he sent Lunzy instead," Torina offered.

Zeno sniffed. "To be his enforcer for the, ah, questioning?"

I lifted one shoulder, watching Torina. Her eyes betrayed nothing as she was getting into character for our interrogation, but she was close enough to me that our fingers brushed with each move of the ship.

That, in itself, said more than any words could.

We docked, and the airlocks opened. I stepped aboard Lunzy's ship in company with Torina and Perry. Zeno and Icky stayed aboard the *Fafnir*, doing some routine maintenance—with Icky under Zeno's careful eye and the detailed work register Gerhardt had decreed close at hand, of course.

Lunzy smiled as she greeted us. "Been a while, Van," she said, leading us into her comfy lounge.

"It has," I agreed, then stopped in the doorway. Gerhardt was sitting in one of the big, overstuffed chairs. Another figure in a nondescript suit sat in a corner.

They were a Grendu.

Wary, I sat down. Gerhardt wasted no time.

"That was quite the intelligence coup you managed, Tudor. I'm surprised your prisoners were so forthcoming, especially considering one of them was a Sorcerer."

I shrugged. "I'm just a persuasive guy, I guess."

Gerhardt smiled in his thin, humorless way. "Yes. *Persuasive.* That must be it."

I inclined my head politely, and Torina did the same. We were in tune, and I admit, the sensation gave me a rush of confidence I'd not had moments earlier.

Gerhardt gestured at the Grendu. "Tudor, there's someone I'd like you to meet. This is Puris-Tar, of the Unity Joint Operations Counter-Intelligence Branch."

Puris-Tar nodded, once. "Your report was quite a gripping read, Peacemaker Tudor."

"Please, call me Van." I turned to Gerhardt. "Forgive my ignorance, but I thought there were no formal relations between us and Unity."

Gerhardt gestured around. "We're having a surreptitious meeting aboard a ship that isn't mine, on the edge of a system that's rarely visited by anyone except Peacemakers, about a subject that transcends Guild jurisdiction by more than a few light-years. Does anything about this strike you as formal?"

Puris-Tar leaned forward. "Your report couldn't have come at a better time, Peace—ah, Van. We've been catching hints of some sort of espionage campaign underway in our space, as well as unusual movements of ships belonging to Group 41 along our borders. I'd been sent on an"—he grimaced in what I guess was a smile, but it was hard to tell on his Grinch-esque face—"informal mission to liaise with your Guild to see if we could start filling in some of the gaps."

He leaned back. "So imagine my surprise and delight when, little more than a standard day after my arrival on your Anvil Dark, your report arrives full of answers, including to questions we weren't even aware we should be asking."

"You're welcome?"

Perry immediately latched onto a crucial point. "In other words, what you're telling us is that you can effectively corroborate what the Sorcerer told us. And that means he was telling the truth. Have I got that right?"

I glanced at him, but his lack of any changing expression told me nothing. Was he saying that for my benefit, to make me feel better about strong-arming the Sorcerer into talking? For Gerhardt's, for much the same reason? Maybe Torina as well?

"It would certainly appear that way," Puris-Tar answered. "The question now is, what to do about it?"

I looked around and saw everyone was waiting for me to speak.

So I shrugged. "I secured the info. I'll leave the next steps to my superiors," I said in a rare moment of humble gallantry.

It was Gerhardt's turn to smile. "Don't worry, Tudor, we're not expecting you to come up with a solution. We are, however, expecting you to be part of one."

"That I can do. What did you have in mind?"

Puris-Tar once more leaned forward. "We're proposing to deal with this swiftly and efficiently. To that end, we are asking you to provide us with a list of those targets whose removal would be most likely to disrupt these nefarious plans. And then, we are going to remove them."

I exchanged glances with Torina. "And by remove, you mean—?"

"Why, kill them, of course. We are hoping that one decisive wave of assassinations across your known space will be able to stop this conspiracy before it can start doing any real, lasting damage."

Silence hung like the sword of Damocles, and no one made a sound. I looked at Gerhardt, expecting him to begin objecting. A series of raids and arrests were one thing. A wave of assassinations —of murders—was something else entirely.

But Gerhardt's expression was as unreadable as Perry's. But he wasn't surprised or taken aback, meaning that he'd known this was coming. Lunzy was the same.

I glanced at Torina and found yet another face set in flat, stony dispassion. It was like sitting in a room full of mannequins.

"Okay, since no one's going to mention the elephant twerking in the room, I will. Isn't that, like, illegal? You know, killing people without due process? Isn't there a word for that, begins with m, rhymes with holy shit you really want to just straight up murder a bunch of people?"

Gerhardt's face was impassive, save for some of his trademark chill. "Seeing you with a desire for accuracy is, to be blunt, refreshing."

"Refreshing?" I asked. If clarity was going to change my life and career, then it was damned sure going to impact Gerhardt. And often.

He turned to Lunzy, who handed me a data slate. A formal document glowed on the screen.

"That's a Special Instrument authorizing this operation, duly drafted and signed-off by the Masters. It's a recognition, Van, of the point you just raised," she said.

I skimmed the document, then transmitted it to Perry and handed it to Torina. "A recognition, and then a complete erasure of galactic law as I know it. Here. In this room. I've been given the power to... to make a call on whether someone lives or dies?"

"Under certain, very specific conditions, it does, yes. Those are normally related to things like periods of emergency or in order to forestall particularly egregious crimes. It's kind of like declaring martial law, but only with respect to the Special Instrument's restrictions."

I looked at Perry. "Uh... anything to add?"

"It's all in order, Van. A Special Instrument is perfectly legit. I'm not aware of one being issued for nearly three hundred years, though, so this is... definitely unusual."

I sank back in my seat, the moment's weight pushing on me in an unrelenting wave. The Special Instrument had named such targets as those specified by the principle Peacemaker assigned to the case—that is, me. Which meant I suddenly had the power to point at people, ships, or anything else I considered to be vital targets and mark them for destruction and death.

I needed to buy some time just to absorb this. "I'll have to approach this carefully. Any list *must* be researched. And double checked. Hell, triple checked, for that matter."

Gerhardt's face softened, if barely. "You'll also need to come to grips with what is being asked of you. And the fallout of that action. Or actions."

I stared at him. "That too." I paused, then added, "if I even can."

"Which is why you are the one I trust to do this, Tudor. For all your willingness to dodge and weave through the correct process, I never believed you were motivated by anything but a desire to do the right thing. Nor did I believe you had any intention of ever abusing your authority."

He leaned toward me. "In other words, the right person to deal with this unfortunate matter is you, precisely because you are reluctant to do it."

I offered a weak smile. "Well, if reluctance is a qualification, then you've definitely found your guy."

I SAT in the *Fafnir's* pilot's seat, staring out into the void. I remembered the first time I'd planted myself in this chair, right before Netty lifted us into a single orbit of Earth and me into a radically new understanding of the universe, and life, and what my future held.

It was a hell of a path from that moment of wide-eyed wonder to sitting in the same seat contemplating whom, exactly, I should kill.

"Van?"

I turned. Perry hopped into his accustomed place. "All of us AIs have put our virtual heads together, pored through all the available intel, and come up with a preliminary list of targets for you to review."

I nodded. "And this doesn't bother you?"

"Why would it?"

"Perry, this is—this is state-sanctioned murder."

"No, Van, it's not. Murder is, by definition, illegal. It requires two things—an act that results in a death and, to use the Earthly term, a mens rea, a guilty mind. The Special Instrument removes the latter."

"So, wave a magic wand and poof, it's not murder anymore?"

"Van, how many people have we killed in the course of this investigation?"

"Those people were out to kill us, Perry. Self-defense is a different matter."

"So killing a guy who broke into your house, clearly intending to kill you, is okay."

"It—yeah, it would be."

"You catch the same guy out in your front yard, his intent just as clear. Still okay?"

"I... guess."

"Now he's out on the street—"

I held up a hand. "Yeah, I see where you're going with this, Perry. The trouble is, where does it stop? At the moment the guy leaves his house? When he first clearly decides to kill me? When he first thinks about it?"

"You tell me."

I blinked.

"Now, let's bring in the whole idea of realpolitik—you know, the pragmatic reality of how the world works. The Sorcerers and the rest of the Trinduk, and Group 41, and maybe even the Victory Supernal have all clearly indicated their intentions to start attacking Unity. They intend to seize territory, kill Unity citizens, and scoop up more innocent people and use their horrific deaths as DLC for those damned Cusp machines of theirs."

He leveled his amber gaze right back at me. "I'll say it again. You tell me."

Netty spoke up. "Van, these are monstrous people intending to perpetrate *monstrous* crimes. Crimes Against Order, in fact, which are universally recognized as the most egregious of all. The reality is that waiting until they've actually started perpetrating them before taking action is saying that we're okay with a certain number of innocent lives being lost—or worse."

"There's another reality, too," a new voice said. Torina clambered into the cockpit and sat in the copilot's seat.

I gave her a lifted eyebrow. "What would that be?"

She shrugged. "They're going to go ahead and do this anyway. We can certainly choose to have no part of it, but we'll have no influence on the outcome and, realistically, no further involvement in this case."

I could only shake my head. "Really? After your reaction to our acting in the storage unit at Dregs, I'd have thought your objection to it a given."

She sighed. "Don't get me wrong, Van. I'm still deeply, deeply uncomfortable with all this. But I can't argue with the results of that acting, as you call it." She rubbed her eyes. "And yes, I'm really torn over using the results of our subterfuge to preemptively kill a bunch of people. But then my moral outrage smacks headlong into the reality of what happened to Schegith's people, and Fostin, the

Wu'tzur, and So-metz the S'rall princess—not to mention all the ones we couldn't save."

She crossed her arms. "Faced with that kind of barbarism, my moral outrage feels like a bit of a self-indulgent luxury, if you know what I mean."

I took her hands in mine, looking down at her slender fingers as I considered what she'd said. Torina neatly encapsulated my feelings not just about this targeting list for the Unity assassination effort, but everything B had said about the Galactic Knights Uniformed.

Sometimes there are things that need to be done, and in certain cases, the Guild isn't a viable option.

Except, as it turned out, the Guild could do at least some of those things, thanks to that Special Instrument. But wasn't that just a way of letting the Guild assuage its own moral outrage? What about all the times a Special Instrument would have been just as effective in saving lives but hadn't been used? Why did some people rate its preemptive protection but others didn't?

The GKU was the answer to that question. The worth of people's lives shouldn't depend on political—and too-often corrupt—machinations of the Peacemaker Guild.

I sat up, feeling the heft of my decision come to rest. There was no way out but through, and I knew it.

So I made the call.

"Okay, Perry, let's see that list."

24

We ended up selecting our top ten targets that, if taken out, would critically disrupt the plans of the Sorcerers and Group 41. After review by Gerhardt and Puris-Tar, that was reduced to eight targets. They both agreed that one on our list, a refueling depot near Unity space that had clearly fallen under the sway of Group 41, was just too public a target with too much risk of collateral damage. The other Gerhardt nixed, just as I knew he would.

"Jun Torol? The Satrap of the Seven Stars League? Really? Don't you think that condoning the assassination of a head of state might not be a little beyond the pale, Tudor?" Gerhardt asked.

I shrugged. "Actually, I do. But I was trying to make a point. We have to assume the League is effectively a hostile entity and deal with them accordingly."

"I don't disagree. But I think we'll stop short of turning a blind eye to killing off their leadership. That could set a precedent we really don't want to face down the road."

I agreed, but even as I did so I found myself wondering—was the charismatic Satrap with the perfect hair the real threat? He'd been reading from a prepared speech, after all, and I couldn't forget that restless, fidgeting woman in the background of his broadcast with the cold, reptilian eyes. I'd thought at the time that she might be the power behind the throne, as it were. Maybe Jun Torol wasn't the right target.

I refrained from saying this to Gerhardt. Not liking how someone looked in the background of a vid-cast wasn't much of a justification for putting her on a sanctioned hitlist.

When we reconvened aboard Lunzy's ship, Puris-Tar confirmed that of the eight final targets, his assets—clinical, antiseptic spook-speak for assassins—could deal with six of them. These were a pair of spies, one in the Seven Stars League and one in the Eridani Federation, both of whom were superbly positioned to disrupt any military response. The other four targets were ships linked through a tortuous series of ownership cells to Group 41, prepositioned as what Perry and the other AIs considered to be door-kickers.

"They're ready to launch immediate raids on key strategic targets, preempting the Unity response and buying time for their follow-on forces to converge and attack," Perry said.

Torina sniffed. "I'd call them cowards, but that's too simple. They're practical *and* cowardly."

Her flat, hard tone surprised me, but only for a moment. "I said I trust you to make good calls, Van. It's easier with evidence like this, isnt it? These people are showing intent. They're using planning to maximize death." Torina shook her head in disgust. "Someday, we'll be faced with a decision that will cost us a lot of sleep."

"But not this one?" I asked.

"Not with this level of depraved indifference toward life. No, this is simple, if not obvious," Torina said, her full lips pressed together in a bloodless line.

Zeno, who'd joined the discussion, just shook her head. "I find them most unappealing." She looked at me. "Your grandfather would have, too, Van. These are exactly the types of beings he devoted his life to stopping."

"Did he say that?" I asked. I always craved hearing words he'd spoken, like a broadcast from my own history.

Zeno thought, then spoke with care. "His exact words were *I'm gonna put those chicken shits in the ground*, or something almost like it."

I smiled, because that sounded *exactly* like Gramps. "Now I really hate them."

That left two targets. One was another of the door-kicker ships, but it was located in an unclaimed system on the edge of Schegith space. It was poised to take out a key comm station that was guarded by a small detachment of Unity Marines. The other was an apparent Group 41 agent in the Reticulum system, in the orbital station acting as the gateway to the interstellar Las Vegas, also known as Reticulum. The system was nominally unclaimed, but it effectively belonged to a crime syndicate called Mirror, who had grown into a full-fledged, legitimate corporation. His or her purpose for being in Reticulum wasn't entirely clear, but the system was a key waypoint for any possible known space intervention force that might be dispatched to help Unity. The gateway orbital station was the only facility big enough to refuel a large number of ships for three or four systems in any direction, so taking it offline would create a strategic bottleneck.

"Tudor, I'd like you to take out both of those targets, starting with that ship lurking on the edge of Schegith space," Gerhardt said.

"Me? I mean, us?"

"You alone have good relations with the Schegith, who have rebuffed all other diplomatic overtures. As for Reticulum, intelligence suggests that the Group 41 agent stationed there is most likely to attempt some form of cyberattack to cripple the orbital, and that's your area of expertise, isn't it?"

"On top of which, Van, we want to keep the circle of knowledge as small as possible for this operation, for obvious reasons," Lunzy added.

I sighed. "Okay, well, it's not like I had any other plans. So take out a class 9 ship, then go and hunt down and take out a potential cyber saboteur, have I got that right?"

"You have," Gerhardt replied.

"Cool. And just so it's absolutely clear, by take out, we mean—?"

"Preventing these two targets from taking hostile action against either Unity or any entity in known space, by whatever means necessary," Gerhardt replied, his voice flat, his intent ominously clear. "The instrument is hardly opaque, even if your current mindset towards this kind of work is—forming, let's say."

Holy shit, Gerhardt is GKU, I thought, because the martinet who loved paperwork was now directing me to take life, not preserve it.

I had another sinister surprise when I contacted The Hole, the Guild's prison barge orbiting sunward of us, to do some follow-up work with the Sorcerer who'd given us all this crucial intel.

"Sorry, Peacemaker Tudor, but there was an incident," The Hole's operations officer reported back via comm.

"What sort of incident?"

"Typical prison sort of incident. Someone decided they didn't like the look of him. Happens all the time. He's already drifting with the stars."

"You mean he's... dead?"

"Quite dead. I'm stunned he survived for ten seconds, given the blade they used on him. Peeled him like a... some kind of earth vegetable, I'm sure. Same with that other one you brought in with him—the Grendu, was it? Separate incident, while he was waiting extradition back to wherever the hell he came from. Union, something like that?"

"Wait. So you just had two high-value prisoners, who we only transferred to you a couple of days ago, killed? And you don't see that as strange?"

The Ops Office barked out a laugh. "We've got an average of one murder and a half-dozen serious assaults on inmates by other inmates a week. It's only by doing everything we conceivably can that we can keep the number that low."

"But—"

"If you want to complain, aim it at the Masters. The Hole is jammed to the overheads with prisoners. We've got twenty-six hundred on board when our capacity is rated at two thousand. Wanna get the numbers down? Give us another barge."

I signed off with a curse. The deaths of the Sorcerer and the Grendu weren't just convenient.

They were inevitable.

"You could've just stayed on Earth," I told myself, but that was a lie, and I knew it. When I pressed the remote and took ownership of the *Fafnir*, my world didn't shift.

It stopped being a world, and became a *galaxy*.

And now, my life had changed again, but this time, I was being pushed away from enforcing the law. I was about to start making permanent decisions over sapient lives, and doing it with the blessing of an organization far more powerful than my Guild.

I was a weapon now. And soon, I would be playing god.

I HESITATED ABOUT whether to contact Schegith and let her know we were going to run an operation on the edge of her space. On one hand, I felt she deserved to know, despite the fact that it didn't directly involve any of the space she claimed. On the other, there was the issue of operational security. I finally decided it was better to be upfront, since I trusted her implicitly anyway. I didn't give her any of the details, but she seemed to be okay with that, demonstrating an instinctive sense of what I was doing without asking a single question.

"This one understands that some things must not be shared," she said, then gave her blessing to the operation, and that was that. She also offered to assist, but I declined. The last thing I wanted to do was get her and her people implicated in this messy business.

We still had a practical problem. We had no idea how heavily armed our quarry, a class 9 cutter, might be. The *Fafnir* could punch hard for her mass, but a class 9 could, at least in theory, mount enough firepower to counter or even slightly overmatch us. Gerhardt had made it clear that he didn't want to involve Groshenko or anyone else outside the Guild, at least not for the time being. That left the *Iowa* as our only other option, but despite being heavily up-gunned, she still wasn't ready for a fight. Her two-person automation was enough to get her from point A to point B, but nothing close to an actual running battle.

"We need way better automation, and by better, I mean hold onto your ass when you see the price tag," Icky said.

"Or a crew, like Groshenko suggested," Torina added.

I shook my head. "Yeah, well, since we've got about two days of prep time, I'm going to say that finding a qualified crew that's also undergone all the requisite security checks ain't going to happen."

Netty came up with a stopgap solution.

"We showed that the *Fafnir* could perform—if not well, then adequately with that antimatter fuel pod strapped to her when we traversed that nebula," she said.

"True. I'm listening, Netty."

"A standard class 4 workboat is less massive than that pod. We could strap one to the *Fafnir* the same way, then use it as an auxiliary gun platform."

"Ooh, ooh, pick me to be the one who pilots an unarmored class 4 in a battle against a potentially dangerous adversary," Zeno said. "While I'm at it, why don't I put on a wet copper helmet and go stand out on a hilltop during a lightning storm?"

"Good of you to volunteer, Zeno," Netty replied.

"Is your sarcasm subroutine offline?"

"No, and I wasn't suggesting we crew it at all. We can operate it remotely, in semi-autonomous mode. I can copy a stripped-down version of myself into its flight management and fire control systems. Someone on board the *Fafnir* could do the piloting via comm link—Zeno."

She pushed up her lip, whiskers a-twitching, then nodded. "That's actually a damned good idea."

"Uh, Netty, what happens to you—or to the you aboard the workboat—if it gets destroyed?"

"It ceases to exist?"

"Is… that a problem? Losing a digital cousin?"

"If it bothers you, I won't copy my personality module over to the workboat."

I glanced at Torina, who shrugged. "I guess that'll work."

I wasn't sure why it made me uncomfortable if it didn't bother Netty. Probably because it made me think of clones, and how they were separate people from whoever had been cloned to create them.

I shook my head, dismissing it. I had enough moral quandaries and second-guessing going on without adding more of them to the pile.

Then a dolorous guitar chord filled the ship's comms, followed by a man singing something about his wife leaving him and taking their dog, but thankfully, she left his pickup behind.

Torina's eye twitched. "Netty. What *is* that?"

"A sad country song by legendary artist Cledus DuDrizzle. It's a classic," Netty answered cheerfully.

Torina made a new and interesting face, like she'd just tasted sour milk. "May I ask *why* you're subjecting us to this… *music*? And now, of all times?"

"If my cousin is going to die in battle, then I feel that we should have an appropriate soundtrack."

I held my hands up in surrender. "Don't look at me. I didn't pick it."

Icky was tapping her toe, grinning. "Kinda catchy. Does this

Cledus dude have a hammer?"

THE *FAFNIR'S* STEALTH COATING, made of thin, flexible sheets we'd seized from a miscreant we'd arrested, had taken a beating. We had no spares left, and we had enough gaps in the hull's coverage that we were now far from presenting a unified stealth profile. Still, the coverage we *did* have suppressed our scanner signature to the point where we were mostly invisible on the low-power nav systems most commonly used. Against more intense and higher-resolution fire control scanners, though, not so much. So we were still considerably harder to see. But once we *were* seen, we were easier to hit.

All of which was to say that we had to plan our approach to the class 9 lurking in the unnamed system bordering Schegith's space with care. I wanted us to get as close as possible, then deliver a devastating, all-out attack that would ideally disable or destroy our opponents before they could respond—and that included them making a break for it.

I tapped my chin and studied the tactical overlay, which was filled with data from our own passive scanners. It showed an icon that placed the class 9 in orbit among the debris making up the rings of a Saturn-like gas giant, which was a terrific hiding spot if you didn't know what you were looking for. We did, though. Even then, the signature was a weak one, the icon flickering as the returns waxed and waned.

"They're not twisting anywhere anytime soon, not that close to the planet. That gives us the luxury of some time," I said, musing aloud.

"True, unless they get their bug-out order to attack that Unity installation while we're futzing around trying to sneak up on them," Perry added.

I made a sound of agreement. It was a fair point. The Sorcerers and their Group 41 allies were obviously waiting for some event or set of conditions that would kick start their offensive against Unity. I suspected it was something internal, like espionage, sabotage to take a key command, control, and comms systems offline—maybe even a series of strategic assassinations to decapitate the leadership.

Whatever it was, we certainly had no control over it and could only work with what we knew.

"Netty, if we twist again to put the gas giant between us and them, then burn like hell to approach, then coast the rest of the way and slingshot our way around the planet, how long would it take for us to reach them?" I asked.

"Good question, boss. You're getting a pretty good head for this flying around in space stuff," she said.

"I've got a good teacher."

"Flattery will get you everywhere. Anyway, to answer your question, about nine hours. We can shave about thirty-three minutes off of that by doing a second slingshot around that big moon on the opposite of our current orbit. We'll be moving pretty damned fast relative to our bogey when we reach him, though. My math tells me we'd have about a two minute engagement window with the missiles and lasers, and about thirty seconds with the particle cannon. Same with the mass-driver, but unless we pass really close, it's going to be like trying to hit a road sign with a .22 while doing eighty on a county road."

"That's… quite a choice of analogies."

"I've been hanging around in Iowa too long, I guess. I'm *this* close to saying *ope* every time we pass by another ship."

"That's a synthesis of Wisconsin and Iowa, but I get you. Glad to know you're absorbing some of that good old Midwestern culture," I said, laughing. "So that's the plan. As long as these assholes don't decide to launch their operation while we're still en route, this should give us our best shot. Zeno, work with Netty to figure out the best way to employ that workboat we've got strapped to our belly."

"You know, Van, I've got a line on a docking module we can add to the *Fafnir* for cheap. Peacemaker Kntrza't just wants someone to buy out the lien from her at cost. Guess she needs some quick cash," Perry said.

"Not a bad idea. We could use a dedicated workboat," Torina said.

"Agreed. Put it on the to-do list. If it's still available when we get back to civilization, we'll go kick the tires. Anyway, Netty, let's get this show on the road, shall we?"

"Lighting the drive in three," Netty said as the *Fafnir* began to thrum.

Only Zeno broke the silence with an unusual growl of emotion. "Let's *go*."

We prepped the workboat for launch, then swept across the nightside of the vast gas giant, passing between planet and rings. Our trajectory took us so close to the planet that, for a time, it formed a flat plain devoid of anything but a hint of curve, an endless sweep of diffuse clouds shot through with spectacular blasts of lighting. Just one of the colossal discharges would have been a single bolt stretching from Los Angeles to Miami. The closeness of the gaseous surface also gave us something else we rarely had, a clear sense of our terrifying speed as it blurred past, but even *that* seemed wildly off scale due to the sheer size of the planet. Nothing about gas giants fit with my senses, and it was such a compelling sight, I had to force myself to watch the tactical overlay.

Sometime in the next minute, our target should be rising over that distant horizon, climbing into the stunning arc of a sunlit ring already slashing across space above us.

"Doesn't feel real," Torina mumbled.

"My eyes can't make sense of this," I agreed. "Can feel the Gs, though. Launch the boat, Netty. We're past the most dramatic part of this… jaunt."

Zeno resettled in her chair, wincing. "This grav is brutal. Right down to my bones."

Netty had planned the trajectory carefully—not lighting the drive until we had the planet between us and the class 9, then burning like hell straight at the gas giant's moon. We whipped around its barren, rocky surface and shot straight toward the ringed behemoth, then rode the cusp of its gravitation, stealing a miniscule bit of its rotational energy to boost us to an even more fearsome speed. Now traveling too fast for even the titanic planet to hold onto us, we were heading spaceward again, straight toward the rings where our quarry should still be orbiting, awaiting the launch of their evil venture against Unity.

It was masterful piloting—as long as it worked, of course. We'd only have that tiny engagement window before we overshot and raced back starward. So if we missed, we'd need a full day and a pile of fuel to bleed off our velocity and even hope to return and resume the fight. There was also a risk of catastrophic collision. We weren't going to pass through the ring but close enough to it that we might run afoul of stray chunks of rock or ice. At this velocity, it would be like driving a Formula One car at top speed into a stack of cinderblocks.

Yet again, I considered the sheer danger of space, which was neither empty nor benign, and when I made eye contact with Torina, I knew she was lost in the same thoughts. *Sure as hell hope this works*. Then her face brightened, and I knew we had our bogey.

"There he is," Torina said, pointing at the overlay. A red icon had popped onto it, marking the class 9's location. But instead of a docile orbit amid the ring debris, it was accelerating away from the gas giant atop a plume of fusion exhaust.

I squeezed the armrest. "He must have made us."

"I don't think so. His trajectory is consistent with a trip out to a twist point," Netty said.

"They might have gotten their go code," Perry added.

Sure enough, the class 9 was outbound, but at a fairly sedate pace. He wasn't burning like he was trying to escape or evade, just make a fuel-efficient trip out to the closest place he could twist.

"Netty, can we still intercept him?" I asked.

"A full burn directly away from the gas giant for thirty seconds will deflect our course enough to roughly maintain our planned closest-approach distance. There's only one problem," she replied.

I nodded, because I'd been doing this stuff long enough to start visualizing these trajectories in my head. "We're going to have to pass right through the ring, instead of staying between it and the planet."

"Do I even want to know what the risk is of us hitting something?" Torina asked.

"If you feel you need to ask the question, then the answer is probably no," Perry said.

"Not very helpful, bird," I said. "Not that I particularly want to know, either, but Netty, can you give us at least a ballpark estimate?"

"The probability of hitting any debris is one hundred percent. However, about ninety percent of that debris is gravel-sized particles or smaller, which will do some damage, but probably nothing too serious. The remaining ten percent of particles are the ones larger than that, up to a few the size of mountains. Hitting one of those would definitely leave a scratch or two."

"Bottom line it for us please, Netty."

"This is most definitely ballpark, but I'd estimate a ninety percent chance we take superficial to minor damage, about a twenty percent chance we take major damage, and a three to five percent chance we suffer a catastrophic hit. And not to increase everyone's stress levels, but we have to make this decision within the next fifty seconds and start burning, or we won't be able to intercept at all."

"Shit." I glanced around. "Everyone feeling lucky?"

"If someone offered you a bowl with a hundred candies in it and told you five of them were poisonous, would you eat one?" Zeno asked.

"Depends. What sort of candy are we talking about? Because if they're Falaxian spice drops, then yeah, I'd totally take one," Icky replied.

"I… don't think you quite got my point, Icky."

I had to smile, but it sure as hell didn't last. I looked at Torina.

Her reply was simple. "If we don't do this, then we're basically saying those twenty-nine Unity Marines are probably going to die."

I smiled again. "You really have a way of cutting right to the chase. Netty, let's turn and burn."

"ONE MINUTE to what roughly constitutes the edge of the rings. Just like Saturn, this ring system has denser and sparser concentric sections, so I've got us and the workboat passing through one of the latter. We're passing through them at a fairly shallow angle, so our transit time is going to be about twenty seconds."

I nodded. "Everyone brace yourselves for the longest twenty seconds of your life."

We'd done everything we could—suited up, put helmets on, and strapped in, plus the cabin was already depressurized to prevent an explosive decompression if we did take a bad hit. As an added precaution, Icky suggested we flip around and pass through the ring debris tail first, with the drive lit, using the incandescent plasma to vaporize most of what we encountered before we hit it.

"Thirty seconds," Netty said, firing the thrusters and rotating both the *Fafnir* and the workboat a hundred and eighty degrees, then lighting both ships' drives.

I heard someone muttering, like they were… reciting a prayer? It sounded like Zeno.

"Zeno, you alright?"

"What? Oh, yeah. I'm just reciting an old prayer to the P'nosk god of fortune."

"I… didn't take you for a religious person."

"I become very religious when someone asks me to take candy out of the bowl that might be poisoned."

I smiled at that. I'd never been particularly devout myself, but at times like this I could certainly see the appeal—

Something banged into the *Fafnir* like a gunshot. I winced and squeezed the armrests in a deathgrip. The rhythmic rush of blood in my ears seemed to beat out a rhythm, a syncopation of heart-beats and fear and time that slowed to a maddening trickle of distant *thumps*. I could only keep hoping that the next swish of my pulse wasn't also the very last one—

There was another bang, harder, enough to make the *Fafnir* shake with the impact and the detonation of at least two REAB modules. I saw some systems go yellow on the status board, and one red—the thruster cluster I'd been working on when I blew out my knee had just been ripped off the *Fafnir*. That triggered a sudden, stupidly incongruous thought—had anyone ever retrieved the align-ment gauge I left clamped onto it? Because those gauges weren't cheap—

"We're through," Netty said.

We inflated our suits a bit with exhaled breaths as the stress mounted with each passing second. Netty cut the drive and flipped the *Fafnir* and the workboat, which had also survived, around to face the departing class 9. Our own fusion exhaust plumes had blinded us to whatever it was doing while we bashed through the rings. Now we saw it directly ahead—

Along with a swarm of missiles, every one of them streaking toward us at murderous speed.

25

"INCOMING! WEAPONS HOT!" I shouted.

Torina opened up with the lasers, her reflexes nearly machine-like in timing. The incoming missiles immediately began to dodge and weave, reconfiguring their formation as they approached to accommodate any that Torina hit. Of the twelve—*twelve*—missiles that had launched, she'd taken down four. I didn't need Netty's ability to instantly calculate probabilities to know that we were going to be hit.

"Military grade," Zeno snapped, hammering at her console. "Van, next time we upgrade the ship, we should give some serious thought to a decent ECM suite. This off-the-rack stuff we've currently got sucks."

"As of this second, it's on the wishlist," I said, my mind racing. Our ECM suite, a package of emissions intended to jam missiles and tracking systems was... let's say basic and leave it at that. It was an expensive system to upgrade, which made not upgrading it seem like a fiscally responsible move.

Until now.

I shifted my attention from the instruments to the overlay, and back and forth, over and over. I asked if anyone had ideas, but they didn't. Meanwhile, the swarm of red incoming missile icons drew inexorably closer toward the pair of blue ones that represented the *Fafnir* and the workboat—

A pair of blue icons. But we were only one of them.

I feathered the screen, taking manual control of the workboat. The instruments in front of me immediately changed, becoming the workboat's primary console. I jammed its drive to full power, then flicked back to the *Fafnir* and slammed the side stick forward. The starscape blurred as the ship flipped over. I yanked the side stick back when our ass end was just short of being pointed at the enemy class 9, then ramped our drive to full power. The workboat shot forward, rapidly pulling out in front of us.

But I wasn't done. I switched back to the workboat and snapped its active scanners to full power. I stayed with it, activating its single point defense battery while snapping out shots from its laser as fast as the weapon could cycle.

Twenty seconds passed, then a quartet of missiles bracketed it, detonating nearly simultaneously. It vanished into a cloud of confetti-like debris.

But now, only five missiles remained inbound to the *Fafnir*. I grabbed the sidestick and instead of flipping the *Fafnir* again, I rotated her ninety degrees to port and accelerated against our course. The missing thruster cluster made her movements sluggish, but Netty did her best to compensate. With our exhaust plume no longer obscuring the class 9, our point-defenses opened up on the remaining missiles. Zeno took control of the particle cannon and added its fearsome firepower to theirs. Torina, in the meantime, fired a spread of missiles at the class 9, then went rapid fire with the laser batteries.

One of the incoming missiles wove its way through our defenses and detonated close enough to do some minor damage, including a hole punched through us somewhere aft that would have caused a decompression. The class 9, apparently inspired by our rapid succession of maneuvers, tried to slew its own fusion exhaust up and down, side to side, to put off our missiles while pouring brief bursts from its own point-defense. They'd have been better off to just keep their exhaust pointed straight at us because the changing target aspect gave Torina the openings she needed. She landed a hit with the laser, then another, then two more. A fifth hit killed the class 9's drive in a surgical strike that left glowing slag trailing away from their engine bell.

Torina lined up again, then hissed in satisfaction when she scored a *sixth* hit, piercing the enemy ship through and through.

Her power emissions dropped, leaving her coasting more or less dead. I started to tell the crew to get ready to board her—but I stopped myself. We weren't here to risk our lives taking prisoners. Our mandate, per the Guild's Special Instrument, was clear.

I turned to Torina. "I'll finish them—" I said, then cut off as the class 9 abruptly blew apart in a searing pulse of light. She'd lost her antimatter containment, which could have been hard on us if we weren't speeding away from her at such a ferocious rate. We got hit with a brief wave of high-energy gamma rays that exposed all of us to about the equivalent of a chest x-ray, and that was that.

I slumped back in the seat, suddenly aware I was sodden with sweat inside my b-suit. It trickled down my forehead, and I moved to wipe it before it reached my eyes—and effectively punched my own helmet.

"Smooth, dear," Torina said, one lip curled in a wicked grin.

"Especially coming from the pilot who just did *all that*. Van, have to admit, those were superb choices," Netty said.

"Seconded. When did you become such a space ace?" Zeno asked.

I shrugged. "I... honestly don't know. It all just kind of came to me, I guess, sort of unfolding like a puzzle in reverse. Cost us the workboat, though—which means we now owe the Guild a workboat, I guess, since that one was just a requisition.``

"Nah. It was lost in the course of performing a legitimate duty, and under a Special Instrument yet. The Guild'll pick up the tab," Perry replied.

"Not to mention there are twenty-nine Unity Marines who'd probably be willing to take up a collection to help pay for it," Torina said.

"Yeah. Too bad, though. It was a perfectly good workboat."

"Hey, give a keel, save a keel," Netty said. "In this case, mine."

Icky and Zeno unstrapped to head back and do some damage control, particularly to restore hull integrity so we could repressurize the ship. More sweat trickled into my eyes, so I blinked furiously to lessen the sting. "Still, sorry about the version of you that died with the workboat, Netty."

"Just a distant cousin, boss. Like I said, I never copied over my personality module. I don't consider that to have been me but something more like Waldo."

"If you're okay with it, so am I," I said, then held up a finger. "I do have a request, Netty?"

"More sad country songs? Coming right up, Van."

"Actually, I was thinking the opposite was in order. How about we just bask in the glow of our victory and leave Cledus on hold for a bit?"

Zeno reached into her thigh pocket and pulled out a ten-bond note, then handed it to me with a wink. "Good call, boss. Have a drink on me."

WE DIDN'T HAVE time to savor the win. With Zeno and Icky still patching things up, we set course for Reticulum and our second target, the mysterious hacker.

The trip there was uneventful. We twisted into the system and found nothing but the usual traffic, mostly people with too much time and money on their hands inbound on their way to gamble and debauch it away—or sheepishly outbound, having just done that. At the sight of a Peacemaker, a few ships made abrupt changes of trajectory, but we ignored them. We had more important work to do here than round up petty criminals, and candidly, my inclusion in the GKU changed who and what I considered to be priority targets.

Which meant our focus had to be on the Sorcerers and their co-conspirators, and the operative they'd planted on the Reticulum orbital. Sabotage was the only obvious goal, but with a massive, complex system like Reticulum, there were limitless opportunities to disable the orbital and thus remove it from any action.

As soon as the traffic control AI contacted us, I went straight to pulling out my credentials and declaring a state of emergency. A live controller replaced the AI, and I started to explain the situation, but he cut me off.

"I've got two people here waiting for you. They say they're from Unity." He gave me a comm channel to contact them, then a docking port we could use. While Netty handled getting us into the pattern and lined up to dock, I switched to the specified channel. It immediately did a handshake with the encryption module Puris-Tar had given us, then opened the link. The image of another Grendu appeared.

"Peacemaker Tudor, I'm Gauren-Kas. Puris-Tar said I should use the recognition code Des Moines to ID myself to you."

I nodded. "Good to meet you. He wasn't sure whether he could proposition you guys or not in time—"

"Just in time, as it turns out. The conspirators launched their operation just a few hours ago, right about the time we started our operation against them. We're not sure if that was their planned start or if we goaded them into it. In any case, we've taken out five of eight targets so far—"

"We took out that ship intending to attack your comm relay station."

"Okay, six of eight targets. It hasn't stopped them, but it's definitely screwed them up and slowed them down."

"Music to my ears. What's the situation here?" I asked.

"We only just got here ahead of you. We've asked the Sovran Brigade aboard the orbital to keep an eye out for any unusual activity, but that's it."

I nodded. "We'll be docking in about ten minutes. See you then."

We met Gauren-Kas and his colleague, another Grendu, in a remote corner of the docking concourse. Like the domed pleasure city on the planet below, disused parts of the orbital were ritzy, even ostentatious. It reminded me of Vegas or any number of other tourist traps back on Earth—luxurious and mostly clean but with a garish, over-the-top edge.

"We have no idea where the enemy agent is, other than somewhere aboard," Gauren-Kas said, his tone apologetic. I shrugged it off.

"So we need to find him. Netty, any ships at dock right now that might be considered suspicious?"

"This is Reticulum, Van. It would be faster for me to give you a list of ships that *aren't* suspicious, which includes the *Fafnir*. And that's it," she said.

I gave a rueful smile. We'd left Zeno and Icky aboard the *Fafnir* to keep her flight-ready, in case we had to bug out fast. Although, in Icky's case, it was as much to keep her out of sight. She stood out in a crowd, but we'd chosen to stay more circumspect, dressing in civvies like the two Grendu had. The sight of a Peacemaker uniform risked spooking our bad guy, who could be anywhere aboard—even watching us now. Hence, I wore a coat, while Torina had clad herself in a jumpsuit with a tool harness borrowed from Zeno. Tucked away in a pouch was her trusty sidearm, and the two of us were as nondescript as could be, right down to what Torina called *sensible boots*.

"So how do we track this guy down? There're thousands of

people aboard this orbital right now, and they're in motion. Makes a single target that much harder to pin," Torina observed.

She was right. The Reticulum orbital was a small city in space, having expanded over the years to accommodate more and more people who didn't want to make the trip to the surface to get laid and lose all their money.

It was time to channel my inner villain. It was how I'd approached cyber-ops back on Earth, and it seemed to apply here as well, among the throngs of people engaged in everything I'd seen before—and a few things that were immoral, illegal, and new to me.

"Creatively criminal, aren't they?" I murmured.

A true celebration of all things unsavory, Perry answered in my ear bug.

I stared down the concourse. "Well, he wants to shut this orbital down, make it completely unusable, right? The surest way of doing that would be by destroying it. And the surest way of doing that would be docking a ship and setting it to lose fusion or antimatter containment."

Which he might have already done, and the clock's ticking, Perry said.

"Thanks, bird. I needed a reminder that we could all go poof at any second."

Any time, Van. I'm a helper.

I tapped my chin, continuing to mumble. "But I somehow don't think that's it. If it were, there's no reason he wouldn't have done that already, that we wouldn't have already arrived to find the orbital and the agent both long gone."

On top of that, the Sorcerers may not want to destroy this orbital. If it's a good staging point for operations against them, it's a good staging point for operations of their own, Netty added.

"Right. In fact—" I stared at the deck, letting my thoughts flow along like water, following the path of least resistance to getting what I wanted—which was disabling this orbital. But was that all? Again, I went back to the idea of just blowing the thing up. It would be simple, efficient, and reliable. So I wanted to keep it intact and usable, but—

"Van?"

I blinked and looked at Torina. "What?"

"You've been staring into space and mumbling away to yourself."

"Yeah, sorry, it's how I chew through these issues. Well, that and talking to Netty and the bird. I keep coming back to some fundamental points. What do the Sorcerers want? What's their endgame for this place?"

"To disable it but keep it intact," Gauren-Kas replied. "At least, that's what we're assuming."

"Yeah. But if I'm a Sorcerer, I'm greedy and like inflicting the maximum harm possible. I'm a vicious, amoral dickhead for whom simple victory isn't enough. I need it to be *seen*. How could I do that? Destroy the orbital, sure, that's big and showy, but it's also a one-and-done. Cripple the orbital and I accomplish my goal, but that's all. So what if I cripple it in the most horrible way possible? What would that be?"

"Some sort of chemical agent? Or a virus?" Torina suggested.

"Maybe. But it's also complicated, requires some specialized contraband I have to sneak aboard, and would just end up with the orbital being quarantined. I want something bigger that's going to trigger a crisis response. Like you said, there are thousands of people aboard, and if they had to be evacuated—"

"So, shut down water purification—" Gauren-Kas said, but I shook my head.

"No. Air. Disable the air processing systems. You create a crisis, and an awful one. One that's going to require the ships and resources of Reticulum and every nearby system to deal with. That accomplishes my goal and ties up my enemies in a big way, both at once."

"Okay, so let's say it's the air. How do you disable the air processors on a station this big? There must be dozens, maybe hundreds of units scattered all around it."

"We're after a hacker, remember?" I said, starting to walk. "Come on. I need access to a terminal."

IT TOOK us a while to persuade the Reticulum authorities to give us access to their core systems. With each passing second, I was keenly aware that the hacker, wherever they were, could do serious and irreparable harm to the orbital's air processing system, or any number of other systems if that was their intent. It finally took a combination of me pulling Peacemaker rank, the Grendu warning of a diplomatic incident if they didn't cooperate, and the specter of the orbital's breathable air being limited to whatever it currently contained to get them to budge.

I got into the face of an officious Sovran Brigade orbital manager, a Gajur who was trying to project an air of competency—and failing.

"All the ships currently here can take off, what, maybe a couple of thousand people? And you've got probably ten times that on board, at least? Fifty times that? More?" I growled.

"Not to mention that the only place those people could go is down to your domed city. You'd better hope they aren't planning some sabotage down there, too," Torina said, and the Gajur finally gave up.

"Fine. My assistant here will give you access. But I'm going to have my people monitoring—"

"If *your people* impede our work, you're going to see a different side of my sparkling personality," I told the Gajur in flat tones.

"Mine too. But when I toss some busybody out an airlock, I'll *monitor* them as they drift away," Torina said, wearing an impossibly bright smile.

The Gajur wasn't used to a unified front, or more specifically an *aggressive* unified front. So he said, simply, "Fine," before stalking off in a low-g huff.

The manager's assistant took me to a terminal in an outer office, then logged in with full access to the orbital's core systems. Despite this system being so advanced it made Earth tech look like a sundial, I immediately saw a half-dozen flaws in their security protocols.. It turned out the technology could advance by light-years, but the psychology behind its design didn't even come close to keeping up. Human nature, or rather sentient nature, was a persistent flaw that could hamstring even the most elegant of technological designs.

"Perry, lend me a—hand, wing, whatever," I said.

He hopped onto the desk and extended a data probe. Torina snickered.

Perry and I both shot her a glance.

"Really, Torina? Is there no time that a boner joke is inappropriate?" Perry asked.

"I can't think of one."

Perry stared at her, then turned back to the terminal. "Now that you mention it. . .."

"See? Good material *always* has a place and time," Torina said with the air of someone proven right.

"If you two are done, can we get back to saving the world?" I asked, with superb patience and self-control despite the fact they were probably right. After pulling out the set of data-port adapters Perry had me bring, I selected one and plugged it into the terminal, then let Perry connect and get access. He immediately painted the screen with a schematic of the orbital's core systems.

"We want air processing," I said. "You can ignore the rest for now."

He obliged, switching to a new schematic. I studied it.

"Okay, it looks like the data net controlling the core systems is physically separate from the other nets," I said, then noticed a convergence. I pointed. "Except right there. The docking controller has a link to all the core systems. That is an achilles heel if ever I saw one."

"That's so it can adjust the demands on the air processors according to the number of people actually aboard," the orbital manager's assistant said. "It extends the life of the filters and purifiers, which—"

"Saves money, yeah, I know. I swear, every major security hole I've ever found either had something to do with saving money, or boners," I said, touching the screen to slide and rotate the schematic.

"So we're back to that again, I see," Torina said, but I shook my head.

"There are far too many paths for our bad guy to get access, so chasing that angle's going to be a dead end." I bit my lip for a moment. "Okay, so if I were going to shut down the air processors, how would I do it?"

Perry and I spent the next few minutes looking for bottlenecks, places we could shut the system down in a way that would make it almost impossible to bring back online, at least not without a lot of time and work. We finally identified four likely candidates—two AI-controlled routers that directed the flow of air through the purifiers, and two emergency systems designed to shut the system down to prevent the dispersion of things like noxious gases or pathogens. Each pair of bottlenecks was a redundancy.

And redundancies are my specialty. There's nothing like a triple stack of pointless code to let me creep up the back stairway, so to speak. Programmers think they're careful, designers think they're thorough, and guys like me think it's a national holiday when we see layers of security piled in one easy-access point.

It's like they were asking for it. "Perry, how many bonds did they save by doing it this way?"

He replied with the kind of glee that only a morally righteous blowhard can muster, drawing himself up with great dignity.

"Thirteen," Perry said.

"Million?" the assistant manager asked, but Perry waggled his head, slowly.

"Just thirteen. Not hundred, either. *Thirteen*. It's like they used a coupon code for their entire system," Perry said, doing his very best *not angry, just disappointed* tone.

The assistant manager's face fell. "Oh."

"Oh, indeed. Let me look before you run howling into the accounting department, okay?" I said, then tapped the display to bring up the detailed schematics and access logs for each. I decided to start with the flow controllers because they were less protected and easier to access. The access logs showed no obvious intrusions, although there had been a diagnostic run on one of them just a couple of hours ago—

I zeroed in on that log entry, finding it to be a diagnostic, and nothing more. Beyond that moment, the log recorded no access attempts at all. But if the diagnostic had been the access attempt—

"Perry, bring up a list of every piece of software running on this flow controller here," I said. He did, and I scanned the list. There were dozens and dozens of processes running, most of them meaning absolutely nothing to me. But I didn't care about that. I only cared about processes that were, in turn, accessing the network—

"There." I pointed at the screen. "That one, right there, is sending data out of the flow controller. Perry, chase it—"

"To wherever it's going. On it, boss," he said. A moment passed, which for Perry meant a huge amount of effort.

"Yeah, this is convoluted, but I can trace data packets through the water purifying system and a power-distribution controller to that emergency shutdown unit, right there," he finally said, high-lighting one of the other pairs of critical subsystems.

"Well, what do you know," I said, calling up the logs for it. It showed an intrusion in progress, originating at a terminal in the docking concourse.

"We've got him," Gauren-Kas said, starting to turn away. But I stopped him.

"No, I don't think we do. That was too easy to track down."

"Maybe that's the point," the Grendu replied.

I shrugged. "I could buy that if it didn't give his location away so clearly. See, this is the reality of hacking. Maybe three-quarters of it is about computers and software. The other quarter is all mind games. Perry, check all the processes running on this emergency shutdown unit. See if there's anything funny about them."

"Funny?"

"Yeah. Not funny-funny, funny-strange. Meanwhile, I'm going to look at the redundant unit."

Perry and I each did our thing. I could feel the tension mounting in the room as it became ever more clear that there actually was a hacker, and that they had managed to access critical systems, and that we might already be too late. But I forced myself to ignore it. I was looking for something to suggest an intrusion into the second emergency shutdown unit, the one that had apparently been left alone.

"Van, I found your funny-strangeness," Perry said. "All these processes here are running as normal in this emergency shutdown, but these ones that look like they are, aren't. They're doing something else."

"Of course they are. I'll bet they're preventing the thing from operating, aren't they?"

"They—are, yeah. This thing's offline. Do you want me to try and get it running again?"

"Nope. For one, you're going to find it really hard to do that, maybe even impossible. For another, you'll definitely give us away."

"So why would he take that emergency shutdown unit offline but not trigger it? Has it shut the system down?" the manager's assistant asked.

"Because that's not his target. This second one is. He just needed to disable that one and take it completely offline so it can't be redundant to the other one." I spoke as I studied the processes running on the second shutdown unit. Damn. Everything seemed fine. This hacker, whoever they were, was good. Or, alternatively, I was completely wrong and this was the most wild of goose chases—

No. There. I found a process whose use of system resources was swinging rapidly up and down.

"Perry, I want to look at that process right there, but let's make it totally passive, okay?"

"Gimme a second."

We waited. I could feel everyone gritting their teeth. A single process among dozens appearing to behave strangely might mean nothing. I knew nothing about that particular process or what it was for, but it stood out. After all, these emergency shutdown units should just be operating in standby mode, passively awaiting a sudden command to shut the air purifiers, pumps, ventilator fans, and the rest of the system down.

"Got it. That process is actually being accessed from a terminal located in someplace called Unprocessed Sanitation Dump," Perry said.

I looked at the manager's assistant. "There's a certain amount of waste that can't be recycled or reprocessed, so it gets taken there, compacted into dump modules, then shot into a stellar orbit that'll eventually decay and fall into the star, Reticulum."

I stood. "Garbage dump, got it.We pick the most romantic places for crime, don't we? Where is it?"

"Bottom-most deck, sternward—"

"Perry, buy us some time, try to keep him busy without him knowing you are." I turned to the assistant, checking The Drop and the Moonsword under my coat. "Let's go. And one more thing—"

"Yes?

"Whatever happens, when we confront this... person... do *not* get in front of me."

26

THIS PART of the orbital clearly wasn't intended for the guests. It was more typical of a well-used ship—dimly lit, the bulkheads and decks stained and grubby, exposed pipes, cables and conduits snaking off in every direction. The assistant took us to a blast door marked Sanitation Dump—Unprocessed—Authorized Personnel Only, beneath which was a warning about the space beyond the door being subject to depressurization. That meant the blast door was actually the outer barrier of an airlock.

I glanced back. The assistant manager had summoned a security detail, four heavily armed guards. They moved together in a martial efficiency, along with Gauran-Kas and his compatriot. Everyone was in full battle rattle, their faces set in grim expressions that revealed they weren't just armed to the teeth.

They were *itching* for a fight.

It wasn't a straight-up firefight that worried me. I wanted to take our hacker out before he had a chance to do anything that might obscure his digital tracks. It wasn't enough to know that he was out of action—we also had to be sure he hadn't planted any malware that might take effect even if he was dead. To that end, I wanted to seize the terminal he was using intact and unchanged.

"How do you want to do this?" Torina asked.

I stared at the imposing door. "I don't want to do it at all. But if we have to, I guess…"

My voice trailed off as the words under Authorized Personnel Only sank in.

This space is subject to depressurization during dump cycles. Obey all warnings and do not enter if in doubt.

I tapped the comm. "Perry, update?"

"My confidence level's dropping here, Van. Sometime in the next couple of minutes, he's going to realize I've been leading him on, making him think he's injecting malware into the unit's core processes when it's just going into a sandbox of protected memory I created. Once he does, all bets are off."

I stared at the door.

This space is subject to depressurization during dump cycles.

"Perry, can you access the dump system? The one used to shoot unprocessed waste into space?"

"Yeah, it's not protected—oh."

I took a breath. What I was about to ask Perry to do was, if not murder, then an execution. It was exactly the sort of thing Gerhardt would have used to investigate and possibly court martial me not that long ago.

I glanced at the assistant. "Is there likely to be anyone else in there?"

He shook his head. "There shouldn't be. If there is, the airlock should be open and locked in a preventive position—" He stopped, getting it. "No, there shouldn't be."

I felt Torina looking at me and turned to her.

"Special Instrument, remember?"

She nodded, once.

"Okay, Perry, do it."

He didn't respond. Instead, a shrill alarm sounded and a pair of lights flashed over the blast door. A faint, distant rumble followed, then quickly died away.

And that was it.

"Okay, Perry, repressurize it and open it up."

I drew The Drop, which signaled everyone else to draw and ready their weapons. We waited for the pressure indicator to show the atmosphere was equalized on both sides of the lock. When it did, the inner and outer doors slid open. The security detail charged in, boarding shotguns at the ready. Torina and I followed, with Gauren-Kas and the other Grendu right behind us.

The waste dump system was in the process of moving another module into place from a rack of empties, to replace the one it had just dumped. I heard the security guards shouting over the hum and whine of working machinery.

"Clear left!"

"Clear right!"

The detachment commander, a gruff Nesit, turned to us. "All clear."

I hurried over to the only visible terminal. Sure enough, it showed an intrusion in progress. But it wasn't the screen that caught my eye. It was the thing wedged into a gap on the edge of the terminal's case.

A bloody fingernail, ripped out at the root, testament to a desperate but ultimately futile attempt to hang on as the compartment opened to space.

Torina turned away, her face gone bone white, but I walked over, removed the fingernail, and gave it a casual examination.

And then I dropped it.

Perry tilted his head, then spoke. "Are you—disregard. That's irrelevant. I know you're not alright. Are you at least functional?"

I gave it some thought. "Yes. This was never going to be all swashbuckling and repartee." I glanced at where the nail had wedged and saw a small scar in the terminal cover. "Perry?"

"Yes, Van?"

"I think this is the last stage of adulthood, at least in this profession."

"I'd say you're right," he agreed.

I sighed, staring at everything and nothing. "Right now, it sucks. But it also hurts."

"That's why you have friends, Van. To spread it around and make your burden lighter. Now, one last question?"

"Sure."

"Can you do this all over again?"

"So he was trying to shut down the air purifiers and asphyxiate everyone but ended up being sucked into space himself? You wield irony like a blade, Tudor," Gerhardt said over the comm.

I shifted in the *Fafnir's* pilot's seat and shrugged. "Right? Total orchestration on my part."

"Of course it was. In any case, well done completing the two assignments given to you. That makes seven of the eight that were successfully carried out. It appears to have provoked the Sorcerers and their conspirators into attacking targets both inside and outside Unity."

I frowned. "So… did any of what we did end up making any difference?"

"Absolutely. The attacks have been sporadic and uncoordinated. Some have even assaulted targets clearly meant to be left vulnerable by some of the attacks we did thwart, meaning they struck intact and prepared defenses. We managed to preempt and disrupt the conspiracy across the board—thanks to the information you extracted from that Sorcerer you captured."

I nodded. "Yeah. The one that ended up dead right after we transferred him to The Hole."

"We don't generally imprison people for being too kind and gentle."

I spent a couple of heartbeats trying to study Gerhardt's face for a hint of what he might have known. Had he been surprised about the Sorcerer's death in custody? Had he known it was going to happen? Had he been involved? He was a Master, so he presumably knew something about the secretive Galactic Knights Uniformed. Was he one of them? Because killing the Sorcerer to prevent word of his effusive testimony from getting back to the conspiracy sounded exactly like the sort of thing they'd do.

"If I had to guess, I'd say he was killed by his compatriots before he could reveal anything else—which is unfortunate, because your report suggests that he might have known even more."

I waved that off, but gently. "Honestly, I wasn't even sure if what he had told us was true. Until the Unity agents corroborated most of it, I wondered if he'd just told us things he thought we might want to hear."

"And that, Tudor, is the problem with coerced information—"

Netty cut in. "Van, we have a problem." As she spoke, the tactical overlay came to life, painting a jarring picture. Eight red icons had popped onto it, each a ship inbound at high speed and roughly matching configurations known to be used by the Sorcerers.

"Uh, Master Gerhardt, gotta go. We've got a flotilla of incoming bad guys. Eight of them. It looks like they mean to destroy this orbital one way or another."

"Suggesting it's crucial to their plans. It would be interesting to know why."

"I can ask them if you like."

"I'm dispatching everything I can to assist you, Tudor," Gerhardt said, then frowned offscreen. "Unfortunately, it looks like you'll be on your own for at least five or six hours."

I didn't have to do any calculations to see the grim truth. "It'll be decided long before then."

"Tudor—" Gerhardt started, then stopped. "Van, you're not obligated to confront eight-to-one odds. Your mission was already a success."

I stared at the overlay. The inbound ships would be in range to bring the orbital under effective fire in about three and a half hours.

Eight-to-one odds.

"We're going to do what we can," I finally said. "We'll try not to get ourselves killed in the process, but I'd hate to have saved this place from an ugly, lingering death just to lose it in a violent cataclysm. Lotta innocents on this flying deck."

Gerhardt stared out of the screen for a moment, then nodded. "Understood. We'll get help there as soon as we can. Good luck, Tudor."

Back to my last name, which meant back to business. Later, assuming I survived the next few hours, I'd let myself be warmly surprised at that moment of actual, personal connection between Gerhardt and me.

I fought the urge to salute and went for a single nod of thanks. Gerhardt understood. It was time to go to work. "We're going to need it. *Fafnir* out."

I BRIEFED the crew as we were getting underway. I'd told Netty to burn as hard as she could to give us the highest possible closing speed with the approaching Sorcerers. It meant we'd have a head-on engagement with a brief, fast pass, so we had to do the maximum damage possible in that limited window. There wasn't time for any more sophisticated maneuvering than Charge!

"Kind of reminds me of Joshua Chamberlain at the Battle of Gettysburg," Perry said, and we all turned to him.

"Joshua Chamberlain? No? Van, it's one of the most dramatic moments of your whole Civil War."

"Pretend I'm not familiar with it, which should be easy, because I'm not."

"Joshua Chamberlain, Colonel, commander of the regiment designated the 20th Maine in the Union Army. On the second day of the Battle of Gettysburg, his regiment was holding the extreme left flank of the entire Union army, on a key hill called Little

Round Top. His regiment was attacked again and again by the opposing Confederate forces and would eventually have to give way. If he had, it would likely compromise the Union flank and the entire army. He couldn't retreat, and his troops were virtually out of ammunition so he couldn't just stand, so he ordered a charge."

"Let me guess—he saved the day but died heroically in the attempt?"

"Nope. Well, he did save the day, but he survived, was awarded the Medal of Honor, ended up being promoted to General, served twelve years as Governor of Maine, and died at the ripe old age of 85," Perry replied. "The old boy was kicking for a good long while."

"So… what you're offering, bird, is some hope that we're going to survive this?" Zeno asked.

"I… was going to say that it shows that sometimes the best strategy is to attack regardless of the odds, but if that makes you feel better, then yes, that's exactly what I meant, absolutely!"

Torina rolled her eyes. "I'm convinced."

"I'm not worried about a medal or becoming governor of anywhere or living to 85. Just my next birthday would be nice. But I agree about the attacking part. There are thousands of lives at stake, and offense is our best strategy right now."

I looked back at the crew. "That said, is there anyone who thinks this is a bad idea… that there might be a better way to do this?"

"It's a terrible idea," Icky replied.

I stared at her, waiting for her to go on.

She blinked back at me. "What? I think it's a terrible idea. I think lots of things we do are terrible ideas. I was, you know, just saying."

I smiled but looked from face to face. "Guys, look, if any of you—"

"Van, would you just shut up and drive?" Zeno snapped. "The rest of us are going to try and figure out how to win this battle."

I had to grin. "Alrighty, then."

We flew on for a bit, then I turned to Perry. "So you're a Civil War buff on top of everything else?"

"I can't believe I have to keep saying this—hello, AI bird here, Van! I literally can't forget anything I learn. I'm an adorable version of Wikipedia but without the snarky comment section on every page."

"You're your *own* comment section, bird."

Perry's beak opened. "As you like to say, hurtful but fair."

———

No matter how we did this, we were not going to be able to destroy all eight of the Sorcerers' ships. Unless they cooperated by letting us hit one of them with each of our six remaining missiles and made no defensive moves at all, the *Fafnir* couldn't unleash enough destructive power to destroy eight ships—not in the window of engagement time we had.

Torina, Zeno, and Perry instead focused on what we could do and designed the most efficient use of our weapons during our insanely high speed pass. Icky was in the back, trying to coax a little more performance from the power plant and drive—and dutifully recording it all in the maintenance log. I watched the tactical overlay and tried to maintain an overall situational awareness.

At the moment, though, I was on the comm with Gauren-Kas.

"We've marshaled every ship that's capable of fighting, less a few that decided they could best contribute by running away. In total, along with my ship, we have nine vessels standing ready."

I smiled. It sounded good—nine ships, but the largest and most powerful was Gauren-Kas's, and it was just an unusually heavily armed class 7 cutter. The remaining ships were all class 6 and smaller, including four more armed cutters used by Mirror to guard against piracy in the Reticulum system. Which was ironic, considering they'd pretty much started out as pirates, and now had to protect themselves against their one-time buddies.

"Mirror also has two class 12 corvettes registered, both fully armed. Where are they?" Netty asked.

"One's apparently involved in a trade mission to Tau Ceti, and the other's in dock for repairs with her drive in pieces," Gauren-Kas replied.

I swore under my breath. "We could have used a couple of class 12s. They might have been enough to make these Sorcerers think twice about attacking."

Gauren-Kas nodded. "I think the Sorcerers would agree, which I suspect is why the drive maintenance was abruptly rescheduled. It wasn't supposed to happen until after the other class 12 had returned from Tau Ceti."

I sighed. "Yeah, things that make you go hmm. Doesn't surprise me they'd have influence inside the Sovran Brigade."

"In any case, that's all we have to protect the Reticulum orbital. We're going to form a defensive line and keep our velocity low so we can maneuver into blocking positions, but—"

I sighed. He didn't need to say the grim finish to that sentence out loud.

I was curious about something, though.

"I've got to ask—you're putting your life on the line here, Gauren-Kas, when you really don't have to. Don't get me wrong, it's noble and damned welcome, but—"

"But you want to know why. It's very simple, Peacemaker Tudor. It's not because I have any particular fondness or loyalty to this place. Rather, it's about you. You risked your life for my people in stopping the attack on our comms installation—to save the lives of Unity Marines that you didn't even know. How can I do any less in return?"

I nodded but a little uncomfortably. I wasn't sure I was thrilled with the idea that Gauren-Kas was risking his life out of some sense of obligation to me. To my crew? Maybe. To me? That veered into places my Midwestern heart found dangerously close to a compliment.

"Well, we appreciate it. It would be nice to get to know you and your people better."

"I agree. Perhaps the Sorcerers and their evil conspiracy has achieved what years of diplomacy couldn't—a closer friendship between Unity and the powers of known space. Wouldn't that be ironic?"

I smiled. "It seems to be a day for irony. Anyway, we'll see you on the other side of this."

Gauren-Kas offered a thin and somewhat enigmatic smile. "Indeed you will."

He signed off. Torina made a *hmph* noise. "He sounded pretty sure we were going to get through this."

"What was he going to say, sorry, you're all gonna die?"

27

"Van, Netty and I have noticed something interesting," Perry said when we were about ten minutes from engagement range. By that time, our closing speed with the Sorcerers was an eye-watering many kilometers per second, and since we were all still burning at full power, that number was only climbing.

I glanced at Perry. "Okay—and?"

"And, that lead Sorcerer ship, the class 10 on point, is transmitting repeated, encrypted traffic to which the other Sorcerer ships are responding."

"Huh. That is interesting—although I'd be awfully surprised if it's a destroy-the-mothership kind of thing."

"A what?"

"Really, oh Winged Wikipedia—hey, Wingapedia! I like that."

"Van, you were ambling toward a point?" Perry asked.

"Oh, yeah, it's a dumb sci-fi trope. Aliens attack with overwhelming power, but if you destroy their mothership, all the aliens die."

"That's… not how it works, not at all."

"No shit. So what do you think it does mean?"

"Targeting data. The lead ship is probably going to coordinate the fire of all of them. It means we're likely going to get hurt pretty badly flying right through their formation—which, I might point out, is not inevitable."

I glanced at Torina. "I think you've got your priority target."

She nodded. "My recommendation is we go all in on crippling or destroying that one ship. It might disrupt their attacks enough for us to survive beyond the first three minutes."

"Agreed. Netty, at the *very* last moment, veer us to pass as close as possible to that lead ship. We're going to hit it with everything, even point-defenses. Hell, Icky, if we pass close enough for you to whack it with your hammer, feel free."

"If I could, I would, Van." Her face beamed. "Can you *imagine* a hammer at half light-speed? Bro!"

"Bro?" Torina asked, one brow raised.

Perry waved toward a back screen. "She found some reality TV from a place called Malibu. Trust me, you don't wanna know. I had to talk her out of finding—and using, I might add—hair gel."

"It makes waves, and it looks cool. Don't hate what you can't have, Metalboy," Icky said with glee.

"See?" Perry asked.

I cut my eyes at Zeno. "When we get out of this, I want her watching British murder mysteries, documentaries about cheese, and vintage music videos. *No* reality TV."

"I'll do my best," Zeno promised.

We watched as the range ticked down. Four minutes away from maximum engagement range, Netty applied lateral thrust, and she had to roll the *Fafnir* to do it, to accommodate the thruster cluster we'd lost. With Netty's delicate touch at the controls, she nudged us into a close pass by the lead Sorcerer ship. I waited for it to maneuver to keep the range open, since our opponents had no need to turn this into a knife fight and could just pummel us from a distance.

But he didn't. Instead, he adjusted course to come at us almost head-on, a game of chicken at a measurable fraction of light-speed in our combined velocities. There was even some time dilation going on. Not much—for an observer back on the Reticulum orbital, about 1.01 seconds would pass for every second that we experienced—but over a day that would add up to about a fourteen minute difference. More importantly, though, it told me something about Sorcerer psychology. Offer them a challenge, and they'll take up the gauntlet.

Good to know.

"Van, I just had an unpleasant thought," Netty said.

"FYI, I do not like when my ship says it has an unpleasant thought two minutes from battle. What's on your mind, Netty?"

"That lead Sorcerer ship may be intending to collide with us."

I blinked. Well, shit. I hadn't considered that. Now that Netty had said it, though, it wrenched my already tight gut down to a painful nub.

"How likely is that?"

"If we don't maneuver, it's one hundred percent, since our position can be accurately projected for each instant of time."

"What if we just start varying our thrust and using the thrusters to accelerate side to side?"

"That wouldn't hurt."

"Okay, do it." I turned to the others. "Everyone ready?"

I received nods and affirmative mutters. Again, we suited up and depressurized the ship. As we did, I had another thought.

"Netty, bring the glitter caster online. As soon as we've passed that lead asshole, fire it."

"To remain inside the glitter's envelope, we're not going to be able to vary our speed or course. It's going to make targeting us a lot easier for the rest of the enemy ships. I'm not sure the added protection from laser fire will be worth it."

"Maybe not, but if I understand these numbers on the overlay correctly, this whole thing is going to last about twenty seconds, right?"

"And change."

"And change. So we'll fire the glitter, give them an obvious target, then slide back out of it. Even if it only confuses them for a couple of seconds, that's ten percent of our engagement time, right?"

"I'll say it again, Van, you really are getting good at this," Netty said.

But Perry leaned toward me. "Don't get cocky, kid. That's how skilled and experienced pilots end up as clouds of ionized gas."

"Copy that, mom."

The range ticked down. At fifteen seconds out, I braced myself —for what, I wasn't sure, because it wasn't like tensing up my knees was going to help me survive a missile to the face.

Torina and Zeno kept their focus on the fire control system since they'd divided the weapons between them. Icky was again somewhere in the back, ready to stitch things back together that came apart.

I was under no illusions, though. This was going to be so quick that things like damage control would be an afterthought.

Five seconds.

When the time hit zero, all hell broke loose.

THE BATTLE WAS an *orgy* of violence.

Space abruptly filled with crisscrossed beams of laser energy and a swarm of mass-driver and point-defense slugs. Our fire control system worked overtime, delivering firing solutions that poured streams of accurate shots into the Sorcerers' leading class 10. Our particle beam did the most damage, lancing out and tearing into the lead Sorcerer ship like a filet knife gutting a fish. An instant later, the glitter caster fired, surrounding us in a sparkling cloud of chaff. Something slammed into the *Fafnir* aft. REAB modules detonated. More things crashed into us. Systems went yellow, red, or dark. The lights flickered. I was just a passenger and could only hang on and hope a mass driver round or shrapnel slug from a missile didn't turn me into pink mist.

And then it was done.

I looked around. Smoke fumed the *Fafnir's* cockpit, hanging utterly still with no air currents to move it around.

"Everyone alright?" I shouted—unnecessarily, since we were all on the comm.

"Okay here," Torina said thickly. "Bit my tongue. Twice."

"Yeah, I took a hit—damn it, that hurts," Zeno snapped. I looked back and saw her applying sealing foam to her upper thigh. A fragment had apparently entered the cockpit beside her, grazed her leg, then punched out the opposite side and took out Icky's panel on the way. If Icky had been sitting there, it would have passed right through her.

Speaking of Icky—

"Icky, you still with us?"

Nothing.

I swore and started to unstrap, but she poked her head into the cockpit. "Van, think fast," she said, tossing me something. I caught it and found myself holding a piece of a metal rod a few centimeters long. It was heavy as a son of a bitch, hinting at depleted uranium or something similar.

"That came through the hull, banged off the starboard main spar, then ricocheted around me a few times," she said. "On an unrelated note, can we get repressurized soon? I've gotta change my undies."

ICKY WAS SPEAKING FIGURATIVELY—A fact I was eternally grateful for. Still, the *Fafnir* had taken a beating during our brief and intense firefight with the Sorcerer ships. We were lucky that Zeno's wound from a splinter of hull plating was our only injury. The *Fafnir* herself needed some serious time in a maintenance hangar to deal with a multitude of damaged systems and components, including a partial loss of flight controls. Until Icky, half-buried in the crawl space under the deck at the back of the galley, could effect repairs, we could only roll the *Fafnir* very slowly and couldn't yaw her at all.

"She feels like a ship with her bilges full to the brim," I said.

Perry cocked his head at me. "You an old salt?"

"No. Sank a rental pontoon boat off Cedar Key. I can remember it like it was yesterday. The lack of steering. The screams. Drinking beer while we waited for the Coasties to show up."

"Okay, Magellan. How deep was the water?" Perry asked.

"Almost five feet. An ordeal, I tell you. If I didn't have a cooler full of beer and Publix subs, I'd be in Davy Jones's locker," I told him with all the seriousness I could muster for a blatant lie.

"Thank you for your service, sailor. Now, what about the next round of brawling?" Perry asked.

"You're watching it with me. Only hoping that Gauren-Kas can punch above his weight," I said.

The Sorcerer's flotilla bored inexorably sunward, now only minutes away from engaging the meager defensive line around Gauren-Kas. We'd effectively destroyed the lead Sorcerer ship, which was also their heaviest at class 10, but the remaining seven class 8s and 9s were much more than a match for the motley gang of last-ditch defenders. And while the loss of the class 10 seemed to have degraded their overall performance, it wouldn't matter much given such overwhelming odds.

Despite her damage, we flipped the *Fafnir* over anyway and decelerated for a return back to the Reticulum orbital, but it was just for show. It would take us an hour just to bleed off our outbound velocity, and then we had to accelerate back in-system. By then, it would be too late.

"Maybe we should have just stood and fought, instead of trying to get fancy," I said, voicing the second-guessing now rattling through my mind.

"Van, even including the *Fafnir*, that defensive line wouldn't last long. Instead of stupidly outmatched, it would have been ridiculously outmatched," Perry said.

I stared hard at the overlay and its implacable truth. "I know. But this feels like—I don't know. Like we abandoned them."

"Do you really think even the Sorcerers would destroy that orbital, though? Kill thousands and thousands of people for… what?" Torina asked.

"For sheer stubborn douchebaggery," I replied, unable or even unwilling to keep the morose tone out of my voice. "We got ahead of them and their evil schemes, so they're just going to want to kill things out of simple revenge."

"I think there's another message here, too," Zeno said, looking up from her panel.

"What's that?" I asked.

"They'd planned to attack Unity, not known space. We thwarted them, so they're telling us that if we're going to interfere, then they are going to focus their wrath here at home."

"Uh, excuse me, but they planned to asphyxiate thousands of people on that orbital. I think that constitutes an attack."

"An attack with a purpose. That purpose doesn't even exist anymore, so this attack is pure, white-hot retaliation."

"What a dick move," Icky hissed.

"Yes. That's exactly what it is," I agreed.

I thought about the way the lead Sorcerer ship had turned into our approach, as though daring us to a game of hyper-velocity chicken. I'd mused that it told us something about Sorcerer psychology, and this certainly seemed to bear that out.

I sighed. "It's like these asshole Trinduk are all about harm and not much else."

"I think it's their major export, actually," Perry said. "I know they don't manufacture anything of note, except despair and pain."

"It's probably xenophobia, but not the insular, hide-from-the-universe type we normally see. This is an outward-focused, let's wipe everyone else out sort," Torina offered.

I nodded glumly. This was all very interesting and would potentially be useful down the road, but right now it didn't help us—or the people aboard the Reticulum orbital, or those defending it.

Which meant we had ringside seats to the death of thousands of innocent people in the worst show on earth.

Or the known stars, anyway.

THE FIGHT between the Sorcerer flotilla and the handful of defending ships went as expected. The Sorcerers broke off four of their ships to engage them, while the other three charged on toward the orbital. A ferocious firefight erupted, which quickly went one-sided. The smaller, lightly armed and armored ships that had been scraped together to defend the orbital were crippled or destroyed in just a few minutes of fighting. One ship broke off to chase the three Sorcerer ships bearing down on the orbital, snapping out and landing shots on both.

"That's Gauren-Kas," Perry said.

I stared at our scanner returns, fascinated by the detached, grim details filtering over the miles. It was an impressive display of flying and fighting. Gauren-Kas did a superlative job of dodging return fire and kept landing hits in return. He actually managed to damage one of the Sorcerers enough that their acceleration dropped by more than half.

Unfortunately, by that time the other four ships had finished up with the other defenders and raced in after their fellows. Gauren-Kas was suddenly caught in a crossfire that could have only one outcome.

I saw his ship take a missile blast close by, quickly followed by another. His drive died, and the Sorcerers pounced. In less than thirty seconds, his ship had been battered into a wreck. Ten seconds later, it exploded.

"*No.*"

My single word had been the only sound in the *Fafnir's* cockpit, aside from the usual sounds of her workings and her drive. Everyone had been glued to the overlay, hoping against hope that the defenders might pull off a miracle. Even Icky had taken a break from her work to poke her head back inside and watch.

But there was no miracle today. The Sorcerers' ships reformed and resumed course toward the orbital. There was nothing to stop them now. The orbital was a flying pleasure city, an annex to the one on the planet, not a fortress. Anvil Dark could have shrugged off an attack by seven Sorcerer ships without breaking a proverbial sweat. The Reticulum orbital, though, was essentially the Vegas strip in a massive tin can.

We waited.

"In case you care, the Sorcerers will be in effective weapons range in ten minutes," Netty said. I glanced at the *Fafnir's* chronometer and noted everyone else did the same. It was just a reflex. Our time to engage was still nearly three hours, by which time the orbital would be destroyed and the Sorcerers long gone—

"Woah. What the hell is that?" Icky asked.

I followed her gaze back to the overlay. A new icon had popped into existence, between the Sorcerers and the orbital. It was something big—huge, actually—and it had twisted into being deep in a gravity well, where twisting shouldn't be physically possible at all.

The newcomer's data appeared a few seconds later. It was the *Righteous Fury*, the Peacemaker Guild's enigmatic battlecruiser.

"How—?" Zeno started, but that was as far as she got. The rest of us just shook our heads.

As suddenly as she'd appeared, the *Fury* erupted with a hurricane of fire that engulfed the lead Sorcerers. Her raw weight of firepower was stunning, and for the first time in my career, I truly understood the distinction between Dragons and ships made for the purpose of war.

One of her broadsides outmatched the *Fafnir* by a factor of ten, and in rapid succession, three of the Sorcerers' ships were torn into pieces or had sections simply vanish in hot flares of gas. The other four enemy craft demonstrated a remarkable survival instinct and began burning hard toward the down side of the system's ecliptic plane.

Even as that quartet fled, the *Fury* launched three weapons systems at once, overwhelming a hapless pair of enemy ships in a matter of seconds. One ship simply vaporized; the other, turning to present her flank, was gashed open to hard vacuum even as dancing blue flames raced along the exposed bulkhead. Van saw several small objects expelled into space at high velocity.

And the shapes were moving, but not for long as they all passed through a beam weapon that made them vanish in white flashes of elemental rage.

Those are—or were—people, Van mused, as the vicious finality of warfare unfolded before him.

Then, the terrible, beautiful warship punched her thrusters and hung by the orbital like an implacable wall of dark alloy and menace.

Perry finally broke our silence.

"Well, that was unexpected."

I blinked a few times at the overlay and the zoomed imagery of the battle. "Uh, Netty, correct me if I'm wrong, but isn't it impossible to twist so deeply into a gravity well?"

"Apparently not," Torina muttered.

"I mean, there's a big-assed gas giant *right there*," I went on. "How—I—" I shook my head in wonder.

"Twisting is governed by a complex but rigid system of spatial and temporal laws," Netty replied. "Which apparently means nothing, based on what we just saw, so my answer to you, Van, is I've got no damned clue what just happened."

A chime announced an incoming comm, on an encrypted Peacemaker channel. I answered it, kind of expecting it to be Gerhardt. But it wasn't. It was a human woman I'd never seen before, dressed in an ominous black uniform. I didn't recall if I'd ever before encountered someone I'd describe as regal, but I had now. This was a commander, in every sense of the word.

"Peacemaker Tudor, I'm Stosa Brunel, Captain of the *Righteous Fury*. What's your status?"

"Uh—aside from stunned as shit, not too bad. Let me get right to the point. How did you twist into the middle of a battle occurring in the gravity well of a gas giant?"

She granted me a thin smile. "Not only is that not relevant to the current situation, but it's also a matter of operational security. Oh, and incidentally, per Guild Protocol Two, Section Six, you are forbidden to speak of or refer to the matter any further."

I glanced at Perry, who nodded. "She's authorized to invoke that Protocol, and we—all of us—are bound by it."

I turned back to her, tempted to press her for... anything, because I still believed in the laws of physics despite what I'd seen with my own eyes. A twist drive that could insert a ship into a gravity well was a complete game-changer. The implications were clear even at a casual glance. It meant the Guild had a drive that performed according to some completely different and novel physics—physics that the builders of the *Righteous Fury* had monopolized to maximum effect.

I decided not to ask further questions because Brunel didn't seem chatty or open to the discussion of classified drive technology. I had my crew. If there were secrets to unspool, we would do it as needed. For now, I launched into a dry, unemotional report on the progression of the battle, ending with what I considered the most critical point.

"... thus, my crew and ship are in fighting form, we've turned away a significant Sorcerer force, and the population is safe from cybernetic attacks," I concluded, doing my best to keep it short and professional.

Brunel nodded brusquely.

"That was good work, Peacemaker."

"Not good enough. I'm... glad you came along when you did,

although glad doesn't really do it justice. Euphorically relieved, maybe?"

She smiled, a brittle, porcelain expression that stopped short of her eyes. "We're dispatching boats to retrieve any survivors, friendly or enemy. In the meantime, we'll stay on-station awaiting the arrival of a relief force from the Eridani Federation. They've offered to secure Reticulum for the time being, at least until the present threat has abated."

"Speaking of the present threat, are the Sorcerers attacking anywhere else?"

"There've been reports of several incursions, including one directed at your home system, Sol."

I stiffened. "What?"

She raised a slender hand. "Petyr Groshenko anticipated it and was waiting with a flotilla of mercenary ships near that gas giant with the rings—"

"Saturn."

"Saturn, that's it. Regardless, he ambushed the Sorcerers heading for Earth and managed to destroy all but two of them, who fled—just like these are doing."

I looked at the overlay. The surviving Sorcerers were now heading directly down relative to the ecliptic plane of the Reticulum system.

"I wonder where they're going, or where they think they can hide?" Zeno asked.

I shrugged. "Probably back to that nebula."

"We'll be able to find out once they twist," Netty put in.

I frowned. "What, you've figured out how to track ships when they twist now? Did all the laws of physics get some sort of update today?"

"Nothing so fancy. As we were flying through the Sorcerers' formation, I took the liberty of firing a tag missile that planted one of our experimental twist trackers on one of them."

Torina made an impressed face. "I hadn't even noticed."

"You were busy trying to turn the enemy into plasma. Anyway, it was a long shot, particularly since most of the Sorcerers were destroyed. But I'm getting a ping from one of those survivors, so the tracker's still active."

"We got lucky," Zeno said.

Brunel cut in. "If I understand what you're saying, and you'll be able to get some sense of where they're going to twist to, please make sure you share that information with us."

She'd said please, but it wasn't really a request. I just nodded.

"Of course. What's ours is yours," I said, earning another of those wintry smiles.

Brunel signed off. While we kept decelerating and effecting whatever repairs we could, I watched the overlay. The Sorcerers stayed their course and, about an hour later, twisted away, their icons blipping out as they did.

"Netty?"

"One moment."

We waited.

"Alright, based on the twist parameters the tracker was able to transmit, it seems that the Sorcerers have gone into the region known as the Deep Shadows," she finally said.

I looked around but just got blank looks and shrugs from the others. "The Deep Shadows? Where and what is that?"

"It's a region below the galactic plane that's heavily obscured by dust with a high metal content. That makes it more or less impervious to scanners."

"So another nebula."

"Yes and no. It is a region of dust like a nebula, but it has properties that are wholly unlike any other astronomical feature. More to the point, its closest edge is nearly one thousand light-years away. From our perspective, those Sorcerers are going to be in-transit for months."

I sat back. "They're in no hurry."

"So it would seem."

Netty expanded the overlay into a star chart extending to the Deep Shadows, which formed an impenetrable barrier to thousands of cubic light-years of space beyond it. Not a single byte of data had ever been collected from the far side of that blank veil, simply because it was too far away to bother.

That was going to have to change.

Zeno must have seen the look on my face.

"Van, we'll get them another day."

I nodded, my eyes locked on the words Deep Shadows and the utterly blank space beneath them on the display.

"Yes, we will. And soon."

EPILOGUE

I WANTED to return to Earth, but the *Fafnir* needed more and heavier repairs than we could carry out in the barn. So we limped back to Anvil Dark instead, tucking the ship into a pressurized hangar, then dismounting to survey the damage.

"She's a tough bastard, isn't she?" Icky said.

We all stood in a line, nodding. The *Fafnir* had taken worse damage, but I didn't think she'd ever taken so much. More of her REAB modules had been blown out than not. Dents and scrapes scarred her armor. A long, straight gouge across her dorsal hull just ahead of engineering shimmered with heat-crazed colors, the record of a laser hit.

But those were just the things that hadn't actually penetrated her. It had taken us most of the trip back to Anvil Dark patching her actual holes just to get her airtight integrity restored. We repressurized her, but even then she had a slow leak somewhere. Nearly a third of the thrusters were offline, as were a dozen of her internal systems. Just docking her in the hangar had been a tedious, nerve-wracking adventure, requiring the assistance of an AI-controlled tug.

"The other ships' AIs are never going to let me live that down, having to use a tug," Netty had complained.

"Really? Why not?" I asked her.

"A tug, Van? Tugs are for freighters and bulk carriers. It's a point of pride among us AIs not to have to use them."

I smiled. "If you get any shit about it, Netty, just point out that the only reason we did need a tug is because of battle damage. And if they keep giving you any shit about it, just let me know."

Netty sniffed. "I can fight my own battles, thanks, Van," she said. She paused a moment, then added, "But seriously, thanks."

Now staring at the damage, all I could do was sigh. "This is going to cost us a fortune to fix."

"I'm estimating two hundred and six thousand bonds," Perry said.

I shot him a glance. "That's awfully specific for an estimate."

"So it's a specific estimate. A prebill, if you will."

A new voice cut in. "Peacemaker Tudor, Gerhardt here. Please come to my office at your earliest convenience."

I sighed. "On my way."

"He might not be intending to give you shit, you know," Torina said.

"That's the problem with Gerhardt. I never know what to expect, despite how our interactions began. He went from a ruthless taskmaster to an ally," I replied. "On top of that, his poker face is next level."

She returned a puzzled smile. "What do you mean?"

"Unlike me, Gerhardt can hide any and all emotions. I'm not inclined to sit and wait for his intentions to unfold. Not after what we just saw. Not after what we just *did*. That was war, Torina. Not law enforcement."

She took my hand, her fingers interlocking with mine of their own volition. We fit. "I admire Gerhardt, but not that part. I'd prefer to show my emotions. To you, anyway."

"Same," I said, as she leaned into me, and for the moment, it was enough.

I sat down in Gerhardt's office. Aside from the two of us, Puris-Tar sat nearby, looking as inscrutable as ever.

"I would have gotten to work on my after-action report on the way back here, but we were too busy trying to plug holes in the *Fafnir*—"

Gerhardt waved a dismissive hand. "In due course, Tudor. Just tell us what happened during—was it two operations, or three?"

"Well, there was the class 9 we took out, then the hacker on the Reticulum orbital we took out, and then the Sorcerers' ships attacked, so… I guess it was three," I said.

"Very good. I'll expect a separate report on each then. In detail."

I sighed. On top of everything else those vile, murderous bastards had done, they'd increased my paperwork.

I launched into a recounting of what had happened in each successive operation. I ended up talking for nearly half an hour straight, with Gerhardt and Puris-Tar only interrupting for clarifica-tions. When I described Gauren-Kas's sacrifice on behalf of the orbital, I spoke directly to the Grendu.

"I highly recommend you honor him as a hero. We'd preempted the Sorcerers by then, so he didn't need to do what he did. It was a sacrifice of pure nobility."

Puris-Tar tilted his head. "Peacemaker Tudor, nearly fifty citi-zens of known space died in the course of stopping these criminal operations by the Sorcerers and their co-conspirators. They died in an effort to save my people. Gauren-Kas did die a hero, but how could he not?"

I inclined my head. "I couldn't agree more.".

"I do have a request, however. I would like you to come to my homeworld and offer your testimony regarding his actions. I think it would have much added weight, coming from someone else consid-ered a hero among my people."

I glanced at Gerhardt, then back to Puris-Tar. "I… don't really think I'm a hero—"

"We Grendu do not like false modesty, Peacemaker Tudor. In any case, that's not your decision to make. We consider you a hero, so a hero you are."

"This would be the first formal diplomatic contact between known space and Unity, Tudor. I'd particularly note that it would involve the Guild, which, quite frankly, won't hurt our standing here in known space."

What could I say? I turned back to Puris-Tar. "I'd be delighted to do this. Well, just as soon as my ship's flying again, and with one condition that I'm afraid is not negotiable."

"Making demands, Tudor?" Gerhardt said, his voice neutral.

"Yes, sir. If there is honor to be given, it'll be shared with my crew. We're a package deal," I said, smiling to take the edge off my words.

Puris-Tar leaned forward with the body language of agreement. "That is the just thing to do, Peacemaker. And regarding your ship —I understand that, given the way your Guild operates, you bear the burden for the repairs? To the *Fafnir*."

"Less an allowance provided by the Guild for damage incurred during legitimate operations, but that's generally true, yes," Gerhardt said.

"Then the least we can do is assume that burden for ourselves. I will arrange payment for all of the repairs you need to make to your ship, and I will also fund the next upgrade you wish to make to her."

I stared blankly for a moment. "That's very generous. Thank you."

Puris-Tar stood. "Don't thank me yet, Peacemaker Tudor. I have a feeling we're going to need you and your ship again. The Sorcerers, Group 41, and the various other conspirators have lost this battle, but the war is far from over, I'm afraid," he said, then left.

I looked at Gerhardt. "If there's nothing else, I should get back to my ship."

"And completing your reports, yes."

I kept my voice devoid of any emotion, a feat given my antipathy for paperwork. "And completing my reports," I said, standing and heading for the door.

"Tudor?"

I stopped and turned back.

Gerhardt smiled. "That was damned good work."

"Thank you, sir. Truly." I started to turn away but didn't. I had a question I wanted to ask.

"About the *Righteous Fury* and her… ah, timely arrival. That was your doing, wasn't it?"

"I am involved in many operations, Tudor."

"Uh-huh. As a Peacemaker? Or as something more?"

Gerhardt smiled again. "Three after-action reports, Tudor, by—I'll be generous. By midday tomorrow. That should give you an opportunity to unwind in The Black Hole tonight." His smile widened. "I may even buy you a drink."

I smiled back, shook my head, and left, heading for the *Fafnir*.

It was a good thing the Grendu agreed to pay for the *Fafnir's* repairs because they ended up being even more expensive than Perry had estimated. The piece of shrapnel Icky had given me—which I kept as a souvenir mounted on the top of the *Fafnir's* instrument panel—hadn't just ricocheted off the starboard spar, it had damaged and deformed it. Since it was one of four main structural members carrying loads through the *Fafnir's* hull, it had to be replaced. Guild policy, not to mention common sense, didn't allow ships to fly with a key part of their structure compromised.

It wasn't a small job. It meant removing the hull plating on the starboard side, disconnecting the spar from all of the other structural components linked to it, swapping it out, and hooking everything back up. It took a heavy maintenance team a full day and jacked the bill up by an eye-watering hundred thousand bonds.

I scanned the final repair manifest and shook my head as I

signed it off. "Don't know how we could have afforded this on our own."

Torina gave me a coy smile. "You could always trade on your good looks."

"Yeah, that should be worth a couple of hundred bonds," Perry said from his perch on a nearby tool cart.

She scowled at him. "You know, it's like having a toddler around, ruining all my attempts at romance and emotion."

"Hey, this toddler is equipped with hyper-sensitive aural inputs. Maybe try keeping your sweet nothings behind closed doors."

I narrowed my eyes at him, thinking of the few times Torina and I had had a closed-door meeting aboard the *Fafnir*. Netty was careful not to intrude, but as for Perry—

"Is that actually enough to block your hyper-sensitive aural inputs?" I asked him.

"Mostly."

"What do you mean mostly—?"

"Sorry, Van, gotta run, big AI meeting starting," Perry said, leaping into the air and sailing away.

Torina sniffed. "Big AI meeting? Really?"

"I… think he might be lying," I said.

The spar replacement wasn't the only heavy job we had done while in dock. We'd pondered Puris-Tar's offer to upgrade the *Fafnir* and what that upgrade should be. We had nearly no end of choices —another weapons module to increase our firepower, an additional crew-hab module for more living space, a service module to give us more power, ship's systems and overall redundancy, even an upgraded ECM suite like Zeno had suggested to improve our defenses, particularly against incoming missiles.

We finally settled on the discounted docking module Netty had mentioned, which would give us the ability to permanently cart along a class 3 workboat in a ventral dock. It wouldn't be strapped to the ship as an afterthought, though, but snuggled mostly up inside her. The module incorporated an airlock, letting people enter and exit the workboat in a pressurized environment. It also offered another weapons hard point on its dorsal or top side, while adding some additional storage for food, water, and pressurized air, extending our flight endurance time. More to the point, it wasn't such an expensive upgrade that it made me feel like we were taking advantage of Puris-Tar's generosity.

It also meant the *Fafnir* was officially a class 10 Dragon, pushing class 11. And that, in turn, meant that the barn back in Iowa was now about a meter too small to hold the ship, unless we parked her diagonally inside. On our next trip to Iowa, we were going to have to land two of us in the workboat, then spend a day or so dragging and heaving junk out of the barn to make way for her. That led me to another of those incongruous moments, visualizing myself hauling out the rusty old spike harrow that had been hunkered in the barn since I was about eight, to make way for a *starship*.

I'm not sure what I envisioned when I was a kid, but I can say for certain it didn't include adding on to the barn because my warship was too big.

As problems go, it was a good one to have.

WE RETURNED to Sol but didn't head straight to Earth. I wanted to check out the site of the battle Groshenko had fought with the

Sorcerers who'd been trying to reach Earth. Brunel said it had happened near Saturn, but it had actually occurred about a third of the way from Saturn to Uranus. More importantly, given that at any moment I'm sure there were hundreds of telescopes on Earth trained on Saturn, it had happened far enough away from the ringed planet that it should have happened outside their fields of view.

As an added precaution, we tuned into Earthly audio, video, and data broadcasts, looking for word of a space battle. Ironically, the best place to get early news about things that might have been noticed on Earth were the tabloids and conspiracy theory websites. Their willingness to immediately publish almost anything lurid made them the most reliable sources of interstellar news on Earth.

We found nothing, though. The battle, which had resulted in the destruction of three Sorcerers' ships in exchange for two of Groshenko's taking heavy damage, had played out unseen by anyone on Earth. That made me breathe a little easier, but seriously —eventually, something was going to happen that revealed the truth to humanity. Something that didn't just flash up on tabloids and wacko conspiracy sites or the breathless newsletters shared among fringe types like Tony Burgess and his associates. It would be something that would hit the mainstream news, and it would fundamentally change how Earthly society worked.

But not today. Satisfied the extraterrestrial cat was still firmly in the bag, we set course for the *Iowa*. I wanted to take a day or two off before heading to Earth and cleaning out the barn, which was going to be a dusty, sweaty, and laborious job.

As soon as we docked with the *Iowa* and moved to the airlock, though, Netty spoke up.

"Everyone, I've got a surprise for you."

We all exchanged puzzled glances. "A surprise?"

The doors opened. "Yes. Please go to cargo hold starboard-two."

"Uh—why?"

"You'll see."

More glances were exchanged. We did as Netty asked, heading for the rearmost of the two cargo holds on the starboard side. I wasn't sure why—it was just a gloomy, cavernous space about the size of the barn back in Iowa. But Netty had never asked us to do something like this before. All of us were intrigued and made our way to the hold.

We stopped at the sealed hatch. "Okay, Netty, we're here," I said.

"Before I open it up, I just want to say I was really just a bystander. The gift itself is from Retta. I have the pleasure of pulling back the veil, though."

I frowned. Retta? Our ball-riding Francophile slug restaurateur? A description which, now that I thought about it, was probably the first time those words had ever been arranged that way by anyone, anywhere.

"Okay, Netty, go ahead. Knock our socks off."

The door slid open. Light spilled out.

We stepped inside and found ourselves in—

A park?

We walked in, stopped, then each of us slowly turned a circle.

A meter or so inside the doorway, grass covered the deck. At least a dozen trees were arrayed about us, sweet with blossoms and filling the air with a fresh, lively fragrance. A small rococo fountain tinkled in their midst, with three intricate wrought-iron benches placed around it.

For a while, we just looked around. Torina finally spoke up. "I don't recognize these trees. They look like they might be from Earth, though—?"

"They are. They are orange and lemon trees cultivated from seeds collected from the Orangery at the Palace of Versailles," Netty replied.

"Well of course." I had to grin. "So you and her were in cahoots, eh, Netty?"

"I don't get a chance to surprise you guys very often. Well, not in a way that doesn't usually involve the sudden appearance of enemies or damage control, anyway. Incidentally, Retta sent a message along as well."

Retta's lilting voice spoke, fancy with her cultured French accent.

"Bonjour, mes amis. I am so glad to give you this gift, to maybe brighten up your time in space, yes? It gets so dreary, staring at nothing but decks and bulkheads, so I thought this could be your own chez soi loin de chez soi, your own home away from home. I have discussed with Netty the needs to maintain it, and she has been un vrai délice, a true delight to work with. Please, enjoy the delicious fruit of these trees!"

I laughed. "Well, I'll be. Our own Orangery in space—Icky!"

She turned from one of the orange trees with flower petals dangling from her mouth. "What? She said enjoy"—she spit out a petal—"the fruit. Gotta be honest, there's not much to it, though."

"That would be because those are just the blossoms. The fruit will come along later."

"Now you tell me."

"Netty, please send Retta our thanks, and tell her I'll give her a call later on to thank her personally. Also, let's send her that last bottle of good bourbon we brought from Earth," I said.

"I thought you wanted to save that for a special occasion," Torina said.

I gestured around. "I think this would count, don't you?"

"On it, boss. I'll make sure the bottle gets couriered to her next time we're at Anvil Dark. I'll arrange to have it sent in a Guild diplomatic pouch," Perry said.

That prompted a puzzled look from me. "A diplomatic pouch? Why?"

"There's a hot market for good booze out there, Van. I'm telling you, we could make a small fortune selling good whiskey across known space."

"You want us to get into rum-running?"

"What did I just say? Whiskey, Van, whiskey. That's where the big bucks are."

I WAS ENJOYING our new orangery, sitting on one of the benches facing the fountain in relaxed dress, just maintenance coveralls and sandals. My duty boots were comfortable as hell, but they didn't compare to the brush of grass under my bare feet. I was working on a follow-up report Gerhardt had requested to clarify some points in my original three reports.

Reports on reports. Did bureaucracy have no shame?

Netty interrupted. "Van, we have a visitor inbound."

I lowered the data slate. "Is this another surprise?"

"It… is, yes, though not one in which I'm a co-conspirator. It's Petyr Groshenko in the *Poltava*. He's asking permission to come aboard."

"Ugh. I can already taste the vodka—and I am not a fan." I stood. "By all means, offer my compliments and have him piped aboard."

"Piped aboard?"

"Eh, something I read once in a novel about sailing ships. I just thought it sounded good."

I went to the airlock where the *Poltava* had docked, waiting for it to cycle. When it did, Groshenko appeared, a broad grin on his face, a bottle of vodka—of course—in one hand, and a small, unmarked box in the other.

"Van, it's good—"

A shrill, warbling whistle cut him off. It was the Boatswain's Call, the familiar low-high-low tune that was also the name of the little pipe that produced it. Groshenko blinked, then grinned. So did I.

"Well, aren't we formal?" He came to exaggerated attention. "Permission to come aboard, Captain!"

"Hmm. I don't know—"

He scowled and lifted the vodka. "Make up your mind. This is getting warm. Oh, and have Perry meet us, but not the rest of your crew."

I opened my mouth, but Groshenko just started walking. I shrugged to myself and followed him.

"Netty, ask Perry to join us in the forward mess. Oh, and the whistle was very cute."

"Perry's not the only adorable AI around here, you know."

"Never for an instant thought that he was, my dear."

We walked to the mess to find Perry already there. Groshenko asked Netty to seal the doors, then he poured vodka, like he always did. I pretended to enjoy it, like I always did. Before I could say anything else, though, Groshenko plunked the small box on the table. It was nondescript metal, a little scuffed on the corners and edges.

"Open it," he said.

I did. Inside, sitting on a tiny red velvet cushion was a black metal star with gold points.

I looked from it, to Groshenko. "You're… giving me an award?"

He glanced at Perry. "Of sorts. There are very few families who can claim Hereditary Status among us, Van, and your, ah, recent change in rank means that star is now yours. I don't recommend wearing it, though, unless you feel it's absolutely necessary. But you've earned it, and not just by riding the coattails of your grandfather."

"Or anyone else," Perry said.

Groshenko nodded. "Or anyone else."

"Okay—so what does it mean, exactly? Is it related to, uh—" I hesitated. As far as I knew, Groshenko was fully aware of the Galactic Knights Uniformed, as B had described them to me. But I wasn't sure of the protocols around even bringing it up in a conversation.

"The GKU?" He nodded. "It's that, but it's also more. And by more, I mean it has special significance for you."

I stared. "Okay, you've lost me."

Groshenko idly tapped the table, a look on his face like he was trying to figure out how to say something. He finally spoke.

"It's a five-pointed star. You'll note that four have gold tips."

I glanced at Perry, then back to Groshenko. "Sorry, it must be the vodka. I'm not following."

"Van, this is the GKU Hereditary Star. It denotes successive generations of Galactic Knights, with each gold point representing one member of one generation," Perry said.

I frowned. "There are four gold points. So, one for Gramps, one for... my grandmother?"

"That's right," Groshenko replied.

"One for me?"

Groshenko nodded.

"So who's the fourth point?"

Groshenko leaned on the table. "That, Van, would be your mother."

I just stared, my voice, and even my thoughts, momentarily stuck. When they came unstuck again, I shook my head.

"My... mother? But she left my dad and I when I was just little."

Groshenko nodded. "She did."

"To... what? Come out here?"

Groshenko's smile widened a bit. "Your family has been doing this for a long time, Van, and you've only ever heard a small part of the story. And that means that now, it's time you know the rest."

I turned to Perry. "Scratch sending that bottle to Retta. We'll get her another one. Meantime, I'll get the bourbon and clean glasses. I think we're going to be here a while."

Amazon won't always tell you about the next release. To stay updated on this series, be sure to sign up for our spam-free email list at jnchaney.com.

Van will return in BLACKEST OCEAN available to preorder now on Amazon.

GLOSSARY

Anvil Dark: The beating heart of the Peacemaker organization, Anvil Dark is a large orbital platform located in the Gamma Crucis system, some ninety lightyears from Earth. Anvil Dark, some nine hundred seventy years old, remains in a Lagrange point around Mesaribe, remaining in permanent darkness. Anvil Dark has legal, military, medical, and supply resources for Peacemakers, their assistants, and guests.

Cloaks: Local organized criminal element, the Cloaks hold sway in only one place: Spindrift. A loose guild of thugs, extortionists, and muscle, the Cloaks fill a need for some legal control on Spindrift, though they do so only because Peacemakers and other authorities see them as a necessary evil. When confronted away from Spindrift, Cloaks are given no rights, quarter, or considerations for their position. (See: Spindrift)

Dragonet: A Base Four Combat ship, the Dragonet is a modified platform intended for the prosecution of Peacemaker policy. This includes but is not limited to ship-to-ship combat, surveillance, and planetary operations as well. The Dragonet is fast, lightly armored, and carries both point defense and ranged weapons, and features a frame that can be upgraded to the status of a small corvette (Class Nine).

Moonsword: Although the weapon is in the shape of a medium sword, the material is anything but simple metal. The Moonsword is a generational armament, capable of upgrades that augment its ability to interrupt communications, scan for data, and act as a blunt-force weapon that can split all but the toughest of ship's hulls. See: Starsmith

Peacemaker: Also known as a Galactic Knight, Peacemakers are an elite force of law enforcement who have existed for more than three centuries. Both hereditary and open to recruitment, the guild is a meritocracy, but subject to political machinations and corruption, albeit not on the scale of other galactic military forces. Peacemakers have a legal code, proscribed methods, a reward and bounty scale, and a well-earned reputation as fierce, competent fighters. Any race may be a Peacemaker, but the candidates must pass rigorous testing and training.

Perry: An artificial intelligence, bound to Van (after service to his grandfather), Perry is a fully-sapient combat operative in the shape of a large, black avian. With the ability to hack computer systems and engage in physical combat, Perry is also a living repository of galactic knowledge in topics from law to battle strategies. He is also a wiseass.

Salt Thieves: Originally actual thieves who stole salt, this is a three-hundred-year-old guild of assassins known for their ruthless behavior, piracy, and tendency to kill. Members are identified by a complex, distinct system of braids in their hair. These braids are often cut and taken as prizes, especially by Peacemakers.

Spindrift: At nine hundred thirty years old, Spindrift is one of the most venerable space stations in the galactic arm. It is also the least reputable, having served as a place of criminal enterprise for nearly all of its existence due to a troublesome location. Orbiting Sirius, Spindrift was nearly depopulated by stellar radiation in the third year as a spaceborne habitat. When order collapsed, criminals moved in, cycling in and out every twelve point four years as coronal ejections rom Sirius made the station uninhabitable. Spindrift is known for medical treatments and technology that are quasi-legal at best, as well as weapons, stolen goods, and a strange array of archaeological items, all illegally looted. Spindrift has a population of thirty thousand beings at any time.

Starsmith: A place, a guild, and a single being, the Starsmith is primarily a weapons expert of unsurpassed skill. The current Starsmith is a Conoku (named Linulla), a crablike race known for their dexterity, skill in metallurgy and combat enhancements, and sense of humor.

CONNECT WITH J.N. CHANEY

Don't miss out on these exclusive perks:

- Instant access to free short stories from series like *The Messenger*, *Starcaster*, and more.
- Receive email updates for new releases and other news.
- Get notified when we run special deals on books and audiobooks.

So, what are you waiting for? Enter your email address at the link below to stay in the loop.

https://www.jnchaney.com/backyard-starship-subscribe

CONNECT WITH TERRY MAGGERT

Check out his website
http://terrymaggert.com/

Connect on Facebook
https://www.facebook.com/terrymaggertbooks/

Follow him on Amazon
https://www.amazon.com/Terry-Maggert/e/B00EKN8RHG/

ABOUT THE AUTHORS

J. N. Chaney is a USA Today Bestselling author and has a Master's of Fine Arts in Creative Writing. He fancies himself quite the Super Mario Bros. fan. When he isn't writing or gaming, you can find him online at **www.jnchaney.com**.

He migrates often, but was last seen in Las Vegas, NV. Any sightings should be reported, as they are rare.

Terry Maggert is left-handed, likes dragons, coffee, waffles, running, and giraffes; order unimportant. He's also half of author Daniel Pierce, and half of the humor team at Cledus du Drizzle.

With thirty-one titles, he has something to thrill, entertain, or make you cringe in horror. Guaranteed.

Note: He doesn't sleep. But you sort of guessed that already.

Made in United States
North Haven, CT
10 June 2022

20102119R00251